Philippa Moseley

EAVESDROPPING

Note

This is the story of my childhood in the Middle East, written in the form of a novel, with most of the names of characters changed. Some of the events have been shifted around, and a couple of dates have been changed. Only two events did not take place: I wasn't born in Haifa, as you know; my mother was ill during her pregnancy and it was decided she should return to the UK for her confinement. After my birth she was too ill to leave hospital, and my father's sister, Reta, looked after me. Three months later my mother was well enough to return to Haifa, but Reta did not go there to look after me.

At the end of the book I was left only partly knowing what had happened. There were many questions I wanted to ask, but the atmosphere was such that I didn't dare do so. Children in those days weren't supposed to ask for explanations about adult behaviour.

In the excitement of the trip to Liverpool, the meeting with my relatives and the travelling around England, there was enough to think about. I didn't know whether my parents had told Reta and Eric about Basil.

Once when I was alone with my mother, I ventured to ask if she was ever going to see Basil again. In no uncertain terms she gave me to understand that she and my father did not want to talk about our time in the Middle East. It was all in the past, and we must forget it. On no account must I mention Basil to anyone in England. She said it in such a way that I knew I must obey.

The years passed, and of course I guessed that relations and friends in the UK had never been told that my mother had left her husband to live with Basil; as Basil had deserted her, there must have been the decision between my parents to keep the whole episode secret. I was aware that if I spoke out it would have been a betrayal. It wasn't until my parents' death that I did tell a few people and decided to write this book for you, and possibly my grandchildren, should they be interested.

But the question of whether my mother had decided to take an overdose to kill herself, or whether she actually took too many pills by accident, has never been solved. I can only be glad that she recovered and returned to my father. He would have had a most unhappy life without her.

Chapter One

Under her mattress, in order of preference, Alex keeps a secret list of the people she loves best in the world. First comes her father, Giles Kinley, then Zilpha, her Palestinian nanny. Mr Gregson, who has promised to make her a dolls' house, comes next, followed by Mustapha the sad gardener, and Fatima, the giggling girl who does the cleaning. Her mother isn't included. She worships her mother, Sheena, but it's worship too mixed with fear to rank as love.

The new Iraqi watchman who inhabits the little tower room at the gates of K3 oil pumping station has recently been added to her list. Saeb is a great improvement on the previous grumpy fellow who rarely changed his sweaty uniform and invariably scowled at Alex and Zilpha as he let them through the gates to take their late afternoon walk in the desert.

Saeb has a big friendly smile. His shirts are dazzling white like his teeth. He sports a large pair of binoculars round his neck. His English is excellent but he's encouraging Alex to learn some Arabic. He tells her jokes and tall stories with such a serious expression on his benign face that she believes everything he says. Zilpha complains to Saeb not to frighten her with his tales of wicked djinns and bandits and wolves in the desert.

When the Kinleys first came to K3, in the autumn of 1937, Zilpha used to take three-year-old Alex as far as the water tank outside the nearby village of Haditha, to watch the fat yellow frogs hopping in and out of the water. But now they go farther into the desert. The flat scrubby land around K3 is dotted with miniature volcanic eruptions known as *'tells'*. Alex enjoys climbing these rocky hillocks.

On their return from these walks Saeb often calls them up the ladder to his tower room to watch the sun set. Through his binoculars Alex can see the distant mountains of Lebanon to the west and those of Persia to the east. Once she is entranced to catch a gazelle in the lens. As the great

5

red ball of the sun sinks behind the mountains, they watch in awed silence as the land briefly retains a vivid pink flush which darkens into purple and then swiftly into night.

'Why can't we stay in the desert after dark?' asks Alex.

'Because the djinn will take you', warns Saeb, making a ferocious face. 'Do you know what a djinn looks like?'

Alex brings her *'Tales from the Arabian Nights'* to show Saeb a full page picture of a djinn – a great burly male figure wearing a white turban trimmed with gold brocade above his cruel, swarthy features. A thick black beard flows over his chest above his baggy blue embroidered trousers. His eyes are large black holes filled with two burning coals. A shiny scimitar hangs from his red belt, inlaid with gold coins, and his bristly hands are like claws.

'Yes, yes, that's him', exclaims Saeb cheerfully.

'Where will he take me?'

'To his cave in the rocks – under the highest tell – look, you can see it over there.'

'That's my own tell, where I go to play. I've never seen the djinn.'

'In the daytime he likes to sleep. He only comes out after sunset, to go hunting for little girls.'

For the first time Alex is uncertain whether to believe him. 'What if he did come out in the daytime?'

'Better run fast!'

'Alex, you mustn't listen to Saeb', grumbles Zilpha. 'There's no djinn under the rocks. Djinns only exist in stories.'

But Alex's imagination is fired by Saeb's assurance that the djinn will cast a spell on her if he gets the chance. 'See those black birds? Well, the djinn might turn you into one of those if he catches you.'

Zilpha becomes angry. But the watchman only laughs. 'Children love to be frightened by stories. Next time I'll tell you where the ifrits live', he whispers to Alex.

'Tell me about the ifrits now!' begs Alex.

'Bukra, bukra.'

'That means tomorrow.'

'Quite right. Now what's this I'm going to give you?', and the watchman holds up a large ripe banana.

'Muz, muz!' shouts Alex triumphantly.

'Have you remembered the words you learnt yesterday?'

'Aiwah – Zayit means oil, and mafish means it doesn't matter.'

'Very good. And the word for good?'

'Taiyib, taiyib, taiyib!' chants Alex, and he laughs at her pronunciation.

Saeb has recently presented Alex with a toy camel, a shabby beige creature with hairy lips, heavy-lidded eyes and a haughty expression. Alex's mother wanted to throw it in the dustbin, it smelt so musty. But Zilpha promised to boil it. The faded toy becomes Alex's major confidant, sleeping in her bed and accompanying her everywhere. Saeb says on no account talk to it in English, it would only understand Arabic. Arabic, he maintains, is the language of the angels, a sacred speech, utilising every sound a person can make in the throat, and comprising the largest vocabulary. Does Alex realise, for instance, that there are more than a hundred words for camel? Alex knows only one word – jemel. Her jemel can't stand up properly. Its legs are floppy after Zilpha's vigorous boiling. Saeb grins. 'Too much whisky-soda!' Alex decides to call the camel 'Whisky-Soda', and later 'Soda' for short.

Alex maintains her camel is clever and kind, but Saeb assures her all camels are stupid and bad-tempered. Their bite is poisonous, and they'll kick their owners given half a chance. When walking they can only travel about three miles an hour, but they can run very fast. 'The camel thinks itself superior to man because it knows a great secret.'

'What secret?' demands Alex eagerly.

'The camel won't tell' replies Saeb.

'If I tell Soda all my secrets, one day he'll tell me his great secret' asserts the child.

Giles has kept his six-year-old daughter well supplied with reading matter in spite of their living on a remote oil station in the Iraqi desert. Until war broke out in 1939, his sister May used to send a children's book from England every month. Alex has become obsessed with fairy tales, devouring all the Hans Andersen and Grimms' fairy tales as well as the Greek myths, the Norse legends and George MacDonald's stories. Her favourite book remains *'Tales from the Arabian Nights'.* She relishes the exotic atmosphere and the romantic names. Her greatest desire is to become an eastern princess – like Princess Badr al-Budur, who married Aladdin – and to wear diaphanous pantaloons and a veil. Her attendants will twine jasmine flowers into her long shining black hair, and she will glide across marble floors in tiny gold slippers, jangling a dozen gold bracelets on each arm.

Climbing every weekday afternoon up the highest 'tell', Alex devises elaborate make-believe games. While Zilpha sits on a flat stone at the foot of the rocky little hillock doing her crochet work, Alex climbs nimbly up to the 'turret room' at the top of her 'castle', with Soda, who participates in her fantasy world of beautiful princesses, brave princes, tyrannical sultans and wicked djinns. The daily outing from the oil station has become a ritual. Her mother can't understand the attraction the desert holds for her daughter. Why doesn't Alex play with Tony Hotchkiss in the garden or go swimming at the club? 'Peter Blake says it isn't safe to allow Alex outside the gates', Sheena tells Giles, 'Especially when the Bedouin are camped nearby.'

'Of course it's safe!', retorts her husband. 'Everyone knows the Bedouin would never harm a child.'

Spring arrives in March, with shoots of brilliant green popping up miraculously out of the scrubby iron waste, followed overnight by a carpet of miniature wild flowers. During this fleeting period Giles sometimes accompanies

Alex and Zilpha on their walks. He carries a book on wild flowers to teach Alex their names. Already she recognises red poppies, clumps of white, blue and mauve anemones, pink mallow, purple iris, white violets and her favourite, yellow mignonette. Such a lovely word, 'mignonette', the way it's pronounced. She wants to gather up armfuls of the tiny blooms but her father says it's better not to pick them. 'Desert flowers are extremely fragile', he explains. 'They wilt and die very quickly.'

Alex refrains from picking the poppies, looking so frail and wispy blowing about on their long thin stalks. But sometimes she can't resist gathering a few flowers to decorate her 'turret room', where they begin to droop immediately.

March brings the Bedouin, heralded by the sound of tinny goat bells in the distance. They pitch their tents in rows within sight of K3 — some fifty black tents made of goats' hair. This is a small tribe, says Saeb; large tribes such as the Ruala, might have several thousand tents. Riding agile little horses and carrying guns slung over their backs and lances in their right hands, the lean, hawk-eyed Bedouin men drive their flocks of sheep and goats to each new settlement, along with a few camels and horses, the long-legged colts galloping ahead.

When Zilpha escorts her out of the gates, hordes of Bedouin children, shouting to one another in harsh voices, come charging towards them, crowding round Alex, trying to touch her hair and her clothes. Grubby brown hands pull at her, grab at Soda, and worst of all, point at her eye patch and laugh: the detested eye patch which she's obliged to wear to correct a slight squint in her right eye. The children gabble so fast that Alex can't pick out a word. Zilpha assures her they want to be friends. She envies them, sleeping in a tent, not having to go to bed at half past six, and having each other to play with. They can sit round the camp fire at night and eat supper with the grown-ups.

When Alex is in bed she can hear drumming and pipe music from the Bedouin camp.

Zilpha likes to chat to the Bedouin women. 'Ahlan wa sahlan!' they shout, and Zilpha replies 'Salaam aleikum!' Once they are invited into a tent full of chattering women. Inside, the ground is covered with threadbare rugs. They sit crowded together on embroidered bolsters and cushions. Zilpha keeps her legs neatly tucked under her skirt. Alex's bare legs stick straight out from her skimpy shorts. She guesses the women are making remarks about her grazed knees and her Clark's sandals, and wishes she could go barefoot like the Bedouin children. The women's faces are unveiled and their arms are tattooed with strange patterns. They appear thin and ugly to Alex, with harsh, squeaky voices. She gazes in fascination at their nails painted with henna and their eyes ringed with kohl. Zilpha, too, sometimes paints a line of black kohl around her eyes to make them look larger and more lustrous.

Alex is intrigued by a mother with a baby strapped to her back. It wears a string of bright blue beads round its forehead, and gold bangles on its tiny brown arms. It stares at Alex with huge fathomless eyes under eyelids blackened with kohl. This silent, wise-looking child bears no resemblance to the constantly wailing pink baby belonging to their neighbour, Mrs Jennings, at K3.

On arrival they are handed bowls of warmed goats' milk, smelling sickly but tasting pleasantly sweet. Alex has been warned to take the cup in her right hand to avoid offending their host. The women chat eagerly to Zilpha. Eventually Alex becomes restless, impatient to reach her 'castle' and resume her game of make-believe.

'The Bedouin ladies have real jewels hanging from their belts on silver chains!' Alex informs her father, but Giles says they're probably not valuable jewels – more likely to be agates or cornelians.

'Why are the Bedouin so thin and hungry-looking?'

'Because life in the desert is extremely hard', explains Giles, 'They don't have much to eat. Sometimes they exist for weeks on nothing but milk and a few dates and dried locusts.'

The idea of eating locusts is disgusting. 'Then why do they stay in the desert?'

'They're what we call nomads, people who have to move around to feed their flocks. Over the centuries they've learnt to like living in the desert. They feel free in all this space and they make their own laws. Frontiers don't worry the Bedouin.'

By the end of May the tents have moved on and the land around K3 looks strangely empty. The flowers, too, have withered away to dust, leaving nothing but nondescript thorns and dwarf acacia. The days become sweltering. 'I'm all sweaty' says Alex when they return from their walks.

'Don't use that word', Sheena tells her. 'It's politer to say *perspiring*'. But Alex prefers the word *sweaty*.

One afternoon as Alex and Zilpha approach the tell, half a dozen buzzards rise suddenly from behind the rocks and start circling above. 'Those ugly birds are really people the djinn has cast a spell on', says Alex.

'Don't be silly', says Zilpha. 'They're only vultures, probably waiting to finish eating a dead sheep or gazelle.'

Zilpha sits down on her usual stone and takes out her crochet work while Alex climbs up the rocks with Soda. Pulling off her eye-patch she unplaits her hair and places a cardboard crown covered with gold paper on her head. She keeps this crown in a large square Peek Frean's biscuit tin hidden under a rock. The tin is full of 'jewels' – coloured pebbles, some of Sheena's discarded bangles, earrings and beads, and a piece of broken mirror. Her prize possession is a string of paste pearls her mother threw out when Giles brought her three strings of tiny real pearls from Bahrein. Alex much prefers the large fake pearls.

She stares at her face in the mirror and chants softly: 'I am the Princess Alexandria, surpassing in beauty, with a face as radiant as the full moon. I have all the witchcraft of Babylon in my eyes!' For a couple of weeks now she's pretended to be a princess imprisoned by a wicked djinn. Soon a prince will come galloping across the desert on a pure white stallion to kill the djinn. The black birds still circling above the tell are princes who have already tried to save her and failed. They will swoop down, peck out the dead djinn's eyes and devour his body. The spell will be broken and they will be changed back into princes and return to their own kingdoms, leaving Princess Alexandria to ride away with her deliverer to Babylon. There they will live happily in a palace for ever after.

Alex gazes hopefully out of one of her 'turret windows' at the line of reddish hills to the west, and from another at the flat horizon to the south where all colour seems to melt away and she can hardly discern where the desert ends and the sky begins. She turns to scan the distant hazy shapes of the mountain ranges to the east, west and north. From which direction will her prince come riding? A gentle breeze billows out her white silken gown embroidered with tiny rubies. Her shining black locks flow down her back. In the milk-white sky the birds are still circling.

Suddenly Alex's crown slips off and blows away down the steepest side of the tell, the dangerous side which Zilpha has forbidden her to climb. But the precious crown must be retrieved, and Alex begins to descend cautiously. She can see the crown clinging to a jutting spit of rock halfway down. Searching for safe footholds she becomes aware of a stench which sharpens as she descends.

She's almost within reach of her crown when a second upsurge of breeze blows it further down, out of sight. Alex lies flat on her stomach on the spit of rock and peers over the edge. She can see the base of the tell now where the lowest rocks spread fingers of stone along the ground like tree roots. There's no sign of the crown.

She edges further out and experiences a visual impact so shocking that later she will never be able to describe it in detail to anyone. So paralysing is her fear that movement is impossible. She remains frozen to her perch staring fixedly at the crown which has landed on the massive half-naked body of a man lying on his back, jammed between two rocks. She shuts her eyes tightly, and then looks again, taking in the black beard, hairy chest, torn blue trousers and, worst of all, the gaping black holes in his bloodied face. This must be the djinn Saeb has warned her against, come out of his cave and waiting to catch her. Alex's fantasy world has become grim reality.

The djinn seems to stare straight at her. No movement – is he dead, or is he tricking her? If she descends to retrieve her crown, will he rise up and clutch at her with his huge bristly hands? Will he turn her into a buzzard? She looks up at the birds, settled on the rocks above, waiting to continue their feast, gazing down at her like malevolent old men in shabby black suits.

She shouts to Zilpha but no sound emerges. She must act quickly before the djinn moves. With difficulty she scrambles back up the rocks. At the top she grabs Soda. With loose hair and still wearing the pearls she descends to her nanny and bursts into tears.

'What's the matter, sweetheart?'

'The djinn! I saw him! On the other side of the rocks! Just like Saeb said! With black holes in his face!' gasps Alex between sobs.

Zilpha however has had long experience of Alex's imagination. Putting her arms round the child she says soothingly, 'Djinns don't exist except in story books. It must have been the black birds that frightened you.'

'No, it was the djinn. It was!'

Alex starts to run towards K3 and Zilpha follows, shouting 'Where's your eye-patch?'

'In my pocket.'

'Stop and put it on.'

But Alex doesn't stop until she reaches the gates of K3, which Saeb opens, exclaiming as usual, 'Quick! Quick! Inside the gates or the djinn will get you!'

After this disturbing incident Alex refuses to go for walks in the desert again. For some weeks her dreams are dominated by the image of the djinn waiting to catch her. She hears Zilpha telling her mother that the buzzards have frightened her daughter, and Sheena accepts this reason with relief. Zilpha now takes Alex sedately round the compound for her afternoon outing. They walk past the rows of white bungalows, past the clubhouse, tennis courts, two shops and the storehouse. Then they skirt the airstrip and the high wire fence enclosing the towering silvery oil tanks, the power house and telecommunications: a dull walk but a safe one. No djinn would dare to come inside the station. It isn't the kind of place djinns frequent. K3 is very much a place where nothing frightening ever happens.

Chapter Two

Sheena and Giles decide to give a cocktail party. Would Alex like to stay up late for a treat and help pass round the savouries Zilpha is so clever at making? 'You may wear your new frock, and just for once leave off your eye-patch', says Sheena. Alex is nervous at the thought of appearing at an adult party but desperately wants to wear the pink organdie frock with the intricate smocking which Zilpha has made for her on the Singer sewing machine. Zilpha is an exceptionally talented dressmaker.

Guests begin to arrive, exclaiming 'Hello' in loud voices, and laughing brightly at incomprehensible jokes. Alex takes fright and wishes she hadn't stayed up. The living room becomes choked with cigarette smoke and the odour of powder and perfume. The smiling mouths above her are opening and shutting so fast she can't make sense of the conversations. Two of the ladies remind Alex of her dolls – their bare brown backs smooth and unreal, like wax.

Jaws move up and down as the snacks are devoured. How grotesque mouths begin to look, thinks Alex, if you stare at them long enough!

She edges her way back to the kitchen, where Zilpha chides her gently.

'Oh, sweetheart, don't be such a baby! No one's going to bite you! Take this bowl of nuts and offer it to each guest.'

The child hovers just inside the living room door wondering how to penetrate the nearest group. The glass bowl weighs heavily in her small hands as she worms her way through the bodies. A lady in tight scarlet satin with lipstick and nail varnish to match bends over Alex. The top of her ample breasts burgeon out from her bodice almost brushing the child's cheek. 'Let me pass round those nuts for you, my poppet.'

But Alex, having taken the plunge, is not to be deterred. 'No, thank you,' she replies firmly, 'Sheena said I was to do it.'

'Good heavens! You're not calling your mother Sheena already!'

'She doesn't like being called Mummy.'

'And how about your father?'

'I used to call him Daddy but now I call him Giles.'

'Very grown up, I must say!' The lady laughs, and picking out two plump cashews between scarlet fingernails she pops them between her glossy red lips and totters away on impossibly high heels. Alex is glad her mother doesn't have breasts like the lady in red. She notes with pride that Sheena is by far the most beautiful woman in the room, the only one who could pass as a princess.

Later, in bed, Alex listens to the chatter becoming louder and shriller, and even after the last guest has gone giggling down the drive she can't get to sleep. Climbing out from under the mosquito net she pads along the passage in bare feet to the bathroom. On the way back she stops as always outside her parents' bedroom. The light is still on

15

and she can hear her mother's irritated high-pitched tone. Sheena, who rarely permits herself to argue or quarrel with Giles in front of Alex, will rail on for an hour or more in the privacy of her bedroom, especially after a few drinks.

Alex catches the sound of her own name and strains to hear every word. This isn't the first time she's listened to her parents' discussions behind closed doors. Zilpha has caught her at it more than once and rebuked her sharply, saying eavesdroppers never hear good of themselves. This line of reasoning only makes Alex more inclined to listen. If people are saying things about her, pleasant or unpleasant, she wants to hear them.

Tonight Giles and Sheena aren't having a quarrel, just a heated conversation.

'I'm sick of everyone telling me I should have taken Alex to South Africa! Peter had the bloody nerve to tell me it was selfish to keep her here!'

'Why worry about what Peter says when he's had too much to drink?' says Giles. 'He's just jealous because his wife and kids have gone and he's feeling lonely.'

'He sounds so self-righteous going on about Baghdad being full of pro-Nazis waiting for Hitler's invasion. Iraq will be taken over, he says, and the whole Middle east will follow. Alex and I will end up in a concentration camp and it will serve me right!'

'Peter dramatises everything. The Iraqis are doing far too well out of the oil companies to change sides. We have an excellent relationship with the government and with our Iraqi employees. The PM, Nuri al Said, and the Regent are doing a good job to keep the country in order. You mustn't let Peter provoke you so easily.'

But Sheena is always prickly on the question of what they should have done with Alex at the outbreak of war in 1939. 'And you're just as bad as Peter! You wanted to pack us off to the UK'

'I didn't want to, Sheena. I was simply prepared to do so for your own safety.'

'When I did suggest sending Alex home to my mother you were completely against it!'

'Of course I was. How do we know how long this war will last? I've told you again and again that if you'd opted to go with Alex I'd have accepted your decision. As it is I'm only too glad to have you both here.'

But Sheena won't let this well-worn subject drop. 'How could you expect my mother to put us both up with all the family in that little semi in Glasgow? I'd have gone mad in a week! Anyway, there's my job at the hospital here. They're desperate for trained nurses. It's different for wives who sit around the club all day with nothing to do.'

'You don't have to keep justifying your decision, Sheena.'

'Imagine if we had gone home! It's been the worst winter in the UK for years. Mother said the pipes were frozen for a month. Alex would probably have caught pneumonia.'

'I'm glad you stayed.' Giles' voice is weary. 'There's nothing we can do about it now.'

'Someone said tonight that a pro-Nazi called Raschid Ali is stirring the people up against the British and planning to negotiate with Hitler. Is it true?'

'It might be.'

'If the Germans do invade, we won't stand a chance, will we?'

'Don't worry. The Germans won't get their hands on Iraq.'

Sheena is silent for a moment and then changes the subject. 'If the war does end soon we could send Alex to a boarding school in England next year.'

'A boarding school!' Giles is aghast.

'Yes. She ought to be at school. If she doesn't learn to mix with other children she'll become a problem child. You saw tonight how incredibly shy and awkward she is.'

'Lots of children are shy. Why on earth should she turn into a problem child?' Giles sounds impatient for the first time.

'Because you and Zilpha spoil her. You let her argue and sulk and answer back. You fill her head with adult ideas she doesn't understand, and allow her to daydream when she should be paying attention. All our friends think she's a peculiar child. She never smiles or talks naturally to people. And lately she's bursting into tears at the slightest criticism.'

'You're exaggerating grossly. She is rather shy, and sensitive, but she'll grow out of it when she eventually goes to school.'

Sheena's voice rises in frustration. 'She should be at school right now. If she was a charming, friendly child like Tony Hotchkiss it wouldn't matter so much.'

'Tony Hotchkiss is older and not half as bright as Alex.'

'What's that got to do with it? You must be blind if you can't see there's something very odd about your daughter.'

'I find her intelligent and perfectly likable,' Giles insists doggedly.

'And another thing – she won't wear her eye-patch' continues Sheena. 'Her squint's as bad as it was before her operation. In a few months she'll probably have to wear glasses. What a sight she'll be then!'

'She can't help how she looks.'

'If she had any charm her looks wouldn't matter so much.'

'For goodness sake, Sheena, we're talking about a six-year-old!' Giles sounds angry now. 'Since she's the only child we'll ever have you'd better make the best of it.'

'I sometimes wonder how she could possibly be my daughter.'

A tense silence follows Sheena's last remark, and Alex, standing stock-still outside the door, shivers suddenly, though the night is warm. Then her mother says, 'Sorry,

Giles. Of course I love Alex, and I want the best for her. I just wish she was different. I feel guilty about her but what can I do?'

When Giles answers it's in a strange, sad tone. 'Alex needs lots of affection. If you can't give it she might well become a problem child. She not only needs love, she gives it too.'

'To you she does – and to Zilpha. But not to me.'

'You don't give her a chance. Some evenings you don't even go to kiss her goodnight.'

'She makes it obvious she'd rather have you or Zilpha at bedtime.'

'She likes the stories Zilpha tells her.'

'I'm too tired to tell stories after working all day. Zilpha fills her head with too many stories, some of them quite unsuitable. And shoving all that religion down her throat.'

'There's no harm in her learning about Christianity. She can discard it later if she wants to. We were so lucky to find a nanny like Zilpha. She's a very talented and highly moral young woman.'

'I agree she's reliable, but I find her attitude vaguely insolent. She sets Alex against me.'

'You're wrong. Like most Arabs, Zilpha's very fond of children. There's no need to be jealous.'

'How could I be jealous of a servant?'

There is a pause and then Giles says, 'It was a mistake allowing Alex to call us by our Christian names. It puts us on a par with Zilpha.'

'Possibly, but I did hate being called Mummy.'

Another silence and then her mother says in a cajoling tone, 'We could afford to send Alex to a really good boarding school, couldn't we? If I go on nursing?'?'

'Sheena, this idea of boarding school amazes me. We settled long ago that after the war Alex will live with my sister and go to the local school with her cousins. May is very keen to have her.'

'May will spoil Alex. She doesn't believe in discipline. I bet her children run wild. And the one thing Alex needs is discipline. If I go on nursing, I'm sure we could afford a boarding school.'

'It's too late to discuss it now. But one thing I do know: Alex will never be happy at a boarding school.'

When the line of light under her parents' door disappears Alex continues to stand motionless for a while. Then she returns to her bedroom with a quickened heartbeat, mulling over what she's heard. Deep within her has always been the fear she'll never live up to Sheena's standards. Zilpha has assured her that all mothers love their children, however naughty, stupid or ugly they may be, and in the past Alex has believed her. Now she knows for certain that she herself will have to earn her mother's love. If she's good, works hard and never argues, if she's polite and charming to her parents' friends, if she wears her eye-patch at all times – then Sheena might come to like her, to be proud of her.

How humiliating that her mother approves of Tony Hotchkiss, the eight-year-old boy who lives in the bungalow next door. In Alex's experience Tony is neither charming nor friendly. He is forever taunting her, calling her 'The Pirate' because of her eye-patch, and laughing at her name. She's explained that she was christened Alexandria, after the town in Egypt where her father first met Sheena. But Tony says people are never called after towns. He laughs at the name 'Sheena' too. He says it's showing off to have a fancy name no one's ever heard of.

Alex likes her name – Alexandria Jane Kinley. Her christening took place at a church in Haifa, where she was carried to the font by Giles's sister, her Aunty May, since Sheena had to stay in hospital for two months after giving birth. May, who adores children, came out to Haifa from England to look after her niece. Alex has a photograph of her aunt with her husband, Bill, and their two children, Martin and Caroline, aged three and four. Alex likes the idea of living with this kind-looking aunt who adores children, but wonders how she would get on with the cousins. But now, if Sheena has her way —she'll be sent to boarding school. If only her mother liked May, if only her mother liked all the relatives who live in England and Scotland. But her tone always suggests she has little time for family ties.

Towards dawn Alex finally falls asleep, and dreams that her aunt comes to visit and exclaims 'What a charming little girl Alexandria has turned out to be!'

Chapter Three

Alex is lying in the hammock which Mustapha, the gardener, has strung up for her between two small date palms. Her eyes are half-shut against the glare of the noonday sun stabbing at her through green fronds. She's daydreaming about going to 'Fields' with her father. He's been promising to take her for a long time. She's seen pictures of green fields but Giles says oilfields are quite different.

At this time of day the stench of crude oil hangs over the whole station. Alex loves the soporific, comforting smell she's breathed in for as long as she can remember. When visitors come up the line from Haifa to K3 they complain that even the whisky tastes of oil. An American lady once drawled as she sniffed her hands, 'Just like gasoline's oozing out of my pores!' How odd, Alex thought, that she should call her freckled hands sparkling with diamond rings, *paws*. 'How you folks can live in this place for months on end!' she kept repeating. 'It's no bigger than a summer camp – and all that desert with nothing to look at!'

But Alex is happy at K3. She likes their bungalow with its large garden full of dwarf palms and colourful shrubs – hibiscus, tamarisk, oleander and flowering cacti. A truck frequently brings fresh top-soil from Baghdad and

Mustapha sprinkles the lawn with water every day. In a small patch marked off with yellow stones collected from the desert Alex has created her own vegetable garden next to Zilpha's thriving herb garden. Sometimes if she lies long enough on her stomach in the grass she can almost catch the seedlings unfurling their tiny leaves. The scent of Zilpha's herbs – parsley, coriander, oregano, marjoram, thyme, tarragon, fennel and mint – is intoxicating in the heat. It's a miracle, says her father, what can be made to grow in the desert.

Alex's exercise book of half-finished sums has slipped onto the grass beneath the hammock. On her ribs she's balanced a large book of *Grimm's Fairy Tales* illustrated by Walter Crane. She turns the pages lovingly – *The Golden Bird, Rumpelstiltskin, Snow White, The Goose Girl, The Frog Prince...* Her favourite picture is of Rapunzel letting down her long golden hair from the top of a tower. Any minute now the midday siren will go off and Giles will come home to give his daughter a lesson before lunch, grumbling because she hasn't finished her sums. But he never stays cross for long.

His car is reversing into the garage. He'll wash and change his shirt before coming out to inspect her morning's work. Alex gazes for a second into the white-hot light behind the foliage. She shuts her eyes and opens them again to find him standing beside the hammock looking down at her with his slightly crooked smile and the amused look in his hazel eyes belying a deep compassion. She breathes in the comforting smell of Wright's Coal Tar soap. The edge of Giles's brown moustache is tinged yellow with nicotine. His tanned face is already creased with thin lines; yet her mother's face isn't lined at all. Sheena always wears a large hat in the sun.

Giles says sternly, 'Alex, where's your eye-patch?'

'I don't know.'

He knows she's fibbing. 'Go and put it on at once! You've got to get that lazy eye of yours working.'

She drags her feet across the lawn, stopping to observe a tawny green lizard scurrying off into an oleander bush ablaze with magenta flowers. She climbs the two stone steps up to the verandah and breathes in the honeyed scent of the jasmine twined along the trellis, the only scent that can compete with the constant smell of oil.

Zilpha is laying the wickerwork table with the glass top for lunch. Alex pinches a grape from a basket of fruit and walks through the living room and across the hall to her bedroom. The eye-patch is under her pillow – a shiny stiff pink shape attached to a thin pink elastic. She fits it over her left eye and regards herself in the mirror. Skimpy mouse-coloured plaits hang on each side of a thin sallow face. How very plain she looks! Soon she'll have to wear glasses, and Tony Hotchkiss will think up other rude names to call her. But with luck he may have gone to Egypt by then. She pulls the patch down round her neck and brings her face close to the mirror to look at her squinting right eye. If it doesn't straighten itself in a year she may have to undergo another operation. Will the doctor take her eye out to repair it? She pictures it squinting at the surgeon as it lies in a white kidney bowl like the one Sheena sometimes brings home from the hospital. For the first time she notices that one side of her face is quite different from the other. She pulls the eye-patch back into position as she hears her father calling.

Alex returns noiselessly to the living room. Giles is kneeling with his back to her on a Persian rug beside the overloaded bookcase. She moves carefully between two gleaming brass trays on their wooden stands and jumps at him, growling. They tumble over together, Alex giggling and saying 'I stalked you just like Shere Khan!'

Giles gives Alex her lessons at the walnut dining table with carved legs. This table is the envy of Sheena's friends. 'Bought for a song', she tells people, 'In Cairo after our wedding'. Alex likes the image; what was the song, and who sang it, she wonders. There are six carved chairs to match the table. Zilpha keeps the top polished like glass under its velveteen cover.

When the table is laid for a dinner party Alex is permitted to light the six tall pink candles in their copper holders for a few moments. She loves to watch the tiny flames reflected in the shining wood on either side of a copper bowl of pale pink roses. Beside each place setting stand copper finger bowls and pink damask napkins. A pity the meal will disturb such a beautiful arrangement!

Giles does up the fastening at the back of Sheena's dinner gown and kisses the smooth white nape of her neck. When she bends to light her cigarette from a candle flame her auburn hair, braided intricately in coils around her ears, gleams in the soft light. Alex desperately wants to put her arms round her mother's neck and whisper, 'You're the most beautiful princess in the whole world!' But she doesn't. Instead she hears Sheena say briskly, 'Time you were in bed, Alex'.

During the day the dining room shutters are half closed to protect the Persian carpet from the sun, and Giles switches on a table-lamp. On weekdays he gives Alex arithmetic, writing and literature lessons. On Saturday it's lessons all morning, a mixture of history, geography and nature study. Most of all he enjoys telling her about this own pet subject, ancient history and archaeology. His craze for exploring ancient sites and buildings is one of the reasons he took a job in the Middle East. When Alex is bored with arithmetic she can usually tempt him to talk about the places he's seen. He stresses that two thousand years before Jesus was born the two great civilisations of the world were in Egypt and in Mesopotamia, the old name for Iraq. 'The Arabs, the Chinese, the Jews, the Greeks and the Romans were all civilised centuries before us. So don't ever make the mistake, Alex, as most British people do, of thinking ourselves superior to the Arabs.'

He encourages his daughter to be curious about everything around her, never to be afraid to ask questions.

Sometimes Sheena comes into the dining room during the lessons and listens to Giles. 'It's ridiculous the way you talk to Alex. You fill her head with long words and ideas she can't possibly understand.' She thinks Giles should stick to the textbooks for young children which he ordered from the London bookstore, Bumpus, before the war.

Sheena comes home from the hospital at half past one for lunch, looking smart and efficient in her white uniform. If she can't be a princess when she grows up, Alex would like to be a nurse. Sheena took her to the hospital once to visit Tony after he'd had his tonsils out. She sat for twenty minutes saying nothing to the boy but taking in every detail of the ward. How lovely to wear a starched white veil and a white overall with a row of safety pins attached to the breast pocket; to carry trays of jelly and ice cream to the sick people tucked up so neatly under the crisp white sheets; to pop thermometers into their mouths...

Sheena takes off her veil at lunchtime and unpins her thick plait. If only Alex had hair like her mother's, how happy she would be. How cool and pretty Sheena looks, even in uniform. She never becomes hot and sweaty. Sometimes Alex catches sight of Sheena sitting in front of her mirror in the bedroom, brushing her hair which flows down the back of her black silk housecoat embroidered with big white daisies. She would like to be allowed to brush her mother's hair...

Zilpha has laid out a cold lunch on the verandah: kibbeh (croquettes made of lamb and bulgar wheat), a bowl of glistening tabouleh, stuffed eggs, home-made rolls, a jug of iced orange juice. But Alex isn't hungry. It's too hot. She's still toying with her first course while her parents are having fruit and coffee. 'Stop playing about with your food, Alex', says Sheena impatiently. 'You mustn't waste food when people are being rationed in England.'

'Why does food have to be rationed?'

'Because there isn't enough to go round', snaps her mother.

'The reason is', explains Giles, 'that the ships which normally bring food from other countries to Britain have had to stop in case they get torpedoed by the Germans.'

'In England', adds Sheena, 'Every child has to drink a nasty concentrated orange juice mixed with cod liver oil because there are no fresh oranges. So drink up your juice. You're lucky we haven't any shortage of food in Iraq.'

Giles opens an air mail letter from his sister in Liverpool. 'Your Aunty May mentions the rationing', Giles tells Alex. *'Rationing in Britain gets worse every month'* he reads*.' We get very little butter and hardly any fresh eggs. The margarine and egg powder are disgusting. It's become impossible to ask friends round for a decent meal. How I miss those family parties we had before the war...'*

After lunch Giles insists on Alex finishing her sums. 'You must make more effort, Alex', says Sheena. 'You won't want to lag behind other children of your own age when you go to school.'

'When will I go to school?' asks the child, annoyingly, since she knows the answer already: when the war is over. It is Sheena's answer to most of her questions. If only the war would go on for ever! Then she would never have to go to school.

Giles and Sheena usually rest for an hour before returning to work. Alex goes to her room, where she tries to work out the unfinished sums. She gives up and glances along her bookshelf. She's read all the books over and over again: *The Jungle Book, The Princess and the Goblin, The Little Grey Men, The Land of Green Ginger, Emil and the Detectives, The Cave Twins, The Flower Fairies...* She pulls down *The Princess and Curdie* and pretends she is the Princess of the Silver Moon in her emerald grotto deep within the mountain.

Suddenly the telephone rings in the living room. Sheena shouts 'For you, Giles, a call from Haifa.' Alex slips out of her room and watches her father pick up and later replace the heavy black receiver. He looks very serious.

'What's happened?' asks Sheena.

'The refinery's been bombed again. Two tanks on fire and the recording instruments in the power house damaged. German bombers this time operating from a base in Syria.'

'Will the pipelines have to be shut down?'

'No. But it's a worrying situation. We've always assumed the Germans wouldn't want to destroy the refinery, in the hope of using it themselves eventually.'

'Then you mustn't take Alex with you on your next trip to 'Fields'. They were saying at the hospital there have been riots in Baghdad. The government could fall at any moment. Those fascist generals who've always been against the oil concessions could seize power.'

'If by some remote chance Raschid Ali and his cronies staged a coup and invited the Germans to invade, we'd be in just as much danger here at K3 as in Kirkuk or Baghdad. If there's the slightest hint of trouble I'll drive straight home.'

With a gesture of impatience Sheena returns to her bedroom and puts on her uniform. Then she stands in front of the living room mirror to fasten her veil, saying peevishly, 'Why are these damned Iraqis turning against us? They ought to be grateful for all we've done for them.'

'They are grateful', says Giles. 'But they're also proud. They dislike the way we continue to treat them as inferiors, and even the way we segregate ourselves socially.'

'They'd hate it if we tried to socialise with them. How can you socialise with Muslims? Look at the way they treat their women!'

'There are Christians and Jews as well. We could make more effort. I have several very good friends among the Iraqis in Kirkuk. It's just a question of tolerating their customs.'

'It would take a lifetime to learn their endless customs. Where will you be staying in Baghdad?'

'With Leila.'

'It would be much safer with Terry and Jane at Alwiyeh.'

'And much less interesting, in a Company bungalow. I'd like to show Alex a genuine Iraqi home.'

'All cluttered up with useless ornaments. Leila likes to show off her possessions like all the Arabs. And rats come up to her house from the river.'

'Leila is partly French, and she doesn't show off. As for rats, I've never seen one.'

Giles's calm persistence infuriates Sheena and she raises her voice. 'What's the point of dragging a small child to Kirkuk and driving another five hours to Baghdad and then on to Babylon. Alex won't be interested in your oilfields or your ruins. She'll just be a nuisance.'

Alex wants to deny this but dares not interrupt. She's afraid Sheena will stop her going to 'Fields'. 'It will do Alex good to have a change', insists Giles. 'K3's very limiting. Travel is an excellent form of education, even for a child.'

'And what will she do while you're seeing people in Kirkuk?'

'She can sit in the rest house and do her homework.'

'Won't they think it strange, leaving a child in the rest house on her own. And if you take her to Baghdad she'll probably pick up a tummy bug.'

Sheena looks at her watch and walks out of the house without another word. When Giles has gone too, Alex finds Zilpha sitting on the verandah steps with a large yellow hibiscus flower in her hair, stringing a bowl of green beans.

'Is it yakhne for lunch tomorrow?' she asks.

'Yes.'

Alex loves yakhne, the savoury stew of runner beans, tomatoes, onions and lamb, served with rice. She loves all the dishes Zilpha cooks. Mustapha grows a great variety of vegetables in the garden — okra, egg-plant, peppers, tomatoes, onions, beans, marrow, and Alex's pet hate, spinach. Zilpha combines lamb or chicken with the vegetables in many different recipes. Her greatest culinary talent is for pastries and cakes. Alex helps her make mahmoul with dates and walnuts, and saffron cake with semolina and tahina. 'Always make small pastries for visitors', Zilpha informs her. 'It shows you've taken more trouble. And try to make something yellow. Yellow things are said to bring happiness.'

Giles says Zilpha is more talented than all the wives at K3 put together. The weight of the thick shining braid of black hair hanging below Zilpha's waist fascinates Alex. The ladies at the club spend hours sunbathing, but their skin never looks as smooth and silky-brown as Zilpha's. Sheena is the only woman at the club who doesn't lie in the sun. Her skin remains creamy white.

'I was born in Haifa', says Alex, 'So why don't I look like a Palestinian?'

'Because you inherit your skin colouring from your parents and ancestors, not from your place of birth,' explains Zilpha.

'But I don't look like my mother.'

'No, you look more like your father's sister.'

'Did you know my Aunty May?' Alex enquires eagerly.

'Yes, I met her a few days before she left Haifa when you were six months old. She went back to England to get married.'

'Is she pretty?'

'She has a very pleasant, kind face. She didn't want to leave you. She was in tears when she handed you over to me.'

Alex wishes she could remember being cared for by her aunt. She retains a few hazy memories of the house in Haifa: a monkey puzzle tree, a wide balcony with a high white balustrade onto which her father used to lift her to look at the Mediterranean sparkling in the sunshine below Mount Carmel, and a terrifying bulldog next door.

'Have I been to Jerusalem?' Alex asks.

'No, your mother never wanted to visit Jerusalem. There's always trouble in Jerusalem. People letting off bombs in shops and hotels and cinemas...'

'Why?'

Zilpha, a Palestinian girl herself, tries to explain about the influx of Jewish refugees from Europe. 'Some of the Jews are trying to push the Palestinians out of the country. They want Palestine to be a Jewish state and to call it Israel.'

'But that's not fair!' says Alex indignantly.

'No, it's not. Some of the Jews have formed themselves into a gang to try and force the Palestinians to flee. The Stern Gang, it's called. They blow up Arab houses and murder the people who don't run away.'

'Where do those nasty Jews come from?'

'They've escaped from different countries in Europe because Hitler is trying to kill all Jews.'

Alex's sympathy immediately extends to the Jewish refugees, but at the back of her mind she ponders the logic of the Jews fleeing violence only to mete out violence in their turn. 'Are there some good Jews?'

'Of course', replies Zilpha. 'There are good and bad as there are in every country. Some brave Jews have hidden Palestinians in their houses to escape the Stern Gang. I have some very good Jewish friends. But the Jews mustn't be allowed to turn Palestine into a Jewish state.'

'Why did the Jews go to Europe in the first place?'

'Palestine has been conquered by many countries, and each time the Jews fled elsewhere. Now their descendants want to come back.'

'Where could they go if they don't come to Palestine?'

'A few could come, but the rest should be divided between friendly countries like England and America.'

Alex often thinks about the Jews. If Palestine is such a tiny country with no room for all the Jews and all the Palestinians, why don't the Jews make a country for themselves in the huge Arabian desert which Giles has shown her in his Atlas? Surely the Bedouin could spare some of it? The poor Jews must have somewhere to go. Zilpha says Jesus was a Jew, but the Jews don't believe he was God's Son. But it was only the bad Jews who wanted him dead, the kind of men who are in the Stern Gang. Alex listens intently to Zilpha reading aloud stories of Jesus' life, but she hates the ending. Zilpha has described in detail what a crucifixion entails.

'Why did Jesus let himself be arrested?'

'Because he knew he had to die to save us' says Zilpha.

Alex cannot comprehend this. She wouldn't want anyone to die for her sake. 'Did Jesus feel much pain when he was crucified?'

Zilpha says he did, even though he was God as well as a man. It's possible that he felt more pain than an ordinary human being because he hadn't ever done anything wrong in the whole of his life. But if he was so good how could God let him be crucified? The story remains a puzzle.

On Easter Day Jesus rose from the dead and appeared in the garden, all calm and smiling, dressed in white and looking like an angel. Everyone is happy at Easter but Alex wonders how they can forget about the crucifixion so quickly, and all the torture that Jesus suffered. She wonders what the world would be like if he hadn't been crucified.

Zilpha says Alex was baptised as a baby. That means she is a Christian. Giles says it doesn't really matter whether you are a Christian or not, provided you always treat other people the way you'd like them to treat you. But Zilpha insists you do have to be a Christian if you want to go to heaven and live with God.

'What will happen to my father when he dies?' asks Alex.

'Your father is a good man' was all Zilpha would say. Sheena was brought up very strictly as a Roman Catholic but she won't discuss religion. Zilpha is Greek Orthodox.

Alex doesn't understand why there are so many kinds of Christian.

Giles's mother has sent Alex a large volume of Bible stories with brightly coloured pictures of Palestine which Zilpha dislikes. 'Jesus didn't look like this!' she exclaims. 'He was a Palestinian with brown skin and dark eyes like mine. And the Sea of Galilee doesn't look like this pretty English lake.' Zilpha should know since she was brought up in Galilee in the village of Al Naher. She's promised when the war is over to take Alex to Galilee and show her all the places where Jesus used to go. 'In spring Galilee is so beautiful with fields of wild blue lupins and dark red irises.'

There's a room set aside as a chapel in the K3 clubhouse, where Zilpha once took Alex to a service. On a dark blue carpet stand five rows of polished wooden chairs with pale blue leather seats. Facing the chairs is a table covered with an embroidered cloth, two brass candlesticks, a heavy cross in dark wood and a bowl of white artificial lilies. There are blue leather hassocks to kneel on, and a blue hymn book tucked into a wooden pocket behind each chair. A plump lady sits at a black piano, and a tall thin man in a white robe preaches a sermon in between two hymns. He talks about the war and tells his congregation that if they all pray hard enough 'God will bring victory to our cause'. Alex thinks if God can bring victory why doesn't he do it now before any more people get killed?

On the way out the padre had smiled at Zilpha and patted Alex on the head. But Zilpha wouldn't go again. She doesn't approve of the chapel. A chapel should have a statue of our Lady, a confessional box and a real priest to say Mass. Alex doesn't like the idea of confession. To have to tell all the bad things she's done, and even the bad things she's thought! She could never confess to the padre. Sheena says he's a fool and a crashing bore. Giles says he means well.

Zilpha is very devout, and talks a great deal about religion. Apart from Zilpha, Saeb is the only Christian Arab at K3. All the rest are Muslims. Zilpha doesn't trust the Muslims. She says they hate Christians. But Alex trusts the Muslim gardener, Mustapha, and he likes her. In a history lesson Giles points out that Christians are partly to blame for the Muslims being unfriendly at times. Centuries ago Christians from Europe went on Crusades against the Muslims and treated them very cruelly. Before the Crusades the Muslims were, on the whole, very tolerant towards both Jews and Christians. Their leader, the Prophet Muhammad commanded his followers to respect all human life.

Alex loves her history lessons. Giles has told her stories about the early history of Britain, but most of the time he tells her about the Middle East. Everyone should know the history of the region they live in. He even tells her the story of the oil industry in Iraq and Persia. Sheena disapproves of this. 'You should stick to British history so when she goes to school she won't be at a disadvantage.'

'The discovery of oil in the Middle East is very much part of British history', Giles retorts. 'We ruled Iraq until 1932 – and our discovery of the oilfields is possibly the most important event in our history so far this century. We live on the pipeline so it's logical for Alex to learn what it's all about.'

'Oil is a very dull subject for a child.'

'Not if I show her how an oil well functions. It's a unique opportunity.'

'You'll bore her with it just as you bore me with all those technical terms.'

But Sheena's wrong. Giles is a natural teacher. Alex is rarely bored. He's helped Alex draw a large map of the Middle East, marking in the two main rivers, Tigris and Euphrates, in blue crayon, the oil wells in red and the pipelines in black. The desert area is yellow, the fertile parts green and the mountains purple. Giles has shown her where the two twelve-inch pipelines start at Kirkuk and run through three pumping stations crossing the Iraqi desert, K1, K2 and K3. He describes the difficulties the workers had to endure in building these pipelines in the blazing heat and icy cold, with very little water. Fleets of lorries had to contend with rough tracks and sandstorms in order to bring everything they needed to live for months in the desert. Hundreds of men worked day after day welding, wrapping and burying the lengths of piping.

At K3 the two pipelines diverge. One heads south for six hundred and twenty miles across the huge yellow patch of Jordan, passing through more pumping stations until it reaches Haifa. The other one, only five hundred and thirty-two miles long, crosses the Syrian desert, passing through four stations to the port of Tripoli in Lebanon. 'The two lines were opened at a big ceremony on January 15th 1935, when you were only a year old, and still living in Haifa. King Ghazi came with lots of other important people, and he turned on the tap which started the oil flowing on its long journey to the sea. Ghazi was recently killed in a car accident', Giles informs Alex. 'His son, Feisal, is only a child about your age, so Iraq is being ruled by Abdullah, Ghazi's brother, until Feisal is eighteen. Abdullah is known as the Prince Regent.'

'What about Feisal's mother?' asks Alex.

'Queen Aliyah helps the Regent.'

'Does she wear a crown?'

'She did when King Ghazi opened the pipelines. Now of course the pipeline to Tripoli has had to be closed because Lebanon and Syria have a French government supporting the Germans. We hope the British will soon liberate Lebanon and Syria. Until then the oil can only go to Haifa where it's cleaned and made suitable for the warships and planes and motor vehicles.'

Alex is very excited at the thought of going to 'Fields' with her father. She informs Tony Hotchkiss that they're also going to Babylon.

He isn't impressed. 'Who cares about going to 'Fields'?' He swoops round Alex, arms outstretched, pretending to be a fighter plane. I bet you don't know the difference between a Hurricane and a Halifax.'

'I do!'

'Liar! Bet you've never even seen a Gladiator fighter or a Wellington bomber. Anyway, we're going to Cairo soon in a Hawker Hind.'

What a relief to hear Tony will be departing! She hates being invited to play at his house. She's tired of hearing what he can do, sick of watching how skilfully he can pee from their verandah into the goldfish pond. He says all girls are born stupid. Giles used to give Tony lessons with Alex, but he had to stop because the boy was so slow at reading. Alex can't recall learning to read.

Sheena doesn't like Giles telling Alex too much about the war. 'You'll give the child nightmares.' But the war doesn't upset Alex. She thinks of Hitler and Mussolini as two wicked magicians who want to grab the oil. 'What would we do if the Germans invade Iraq?' she asks.

'We should try to stop them with our Air Force. It's based at Habbaniya. See if you can find it on the map.'

When she's located the place on the Euphrates, not far from Baghdad, Giles says 'The Air Force have had a flying school for years at Habbaniya, so our pilots know more about flying over the desert than the Germans do.'

Everyone at K3 listens avidly each day to the BBC bulletins. The wives who sit around the club pool sipping gin and orange are always talking about the war. Alex remembers the day her parents took her into a crowded room at the clubhouse to listen to a man announcing on the crackling wireless in a very serious voice that war had been declared. People then went home with worried faces. They acted the same way when they heard that a ship called the *Athenia* had been torpedoed. Alex expected something terrible to happen, but life continued as usual.

Alex is sometimes taken to see the Pathe newsreel at the club cinema. Giles tells her Britain is in great danger from German air attacks. She watches planes being shot down in flames, tanks moving across acres of mud, and German soldiers with swastikas on their uniforms marching stiffly across the screen. Names like Churchill, Eden, Pétain, Wavell... are mentioned again and again. But when Alex goes home to find Zilpha waiting with her supper – a boiled egg, hot buttered toast and a mug of cocoa – the war seems very far away.

The *Picture Post* magazines in the club lounge often carry pictures of Britain in wartime – grey double decker buses, queues of drab people outside the shops, broken-down buildings with smoke pouring out of them. Alex is glad she doesn't live there. In her atlas Britain is a tiny pink island. She imagines how it will be, travelling on a boat to Liverpool to meet her relations. She pictures them standing waving on the edge of the pink island as the ship comes into harbour.

A few days before they're due to leave for 'Fields' a sandstorm blows up in the desert. The initial ominous hush is disturbed by a cooling breeze which gathers in strength, throwing up wisps of sand and grit. Zilpha says they must stay indoors until the storm is over. Looking out it seems as though a great wall of black fog has surrounded the bungalow. This passes quickly, leaving the land bathed in an unearthly soft yellow light.

Alex sits in her bedroom peering at her illustrated Bible and talking to her camel. She's found a picture of the hanging gardens of Babylon, and another of the beautiful golden-stoned city itself. 'Look, Soda, what we're going to see!' But she hasn't understood the word 'reconstructed' or taken in the phrase 'as it might have looked' under the pictures. Soda remains impassive as she reads him the story of the Jewish captives who had to march across the desert from Palestine to the Euphrates where they sat down and wept. Zilpha has told her that actually many of the exiled Jews liked Babylon and never did return to Israel.

'And we're going to 'Fields', Soda! Giles says I'm probably the only girl ever to be taken to 'Fields'.'

Chapter Four

Zilpha wakes Alex early the day she's going to 'Fields', while it's still dark. 'Shh!' whispers Zilpha. 'We don't want to wake your mother.'

They move around on tiptoe packing a few last-minute things. Alex feels sick with excitement, but Zilpha insists she eat a bowl of labneh and a piece of toast. Giles is having his usual bowl of labneh with prunes – always six prunes for breakfast.

Outside, the garden is chilly and strange in the still grey light. Zilpha hugs and kisses Alex before she climbs into the black Ford car with her father. Saeb opens the gates, shouting, 'Allah yisellimak! Say a big hello to Baghdad for me! And don't let Soda run away!'

The prospect of four days on her own with Giles fills Alex with a delicious sense of security mixed with the excitement of the unknown. At home the presence of her mother never allows for security. Sheena's moods, the way her enthusiasm and charm can change into sudden boredom or irritation, altering plans or promises overnight, create an underlying tension. Alex hasn't yet learnt to gauge her mother's temper.

The smell of crude oil seems fainter, sweeter at this early hour, as they plunge into the huge, shadowy desert. Far away to the east a bank of dark cloud suffused at the edge with pink is piled above a horizon marked by a sickly yellowish green band of light which gradually widens as if presaging some miraculous happening. Then the cloud lifts and the yellow disappears leaving a pristine shell-pink sky. Presently the sun rises over the distant hills, and the daily wonder is over. The desert assumes its usual aspect, an unending expanse of brown scrubland beneath a glaring sky.

'When will we see a lake?', asks Alex.

'You won't see one.'

'Zilpha said I might see a lake.'

'She meant a mirage. When the sun is high, people often imagine they see water in the distance. Then it disappears.'

Alex looks out for a magic lake but sees nothing but bare brown terrain, absolutely flat except for the occasional horseshoe-shaped dent in the ground. Khaki rocks fling up the heat like a furnace.

'How much further?'

Giles laughs. 'A hundred and forty miles. We've hardly started. You'll have to be patient.' He stops to take another cigarette from a large flat tin of fifty, and places a map of Iraq across her knees. 'You can be our guide. Look, we're driving along this track running beside the pipeline all the way to K2. We'll have lunch there with Mr and Mrs Mason.'

'Do they have children?' Alex asks, visualising another Tony.

'No.' What a relief!.

K2 is like K3 – the same smell of oil, the same rows of neat bungalows and huge oil tanks. But the Masons' living room is nothing like the Kinleys'. The curtains are made of a heavy pink floral cretonne. The same material covers Morris chairs provided by the oil company. Lampshades of stitched parchment are fringed in pink silk. Lacy mats perch on little tables under a number of sepia photographs in heavy brass frames. Alex sits on a plum-coloured velvet pouf and stretches her legs out over a shaggy plum-coloured carpet.

On opening the door Mrs Mason had given a little shriek, crying, 'Goodness, what a big girl! Alexandria doesn't look anything like her mother, does she, Giles?'

'No, she doesn't' replies her father shortly. Alex wants to look like Sheena and for a moment she hates Giles.

Mrs Mason is very friendly and keeps placing a protective arm round the child. Alex doesn't enjoy this.

'What a pretty camel!' ventures Mrs Mason.

'He's not!' retorts Alex, 'He's old and ugly'.

Mrs Mason brings Alex iced lemonade and asks in a babyish voice 'Does camel want a drink?'

Alex stares at her contemptuously and replies 'Soda is a camel and camels can walk twenty-five miles a day for three days without water'. Giles gives his daughter a warning look. Alex knows she's being rude but Mrs Mason is laughing so she can't be offended.

Alex wonders where the Masons keep their books. She can only see a stack of magazines, with the New Yorker on top. The shutters are half closed to keep out the sun, but rather than cooling the room it makes the atmosphere seem hotter and more confined. There's a peculiar smell which she can't name. Her head begins to ache.

Mr Mason tells Giles they have a house guest, an American called Basil Carrington. 'He lived in Beirut until recently. We met him on our last trip to Baghdad at a welcome home party for the American Resident. Basil works for Shell. He'll be joining us in a minute.'

'You'll like him', adds Mrs Mason, 'He's so friendly, like most Americans.'

A moment later Basil Carrington comes into the living room and shakes hands with Giles. 'Hi there!' he says heartily to Alex when Mrs Mason introduces her. 'I have a little girl, not much older than you. Her name is Sally-Ann.' He regards Alex appraisingly with small metallic blue eyes. His eyebrows and eyelashes are so pale and stubby they're barely visible. He takes off his white Panama hat, revealing a bald pink patch surrounded by sandy coloured hair. He sits down heavily in a Morris chair and wipes his flushed face with a large silk handkerchief monogrammed with the letters B.D.C. A strong smell of cologne infiltrates the stuffy atmosphere.

Alex stares at the American and makes an immediate instinctive judgment. Can this man really be a father? Alex looks at her own father, realising for the first time just how fortunate she is, even though his clothes are scruffy compared to the American's immaculate white linen trousers, yellow silk shirt and yellow socks with two-tone cream and brown shoes. Mr Carrington's accent is soft and drawling, and his red lips smile easily. Alex watches his mouth opening and shutting, stretching into strange shapes as he dominates the conversation. How odd faces are, with their two entirely different sides! Giles's right eye, she notices, is higher than his left.

A shaft of sunlight pierces the gap in the shutters and lights up Mr Carrington's heavy gold watch and signet ring and the bristling gingery hairs on his freckled arms. Alex sits bolt upright on her pouf and attempts to look charming. She feels repelled by this man whose presence fills the room. Everyone is listening to him intently, laughing when he laughs. Mrs Mason is positively ogling him. Alex feels guilty as she remembers Zilpha's advice not to be too quick in judging someone at a first meeting. You have to give people a chance. Wait and see how they turn out.

Mr Carrington is telling Giles he sent his wife, Muriel, and his daughter back to the States when the French Vichy government took over Lebanon. 'Do you know Beirut?' he asks.

'No', replies Giles, 'But I've heard it's a beautiful city.'

'The Lebs are doing their best to ruin it. I still have an apartment in Beirut near the American University. I hope to return when your folks send the Vichy packing.'

At lunch Alex's plate has a piece of roast chicken on it, a heap of tinned carrots and peas and a mound of mashed potato. She pours thick brown gravy over it. She's not hungry so she mixes the food together with her knife and then rakes it over with her fork. 'Alex, do eat up your lunch', whispers Giles. She starts to eat but everyone else has finished and Mrs Mason tactfully whisks her plate away and replaces it with a bowl of red jelly and vanilla ice cream.

After the meal the grown-ups sip coffee, except for Mr Carrington who drinks another gin and tonic. He's just come from Abadan in Persia. It seems the Shah is aiding the Germans on the quiet, and some of the oil installations have been sabotaged. German technicians are forming a Fifth Column. 'Sabotage' and 'fifth column' – what can they mean? Alex wonders. Mr Mason says there's a Nazi printing press in Baghdad.

'You people need to be on your guard here', warns Mr Carrington. 'You can bet your bottom dollar the Iraqis will turn against you if they see any profit in it. Everyone in Abadan is gloomy about the future. The women have left for India or South Africa, and oil production is almost nil.'

Alex loses track of the conversation and wishes they could go. But Giles is having an argument with Mr Carrington about the Iraqis. The American maintains they have no loyalty. Britain has given them a modern state with railways and irrigation schemes and education and health care, yet they're not grateful.

Giles replies hotly that many of them are very grateful, but one should realise the British record in Iraq hasn't all been good. In return for their help against the Ottoman Turks in the last war, they were promised independence by France and Britain. When the war ended that promise was never fulfilled. The Kurds rebelled, and were put down with mustard gas in 1919.'

'Quite right too.'

'And when the Arab Iraqi leaders rose against us in 1921, we quite ruthlessly bombed villages full of civilians and livestock to save our troops having to march across the desert to confront the ringleaders.'

'That's history!' snorts Mr Carrington impatiently. 'How else could the Iraqi rebellion have been put down?'

'I find it remarkable that most Iraqis don't bear us a grudge.'

'They would if it suited them. They simply go for the biggest bribe, and the Germans arte bribing them right now.'

Alex can tell her father is annoyed, though his voice remains civil.

As they say goodbye, Mr Carrington mentions he's going on to K3 in the morning and he hopes the resthouse is tolerable.

'It's comfortable enough' replies Giles, 'But the food's pretty awful.' Alex is surprised when her father adds in a friendly manner, 'Why not stay at our house? My wife, Sheena, would put you up. She's always glad to see a new face at K3 and we have an excellent cook.' He telephones Sheena to warn her of Mr Carrington's arrival.

'You didn't smile when you said goodbye to Mr Carrington' Giles remonstrates with his daughter when they've resumed their journey. 'You must try to be polite however bored you are.'

In self-defence Alex says vehemently 'I don't like Mr Carrington. I don't want him to sleep at our house.'

'That's very unkind, Alex. The Arabs could teach you a thing or two about hospitality. One should always offer a bed and a meal to a stranger, especially in the desert.'

As they drive on, mile after mile, nothing relieves the monotonous landscape but the occasional undersized thorn tree and the odd clump of spiny plants. They stop once to look at a well, a deep hole strengthened with granite walls. 'These wells', explains Giles, 'Used to be a life-saver for the camel caravans crossing the desert. And of course the Bedouin still use them.'

'How did they know where to dig?'

'Desert folk have an uncanny instinct for locating water. In fact the more I learn about the Bedouin, the more I realise what an extraordinary people they are. Because desert life is so hard they've become much tougher than we are and their needs are very simple. We should never despise them for not having tiled bathrooms and fridges and electric stoves.'

But Alex is thinking how horrid it must be to have to drink that dirty brown water at the bottom of the well.

At K1, the nearest pumping station to Kirkuk, they spend the night with Madge and Bill Turner. Alex decides immediately that she likes this young, cheerful and unpatronising couple very much. Their bungalow is almost bare compared to the Masons'. Cream curtains of a thin silky material billow at the verandah doors.

'What a welcome breeze' remarks Giles.

'Yes, it's reasonably cool in the evening at this time of year' says Madge. 'But in the summer we often get the most unpleasant strong dry winds. It feels like opening an oven door.'

Alex is offered banana sandwiches and brandy snaps for her supper, and the Turners ask questions about her life. Does she like K3? What does she read? Which is her favourite food? What does she want to be when she grows up? Madge takes her into the garden to help feed six ducks in a pen. She allows Alex to collect the large greenish-white eggs. As soon as darkness falls Alex is ready for bed.

There are two white beds in the guest room and a large picture of a pretty thatched cottage amidst trees and hills. Alex falls asleep immediately but during the night wakes suddenly from a disturbing dream. A wide ribbon of moonlight lies across her father's bed and she can see his face on the starched white pillow case. His features are so motionless she feels sure he must be dead. She jumps out of bed in a panic and bends over him, her cheek brushing his moustache. With relief she hears his breathing and smells whisky and Polo mints.

Before dawn she wakes to the whirr of Giles's alarm clock.

'Why are we getting up so early?'

'Because I want to show you an interesting sight before breakfast, while it's still cool.'

As Giles drives away from K1 he tells Alex they're going to visit the Eternal Fires near Baba Gurgur. Ever since the time of King Nebuchadnezzar and probably before that, a circle of flames a few yards wide has been burning away all by itself in the desert. Alex is filled with excitement, imagining a ring of tall red flames like those that burn forever round the sleeping form of Brünhilde in her *Norse Tales.* But when her father says 'Look, there they are!' she's bitterly disappointed.

All that can be seen is a circle of what looks like the half-extinguished remains of a fire. They get out of the car and approach the 'fires' which emit a low roaring noise, the only sound to be heard in the ghostly half-light. 'These fires are caused by a self-igniting seepage of natural gas from the ground', explains Giles in his guidebook voice, ignoring the fact that his daughter won't understand what he means.

Alex says peevishly 'I hate this place. It smells horrible!'

'Yes, like bad eggs. That's the smell of sulphur.' Then, aware of how unimpressed she is with the Eternal Fires, he adds 'I know they're nothing much to look at. What's interesting is that these 'fires' have been here for so many thousands of years. It was because of them that people guessed there might be oil under the ground in this area. The flames themselves actually produce a substance rather like oil which we call pitch or tar. It's the dark brown stuff they put on roads. Pitch is very good for keeping out water. The Iraqis have always used it on their river boats. Can you guess who might first have used pitch on his boat?'

'I don't know.'

'Someone in the Bible who built a famous boat.'

'Noah?'

'That's right.'

The thought of Noah using pitch from these very flames for his ark intrigues Alex. 'Is this where the flood was?'

'It could well have been. Before people learnt to irrigate this land the rivers Tigris and Euphrates flooded for miles around each year. Families must have built themselves waterproof boats to live in. Of course there are still floods in the spring, but to a much lesser extent.'

Looking across the immense dry desert now it seems impossible to Alex that it could ever have been covered with water deep enough for a boat to sail in.

Giles drives on to Baba Gurgur. Baba Gurgur! Alex repeats the words aloud like a charm all the way, expecting to see black fields of oil on either side of the road. Instead she sees the steel derricks of the oil rigs towering above a dusty little township of workshops, offices, store houses and rows and rows of tiny mud brick dwellings. Giles parks the car and they get out to look at a rig more closely. The smell of oil is overpowering. They walk past a hospital and stop outside a rest-house with a large canteen at one end. Each building is decorated with a string of Union Jacks interspersed with the black, white and green Iraqi flag.

Giles takes Alex into the canteen for breakfast. Burly, unshaven men with loud voices sit crowded round the tables devouring platefuls of bacon and eggs, sausages and tomatoes – and piles of toast. They all look up and stare at the odd-looking child wearing an eye-patch and clutching a shabby toy camel.

'I don't want to have breakfast here' she whispers to Giles.

'Don't be silly. The men are just surprised to see a little girl.'

They order shredded wheat, scrambled egg and orange juice from a smiling Iraqi waiter called Hassan, who greets them warmly. As they eat, Giles tells Alex about the oil-fields.

'Baba Gurgur is a very special place for the Iraq Petroleum Company. Oil was discovered here in 1927, the year I joined the company at the age of 23. The oil rig you see through that window stands right above the well where the first oil was struck on October 14th, thirteen years ago today. That's why the flags are flying. There will be a celebration tonight.'

But at the moment Alex is more interested in her breakfast than in the discovery of oil. There's little to fire her imagination in this ugly township.

'Listen, darling', says Giles when they've finished eating. 'In an hour's time I've got to see various people connected with my work. You can sit in the rest-house lounge and do some work too. Don't look so sulky, you can't waste a whole morning. Hassan will keep a friendly eye on you. Now this is what I want you to do. I'm going to tell you a true story about Baba Gurgur, and then you can write me the story in your own words. It will be something quite new for you to describe. This afternoon we'll go to Kirkuk and buy something nice in the bazaar.'

The bribe works, and Alex prepares to concentrate hard on what her father is going to say.

'In October 1927 when I was living in Baghdad, there were hardly any buildings here – just a few mud huts, some sheds and the drilling equipment. The drillers looking for oil lived in green canvas tents. On the night of October 13th we received a message from Baba Gurgur asking for help. Great excitement! After two years of drilling we had discovered oil at last. Now listen carefully to what happened on October 14th, the day known to us as the Day of Destiny.'

Giles starts by drawing Alex a very simplified diagram of an oil well and a drill, marking in the names of the different parts – derrick, well-head, valves... – 'You drill for oil by pounding away at a hole with a huge piece of steel called a bit. This is suspended on a wire cable which raises it up and then lets it fall with a heavy thud on the bottom of the hole. Gradually the hole fills up with chippings of earth and rock, so every now and then the bit is taken off the wire, and what we call a bailing tool is substituted at the end of the cable to clear out all these chippings. Then the bit is put back and the drilling goes on.'

As her father illustrates and describes as simply as possible what happened on the Day of Destiny and during the days that followed, Alex finds it a surprisingly gripping tale. She takes it all in and is eager to start on her own version. She sits in the empty rest-house lounge with Giles's diagram in front of her, together with an exercise book and three sharp pencils, plus a list of unfamiliar words, phrases, figures and dates. She's always enjoyed writing stories, so it won't be too hard. Yet her first and second attempts are full of crossed-out words and sentences. The third attempt is passable and she presents it proudly to Giles who reads it aloud.

'THE DAY OF DESTINY

'At Baba Gurgur the oil drill has made a deep hole. The driller takes off the bit and clears up the pieces of rock and earth. Suddenly there is a loud hissing noise and a stream of gas and oil gushes up from the hole.

'The oil pours down on everyone like a roaring giant black fountain. Gas floats in the air making a black fog.

'Another driller turns off the boiler and the electricity, so the gas won't catch fire. If it does catch fire everyone will be blown to pieces so it's a very dangerous time. No one's allowed to have a light or strike a match.

'The stream of oil turns into a black river a hundred feet wide running down the wadi. Some of the men dig small dams to try and stop the oil but it's no use. Then a sandstorm blows up. The oil is blown around in every direction. A terrible roaring noise goes on and on and the poor drillers are stumbling round in oil-soaked clothes. They wear tin hats and have black oily faces. Their eyes are stinging and they are coughing.

'Mr Kinch drives into the desert to ask the Jibbour tribe to send eight hundred men to help dig a big dam to make a lake for the oil.

'With the oil and gas blowing about it's hard to block the well hole without electricity. The hole is only three inches wide. The men trying to block the hole can only bear being down in the well for about ten minutes or they faint. For nine days the brave drillers take turns in the well-shaft. They try to lower a four-foot well-head control weighing three quarters of a ton into the tiny hole. The oil is gushing at the rate of 12,500 tons a day. And the gas from a well under pressure is so strong it can cut through steel pipes.

'The column of oil spouting up can be seen five miles away. People come from Kirkuk and other places to watch. No one is allowed to light a fire or to do any cooking. Tins of food which can be eaten cold are taken round to all the mud huts.

'At last at three o'clock on October 23rd the drillers block up the hole and the oil stops flowing. It's very quiet after days of roaring noise. For a little while the people watching from the roofs of their houses dare not move or speak. When they hear it's safe again everyone is very happy.

'That's how oil was discovered at Baba Gurgur on the Day of Destiny.'

Giles is impressed with Alex's description. Driving to Kirkuk after lunch, he tells her that after the discovery of oil at Baba Gurgur, twenty wells were drilled successfully, and the whole area for miles around became known as Kirkuk Fields and then just 'Fields' for short.

Chapter Five

Kirkuk is built on and around a small hill. As they draw near the town the minarets and cupolas of the many mosques rise up between the flat-roofed houses and the trees. Giles parks his car on the outskirts since the winding streets in the town are so narrow. It's exhilarating for Alex to see a place so full of people of all kinds, clad in such a variety of clothes. At K3 the men, including the Iraqis, wear khaki shorts and white shirts, and the women shorts or sundresses. Here, textiles of every colour mingle with exotic jewellery, swishing and jangling along the crowded streets – silky dark pantaloons, baggy white trousers, gauzy veils, shiny green turbans, velvety dark red tasselled tarbooshes, rainbow-coloured shawls, embroidered caps, gold-fringed scarves, long black abbas, red and white checked kaffiyehs and cotton rags; a bewildering moving tapestry of colour into which are woven the contrasting black hejab and veil covering all but the eyes of the Muslim women.

After inhaling nothing but the smell of crude oil tempered by the clean desert air, the rich pungent stench of humanity comes as a shock to Alex's senses. This and the deafening noise: people shouting, donkeys braying, wirelesses blaring, cars honking. She clutches her father's hand as they inch their way through the thronging masses to the bazaars spread out round the hill.

'Before we go shopping', says Giles, 'We'll have a look at Muhammad's carpet. I've been meaning to go and see it for years.'

'Why do we have to see it?' asks Alex, who is longing to stop and look at the goods in the bazaar.

'Because, just think, it's the very carpet on which Muhammad used to pray. It's well over a thousand years old.'

Alex cannot share her father's enthusiasm for objects of antiquity, but she knows it's useless to argue once Giles's sense of history is aroused.

Passing through caravan yards and courtyards full of weeds, they make their way along a narrow lane with a smelly gutter running down the middle. It becomes hard work to avoid stepping in something nasty. The houses on either side have mud walls and overhanging roofs, with rags hanging across the windows instead of glass panes.

Outside one house a miserable-looking skeletal horse is hobbled to a post by its foot. Alex is horrified.

Eventually they reach a house with a yard in front of it dotted with dusty orange trees in blue tubs. Above the gate on a pole hangs a faded Iraqi flag inscribed in flowing Arabic script, *'La illaha illa Allah'*. 'That means God is great, there is no God but God', says Giles. 'You'll see and hear those words a great deal in Iraq. It's known as the Shahada, part of the call to prayer we hear chanted from the minaret on every mosque.'

They cross the yard, mount a few steps and knock on a door. At first no one opens it. 'An old sheikh lives here to guard the carpet and show it to visitors' says Giles. 'I hope he's not sleeping.' Alex hopes he is so that they can go away. As they're about to go down the steps the door is opened by an old man wearing a white turban, with spectacles slipping off his nose. He mutters angrily at his visitors and it's clear to Alex he doesn't want to let them in. Alex recognises the word besât for carpet, as Giles protests in Arabic that they've come a long way to see this precious relic. Eventually the grumpy old custodian gives way and leads them into a stuffy bare room surmounted with a blue dome and carpeted with a few tattered rugs. The sheikh unlocks an iron grill and then a cupboard built into the wall behind it. Still grumbling away to himself he lifts out a heavy object wrapped in a cloth. Inside the cloth is a large red box bound with strips of brass. He opens it and very reverently removes coverings of white silk one by one.

Now Alex becomes excited at the thought of its contents. But when the final wrapping is taken off all they can see is a threadbare matted camel hair rug.

'Just a dirty old mat!' exclaims Alex before her father can warn her. With angry words and trembling fingers the sheikh starts to rewrap the carpet.

'I feel sick!' says Alex, and Giles, after hurriedly pressing some money into the old man's hand, takes her outside.

'Why does anyone want to see that ugly carpet?'

Giles grins. 'Maybe you're right. Now let's go shopping. We've got to buy a rug for Sheena and a present for Zilpha – and perhaps something for you!'

On their way to the carpet bazaar they pass dark cupboard-like shops stacked high with blue, green and white pots and blue faience vases – then stalls glittering with bangles and bracelets and necklaces. Giles stops to pick out a silver filigree bracelet for Zilpha and tells Alex she may choose something for herself. The stallholder is quick to find a small bracelet to fit her wrist, but Giles will not pay what he asks. He argues with the seller in halting Arabic and finally starts to walk away, much to Alex's consternation. The stallholder immediately calls him back in honeyed tones and a price is settled. This is her first experience of haggling and she feels it's a waste of time. Think of having to haggle for a packet of Rowntree's fruit gums at the K3 store!

'Arabs enjoy haggling', says Giles, 'They usually like to make things more difficult than they need be. They'll never make a quick decision if there's time to make a slow one.'

They move on to the copper bazaar. Shining swords and daggers hang dangerously from shop doorposts and copper pots gleam warmly in dark recesses. 'This way' says Giles and they dive down a narrow alley-way, almost tripping over a couple of mangy dogs sniffing at a pile of scrawny hens lying with their claws tied together. Alex is outraged. 'Look at those poor chickens! Why do they tie them up like that?'

But Giles pulls her away. 'There's nothing we can do about it. We must hurry if we're to buy a rug for Sheena.'

The carpet bazaar is enormous. On every side and across the roof hang carpets of every size and hue. Some of the colours are so bright and glowing they light up the dark walls. Giles has brought a little book with him, describing the different kinds of carpet with pictures of the various patterns. The carpets from Kashan are said to be the softest.

'Feel how silky this one is! It's like stroking a lovely smooth cat!' enthuses Alex. She's particularly attracted to a carpet with a pattern of blue arches and red tulips. 'Can we buy that one for Sheena?' she begs.

'That's a holy rug from Turkey. It wouldn't match the rugs we already have, and it's much too expensive.'

They continue to browse among the carpets, enjoying the smell of wool and silk. Giles points out the carpets whose place of origin he knows. One, resembling loose knitting, comes from Kazal; another, with squares and circles, from the Caucasus. Hunting rugs and saddle bags come from Shiraz, those patterned with garlands of roses from Kirman. Alex reads the names in her father's book... Dozar, Tabiz, Zaronim, Isfahan, Bokhara... it will be so difficult to make a choice.

'Excellent rug from Gabistan, very cheap!' urges a carpet seller. The silk rug is patterned with strange birds in pale colours. Alex much prefers the carpet with red tulips but Giles thinks Sheena will like the silk one. He starts to haggle with the carpet seller. Why can't they decide quickly? At last the rug is rolled up and tied with string. 'Gabistan carpet very good for keeping colour' the beaming carpet seller informs them as they walk away with the rug under Giles's arm.

In the adjoining bazaar Alex spots a small pair of shiny wooden clogs painted with pretty blue butterflies. 'Please, please buy me those shoes!' They are frivolous and impractical, but she wants them desperately.

'Your mother would never let you wear them', says Giles, but he allows her to try them on. They seem to be a perfect fit. He gives in, knowing that Sheena will complain he spoils her. For Alex this purchase has transformed a pleasant day into one of sheer bliss. Every now and then she peers into the bag to look at the precious clogs.

'We must go quickly to the spice market, to buy some ginger and cinnamon.' Alex loves the smell, and watching dried pods, bits of bark, roots, bulbs, berries, resins being crushed in a mortar and each spice presented in a little cone of white paper. They walk past stall after stall – gold, glass, leather, perfume, textiles, papyrus and incense, and finally emerge from the gloomy light of the bazaars blinking painfully in the brilliant sunshine. The muezzin is calling the faithful for afternoon prayers. They pass close to three men on their knees, their green turbans touching the dust.

'What are they saying?' asks Alex.

'Allahu Akhbar – *God is great* – is all I can make out.'

How tired they must get of having to pray so often, thinks Alex. 'Who said they had to pray five times a day?'

'It's the Hadith, the holy instruction of Islam. Wearing a green turban means you've made the pilgrimage to Mecca. You remember, Alex, I told you Mecca is where the prophet Muhammad received the word of God, where he built the holiest mosque of Islam.'

'Have you been there?'

'Goodness, no! Non-Muslims are not allowed into Mecca. One or two Westerners have managed to get in by disguising themselves as Arabs, but I certainly couldn't do it. My Arabic would give me away. Very few Europeans are fluent in Arabic.'

'Are Muslims very good people?'

'Most of them are trying to be. Muhammad himself in the seventh century wrote a whole book of just laws and wise advice, but his followers haven't always carried out his commands.'

On the way back to the Turners' bungalow at K1 Alex is dozing when Giles says, 'Look, there's a quail!' She rouses herself to pick out a small reddish-brown bird with a white throat and a yellowish belly, standing motionless on top of a rock. Her father says it's unusual to see one at close quarters. The Bedouin shoot them to eat, and you need a great many quails to feed a family. They thread them onto a skewer and cook them over charcoal, and then eat them whole.

Mrs Turner takes Alex into the garden to see what she calls her 'little forest'. Alex has only seen a forest in pictures. 'It's only a copse at the moment', explains Mrs Turner. 'We've planted saplings Mr Turner brought back from the mountains of Kurdistan.' She moves among the tiny trees telling Alex their names – oak, maple, juniper, wild pear, pistachio, walnut... 'We hope, one day, to have a stream running through our garden. Then we'll plant mulberry and tamarisk and willow.' Her face is full of enthusiasm, but then she says wistfully, 'Of course now there's a war on we may have to leave K1.'

'What will happen to the trees if you go?'

'They'll die with no one to water them.'

'My father says the Germans won't come to Iraq.'

'I do hope he's right' replies Mrs Turner sadly.

They sit on the verandah and watch in awed silence as the sun sets in an opal sky. 'It's worth all the inconvenience of living at K1 just for that sight' remarks Mr Turner. 'Sunrise and sunset allow one to forget the heat and savagery of the desert.'

At dawn the following morning they set off south for Baghdad, bumping along a flinty track through fields of rushes. Far away to their left a line of purplish mountains rise up on the border of Persia like cardboard cut-outs and in the distance they can see the familiar black specks of Bedouin tents. After crossing a little river, the Surwan, they continue across a flat scarred landscape divided up by water courses which Giles says is mosquito country. They pass slowly through a village where half a dozen scruffy dogs lie asleep in the sun. 'Those are Saluki dogs, one of the oldest breeds in the world', says Giles. 'They're used to hunt gazelles as they can run very fast. Sometimes you see Salukis carried on camels to the hunt to preserve their feet from the burning sand.' He stops the car and one of the dogs gets to its feet, stretching lazily. Its long drooping ears are covered with straight golden hair hanging on either side of two expressive hazel eyes. Its long bushy golden tail is matted with dirt.

'Can we get out and stroke it?' pleads Alex.

'No – never touch a strange dog in the Middle East.'

'Because of rabies?'

'That's right.'

'I'd love to have a puppy of my own.'

'Maybe you will, one day.'

The five-hour drive to Baghdad is long and tedious. Alex checks the villages they pass through on the map – Tauk, Khurmatli, Tuz, Baquba – each one consisting only of a little group of mud hovels with hardly anyone in sight. Alex's mouth is coated with dust and there are bits of grit in her ears. They stop to drink weak lemonade from the icebox but Alex can still taste the dust.

'Baghdad is famous for its dust', says Giles. 'You'll get used to it.'

Gradually the grey scrubland gives way to red earth with palms and olive trees. Then, driving along the River Tigris, Alex notices black men as well as brown working beside the water. 'They're building dykes. You'll see all colours and races in Baghdad. It's an interesting town. Those animals lying in the mud are water buffaloes.'

Further down the river, women are doing their washing, beating the garments with flat wooden bats. Behind the women, mud houses are so crowded together along the bank that one could easily leap from roof to roof. Alex is puzzled by slow-moving circular objects spinning round and round in the water. 'Those are wicker basket boats called *guffa,* coated with pitch to keep the water out. Pitch from the Eternal Fires. Steamboats can't come up here owing to the mud flats in the river.'

Two white donkeys stagger along overloaded with heavy baskets, their bones almost protruding from their hides. A man is beating them ferociously with a palm stick.

Yet again Alex is outraged at the cruelty but her father insists that nothing can be done. 'They don't realise they're being cruel, they don't think of animals as feeling pain. Many of these people are so poverty-stricken they can barely afford to feed themselves, never mind their donkeys. If you lead a very hard life yourself you're unlikely to worry about the suffering of animals.'

'I still hate that man, I really hate him!' mutters Alex. 'And he's stupid because they'll die soon and then he'll have no donkeys.'

Baghdad is a flat town built on both sides of the Tigris. Beyond the clusters of mud huts stretch mile upon mile of date palm groves, out of which poke a golden dome and four minarets. In the city centre Giles has to slow down to a crawl to avoid running into throngs of people pushing their way between carts, donkeys, camels and street vendors. On each side ugly blocks of flats rise ten storeys into the sky.

A small girl passes close to the car and presses her face hard against the window. Alex is fascinated by the silver ring in her nose. They smile at each other and the car moves on. Alex envies the dozen or so silver bangles the child wears above each elbow.

They see a small boy staggering along with a bulky brown parcel on his head. 'That's a messenger boy', explains Giles. 'You often see them in Baghdad. It's quicker than sending the parcel by car.'

They trail behind a shiny official-looking car, a Humber Hawk, and a taxi honks hideously on their tail. Giles crosses a bridge and drives into the Old City down a narrow street beneath iron balconies with peeling green paint which jut out from the rickety wooden houses. Old men are sitting in the shade of these balconies selling mounds of lurid-coloured sweets laid out on wooden boards. Further on a woman squats beside a tray of flat loaves, shouting what sound like insults to a man repairing upholstery on the pavement opposite. Gigantic water melons are heaped against the walls, some of them cut into juicy red slices crawling with flies. The tantalising charcoal scent of kebabs stimulates their hunger.

Eventually the car edges its way into a deserted street with high ochre walls on either side. 'Here we are', says Giles, as they pull up in front of a large studded door with a bell hanging down beside it. Two small arched and latticed windows are set into the wall on either side of the door. 'This is one of the oldest parts of the city. We're going to stay a couple of nights with a friend called Leila Hammady. She's a widow, half Iraqi, a quarter Lebanese and a quarter French. I think you'll like her.'

Giles lets Alex pull the bell-rope and a moment later the heavy door opens. A sallow-skinned, broadly smiling lady, who looks older than Sheena, gives Giles a big hug and then kisses Alex. 'Welcome to Baghdad!' she says in a husky voice with a strange accent. Leila is a tall, well-built, elegant woman attired in a long embroidered Arab dress in rust and black. Her mass of jet-black hair is swept up into thick coils held by long tortoiseshell combs inlaid with a row of seed pearls. She surveys Alex closely with her dark eyes, but for once the child isn't overawed. 'You must say what you think here, don't be afraid', Leila tells her with a grin, and a rapport is established at once. She's not pretty enough to be a princess but Alex is drawn to Leila whose face is alive with intelligence and kindness.

Giles presents his hostess with a box of baqlawa.

'Oh, my favourite pastries! How kind!' Then, taking Alex's hand, 'Come and let me show you my house. This is a real Baghdadi house, not like your English bungalows!' Alex moves at ease with this lady who treats her like an equal.

Leila leads her visitors through an entry hall into a courtyard paved with coloured stones, where a diminutive fountain tinkles into a delphinium-blue bowl surrounded with dwarf-sized pomegranate and lemon trees. Jasmine cascades down one side of the courtyard, forming a curtain over stone arches under which they pass into the living room.

Giles is delighted to be in Leila's home again. 'Isn't it a lovely old house, Alex?' he enthuses. 'Look at the mosaics and mouldings on this wall.'

All the floors downstairs are made of pale marble slabs over which small eastern rugs are scattered. They look upwards to a high ceiling carved in cedar wood. A gargantuan black piano fills an alcove. 'Yes, I do still play', Leila says to Giles.

Alex longs to hear what this huge piano sounds like. 'Play it now', she begs.

'Not just now, maybe later.'

Leila's living room is so full of lovely things that Alex hardly knows where to look. She is guided among the exquisite possessions as her hostess tells her what each object is made of – a silver filigree box, a Chinese porcelain dinner service ornamented with peacocks, an antique brass coffee pot, a mother of pearl circular box containing a phial of attar of roses, a sandalwood table inlaid with ivory, a wicker screen with a delicate weave of leaves, a pattern of flowers in black antimony on a silver wall mount, a statuette in jade... and best of all, beyond her wildest dreams, a tall cabinet crammed full of dolls from every country.

'When you've washed your hands you may take out the dolls', Leila tells her. The twenty Arab dolls are intricately dressed, each garment cleverly embroidered, some with real gold ornaments. Alex's favourite is a Bedouin girl with a long black plait who reminds her of Zilpha. She wears a dress of pink, red, blue and green stripes under an orange cloak. A veil of gauzy cream material covers her head, and round her neck hang six tiny gold coins on a gold chain. Her arms are covered with silver bangles and she wears the inevitable bracelet of blue beads.

While Alex is absorbed in the dolls Leila and Giles drink clove-scented coffee from black and gold cups. Leila watches the child admiring the Bedouin girl and says 'You may keep that doll if you like it the best'.

'To keep for ever?'

'Yes, of course.'

As Alex carefully replaces all the other dolls in the cabinet she hears Giles say 'Where did you conjure up these biscuits from? I haven't seen a Peek Frean's custard cream for years!'

'My secret' laughs Leila. 'You can get anything in Baghdad if you know the right people.'

Towards dusk they sit on Leila's balcony overhanging the Tigris. A beautifully groomed white Saluki dog comes to lie at Leila's feet, its head resting on her soft yellow leather slippers trimmed with gold thread. This time Giles doesn't forbid Alex to stroke the long silky hair.

'What's your dog called?'

'Mimi.'

A tall lad dressed in a dazzling white robe serves them with spicy lamb stew, sautéed chicken livers, rice and nuts, and roast fish from the Tigris.

'This fish is delicious', says Giles.

'It's a kind of carp, the speciality of Baghdad. We shall have a special Iraqi dessert, Alex', promises Leila, 'Called mahallabi, a kind of blancmange made of rice flour, almonds, cardamom and cream, which your father loves.'

Alex likes it too, much more than ordinary blancmange. When the meal is finished the servant brings each of them a copper bowl of water and a miniature napkin to wipe their fingers.

'What about your camel?' enquires Leila, 'What does he eat?'

'I don't have to feed him', explains Alex seriously. 'He eats thorns and other plants in the desert. But sometimes I do give him a Polo mint.'

Leila laughs. 'Has Alex inherited your craze for those awful Polo sweets, Giles?'

The sky has turned a sultry pale yellow splashed with pink above the date palms on the opposite bank, but the view is spoilt by a spicy, rotting-fruit stench rising from the river with a hint of something more malodorous behind it. 'I'm told it's the smell of ammonia and saltpetre', says Leila, 'I've got used to it.'

Leila says to Giles 'Your wife won't like it when she hears you've brought Alex to stay in the heart of dusty old Baghdad instead of in the nice clean suburb of Alwiyeh.'

'I'm afraid Sheena is ultra-sensitive to dirt, probably due to her rigorous nursing training. She's never tuned in to the Arab temperament. She becomes very impatient with the nonchalant attitude of the Iraqis towards accidents and jobs that should be attended to immediately.'

'You can't relax and begin to enjoy the Middle East if you worry too much about dust and flies and smells and delays. It's a pity the British gather at Alwiyeh. They miss so much. You have to live on the river to savour Baghdad. Once I saw a corpse washed up in the mud across the river. It was two days before anyone removed it. If I sit here long enough I see all there is to see, except for the British!' As she speaks a raft drifts by, overladen with people and poultry and camel-hide sacks full of dates. 'Those rafts are made of rough planks nailed together and kept afloat by inflated sheep bladders. It's astonishing they don't sink!'

The sun sets, and the sky changes from yellow to a pale violet which gradually darkens. The golden dome of a mosque still shines vividly among the palms. The water swirling below the balcony quickly becomes dark and forbidding.

A boat glides by, lit by many candles. An overpowering whiff of gardenia assails their nostrils. They can just make out dim veiled figures chanting in a monotone. 'Prayers', explains Leila. 'A Muslim family taking a relative down the river for burial.' Alex is both fascinated and frightened by the strangeness of the lives of these people, so unlike those at K3.

Suddenly, in stark contrast to the mysterious funeral boat, a boisterous noise assails their ears – the sound of a brass band in the distance. 'Isn't that a German tune they're playing?' asks Giles.

'Naturally', replies Leila. 'Our royal band is German-trained; very well trained, in fact.' And the conversation turns to the war.

'Are the Iraqis really on the point of rebellion? Do they think the Germans will benefit them more than the British?'

'The Germans would be a disaster, but all the while the British regard our people as stupid and lazy, incapable of organising anything efficiently, and not educated enough to mix with socially, many Iraqis will persuade themselves that Hitler might treat them better.'

'You're right', admits Giles. 'Why do we British always look down on foreigners? It's fear, I suppose, of losing our British identity when we're outnumbered.'

'You keep it at the expense of being arrogant and rude. You're so anxious to reform our eastern vices that you don't notice we have virtues which you lack.'

'You don't need to tell me, Leila. If Jesus Christ himself were to request membership of any British club in the east he'd be sent packing.'

'We do realise we don't govern ourselves as efficiently and honestly as we should. But the truth is we don't worry all that much if the government is a little corrupt or even tyrannical. Democracy isn't such a vital issue with us. The extreme passion and the extreme lassitude of the Arab do not marry well with your system.'

'Yet Iraqi men are for ever debating the merits of western political systems.'

'It's just a pastime, they don't always mean what they say. Our main problem now is that the young men are too interested in western luxuries, particularly in western arms. They all crave guns, and the Germans promise more and more weapons. If the bribes become too large, who knows what will happen? And once the public realises just how hard-pressed the British are in the Mediterranean, they might just decide not to be on the losing side.'

'A lot will depend on Russia', says Giles.

'And on the Palestinian problem', adds Leila. 'The Germans are stirring up anti-Jewish feeling here by emphasising the plight of the Palestinian refugees. Many Jews have decided to leave Iraq. Just think, families who have lived here since the Exile to Babylon! And naturally these Iraqi Jews go to Palestine and help to aggravate the overcrowding. I feel that in the end Britain will be forced to back a purely Jewish state in spite of her promise to the Arabs.'

'It's an impossible situation! How can we prevent Jewish refugees pouring into Palestine after what they've suffered at the hands of the Nazis?'

Alex listens to her father and Leila talking on and on about the Jews and the Palestinians. It's hard to follow much of what they say. Soon she can't keep her eyes open and nearly topples off her chair. 'Oh, you poor darling!' cries Leila. 'It's eight o'clock, long past your bedtime, I'm sure.'

Alex follows Leila up a wide staircase, almost too tired to enjoy the novelty of going to bed upstairs after living in a bungalow. Her room is pale blue, one wall filled by an enormous gilt-framed mirror hanging over a marble-topped washstand. 'There's no bathroom upstairs, but there's hot water in this jug.' Leila tips steaming water into a bowl decorated with large yellow roses, and rubs a hot flannel over Alex's face and hands. Pointing out a large chamber pot in a cupboard beside the high, giant sized bed she tucks Alex up with Soda under the white lace-edged sheets.

Alex falls asleep before Leila has let down the mosquito net.

Chapter Six

Later Alex wakes abruptly and wonders where she is. A clock outside the bedroom strikes twelve and is immediately joined by two other clocks downstairs. A night light flickers dimly on the washstand.

She gets up and catches sight of herself in the vast black depths of the mirror – a thin wispy figure in pink pyjamas with white spots. Her mouth is parched. She must have some water. Tiptoeing out onto the landing she holds her breath and listens. Voices can be heard below. Her father and Leila are still up. Noiselessly her bare feet pad down the stairs and over the silky rugs into the living room which gives on to the balcony where they're still sitting, unaware of her standing in the dark room behind them.

She's about to ask for a drink when she hears her mother's name mentioned. Out of habit she can't resist eavesdropping.

Giles is saying 'I'm afraid Sheena will never be content with what I can offer. She's frustrated by my lack of ambition. She made a mistake in marrying me.'

'Why did she, d'you think?'

'When we first met, in Alexandria, she'd recently escaped from a large, very hard-up family in Glasgow. She'd fought her way through a London school of nursing and got herself a job in Cairo. She was full of plans to educate herself, to travel, to learn French and Arabic. I was only too anxious to help. She regarded me as a kind of mentor.'

'What went wrong?'

'The glamorous colonial-style life snared her. Parties every night in romantic settings. Rich empty-headed men admiring her beauty, fawning around her. You can imagine the high life in Cairo. There was simply no time for education. She found she could mix successfully with the snobbish and even the clever people on a superficial level. Being married to me had its uses at first because people assumed she was well educated. She proved to be a good hostess and soon lost the will or even the desire to educate herself. My intellectual interests bored her, especially my passion for archaeology and literature. As long as there's a good party going on Sheena doesn't care whether she's in Cairo or Baghdad.'

'How do you see your future together?'

'Because of her background, Sheena will always have an underlying sense of insecurity. She doesn't make close friends. To some extent I still give her confidence. While she needs my support I'm only too happy to provide it.'

'You give Sheena a lot, Giles. But what can she offer you?'

'Just being with her is enough for me.'

'Still so much in love after so many years of unhappiness. That's amazing!'

'Yes, it's a kind of madness. I have no illusions about her. But I do have an image of what she could have been. Don't mistake me; on the practical side she's a good nurse, excellent at organising domestic life and brilliant at entertaining. And I like her sense of humour. When she's had one or two drinks she can be quite amusing.'

'Does she drink a lot?'

'Too much for her own good, like most people in K3.'

'My poor Giles. Not an easy life.'

'I manage. Most of the time I'm reasonably content – and I have Alex.'

'They fall silent and it is then Leila becomes aware of Alex's presence. She turns her head and calls her name. Covered in confusion Alex emerges from the darkness of the living room.

'What's wrong, Alex? Can't you sleep?'

'I want a drink of water.'

Leila rises and leads the child into the kitchen. She takes out a water bottle from an ancient icebox on stilts. Alex sips the water which tastes vaguely unpleasant. 'Not very nice', agrees Leila, 'Come and have a cup of tea with us.'

Surprised and excited at being permitted to join the adults at this time of night, Alex clambers into a cushioned wicker chair. Leila and Giles are drinking tea made in a samovar heating on a small charcoal brazier. Leila fetches another cup and pours tea for Alex over three lumps of sugar and a slice of lemon. She's also offered a piece of bread to dip in a date syrup or, if she prefers, zahtar, a mixture of thyme, sumac and toasted sesame.

Alex stares out over the river, fascinated by the gigantic yellow moon floating in the water between the reflections of twinkling lights. She imagines diving through the moon down into the inky, murky depths amongst unspeakable horrors, and a shiver runs down her back.

As they sit bathed in moonlight bright enough to read by, their features sculpted in gold, Leila says impetuously, 'Listen, why don't we take Alex to visit a date garden? This is just the night to see it.'

'What, now?' Giles is astonished at her suggestion.

'Yes, why not? I know the owner of the garden close by. He lets me walk in it any time.'

Alex is enthralled, scarcely able to believe that a grown-up could be capable of such an unconventional idea. Leila wraps a light woollen shawl round the child's shoulders and bundles her into Giles's car. A few minutes later they slip into the date garden and stroll along a corridor of moonlight between the tall palms. A light breeze has come up and they can hear the eerie creaking of the palm fronds intermingling high above their heads. Looking up, Giles says, 'It's true what they say. It's like the roof of a Gothic cathedral. But it hasn't quite the atmosphere of a church. It's too pagan.'

'Definitely pagan', says Leila. 'Date palms were being grown long before Christianity. Some of these trees are a hundred years old. This is the perfect place for them to thrive, with their feet in the water and their head in the sun. Dates are the most extraordinary fruit. Like bananas, they're one of the few complete natural foods. Did you know there are about a hundred and forty varieties of date?'

'I'd no idea there were so many.'

'And about seventy kinds of arak are made from dates.'

'The fruit mentioned in the Garden of Eden is probably the date, yet oddly enough, the word never occurs in the Bible. Everyone living here at that period must have eaten dates, not to mention the livestock.'

'Yes, it's strange they're not mentioned. I watch the palms all the year round from my balcony through binoculars. They blossom in February. The dates ripen in May, hanging from the thick yellow stems, and by August they're soft. Most of them are left on the tree to dry until September. A cluster of dates can weigh up to eighty kilos. Date stones are ground up for cattle feed. Nothing is wasted. It's a miracle of nature.'

For Alex the date garden is like a bewitching yet frightening dream. Think of being lost here alone, walking through these endless ghostly moonlit aisles, hemmed in by so many tree trunks all looking exactly the same! She clings more firmly to her father's large and comforting hand as the three of them begin to retrace their steps in silence towards the entrance.

It is then that they hear the clear thin sound of a bird. It comes a second time and a third, yet it's hard to tell from which direction. 'A bulbul!' gasps Leila in delight. 'I've only heard it once before. Aren't you lucky, Alex? It's so very rare to hear a bulbul.'

'A nightingale', says Giles. They listen intently for a while but hear nothing more.

Back at Leila's house Alex is carried to bed by her father, and by morning the midnight excursion has become entwined with her dreams.

'We're going to Babylon today' says Giles, who is up and ready by six-thirty.

'I'm too tired' complains Alex.

'Don't worry, you can sleep in the car.'

It's impossible, however, to sleep in the car. Their heads bump against the roof as the tyres bounce along the uneven track. In two hours they reach the Hindiyah Barrage where the Euphrates is dammed. The water runs over a weir into a flat landscape where Giles tells his daughter to watch out for a kingfisher. But although she keeps a lookout for the spark of brilliant colour she's disappointed.

'How much longer to Babylon?'

'About fifty miles. It seems a long way driving across desert. In winter and spring this track would be too muddy to drive along. Now it's too hard and bumpy. The only pleasant way to travel in Iraq is by boat.'

Alex catches something of Giles's sense of expectancy, his boyish excitement as they near the end of the journey. Will they arrive at a wonderful garden city enclosed by shining white walls, with a river running through the middle, and fountains playing?

On arrival she feels cheated. The 'city' is nothing but a harsh, barren stretch of land strewn with enormous blocks of stone and piles of broken clay bricks and rubble. Dust-dry tussocks of scrub and rush grow everywhere. Only a desecrated granite statue of a lion and the remains of a huge gateway still stand. 'That's known as the Ishtar Gate', Giles informs her. 'Ishtar means Goddess. King Nebuchadnezzar rebuilt Babylon three times, each time raising the new city on top of the old, trying to make it bigger and grander. When you look at these huge blocks of stone lying around you can imagine how massive the buildings must have been.'

Alex can't imagine it. Her mind registers only heat, dust and emptiness.

'Just think, Alex, of moving those blocks without the help of modern machinery. It's absolutely amazing how they managed to build on such a large scale. And much of the city would still be standing today if people hadn't pinched the stones over the centuries.'

Still Alex is unimpressed. Babylon is boring and she feels nauseated. It's galling to realise her mother was right about it not being a place to interest children. She can't think why her father is so moved by these stones and mounds and pits. She trails round after him for an hour, becoming more peevish by the minute. Her hair clings hot and sticky to her head under her white cotton sun hat, and her eye-patch is giving her a sweaty itch. 'I hate ruined cities!' she exclaims. 'I hate Babylon! I wish we hadn't come! I want to sit down.'

Giles lifts Alex onto a block of stone. 'Be patient for just a little while longer. Then we'll go.' All around her great mounds rise up from the scorched plain and the sun glares down, draining nearly all colour from the land. Beyond the mounds the endless vista of heartless waste tires her eyes.

When Giles returns he says cheerfully, 'Come on, we'll go and find a drink. Perhaps it was a mistake bringing you to Babylon. You're too young to appreciate it.'

But contrary as always, she protests, 'No, I'm not too young, I love Babylon!'

Giles grins. 'Well, at least you'll be able to tell people in years to come that you've actually seen the site of Babylon. You may never have another chance.'

He lifts her down and says 'I'll race you back to the rest house.' Alex is galvanised into action, but it's not easy to run fast across the rubble. Tripping over and grazing her knees on some shards she bursts into loud tears of frustration. Her father consoles her patiently but the day is spoilt – he with guilt for taking her, and she with shame for not being grownup enough to enjoy it.

She dozes fitfully on the back seat of the car all the way back to Baghdad.

Leila commiserates with Alex over the trip, teasing Giles for his enthusiasm for ruins. 'Your father once tried to take me to Babylon, Alex, but I resisted the temptation. I hate the desert. Give me trees and water any day!'

The following morning Alex feels sad at parting from the warm-hearted Leila. She plans to put Leila's name on the list under her mattress – possibly above Saeb – or maybe jointly. The journey back to K3 is long and tedious. First they drive to a village on the Euphrates called Felluja, passing a lake on their way.

'It's an artificial lake' says Giles, 'The dam across the Euphrates channels the water to fill it. At the end of the winter when the snow melts on the Turkish mountains, millions of tons of water flow down the river. All this extra water has to be directed across the land in an organised system of channels, just as it used to be in ancient times, to avoid flooding the whole valley each year.'

After Felluja a two and a half hour ride takes them to Ramadi on a road whose surface becomes worse as it curves between the heaving waves of sand hills. Giles is constantly looking out for signs of ancient civilisation. 'Just think, Alex, once there were towns and villages all over this desert!' But looking at the low mounds and ridges devoid of any discernible vegetation, Alex doubts her father's words for the first time.

Ramadi is the most miserable of villages, even worse than Hit, where at least they had the interest of seeing hundreds of camels grazing. How terrible to live in one of these mud boxes with nothing but mud-coloured hills and mud-coloured camels to look at. And not a tree in sight!

They stop several times to take a drink from the thermos flask Leila has filled for them. Sitting in the shade of the car on the rusty red earth dotted with stones, Alex suddenly feels like an insignificant insect in all these miles of desert. It's a terrifying place. Nowhere to run to, nowhere to hide. The sky stretches in a great pitiless swathe of stainless blue.

When they reach K3 Saeb waves and grins as they enter the clean, orderly world of white bungalows and neat gardens. She can hardly wait to tell Zilpha all about the trip, to show her the Arab doll Leila has given her, and to present the gifts.

Sheena has been resting and she comes out of the bedroom smiling. 'Did you have a lovely time, darling?' she says, kissing her daughter lightly on the forehead. She looks more beautiful than ever. And there's something different about her. She seems unusually gentle, even serene. Giles and Alex are both conscious of her happiness and assume it's because they've returned. Zilpha joins them and they all talk and laugh at once.

Later Giles asks 'Did Basil Carrington turn up?'

'Yes, he stayed a couple of nights. He was very charming and left us two bottles of gin.'

'That was generous.'

Without thinking, Alex blurts out, 'I didn't like Mr Carrington.'

Sheena looks irritated. 'Why not? You hardly know him.'

She's unable to put into words why she dislikes the American. But she has to give some reason. – 'Because he has a red neck and small eyes.'

Sheena laughs but not with pleasure. 'Don't be silly, that's not a reason.'

In the kitchen Zilpha says sternly to Alex, 'That Mr Carrington was a very nice man, very kind. Remember, sometimes the ugly people turn out to be much nicer than the pretty ones.'

Alex knows this could well be so but she still dislikes her memory of Mr Carrington. In bed she becomes aware that her pillow smells faintly of his cologne. 'You didn't like him either, did you?' she whispers to Soda under the bedclothes. The camel is noncommittal but Alex takes his disdainful silence for assent.

The excitement of the trip and the homecoming have been marred by an undefined foreboding.

Chapter Seven

The expedition has unsettled Alex. For the first time life at K3 seems tedious in its repetition of uneventful days in limited surroundings. She learns what it is to be bored. Her father is away down the line now for part of every week, lessons are neglected, and the hours, sometimes even the minutes, stretch as endlessly as the desert into which she's still afraid to venture.

Christmas relieves the monotony, and for a few evenings the house becomes full of noisy adults amidst coloured lights, tinsel, red ribbon and greenery. Zilpha spoils Alex with bits of home-made fudge, gingerbread and ice cream. Santa Claus leaves a bulging stocking on her bed and the breakfast table is laden with shiny red and silver parcels. Now that Tony Hotchkiss has departed, Alex is the only child at K3, apart from several babies, and people take pleasure in bringing round presents for her. She wears pretty frocks with white sandals and white socks. Her hair is tied with a big white bow and she's permitted to leave off her eye patch.

This Christmas of 1940 passes without Sheena scolding her daughter once. It's a time of unalloyed delight with Giles at home every day. The war is scarcely mentioned. When Alex's parents go off to the club party on New Year's Eve, Zilpha plays board and card games with her on the carpet until ten o'clock. Then suddenly Christmas is over and a gloom settles over the station. Alex is aware that the residents have become restless, anxious, abstracted and irritable, as though waiting for a disaster to occur.

During the first three months of 1941 the talk at the club is mainly concerned with whether Hitler will invade Iraq. Giles explains to Alex that the Allied forces in North Africa are having a hard time. He shows her Greece and its many islands in his Bartholomew's atlas and tells her the

Germans are trying to capture it. There aren't enough British troops to fight in North Africa and defend Greece at the same time. Looking at the map it's easy to understand how much Hitler would like to get his hands on the oil fields in Iraq and Persia.

At the end of March the German Air Force begins to attack the Suez Canal from bases in Greece. Giles admits to Sheena one lunchtime that the mood in Baghdad is changing for the worse. Nuri-Said's pro-British influence is losing ground and Raschid Ali and his pro-German generals encouraged by the Vichy French in Syria have attempted a coup. It's been put down but people are sure he'll try again before the spring floods have subsided. Ironically Iraq is having its worst floods for years and all the roads into Baghdad are impassable. Even the railway has been breached. It couldn't be a better chance for Raschid Ali.

Sheena becomes bad-tempered. She says the RAF should have airlifted the women and children out of Iraq by now. Alex hears the ladies at the club saying the same thing, and snatches of worried talk filter into her mind: – 'Why are they so anti-British?' – 'Our government has given no assurances over the question of a state for the Palestinians.' – 'They think Britain and France will carve up the Middle East again after the war.' – 'We've turned the Arab world against us.' – 'What will happen if Raschid Ali does take control?' – 'He'll put the pumping stations out of action.' – 'If the RAF doesn't have enough planes to evacuate us, we'll be murdered in our beds!'

'And what about the men?' Sheena asks Giles. 'Presumably they won't be able to leave the oilfields?'

'No, we'd have to stay and face the music.'

The tension rises every day but fortunately Alex has something other than the war to think about. A friend of her parents, Mr Gregson, renowned for his carpentry skills, has been making her a dolls' house, working patiently at it for nearly two years. It was intended as a Christmas present but Mr Gregson wanted more time to finish off the details and to make some wooden furniture. It will now be a present for Alex's seventh birthday on April 29th.

'You don't know how lucky you are, Alex', says her father. 'Mr Gregson is a perfectionist. His dolls' house is far superior to any you'd find in a shop, and he's not charging us anything for the labour, only the materials. Isn't that generous of him?'

Alex can think of little else. The idea of a dolls' house fills her with intense pleasure as she watches Zilpha making tiny knitted dolls built up on pipe cleaners, and soft furnishings for the two-storey Victorian house which has an attic and even a balcony.

From time to time, however, the general uncertainty about the future intrudes upon Alex's anticipation. If they have to leave K3, will she be able to take the dolls' house?

'I expect so', Zilpha reassures her. 'It can be loaded onto a truck with the furniture.' Yet the nagging doubt remains. And a further thought begins to worry her. She remembers that her father won't be able to come with them if they have to leave. Losing Giles will be even worse than losing the dolls' house. She begins to cling to Zilpha for reassurance until Sheena tells her off. 'You mustn't bother Zilpha all day, Alex. She has other work besides attending to you.'

The desert spring has come round again and from behind the station's high wire fence Alex watches the Bedouin putting up their black tents. Then on April 1st, Giles comes home with the news everyone has been dreading. Raschid Ali and his generals have staged a successful coup and his troops have taken over the palace. The Regent, Abdullah, has fled to Habbaniya. It seems the boy King Feisal, his mother and their English nanny are still in the palace. Very few roads towards the south are passable.

'What are we to do now?' asks Sheena.

'It's hard to say. We must wait and see. At the moment nothing has changed at Kirkuk. The RAF at

Habbaniya will no doubt want to deal with Raschid Ali, yet it's a tricky position. They can hardly bomb Baghdad, and ground troops can't get through till the floods have gone down. The rebels have timed it well. But we mustn't panic. It may be that public opinion will swing against the generals.'

The following morning Giles drives off to Kirkuk to assess the situation. After a week he still hasn't returned. He telephones Sheena each day, and Alex waits for her turn to speak. 'When are you coming home?' is all she wants to say.

'I hope in time for your birthday.'

After each call Sheena tells Zilpha the latest news. 'It seems no one's sure yet what's going to happen. The atmosphere is very tense, even in Kirkuk. So far Raschid Ali hasn't interfered with the British residents or with the oilfields. But when the new Ambassador, Sir Kinahan Cornwallis, arrived in Baghdad on April 4th he wasn't given the customary official welcome. Anglo-Indian troops are due to arrive in Basra, but won't be able to reach Baghdad till the floods go down.'

Another week goes by and the tension relaxes. More time passes, and still Giles doesn't come home.

Alex discovers that the spare bedroom is locked and the curtains drawn even in the daytime. Mr Gregson must have installed her dolls' house in the room. She makes a calendar of the hours until Tuesday April 29th, and ticks them off as they pass. On the Sunday before Alex's birthday her mother takes her to the club to have lunch and swim. Sheena wears a pale lime swimming costume and her usual large sunhat. They sit down at a vacant table by the pool, and several friends bring their chairs over to Sheena's table.

Someone says 'The floods are subsiding at last. Our troops will send Raschid packing.'

Other voices join in: 'I hear a force is being sent overland from Palestine; part of the Free French troops under General Catroux who've been preparing to relieve Syria.'

'My husband says John Glubb's Arab Legion is coming with a British Army force.'

'I'm still afraid we'll have to leave. I've been packed ready since the beginning of April.'

'Where would they fly us to?'

'To Haifa in the first instance.'

'Perhaps they'll take us to India by boat.'

'I'm not being packed off to India' says Sheena sharply. 'Once they get us to India we'll be stuck there for the rest of the war.'

That evening Sheena telephones Giles. Alex hears her shouting down the receiver, 'Not coming home! For heaven's sake, you've been gone nearly three weeks!' A long pause ensues, followed by Sheena saying in a low voice, 'If I go to Haifa we'll have to get rid of Zilpha. We can't afford to keep her without my salary. What are the chances of my finding something to rent in Haifa? God knows where we'll end up. How shall I manage in some overcrowded pension with a child on my hands?'

At Giles's reply Sheena explodes with annoyance. 'No, I refuse to be herded with a crowd of women to India. I tell you, Giles, I'm staying in the Middle East, come what may!'

Overhearing this conversation, Alex realises for the first time that leaving K3 is an imminent possibility. The remark about Zilpha fills her with dismay. Only when she finds Zilpha in the kitchen the following day icing her birthday cake is she able to dismiss her fears for the time being. The dolls' house is waiting in the locked room, and her father has promised to be home. Everything will be all right.

Alex has to be forcibly chased to bed on Monday evening, and as Zilpha is kissing her goodnight Sheena calls her urgently from another room. The girl gets up hurriedly and deep anxiety replaces Alex's hopes of all being normal the following day. Then Sheena herself comes into the bedroom. Her voice has an unusual tinge of hysteria as she says 'I'm afraid your father won't be coming home tomorrow. And it seems likely we shall have to leave K3 by the end of the week.' Thinking of her dolls' house Alex begins to sob. But her mother has no patience with her. 'It's no use crying. This is wartime, Alex. Things go wrong in wartime and we all have to put up with it....'

Alex eventually falls asleep and dreams about the dead djinn for the first time since the trip to 'Fields'. In the early hours she's awakened by Zilpha's quiet but desperate voice in the darkness. 'Alex, sweetheart, you must get up. We have to leave K3 in two hours, to fly to Haifa.'

Alex struggles into consciousness, saying 'It's my birthday!'

'I know, sweetheart, but you're going to be very grownup, and very brave. It's too dangerous to stay here.'

Sheena comes into the room and switches on the light. She carries a holdall in her hand. Her worried, strained face is a warning to Alex not to complain. She must do as she's told, and quickly. Her mother starts to open drawers and to bundle the child's clothes into the holdall. At the same time Zilpha strips the bed. Her birthday isn't mentioned.

In the kitchen Alex is urged to drink a glass of milk and to eat a piece of bread. In the living and dining rooms white sheets have been draped over the furniture. Pictures, ornaments and books have been packed into boxes. Alex sits in sleepy bewilderment while her mother and Zilpha move swiftly from room to room until everything is packed and the luggage stands by the front door.

At last Sheena says 'We've got nearly an hour before Peter comes for us. You may go and look at the dolls' house now, Alex.'

Mr Gregson's creation exceeds Alex's wildest expectations and for a while she's at a loss for words. He's made a perfect replica of a Victorian house complete with conservatory and garden. The roof lifts up and the front swings open, and in the dining room the four dolls Zilpha has made are sitting at the table having breakfast. Alex takes in every detail, hardly daring to touch the intricate, fragile miniatures. Her fingers are trembling as she begins to handle the furniture, to switch lamps on and off, to pull out tiny drawers, to rock the cradle in the nursery, to assist the dolls up the steep staircases....

Zilpha appears in the doorway and Alex exclaims over and over again 'Isn't it lovely! Isn't it lovely!'

'Aren't you a lucky girl! It's so beautiful I'd like to play with it too.'

The hour passes in a flash and all too soon Sheena shouts 'Are you ready, Alex? We're going in a minute.'

'Why can't we stay another day?' Alex asks Zilpha tearfully.

'You'll see your dolls' house again in a few weeks. It will be sent to Haifa by truck. That will be something to look forward to. Or we may be able to come back to this house in a while.'

'Which day will that be?'

'No one knows, sweetheart, in wartime no one knows.'

But Alex wants a precise answer.

'We have to go outside now. Your mother says you must choose two or three books to take with you. Each person is allowed to take one small suitcase on the plane.'

'I don't want books, I want my dolls' house' cries Alex.

Zilpha kneels and clasps the child very tightly in her arms. 'Listen, darling, your mother is very upset, very worried. She won't like it if you make a fuss. Remember she's having to leave behind all the precious things she'd like to take with her, And your father will be so proud of you if you're brave.'

'He won't know I'm being brave' wails Alex through her tears.

'Yes, he will. Your mother will tell him.'

Alex returns to her bedroom and picks up Soda. Then she follows Zilpha into the strange half-light before sunrise where the vivid line of yellow divides the pearl-grey sky from the dark land mass. The lawns sparkle with dew and the scent of jasmine vies as always with the familiar, comforting smell of oil. Alex shivers although it isn't cold.

Sheena comes out of the house and says, 'You're not taking that camel on the plane.'

'I am! He can come instead of my books.'

'No, he can't!'

'I won't go without Soda, I won't!' shrieks the defiant child. Sheena's friend, Peter arrives at that moment to drive them to the air strip and she gives in.

As Peter is loading the luggage Alex suddenly remembers her garden. She must say goodbye to her vegetable patch. She dashes round to the back of the house and surveys her row of tomato plants, heavily laden with clusters of ripe fruit hanging motionless in the still air. She has promised to take Saeb her first crop of *banadoura.* And two rows of brilliant green lettuces are pushing their way out of the dark earth. They will be ready to pick in a few days and the thought that her cherished plants will wilt, unwatered in the sun, is unbearable. She picks a couple of lettuces and crams them into her mouth – then another two as Sheena comes to find her.

'What on earth are you doing, Alex? Look at your dirty hands.'

I don't want the lettuces to be wasted.'

'Don't be so ridiculous!' She grabs the child's hand and hurries her into the house.

'I haven't said goodbye to Saeb', says Alex. But Sheena refuses to enter into further argument.

Ten minutes later they're standing on the airstrip with the other ladies from K3. As they wait to board the plane Sheena suddenly hisses furiously, 'Where's your eye-patch?'

Confused, Alex falters, 'I don't know, I left it by accident.' But her face gives her away. She's deliberately left it on the bathroom shelf.

Sheena glares at her. 'You wretched child! That squint will never be cured now.' *She hates me for having a squint*, thinks Alex. *She thinks I'm ugly and she's spoilt my birthday!*

They wait for a long time on the airstrip. The sky turns pink and then the great ball of a sun bursts from the horizon to provide half an hour of pleasant warmth before the heat of the day. They climb a flimsy ladder into the tiny plane and Alex can't help but feel excited at the thought of flying. On board they sit squashed together along the sides of the plane facing each other. No one speaks. Alex clutches Soda and someone passes round strong brown paper bags as the plane heaves itself into the sky. Alex notices that Zilpha is carrying a square biscuit tin. Air fills her ears and she feels sick. Then her ears 'pop' and she begins to enjoy the first leg of the journey, to Habbaniya.

'Will Giles be meeting us?' Alex whispers hopefully to Zilpha.

'No, he'll stay in Iraq for the time being. He'll join us later.' Alex catches her mother giving Zilpha a warning look and wonders what they're hiding from her.

Turning her head she can just see out of one of the windows. The desert has been left behind and they are now flying over green marshes and patches of water. She can see the Euphrates winding its way to the sea. As the tiny aircraft comes in to land at the RAF base it seems to Alex as though the world is standing on its side. Her stomach lurches horribly and she leans over her paper bag.

The passengers wait on the hard-packed sand in dazzling morning sunshine, surrounded by runways, hangars, sheds and long, sausage-like streamers. They join several other groups of women with toddlers, babies and more piles of luggage. Someone in uniform herds them into a large empty shed where, for the first time, the women all talk at once. There's an exchange of news, opinions and complaints. Alex listens to the shrill female voices: – 'Have they interned the men at Mosul?' – 'Yes, but conditions aren't too bad. The Iraqis are allowing rations to be taken into the consulate, even whisky!' – 'They still have water and electricity and can telephone the embassy.' – ' much worse at Baquba. There our men are shut up in a room above a coffee shop with no sanitation and an ugly crowd outside. It must be hell.' – 'Apparently Raschid's gang is bribing the tribesmen to attack the oil stations.' – 'The Iraqisguards at K2 have sworn to protect our property. They'll shoot anyone who tries to get past the gates.' – 'Where's Major-General Clark now?' – 'God only knows. Stuck in the desert somewhere. It's over six hundred miles from Haifa to Baghdad.' – 'The RAF should have bombed Baghdad instead of waiting for ground troops to arrive.' – 'They can't possibly bomb civilians. The RAF bombed civilian tribes in their villages after the last war, and that's probably why those same tribes are supporting Raschid now.' – 'I wouldn't bank on the oil stations being protected by the Iraqis. '

Alex gathers enough from these remarks to realise her father might have been imprisoned. Kirkuk hasn't been mentioned, but she ventures to ask Sheena, 'Is Giles in prison?'

'No, of course not. He's just not allowed to leave Iraq at the moment.'

'But is he in danger?'

'No, he's perfectly safe. The Iraqis wouldn't dare to mistreat the British.'

As if to contradict Sheena Alex hears another woman say, 'The Iraqi police have taken over the refinery at Khanaqin. Wellington Dix and his British staff have been put in jail.'She suspects her mother isn't telling the truth about Giles.

Men in uniform enter the shed and hand out packets of sandwiches and tepid fizzy lemonade. There's nowhere but the dusty floor to sit on. Sheena remains standing to eat her food, carefully wiping her fingers on a large hanky. They're waiting to fly on to Haifa. The heat is intolerable, babies are crying, the queue for the toilets gets longer, and someone faints. Alex keeps thinking, My birthday is going by and no one has even said 'Happy birthday!'

Zilpha squeezes her hand and whispers 'Guess what's in my tin?'

'Biscuits?'

'No, it's your birthday cake! When we get to Haifa we'll have a celebration. I've even brought seven pink candles.'

By the time they board a plane for Haifa, everyone has fallen silent. Looking down they can see nothing but brown desert until some time later Zilpha cries out, 'Look, Alex, there's the Jordan valley and the Sea of Galilee.' Alex can make out a dark patch in the brown expanse far below. It doesn't look very interesting. Far more exciting a few minutes later is the sight of the Mediterranean sparkling in the afternoon sun. In no time the plane is juddering along the dunes at Haifa airstrip.

As they emerge from the aircraft the heat and the smell of melting tar seem to rise and hit them in the face. A confusion of exhausted and irritated people mills around the airport. Once more they're herded into a room, this time with chairs and tables, a room heavy with stale air and buzzing with flies.

'Why do we have to wait in this horrible place?' whines Alex.

'They're trying to fix us up with accommodation in Haifa tonight until they decide where we're to be sent', explains Sheena. Alex looks at the tired, dishevelled women, some trying to console crying babies, others to control unruly toddlers. Zilpha gets Alex some water, but even after drinking the taste of dust remains in her mouth. They wait for two hours and then Sheena says to Zilpha, 'I'm not putting up with this any longer. Let's find a taxi into town and try to find somewhere to stay.'

The taxi driver wears a tarboosh which reminds Alex of a dark red bucket with a tassel. As he drives dangerously fast along a tree-lined road, Sheena asks to be taken to the Windsor Hotel. He laughs. 'Windsor Hotel? No room at all!'

'How about the Appinger?'

'No room in any hotel.'

'Never mind', snaps Sheena. 'Take us to the Appinger.'

The taxi worms its way slowly through streets crowded with convoys of trucks and people of every nationality, including soldiers in khaki and a number of British police in blue uniforms. 'At least we can have a proper meal at the hotel', says Sheena. 'Then I'll try ringing a friend of mine who lives on Mount Carmel.'

The Appinger has a large shady garden of pine trees surrounded by a box hedge. Graceful wrought iron tables and chairs painted in dark green are dotted about on the thick carpeting of brown pine needles between the gravel paths. Nearly every table is occupied by servicemen. There are no vacant tables but as Sheena and Zilpha struggle through the gate with the luggage, two soldiers leap up and offer their table. Sheena smiles gratefully and says to Zilpha, 'You sit here with Alex and I'll go and order some food and ring my friend.'

As Sheena walks away a voice with an American accent comes loud and clear across the garden: 'Mrs Kinley!'

Zilpha and Alex look round to see Mr Carrington moving towards Sheena who turns to greet him with a sudden charming smile. They return to the table. A waiter is summoned and drinks are ordered while Sheena, looking flushed and relieved, tells Basil Carrington why they've come to Haifa and how impossible it is to find accommodation.

'Don't worry, you can have my room here. I can find a bed with a friend for tonight.'

Sheena protests but Basil insists. 'I'll go and clear out my things right away so you can put your tired little girl to bed after dinner.'

Alex sits in dazed silence as food is placed in front of her. Even Zilpha has nothing to say. By the time Basil

Carrington returns carrying a small suitcase, they have revived a little. Sheena explains the situation in Baghdad.

'Yes, we heard that Raschid has taken over. I'm not surprised', says Basil. 'It was bound to happen.'

'We never realised we might have to pack and get out at a moment's notice.'

'Where is your husband?'

Sheena hesitates, unwilling to tell Basil in front of Alex that he's under house arrest. Then she says, 'He's safe in Kirkuk.'

Basil understands, and doesn't press her further.

'What are you going to do?'

'Anything to avoid being sent to India or South Africa. I'll try and hang on here for the time being.'

'Not so easy with a child.'

'No, I realise that.'

'I'm trying to get home to Beirut soon', continues Basil. 'Apparently an Australian division's being sent to help relieve Syria and Lebanon. I'm worried about my flat.'

Alex remembers that her birthday is nearly over – in a minute she'll be sent to bed.

'Are we going to cut my cake?' she whispers to Zilpha.

'Yes, of course.' Zilpha lifts the iced cake out of the tin and places it on the table. Sheena looks surprised and embarrassed as several people stare at Zilpha inserting the candles into their holders.

'Well, well, birthday girl!' says Basil heartily, lighting the candles with a slim gold lighter. 'Let's see you blow out these with one big puff!'

Alex is overcome with shyness as everyone in the garden turns to stare at her. 'Come on, blow them out!' urges her mother. As she does so people begin to clap and sing *Happy Birthday.* Zilpha cuts the cake and Alex starts to eat her slice. But before she's finished she drops into a deep sleep.

Chapter Eight

Alex wakes to find herself lying on the floor in a strange room tucked up on two thick sofa cushions. Zilpha is sleeping on the sofa itself and her mother is in the single bed. A stream of brilliant sunshine penetrates the half-open shutters.

When they are all washed and dressed Sheena orders a tray of breakfast to be brought to their room while she goes to make a telephone call. Alex eats cornflakes and scrambled egg listening to the constant cacophony of sound outside in the street: a mixture of shouts and traffic, harsh Arab music and animal noises. The agonised braying of a donkey is shattering compared to the peace of K3.

After breakfast Sheena tells Alex her plans. 'I've decided to go to Jerusalem. Mr Carrington thinks he can get me a room at a pension in the American colony, and there's a good chance of my finding a temporary job in the military hospital.'

Alex doesn't welcome the thought of Mr Carrington helping to solve their problems. 'What about Giles?' she asks. 'When will he come?'

'He's got to stay in Iraq to work.'

'Is he in prison?'

For the second time Sheena denies it, but Alex doesn't believe her.

Zilpha has scarcely eaten any breakfast. She looks very subdued. 'Is Zilpha coming with us to Jerusalem?'

'No, I'm afraid not. Zilpha and I have talked it over. She's decided to go back to her own family.'

Alex stares at Zilpha, unable to take in that her inseparable companion and ally could be deserting her – and at such short notice. Zilpha puts her arm round the child. 'When your mother's found somewhere for you to stay in Jerusalem I'll come and visit you, and later you might be able to come and meet my family. It's not so far.'

At this confirmation of her departure Alex is stunned; Zilpha can't be serious about going away permanently.

Her mouth begins to tremble. Zilpha looks anxiously at Sheena, who says briskly, 'You're a big girl now, Alex, you don't need a nanny any more. You wouldn't want other children to laugh at you.' But Zilpha is not just a nanny. She's an integral part of Alex's life, as important as her father, and on a day-to-day basis more important than her mother.

There's no time to dwell on the fateful news. They are to say goodbye straight away. Tears are pouring down Alex's face as she clings desperately to Zilpha, who, smelling of laundered clothes, of lavender and almonds, represents everything safe and good and loving and utterly reliable. The Palestinian girl is weeping too, as she kisses and hugs Alex. 'I'll write to you, sweetheart, and come to see you soon.' Sheena watches the parting with much anxiety and a certain distaste. It's not going to be easy to cope with her bereaved daughter. Zilpha must go, and she mustn't be allowed to reappear in Alex's life to create further emotional upsets.

Zilpha picks up her case and hurries out of the bedroom without saying goodbye to Sheena. Alex continues to sob hysterically until her mother says, 'For goodness' sake, my dear, do cheer up. After all, Zilpha was only a servant. She's not part of our family. Servants usually have to leave in the end. If we'd returned to England before the war Zilpha would have had to stay behind.'

Alex withdraws into a sulky misery, making Sheena even more exasperated. 'Dry your eyes and wash your face, and do try to be nice to Mr Carrington when he comes. He's putting himself out a great deal to help us.'

Basil arrives in a gleaming black Buick driven by a uniformed chauffeur who leaps out and opens the door for him. 'This is Claude, who will drive us to Jerusalem', says Basil as the chauffeur puts the luggage into the enormous boot. Claude strokes Soda and then pulls his hand away quickly, grinning. 'He won't bite', Alex assures him, smiling weakly at him as she detects a possible ally.

Sheena and Basil with the child between them sink into the soft leather back seat. Alex is momentarily intrigued by the row of small woolly toys hanging above the windscreen. In a while Sheena exclaims, 'Look, Alex, we're going up Mount Carmel!' and a few moments later, 'That's the house where we used to live when we first came to Haifa. Isn't it lovely?' Alex sees a white house set amongst monkey puzzle trees and slender cypresses. It's an attractive house but it means nothing to her. 'I'd forgotten just how green and beautiful Mount Carmel is', Sheena enthuses, 'How did we ever survive in the desert? It's wonderful to be back.'

At the summit of the ridge Basil asks Claude to stop. Sheena wants to look at the view along the coast to the lighthouse at Tyre. She persuades Alex to get out of the car with her. Seeing the town spread out below Mount Carmel and the vast blue stretch of water stirs a vague memory from her early childhood. In spite of her misery she's entranced by the sea.

They drive on through terraced hillsides and villages of honey-coloured limestone, then along a steep-sided valley. Basil talks of Jerusalem, of the constant tension between the Arabs and the Jews, and the danger of bombs. 'There's the Arab Freedom Movement, which is in sympathy with the Germans, and various gangs of Jewish terrorists who accuse the British of being pro-Arab. The British police try to keep order as best they can.'

Without her father to point out the well known places they're passing through on the way to Jerusalem, Alex is only half attending to the journey. Her mind is still on Zilpha. Then she hears Basil mention her name and realises he and Sheena are discussing her future.

'There's going to be a problem with Alex. I'm afraid the pension doesn't take children. I've persuaded them to have her for a night or two until we can make other arrangements. Are you thinking of sending her to school?'

'Yes, if I can find a school', replies Sheena. At these words Alex is all attention.

'You might possibly get her into St. Mary's Roman Catholic Convent', says Basil. 'I sent my daughter there as a boarder for a while. She enjoyed it very much.'

'Isn't it only for Catholics?'

'Mainly Catholics, but they're taking a number of non-Catholics at the moment. There aren't many English-speaking children left in the Middle East.'

'Would they take a child of seven?'

'The official age is eight but I daresay they'd relax the rules if I explain the situation. If they'll take her as a boarder it would solve your accommodation problem.'

Sheena looks down at Alex and says brightly, 'How would you like to go and live with a lot of other little girls for a few weeks?' When her mother uses this cajoling tone of voice Alex knows that her mind is already made up. Asking her daughter's opinion is a mere formality.

'No, I want to go back to K3 with Giles and Zilpha.'

'Oh, do try to be sensible, Alex. You've known for a long time that you'd have to go to school soon.'

'St. Mary's is one of the safest places in Jerusalem', continues Basil, 'What with the bombs and street fights and drunken soldiers. The living quarters of the convent are mostly underground, and the children take recreation in a high-walled courtyard.' Before they reach Jerusalem Sheena has decided to try and board Alex at St. Mary's.

From one of the long brown ridges above Jerusalem they begin to descend in a series of hairpin bends towards the town, each bend giving them another view of the beautiful town dominated by the golden dome of the Mosque of Omar. 'Unlike other Middle Eastern cities', remarks Basil, 'They've had the sense in Jerusalem to forbid building in concrete.' Alex has always thought of Jerusalem as being an ancient city untouched by modern life. But as Claude drives along the streets it seems to be just another crowded modern town, with blocks of flats, hotels and cinemas, and cars and lorries speeding in every direction.

'It must be terrifying driving here', remarks Sheena.

'I guess it is', says Basil, grinning. 'But not as bad as Beirut, where the taxi drivers think nothing of doing ninety kilometres in reverse on two wheels!'

Basil suggests lunch at the King David Hotel. Claude knows the town well and soon they are sitting in a shady garden waiting for their meal to be served. Basil takes off his Panama hat. Alex wishes he would keep it on, she doesn't like the way his bald patch glistens. Sheena settles herself in a cushioned basket chair, looking fresh and relaxed in a smart navy dress with white polka dots and a hat to match. Alex toys with her food. It's said to be lamb, but Basil remarks it could be camel, you never know these days. Alex is put off, thinking of Soda squashed between her knees and the table. Basil and her mother chat about mutual acquaintances in Haifa and Cairo. Sheena laughs frequently as she sips thick sweet Turkish coffee with a brandy, and blows cigarette smoke-rings, a trick she's recently perfected.

It would be interesting to explore the hotel garden but Sheena says there's no time. They get back into the car and join the honking cavalcade of traffic. In some ways Jerusalem reminds Alex of Baghdad – the same impression of beggars and donkeys and garish clothes and vivid bougainvillaea spread over white walls – and everywhere the smell of warm dung and spices.

They turn into a quiet street with neat box hedges. The pension is a long, low building tucked away in a haven of cypress and orange trees, lavender, rosemary and lilac bushes. An apron-sized lawn surrounds a fern-fringed pond in which a fountain sprays an arc of water from a stone trumpet blown through the stone lips of a boy. Alex falls in love with this little garden. If only she could stay here and not go to school!

They are shown into a large, airy spotless room with long windows through which wafts the fragrance of lilac. 'From the lounge you'll have a wonderful view of the Mount of Olives', Basil tells them, 'It's very quiet here; you'd never guess you were right inside the city. You two take a rest now and I'll ring the convent and the hospital and see what can be done.'

Alex takes off her sandals and her dress and lies down on one of the twin beds. Her mother sits on the other bed and says persuasively, 'Listen, Alex. If St. Mary's will take you as a boarder you'll have to go because I can't keep you here. I'll be out all day and often at night. You'll enjoy school once you get to know the other girls. Nuns are particularly kind and gentle ladies who'll look after you very well until your father arrives and we find out where we're going to live. So please don't make a fuss. If you've had a taste of boarding school in Jerusalem it won't be so strange for you to go to boarding school in England.'

Alex doesn't reply. Within the space of thirty-six hours she's learnt that nothing is predictable. Grownups are in control of events and have little interest in her fears or desires.

The following morning Basil comes to take them to the convent near the Jaffa Gate for an interview with the Mother Superior. The car draws up outside a high thick wall. The words *St. Mary's Convent* are carved on a wooden door set into an arch. Basil pulls the bell-rope hanging beside the door. They are let in by a very young nun who escorts them across a lawn and through a dark hallway into a cool, shady room with bare stone walls.

A large imperious-looking lady in a dark blue robe and veil with a wimple of dazzling white across her wide, smooth forehead, is seated at a massive oak table raised on a dais. She addresses them softly, precisely, seeming to smile but never quite smiling. Her huge bovine eyes speak of the life of selfless sacrifice but these eyes are also busy summing up her three visitors. She makes it clear she's doing Sheena a great favour in taking in her daughter at the age of seven. She enumerates the many rules and conditions for pupils. Uniform isn't compulsory while the war is on but on no account are shorts to be worn. Alex senses that her mother's ill at ease in this formal situation, and isn't really listening. All she wants to do is to escape as quickly as possible.

'...As you know, term has already commenced. Alexandria may join us at five this evening' concludes Mother Superior, and the interview is over. So soon! Until this moment Alex hasn't quite believed in the reality of going to a boarding school. She feels certain that if her father had been present, there would have been no question of her attending this convent. Her old life at K3 has receded beyond recall and in a moment of panic she's unable to picture Giles's face clearly in her mind. And it is Mr Carrington who has decreed she shall live in this dark, forbidding place.

Sheena takes Alex to buy clothes – two gingham dresses with buttons down the front, some underwear and two pairs of pyjamas. When her mother packs a suitcase for her, back at the hostel, Alex asks 'Can I take my birthday cake to school?'

'Yes, if they'll allow you to take it.'

'And I must take Soda.'

'They'll probably expect you to have grown out of woolly toys.'

As she's being driven to the convent just before five, the thought of meeting a schoolful of girls fills her with terror.

Inside the convent events move quickly. A nun in blue, who introduces herself as Sister Theresa, receives Alex. Her mother gives her a quick kiss, saying 'Be good, darling. I'll see you at half term, in a month's time.' A month! She might as well have said *a year*. Mr Carrington smiles and pats her on the head. Suddenly she's alone with the nun, who leads her along a stone passage lit by two small high windows; then down some steps into a darker underground passage lit by a single dim bulb. This takes them into a long, stone-flagged dormitory furnished with two rows of narrow iron bedsteads. At the further end of the room a heavy black curtain hangs over an alcove. Beside each bed stands a small chest of drawers. In the top drawer is a card with a list of rules written on it. Sister Theresa opens Alex's suitcase and tells her to put the clothes neatly in the drawers. Dirty clothes must always be placed in the big linen hamper by the door.

'I hope everything is clearly name-taped', she says, looking at a pyjama jacket. Alex doesn't know what she means but the nun is clearly annoyed. At the bottom of the case are her shoes and slippers and Soda. 'I'm afraid you won't be able to keep your toy', Sister Theresa says gently. 'Girls aren't allowed personal toys. There are plenty of games and sports equipment in the recreation hall. I'll keep your camel safely locked away until half term.'

To Alex this rule is an outrage, and tears trickle silently down her cheeks. 'You mustn't cry, Alexandria. You're a schoolgirl now, not a baby!' When Sister Theresa sees Zilpha's tin she says, 'You can't keep food in the dormitory because of mice and cockroaches. All food is kept in the cupboard in the refectory and shared out between the girls at your table.'

The enormity of this idea enables Alex to protest 'It's my birthday cake!'

'At this school, Alexandria, we learn to share the good things of life. There is no place for selfishness. Now you'd better wash your face and hands before chapel. I'll show you the washroom.'

She leads Alex into a gaunt grey room where six small hand basins protrude from a peeling wall covered with a maze of rusty pipes. At the far end of an expanse of crumbling dark green linoleum are two shower cubicles.

Three toilet cubicles opposite the basins emit a strong odour of disinfectant. A weak light bulb hangs bleakly from the high ceiling.

Alex washes her hands with a square piece of yellow soap and dries them on a rough-textured white towel which the nun produces from a large walk-in cupboard in the wall.

'Hang that towel on the hook under your name.' Alex is surprised to see her name, *A. Kinley,* written in bold Gothic script on a label above the hook. How long has it been there? she wonders. Have they always known at this convent that she was going to come? The name next to hers has the name *B. Marshall* written on it.

A bell clangs near at hand. 'Time for evening chapel', says Sister Theresa, and ties a blue scarf round Alex's head.

On the way Sister Theresa unlocks a large chest standing in a recess in the passage, and Soda disappears into it. Alex is distraught. How will he manage without food and water? He'll be in the dark with no one to talk to. It seems monstrously unfair.

But there's no time to dwell on Soda's fate. Footsteps can be heard behind them and a line of girls of all ages passes by in silence, each wearing a blue scarf over her head. They are holding their hands together and keeping their eyes down as though already at prayer. Alex follows the girls into the chapel, a shadowy underground space with pillars and arches and tall candle holders. Rows of long narrow benches face an ornate altar covered with glittering objects. A white statue of a lady wearing a blue robe and a golden crown stands at one side of the altar. It must be the Virgin Mary because Zilpha used to keep a smaller version on her dressing table.

Half a dozen girls seat themselves apart from the rest on a bench at the back of the chapel. Sister Theresa indicates that Alex should join them. She sits down, hardly daring to glance at her companions, and wondering why they aren't together with the other pupils.

There follows a strange half hour of singing and chanting and prayer in a foreign language. The girls on the bench don't join in the service, they just sit quietly with their hands folded in their laps. Alex becomes aware of an odd smell, musty yet pleasant, which comes in waves of wispy smoke over the heads of the girls. She wonders why they're having a service on a weekday.

Then it's all over and the girls are filing out of the chapel. Those on Alex's bench wait until last and then move along the passage to the refectory, which turns out to be a dining room with long trestle tables and more benches. There are bowls of steaming lentil soup and a basket of dark bread on each table. Everyone remains standing until a nun has said a prayer. Then there's a shuffling of benches and a deafening chatter breaks out. Alex has never heard such a noise. She's told where to sit and the girls at her table bombard her with questions.

'How old are you?'

'Seven.'

'You can't be. Boarders have to be eight.'

'I'm seven.'

'You'll be in Class One with the day girl babies!'

The questions are fired relentlessly: Why didn't you come at the beginning of term? – Where did you get that funny name? – Where do you live? – What does your father do?... Then someone whispers, 'The new girl's got a squint', and they all stare and giggle.

Alex flushes a deep pink as Sister Theresa leans over one of the girls at her table and says, 'Bridget, I rely on you to look after Alexandria. Show her what to do and where to go for the rest of the week, until she settles down. Tomorrow morning see that she gets to Mrs Jones' classroom.'

After supper Bridget escorts Alex to the recreation hall, which has a glass roof like a conservatory. Here some girls are playing games or reading, but the majority are simply standing in groups gossiping loudly as though they could never have enough of talking. Alex hovers awkwardly near Bridget, saying nothing. Her whole body aches with misery and confusion. A bell clangs and Bridget takes her by the hand and leads her back to the dormitory.

Every girl is expected to kneel by the bed and say her prayers. 'Please, please, God, let Giles come and take me away from this horrible school' is all Alex wants to say, but she knows her prayer won't be answered; God doesn't stand a chance once Sheena has made a decision.

Chapter Nine

During the night Alex wakes from a disturbing dream. A nun with Mr Carrington's features has been chasing her along an endless dark passage. She lies rigidly in the narrow bed remembering where she is. She can just make out the hump of Bridget's body under the blanket in the next bed. Then she becomes unpleasantly aware that her sheets are wet, and sodden pyjamas are clinging to her skin. The damp under her body is warm, but near the edge of the mattress it's cold. She's mystified until the odour informs her she must have wet the bed. For a while shock and overwhelming shame prevent her from moving. Why has it happened? What is she to do? She's never been in this position before. It's a catastrophe too vast to contemplate. She knows she'll be in disgrace in the morning.

The damp becomes unbearable, so she gets up and sits shivering at the foot of the bed, eventually falling into a doze. She comes to herself an hour later when instinct warns her the night is nearly over. Moving her stiff limbs back into the damp bed she waits for the worst to happen.

A bell begins to clang harshly in the distance. Moments later a nun appears and switches on the lights. Is it Sister Theresa or another nun? They look so much alike. Alex ducks under the sheet to avoid the merciless glare of the naked light bulbs.

'Time to rise, quickly now, girls!'

With the sodden pyjamas concealed under her dressing gown she joins the silent queue for the washroom. Bridget, who's standing at the next basin drops the chunky bar of yellow soap on the floor and retrieves it with a loud giggle. The nun on duty snaps, 'No noise if you please, Bridget Marshall!'

Back by her bed Alex scrambles into pants and vest and cotton frock, and then plaits her hair. One of her ribbons is missing but she finds it under the bed. Bridget is stripping and folding the blanket and sheets off her bed and laying them neatly over her chair. The nun approaches Alex and whispers 'Strip your bed onto your chair as Bridget has done. After breakfast you will return to make your bed.'

Alex pulls off the bedclothes and sees with horror how the stiff mattress ticking is marked with a huge brown-edged stain. There can be no question of concealing it. Bridget spots it immediately and gives Alex a look of amazement and disgust. Within minutes, without a word being said, the whole dormitory seems to know the new kid has wet the bed. Everyone comes to stare at the tell-tale stain.

Then like silent clockwork the girls file out of the room to the chapel for early Mass. Alex perches on the bench for non-Catholics, and dreads breakfast, when Bridget will no doubt spread the news verbally round the whole refectory.

After grace has been said the usual hubbub breaks out as the girls scrape back their benches and sit to attack their food. Bowls of grey porridge alternate with plates of bread and jam up and down the scrubbed wooden tables. As Alex feared, Bridget loses no time in delivering her news more widely. Soon every eye is fixed on Alex. She bends her head over her bowl and one of her plaits dips in the porridge.

If only she could speak to Giles. He'd know exactly what to do about her plight. He would explain that she'd never wet the bed before.

Back in the dormitory several girls walk past her giggling and holding their noses. Sister Theresa appears at the door and tells them to hurry up. Please, God, begs Alex, don't let the girls tell her about my bed!

Hands have to be washed and nails presented for inspection as they leave the dormitory. By some miracle Alex passes the test and follows Bridget through a network of underground passages, up steps, along a corridor and across a courtyard adjoining a long, modern block of classrooms.

'That's Room One, your class', says Bridget, half pushing Alex through the door. She finds herself among rows of desks occupied by children of her own age. They stop chattering and stare curiously at Alex. Then she's rescued by a tall lady in steel-rimmed spectacles, dressed in a grey skirt and high-necked white blouse, who smiles kindly at Alex. She introduces the child to the class, finds her a desk, hands out paper, pencil and crayons, a ruler and rubber, together with a reading and a sum book. All morning she explains carefully what Alex is to do next as she completes each piece of work. She praises her efforts so that Alex is sorry when the recreation bell rings. She'd prefer to stay in the classroom with Miss Jones and continue working.

All the girls in Class One are day girls except for Alex. They've brought sandwiches and fruit to eat in the courtyard at lunchtime. Bridget doesn't arrive and the teacher has disappeared. One of the girls offers her an apple which she accepts with relief.

'Boarders have to go back to the convent for lunch', she informs Alex.

'I don't know the way.' How feeble it sounds. If she's not allowed to speak in the corridor how can she ask the way?

Later, when lessons are resumed, Alex wonders if Bridget will ever return to guide her to the refectory. During the afternoon a bell rings once more and they all follow Mrs Jones to an enclosed square of grass. Here Alex learns the rules for playing the game of rounders. But she has no eye for hitting or catching the ball and her team groan every time she misses. Demands to run or to stand still are flung at her in urgent high-pitched tones. She becomes confused, she can't relax, there's always another inquisitive question to answer. It's a relief to return to the classroom where she can concentrate on a row of sums.

As the afternoon progresses the children become lethargic in the heat. Mrs Jones's face glistens with moisture. Alex finds it hard to keep her eyes open and eventually her head drops onto the desk top. She's jerked awake by the thud and strives to keep alert until the last bell when the school day is over. Freed from restraint the small girls rush about, banging desk lids and shouting goodbyes. Within five minutes the room is empty. It's the first time Alex has been alone since arriving at St. Mary's. But she's too hungry and thirsty to savour this brief solitude.

She moves along the corridor and round a corner. Did she come this way in the morning? She isn't sure so she returns to the classroom in the hope that Bridget will turn up. She waits for an hour and wonders if she will be left here all night. At last a sharp-faced nun appears. 'You silly child! What are you sitting here for? You've missed tea and recreation. And now you should be in the needlework room.'

'I was waiting for Bridget to show me the way.'

'You can't expect Bridget to take you everywhere. You should try and remember the way after she's guided you once. We can't always be running around searching for you.'

Alex follows the nun back to the main building, almost running to keep up with the swift blue figure which seems to glide rather than walk along the passages. She attempts to take in one or two landmarks along the way so as to find her classroom the following morning. There are several wall niches containing statues of the Virgin Mary, but nothing else to distinguish one passage from another.

Her guide thrusts her into a room where Bridget and the other girls from her dormitory are sitting round a table on which stand two enormous black sewing machines. Another nun looks up and says, 'Ah, there you are, Alexandria. Better late than never. Here's your piece of linen. Have you ever done any embroidery?'

'Yes.' Zilpha has shown her how to sew cross stitch and chain stitch. The girls are each embroidering a religious text. The first letter of every line is decorated with scrolls and flowers and leaf patterns. Alex looks forward to beginning hers but it takes her so long to thread the needle that the girls are packing away the sewing silks before she can get started.

At last they go to the refectory. The two slices of bread, a boiled egg and a glass of milk aren't sufficient to satisfy the aching void in Alex's stomach.

'I came to your classroom at lunchtime but I didn't see you', says Bridget crossly.

'I was there.'

'No, you weren't. Anyway, you didn't miss much. It was gristly liver for lunch.' Alex's mouth waters as she sees a platter piled with slices of cake being passed round her table. She recognises some slices as being part of her own birthday cake. But by the time the platter reaches her end of the table there are only two pieces of dry sponge cake left. Her face flushes with the injustice of it. How can they call this *sharing*?

'We go to Mother Superior's room after supper today', Bridget informs her. 'She reads us Bible stories.' Mother Superior's private room is carpeted, the only carpet Alex has seen at the convent. The girls sit cross-legged on the floor in front of her. Behind her rises a slender lancet window above yet another, larger statue of the Virgin.

Mother Superior reads in a sonorous voice while Alex stares at her large, strangely flat face and gradually sinks into sleep. Eventually her body keels over and Bridget pokes her awake. She hears a voice saying 'It's not bedtime yet, Alexandria.' The words are spoken quietly but the glance is terrifying. Alex sits bolt upright, flushing deeply, tears pricking her eyelids. Behind her several girls are trying to suppress their giggles.

The reading continues. Alex is wide awake now and listening, but she doesn't hear the story. At last Mother Superior finishes and the girls rise to go. Then the blow falls. 'Alexandria Kinley, will you remain behind please.' She stands trembling in front of this forbidding woman. 'What was the reading about, child?'

But Alex's mind is a blank.

'You must listen carefully to the words of our Saviour. You must not daydream.' The light from the reading lamp shines directly on the calm features. The nun's face betrays neither anger nor kindliness. Alex, who's used to adults being momentarily angry with her, cannot fathom this neutral displeasure. 'Sister Theresa tells me that your bed was wet this morning. I wonder why your mother didn't tell me you are incontinent. Your mattress is stained and will not be suitable for another girl. Your mother will have to pay for a new one. If only you had told me yourself we could have placed a rubber sheet over the mattress to protect it.' She pauses. 'Have you nothing to say?'

Alex is silent with shame, thinking of what Sheena will say.

'At the age of seven', Mother Superior continues, 'You should really have grown out of this babyish habit. Bed-wetting can easily be overcome if you don't drink at supper time. Make quite sure you go to the toilet just before lights out. And should you wake up later and need to go, you mustn't be lazy. You must get up.'

Alex wants to tell her that it's never happened before, so her mother had no reason to warn the school. But she's tongue-tied.

'It would be polite, Alexandria, if you were to say how sorry you are to have caused so much trouble. And crying won't help.'

'I'm sorry', Alex chokes through her tears.

She flees from the room and down the passage and by some good fortune comes across the line of girls going to the chapel. 'Did she give you a penance?' murmurs Bridget.

'No' replies Alex, wondering what a penance might be. Some kind of punishment, no doubt. She's sure it was Bridget who told Sister Theresa about her bed.

'You were lucky', says Bridget, 'It's your first day.'

Later in the dormitory Alex is desperate for some water but dare not drink from the tap. When she kneels to say her prayers she has only one plea: 'Please, God, don't let me wet the bed again.' Her sheets are clean, her mattress has been replaced, her pyjamas have been washed. She can feel a thick rubber sheet beneath the linen sheet. This will protect the mattress, but if she were to wet the sheets the disgrace would be the same. The girls would still make fun of her. She would be summoned to Mother Superior again. She's been to the toilet, but as soon as the lights are out she immediately feels the need to go again. To be safe she will have to get up during the night. But how to stay away until eleven or twelve?

For a long time anxiety keeps her awake. A clock strikes nine and then ten. There are still so many hours of night left. She must rouse herself before she drops off to sleep. The dormitory is so quiet she hardly dares get up for fear of waking someone. She pads stealthily to the washroom and into a toilet cubicle. Sitting on the wooden seat she ponders over how she's going to avoid wetting the bed. Trying to stay awake while lying down isn't going to work.

Suddenly an idea comes to her – why not stay in the toilet? She can doze with her head against the partition until about three in the morning, and then return safely to bed. She remains in the cubicle taking snatches of sleep alternating with prolonged daydreams about her dolls' house. At last the clock strikes three. What relief to be able to go back to a dry bed without worrying!

She dreams Sheena is a nun telling her off for ruining a mattress, and she wakes in panic at the rising bell. But no, the sheets are dry. She's safe for today! Her mind is now geared solely towards avoiding trouble at this convent where it's so easy to break a rule. Her fear of the nuns has lent her a new mental agility as she realises no one is going to help her. She must look after herself.

After a day or two of teasing about the ugly rubber sheet in her bed the girls largely ignore Alex. She tags along from dormitory to chapel to refectory to recreation to classes, intent only on being in the right place at the right time. At recreation she sits pretending to read, hoping no one will speak to her. Fortunately lessons are easy and Mrs Jones continues to be kind. But Alex makes no friends among the seven-year-olds. Boarders are regarded as a different species. There can be no mixing out of class.

Alex has been at the convent for only a few days, yet it seems like a year. Four nights have been spent propping her head up against the partition in the toilet. On the fifth night someone enters the next cubicle. Is it a nun or a pupil? She freezes with fear. When the intruder has gone she wonders whether it will be safe to remain in the toilet every night. The chance of someone finding out what she's doing creates a new anxiety.

Then a solution occurs to Alex. Several times she's noticed a nun opening the walk-in cupboard in the washroom to take out bars of soap or toilet rolls. There are spare blankets on the top two shelves. There would be plenty of room for her to sit or even lie in this cupboard. It would be a completely safe place to doze. If only she had a torch, like some of the other girls.

For the next two weeks Alex makes use of the cupboard every night, lying on a blanket. It's stuffy and smells strongly of mothballs and carbolic soap, but if she leaves the door slightly open it's tolerable. She often thinks of Soda who spends all his time in a dark chest. During the day Alex finds it hard to keep awake during lessons. It's fortunate that Mrs Jones is such an easy-going person. When she falls asleep the teacher comes to nudge her awake gently, making a joke of it. Her only fear is that Mrs Jones will speak to Sister Theresa, who might then keep an eye on her at night. But nothing is said, and Alex settles into her unorthodox nightly routine as though she's been sleeping in a cupboard all her life.

Chapter Ten

Bridget informs Alex half term is on May 31st. The girls are permitted to spend Saturday night away from school. Sister Theresa tells her that Sheena will be arriving at nine o'clock on Saturday morning.

It comes as a shock to see Basil Carrington waiting in the hall with Sheena, as though he's her father. She's not yet connected him permanently with her mother. She'd been hoping to see Giles. In her mind she always imagines her mother and father together as they used to be at K3.

Basil drawls 'Hi there, Alex!', and Sheena sweeps across the hall and hugs her daughter, enveloping her in the familiar perfume so intoxicating after mothballs and carbolic soap. Bitterly disappointed, she finds it impossible to greet Sheena as she would wish with this alien man looking on.

'Lovely to see you, darling! Have you been having a good time? Made lots of friends?' Alex nods her affirmation, since this is what her mother expects. Sheena looks pleased and continues, 'Basil and I are going to take you out for the whole day. Would you like that?' As always she talks as if to a four-year-old. Doesn't she realise how much her daughter has grown up in the last few weeks? Yet Alex's pride in her mother's beauty puts all resentful thoughts out of her head. Over Sheena's shoulder Alex can see Basil smiling. If only he would go away!

'Cheer up, darling, you mustn't look miserable on your day out.'

They walk out to Mr Carrington's car which today he's driving himself. 'It must be fun sleeping in a dormitory with all the other kids', he says brightly. 'I guess you have a good time when Mother Superior isn't looking!'

Sheena asks 'How are your lessons going? I hope you're keeping up with the other children.'

'I'm ahead of the girls in my class', Alex informs her.

'That's good. So school isn't so bad.'

How to confess her misery? From stories she's read she's gathered that boarding schools are meant to be fun. The other girls at the convent seem happy enough. She wants to please her mother, above all to be 'normal'.

She asks about her father, and Sheena replies, 'Wonderful news! The Iraqi rebellion's been put down. Giles will be arriving in Jerusalem in a few days.'

'Then we can go back to K3?'

'I'm afraid not. We've had some bad news as well. During the rebellion Iraqi tribesmen attacked and destroyed some of the oil stations. K3 was wrecked. They stole everything they wanted, and burnt the rest, including your dolls' house. It was such a shock. We have to be thankful we weren't there when it happened.'

Alex can hardly believe that anyone would contemplate destroying the exquisite work of art that was her dolls' house. Tears pour down her face and Sheena says consolingly, 'One day we'll buy you another dolls' house.' But there will never be another dolls' house. There can only be one Mr Gregson.

After the gloom and quiet of the underground rooms at the convent, Alex is bemused by the deafening clamour of the Jerusalem streets. Sheena tells her she's to have an eye test and will probably have to wear glasses.

'Not today!' begs Alex.

'No, but soon.'

At the optician's she has to try several pinkish-grey frames for size. They all make her look very plain. There seems to be no escape.

Then Sheena takes Alex into a department store. In spite of the overhead fans it's oppressively hot and the atmosphere reeks of cheap perfume. Her mother insists on buying her another dress. Alex hates trying on clothes in the stuffy changing rooms.

'Do stand up straight so I can see how it fits.'

'I'm all sticky. I don't want to try on any more.'

'Just one more. I do want you to look nice today. We're going to a lunch party with friends of Basil's.' Alex's heart sinks. Another roomful of new faces!

Sheena finally decides on a dress and says, ' You may wear it now.'

'Will you buy me a torch?'

'A torch? Whatever for?'

'I just want one.'

They descend to the ground floor in the lift and she chooses a small torch. When Basil sees her, he says 'What a pretty dress!'

The summer heat doesn't suit Basil. His face is red, and beads of sweat stand out on his neck. He drives irritably, hooting loudly, letting the car nudge people and donkeys out of the way. Alex's legs seem to melt into the burning leather seat, and her new frock wilts. 'What's Zilpha doing?' Alex asks.

'I don't know. I haven't heard from her', replies Sheena.

'Can't we go and see her?'

'No, not now. It's quite a long way to her village.' Alex isn't surprised at her refusal.

Suddenly behind the noise of the traffic a dull boom is heard in the distance.

As they pass a bakery wafting out a delicious smell of fresh, warm bread, Alex feels a desperate hunger and wishes they could stop at one of the many open-air cafés. But Basil's car has become caught up in a traffic jam. The cars in front have thrown up such clouds of yellow dust that it's impossible to see what's causing the hold-up.

'What on earth's going on?' Sheena's voice is petulant. The heat's even affecting her.

'Another bomb, I expect', says Basil. 'It's so easy to plant a bomb in Jerusalem and get away with it. The British police just can't cope with the situation.'

After being at a standstill for five minutes the car in front lurches forward and Basil starts up his engine again. Presently they pass a house on their right which has been reduced to a heap of smoking rubble. Then Sheena shouts, 'Oh, my God!' and to Alex 'Don't look!' – but she has already seen. On the pavement sits a blood-spattered man staring ahead with glazed eyes, motionless as though turned to stone. One of his legs has been blown off and it lies a few feet away.

'Damn this traffic!' curses Sheena. 'Why can't it get a move on?' But the cars continue to move inch by inch and Alex has plenty of time to register the horror of the injured man. Her heart is pounding and she thinks, why doesn't someone pick up his leg and put it back in place and sew it up? Surely if they'd been quick enough... Now the poor man is lying in a pool of blood. People are running about and shouting. An ambulance screams its way to a halt. Alex feels sick.

At last the cars move forward and gather speed. They drive into a residential area with wide tree-lined streets. The houses are set well back from the road behind neat box hedges over which acacia flowers hang down in creamy scented tassels. They turn into the open gates of a white house and get out of the car. In a large garden groups of people are standing amidst small garden tables around a kidney-shaped pool. The bottom is painted cobalt blue, giving the water an unnaturally vivid colour.

Several voices greet Basil and Sheena. 'So this is your little girl! My, isn't she cute?' gushes an American lady in mauve chiffon wearing huge dark glasses trimmed with diamanté. Alex is the only child at the party. The guests drink champagne until well after two o'clock, when at last lunch is served. Everyone sits down. For a while Alex is absorbed in chicken salad, followed by ice cream.

After lunch she explores the garden. Soon she's bored, and returns to the table. Sheena's slender white fingers are clasped round a champagne glass. The conversation is loud, punctuated with shrieks of laughter. Alex tries to attract her mother's attention, but is told not to interrupt.

Eventually Sheena says, 'It's half past five, darling. Time you were getting back to school.'

Basil says 'You needn't come, Sheena. I'll run Alex back.'

'I want you to come', demands Alex. She dreads being alone with Mr Carrington. What will she say to him?

'You go with Basil, dear. It will give you a chance to have a chat with him.' And Sheena hands Alex a box of cakes.

'I don't want them!' says Alex rudely.

'Why ever not?'

'We have to share everything at school.'

'And a good thing too', approves Sheena. 'It does no harm to share things.' She kisses her daughter, and Basil puts the box in the car. As they pull away Sheena waves gaily, 'Goodbye, darling, see you soon.'

In the car Basil endeavours to make conversation. 'Have you made any friends at school?'

'Yes', she lies.

'That's good. I knew you'd like St. Mary's. Sally Ann said the nuns were very strict but the girls still managed to have fun.'

At the convent door Alex says goodbye hurriedly, forgetting to thank Basil. Going in she bumps into Sister Theresa on her way out.

'Back already, Alexandria!' exclaims the nun in surprise. 'Aren't you going to spend the night with your mother? The other girls won't be back until tomorrow.'

Alex's first reaction is of disappointment; but on reflection she's glad of the mistake. If she'd gone to the pension with Sheena there would have been the worry over wetting her bed. Think of Mr Carrington knowing about her disgraceful secret!

The convent is even more silent than usual. She returns to the dormitory and switches on the lights. It's strange to see the long line of empty beds, but a great relief to be alone. No bells are rung, and she assumes she'll not have to attend chapel. She sits on her bed and eats one of the cakes, and then hides the box under her clothes in a drawer. She lies down and falls asleep, waking as the clock strikes ten. Her new dress is very creased. She wants to sink back into sleep but the temptation must be resisted. Tonight she need not hide in the cupboard. She can sit on the chair at the end of her bed ready to hop between the sheets should a nun appear.

But no one does appear. She's no longer tired and the night seems to stretch interminably before her. She switches off the lights and flicks on her new torch. To relieve the tedium she decides to explore the further end of the dormitory. She peers behind the black curtain across the alcove to find it conceals a winding stone stairway leading upwards into the darkness. Shining her torch she mounts the steps until she reaches a narrow arched door which she opens cautiously. A short passage and more steps. She's amazed at her own daring and wonders if she'll reach the old lady spinning at the top of a tower like the princess in the story. After stopping to listen intently she goes through another door. She finds herself outside under an immense starry sky, breathing in the fresh night air and the strong scent of geraniums. She can make out the shapes of urns full of flowers and ferns set along the edge of a low parapet wall. The beam of her torch picks out a garden table and bench in the centre of what must be a roof terrace.

For some time she remains standing, half afraid of discovery, half enjoying the beauty and secrecy of this unexpected place. Far below can be seen the lights of Jerusalem spreading in every direction. For a while she sits down on the bench. Looking up at the infinity of the sky she experiences a pleasant detachment from the reality of life at the convent.

Somewhere in the distance a church clock strikes midnight. Three hours to go; but she isn't fatigued and will be content to remain here among the geraniums and the begonias and the canna lilies, daydreaming the time away. The thought comes to her that as a place to spend each night this is infinitely preferable to the washroom cupboard. The summer is advancing and the nights are warm. She could easily slip behind the black curtain without being seen.

At three she creeps down the stairs back to bed and sleeps soundly until the dormitory clock strikes eight. No rising bell has summoned her to early Mass. She washes and dresses and sits on her chair until eventually Sister Theresa comes hurrying in.

'You silly girl, why didn't you come to breakfast? Come along, quickly now!' She leads the way to the refectory, and stands with a long-suffering look while Alex eats some bread and jam and drinks a glass of milk. 'You'd better spend the morning in the library', she says.

The word *library* conjures up a vision of the small library at the K3 clubhouse, a bright room full of novels and travel books, magazines and comfortable chairs. The convent library is a cavernous room lined with dark shelves packed with musty religious volumes. There are two long tables lit by table lamps. Heavy wooden stools are dotted about the stone-flagged floor.

'Now let's see what we can find you to read.' Sister Theresa pulls a large book off a shelf, entitled *Lives of the Saints.* 'I should think this might do.'

When the nun has departed Alex opens the heavy book and turns over its many pages of solid print only relieved here and there by a Victorian engraving. It's amazing to see how many saints there are. The name *Basil* catches her eye – Basil the Great, born at Caesarea. She is pleased to think she knows where that town is. The details of the saint's life are uninteresting. She opens the book at random and reads the lurid, violent story of one of the Saints Katherine, a beautiful girl who suffered the most appalling indignities and cruelties rather than renounce her faith. Alex is not sure what faith is. Was it really necessary for Saint Katherine to die for it? She could so easily have hidden her real thoughts. The wonderful thing about thoughts is that you can keep them secret. This Saint Katherine was beheaded in the end, and it is said that milk instead of blood spurted from her neck. Then her body was taken up by angels to Mount Sinai. Alex feels the angels could have acted sooner. Nearly all the saints seem to have died violent deaths. How can they be happy in heaven after all that suffering? God seems content to look down from heaven and watch the cruel people burning and beheading and torturing the good people. She feels great revulsion at the emphasis on suffering in this book. If you have to suffer so much to be good she doesn't want to be a saint.

At half past twelve Alex goes to the refectory and sits in her usual place. A group of nuns gathered together at another table are laughing and talking in low tones. They don't speak to Alex. Someone brings her a plate of minced lamb, potato and cabbage, and a bowl of pink blancmange. Alex is becoming tired of blancmange. The convent cooks never serve any of the kind of food Zilpha used to make. She slips back to the library, but she's had enough of the saints. Scanning the lower shelves she finds nothing interesting. Dare she go outside or must she stay here until she's told to leave? It's almost a relief to hear a familiar bell clanging and to realise that the girls are returning to school. Anything to break the monotony of this solitary Sunday!

The rigid routine resumes. Every night Alex creeps up to the roof terrace. As time goes by without discovery she begins to feel safe. Lying on the hard bench deep sleep is impossible. She can only doze. The moon fattens out each night until it becomes a huge globe turning the city below into a fairy-tale of bluish-white houses and glistening domes. It's easy to be mesmerised gazing up at the moon. She's terrified of falling asleep until the rising bell and being unable to descend unseen to the dormitory.

One night she's so tired, the strain of keeping awake finally defeats her, and she opens her eyes to find the roof terrace flooded with bright sunlight. It's already very warm, yet Alex breaks out in a cold sweat as she descends the stairs to face the nuns.

The dormitory is empty. All the beds neatly made except for hers. She starts to dress as Sister Theresa enters.

'Where have you been, Alexandria? We've been looking everywhere for you.'

'I went up the stairs to the roof terrace.'

'To the roof terrace! You've been out of bounds into Mother Superior's private quarters? How dare you do such a thing?'

Alex wants to protest that no one told her it was out of bounds, but she says nothing.

'You'd better finish dressing and go straight to your classroom.'

All day Alex waits to be summoned to Mother Superior's study. For the first time Mrs Jones becomes impatient with her lack of concentration. Bedtime arrives and still no summons. Then Bridget tells her that Mother Superior has been away.

Leaving her bed that night is out of the question. She dare not risk even going to the washroom cupboard. She must keep awake, but she falls asleep immediately, exhausted by the anxiety of the long uncertain day. She wakes later on a soaking sheet. The worst has happened. There's nothing to be done about it. When she gets up a nun stands at the door observing her every movement. Her bed will be examined while she's at breakfast. Only the rule of silence stops her from being questioned now.

Chapel, breakfast and half the morning's lessons pass without incident. Then at last the suspense is over. There's a knock on the classroom door and Sister Theresa comes in and asks Alex to follow her. In no time they reach Mother Superior's study and Alex is propelled into her presence. She dare not look up but she hears the soft, measured tones, the deceptively quiet voice. 'Sister Theresa tells me you were hiding out of bounds yesterday and causing a great deal of worry. Why did you go up to the roof terrace?'

Alex is unable to think of a plausible reply.

'And then last night you were too lazy to go to the toilet and you wet your bed again. Sister Theresa says you haven't settled down at all well at St. Mary's. It was a mistake to take you as a boarder, and therefore I have asked your mother to come and see me this morning. I shall tell her we can no longer have you boarding, although you may stay on as a day-girl if she wishes it.' As Mother Superior speaks Alex sees her suitcase standing by the desk with Soda sitting on top of it.

Mother Superior takes no further notice of Alex as they wait for her mother to arrive. Her legs begin to ache and she feels sick at the thought of how angry Sheena will be.

But when the knock on the door comes, and Mother Superior says 'Come in', it's not Sheena who enters, but Giles.

Alex wants to run towards him but the disapproving gaze of Mother Superior prevents her. 'You may wait outside the door, Alexandria', she says before Giles can speak. Alex scuttles out of the room and then strains her ears outside the door to hear what's being said. Relief at seeing her father is mixed with the shame of his knowing of her disgrace, of her inability to fit into school life. At first only the faintest murmur reaches her through the heavy door. Then she begins to make out her father's voice raised in anger. From the few words she catches it seems he's defending his daughter's conduct. He's fathomed her situation, and a great weight is lifted from her. Everything's going to be all right.

Then the door opens and her father marches out carrying Soda and the suitcase. He gives Alex the camel and, taking her hand they walk to the entrance without a backward glance. She'll never enter these walls again. The nightmare is over.

Chapter Eleven

Outside, the glare from the high white walls covered with papery purple bougainvillaea dazzles Alex's eyes. She climbs onto the hot leather seat of the waiting taxi. Giles attempts to dispel his fury as he tries to talk to his daughter in a normal voice, avoiding the subject of the convent for the time being.

'I only arrived in Jerusalem yesterday. Luckily I managed to find a room at the American School of Archaeology, in their hostel. Your mother's working very long hours at the military hospital, so you'll be staying with me for the time being.'

'Have you seen Sheena?'

'Not yet. She'll be coming to the hostel tonight.'

'Has the war finished?'

'No, it certainly hasn't. Things aren't going well for the allies. In May the island of Crete was captured by the Germans. Hitler has invaded Russia and everyone is frightened the Japanese will capture Singapore. I'll show you where that is when we reach the hostel. But one good thing – we've defeated the Vichy French in Syria and Lebanon. Damascus was captured on June 21st. And the Iraqi rebellion is over. So the Middle East is in Allied hands and our oil is safe.'

'Did they put you in prison?'

'Not a proper prison. I'll tell you what happened. The day after you flew to Haifa from the airbase at Habbaniya, there was a battle there between the Iraqis and the RAF. The Iraqis were defeated, but in the meantime all the British people left in Iraq had been put under house arrest by Raschid's soldiers. I was locked up with some men in Kirkuk. The worst thing was being crammed together in the heat in a very small room. Luckily British soldiers eventually arrived at Baghdad on May 30th, and Raschid Ali fled to Persia with his supporters. The Regent, Abdullah, returned a few days later, an armistice was signed and we were freed.'

'What's an armistice?'

'It's a peace treaty where the two sides sign a paper saying they won't fight any more.'

Giles pauses, and then says gently, 'I think your mother told you K3 was attacked during the rebellion and your dolls' house was destroyed. It's very, very sad that you weren't ever able to play with it. Mr Gregson is as upset as you must be. You'll have to write him a little note of thanks. He's so glad you saw it for that short time before you left. I don't suppose we shall ever make friends with such a fine craftsman as Mr Gregson, but we might be able to buy you another dolls' house one day.'

'I don't want another dolls' house', Alex tells him firmly. 'I just want Mr Gregson's house.'

'It's hard for everyone at K3 to get over what's happened. It's going to take us a long time to replace all the possessions we lost, especially my books, and yours too.'

Alex wants to ask so many questions but barely knows where to start. She still feels numbed by her sudden release. 'Where are we going to live now?'

'In Kirkuk. I'll be entitled to a bungalow when you and your mother come back with me.'

'Will you go on teaching me?'

'I think we'll find you a nice day school.'

Giles has a large, pleasant room at the School of Archaeology, built below the Mount of Olives, a bare ridge sloping down to the dry Kedron valley. The pungence of magnolia, white lilac and carnation wafts through the tall windows. Goldfish whisk around among water lilies in a pool and pale yellow butterflies hover over clumps of blue delphiniums and lupins.

'I was lucky to find this room', continued Giles. 'The School isn't functioning at the moment, so that's why the warden has room for us. She's agreed to put up a camp bed for you in here'. It seems like heaven to Alex and without warning she bursts into tears. Giles sits her on his knee and lets her sob. The familiar smell of Polo mints makes her cry even harder.

'St. Mary's wasn't the right school for you', he says, stroking her hair, 'But it's all over now. These things happen in wartime. You must try and forget it. It only took up a few weeks of your life. Later on you'll look back and it will seem like a bad dream. Wetting the bed sometimes happens to older children when they're unhappy. I expect it will stop now. But I'll get you up in the middle of the night just in case.'

Giles takes her to the dining room for lunch, and afterwards suggests she take a rest while he reads in the garden. Alex loses consciousness immediately and sleeps peacefully for the first time since leaving K3. At four o'clock she wakes to find her father smiling down at her,.

'Goodness, you were tired! You used to hate resting in the afternoon.' He takes a small parcel out of a drawer, adding 'I'm afraid your glasses are ready.'

'I don't want to wear glasses. Everyone will laugh at me.'

'No, they won't. Thousands of people all over the world wear glasses.'

She puts them on and scowls at herself in the mirror. 'I look so ugly!'

'Behind the glasses you look just the same. And your lazy eye might improve so you won't have to wear them for long. – Now let's go for a short walk before it gets dark.'

'I must say goodbye to Soda first. He's not very well because the nun locked him in a chest for two months.' She kisses him noisily and tucks him up in her bed.

They leave the hostel by a small wicket gate in the back garden fence, leading up onto a white path which twists and turns among small rocks and stumpy olive trees. As they walk, a little cloud of white dust rises behind their feet

'I'm going to show you the garden of Gethsemane.'

The name sounds so lovely, *Garden of Gethsemane,* which means *Olive Press.* But the actual garden turns out to be a small dry patch of land enclosed within a limestone wall. Eight ancient olive trees shored up with stones and wooden poles stand among a few stunted cypresses. These eight trees are little more than bleached and rotten stumps with green shoots. A few hollyhocks and marguerites struggle to survive in the hard ground round a small Franciscan chapel.

'They say these olive trees were here two thousand years ago, in the time of Christ', says Giles.

This information impresses Alex. 'Is it really true?'

'It could be. Certain trees are known to live for hundreds of years.'

The child puts her small hand on the bark of one of the olive trees. 'D'you think Jesus put his hand on this tree?'

'Perhaps. We do know he stood on this ground.' For the first time in her life Alex feels an intense awe at the way present life can be linked so closely with past centuries. The sense of perpetuity her father had hoped to stimulate in her at the Eternal Fires and then at the site of Babylon has taken hold of her imagination at last.

But as a garden Gethsemane is disappointing. She can see no beauty in this dried up orchard with its trampled dusty paths. They sit on a flat rock and gaze across the valley at the honey-coloured walls and buildings of Jerusalem.

'Of course, the city you're seeing now isn't the same as it was during the time of Christ', says Giles. 'It's been destroyed and rebuilt many times.'

Dotting the sloping land below the city wall, hundreds of upright stones stand out like white bones in the gathering twilight.

'What are those white things?' asks Alex.

'Muslim tombs. And over there is St. Stephen's gate. There are eight gates in the city wall, but one of them, called the Golden Gate, is blocked up. There was a legend that Jesus would re-enter Jerusalem one day by the Golden Gate, so the Muslims blocked it up.'

'Why don't they want Jesus to come?'

'Because they think of Jerusalem as their own Holy City.'

After a short silence Alex says 'The Muslims were a bit stupid to block up the gate, because Jesus will be able to walk through it anyway.'

As the light begins to die they hasten back to the hostel and stand in the little garden to watch the sun go down. The only sound is the tinkle of a goat bell, the only movement the flight of swifts high above.

After supper Alex asks, 'When will we go to Kirkuk?'

'Soon. I have some leave which I'm going to spend here with you before we go.'

'Will you stay with me always now?'

'Most of the time. I'll have to travel around for a few days now and then. We're extremely busy in the oil company. There's a massive demand by the Allies for oil. And now the pipe line to Tripoli in Lebanon is to be opened again.'

Alex puts her arms round Giles's neck and clings to him as though she were drowning. 'I don't want you ever to go away', she whispers in his ear. 'Promise you won't.'

'We'll see. Go to sleep now.'

He leaves the room, and Alex closes her eyes. But she's too restless to sleep. She gets up and opens one or two drawers, to see if her father still keeps a stock of Polo mints. She finds a box in a drawer with hankies and socks, a bottle of Andrew's Liver Salts and a leather-bound diary. Giles has explained what a diary is for. This diary starts in January 1941. The entries for the first three months of the year are of little interest to Alex, but as she looks through April, May and June, certain passages catch her eye.

April 20. Anti-British feeling is building up in Kirkuk. Anglo-Indian troops waiting at Basra can't move to Baghdad owing to the floods. Work here so far is carrying on as usual, but we've been warned not to travel. We've also been told the women and children from the oil stations will be air-lifted to Haifa in a few days.

April 29. Alex's 7th birthday. I've not been able to telephone for over a week, so don't know whether Sheena is still at K3.

April 30. An urgent call came from Baghdad. Crowds have gathered in the streets. The British colony have taken refuge in the Embassy. The women and children at K3 have been flown to Haifa, but where they will go after that, no one seems to know. The Iraqis have taken control of Kirkuk oilfields, and we are confined to our compound in Kirkuk.

Tonight a crowd gathered but was ordered away by Iraqi soldiers.

May 1. Well before dawn this morning soldiers came and ordered us to pack a small holdall each. We were then taken by truck to a house on the outskirts of the town and locked in an unfurnished upstairs room. Food and water were brought to us at 6. pm, and we were told we could buy cigarettes. Toilet and washing facilities in a high-walled back yard are most unsavoury. We are to sleep on raffia mats on the floor.

May 7. We keep asking our guards, a couple of quite amiable fellows, what's going on elsewhere. They told us today with great glee that there's been a five-day battle at Habbaniya. The British pilots are dead, and all the British aircraft shot down. The air base has now been taken over by the Iraqi army, which has artillery and modern aircraft. 'Your planes no good', said one of the guards. 'Leftover rubbish from World War 1.' We're staggered by the news. What can have happened to the relief force we were promised? We sat discussing what might happen to us now. For the first time we wondered whether the Germans would invade before our troops reach Baghdad. Death is something we are having to contemplate, but it still seems unreal. At least Sheena and Alex are safe.

May 25. We're trying to keep up our morale, but it's hard not to quarrel when we're so crowded in this small airless room with no exercise. We've only been here a few days, but it seems like months. It's the uncertainty which quickly drives one crazy.

June 2. We were freed this evening and taken back to our compound. Grinning all over, our guards shook hands with each of us, saying they were sorry to see us go. They'd been looking forward to the order to cut our throats!

June 3. I rang the Embassy at Baghdad, and discovered that Raschid, together with some of his troops, has fled. Major-General George Clark's forces have arrived a few miles from the city, and the Regent has been brought *back, together with the Prime Minister, and reinstated. An armistice has been signed, and some kind of order is gradually being restored. But we were mystified to hear that the British forces haven't occupied Baghdad.*

At this point Alex hears footsteps coming up the stairs, and hastily replaces the diary and shuts the drawer. It isn't her father, but nevertheless she gets back into bed and falls asleep. She dreams that her mother has arrived and is sitting on Giles's bed, talking to him in a very low voice. Her back is towards Alex, her auburn hair lit up by the tiny flame of a night light on the bedside table. Gradually she becomes aware that it isn't a dream, her mother really is there, and they're talking about her. She's now wide awake, but keeps her head under the sheet, listening intently.

'How could you send a child of barely seven to a boarding school, and a convent at that?' her father is saying.

'For goodness' sake, Giles, it was just a temporary solution. She was only there for two months.'

'Two months is a lifetime to a child.'

'What else could I have done? The pension wouldn't have her and I needed a job.'

'Did you try anywhere else?'

'There was no point.'

'I found a room here with no trouble, where the warden's only too pleased to accommodate a child.'

'Do be realistic, Giles. You have contacts in Jerusalem. I haven't. Basil recommended St. Mary's, where his own daughter was perfectly happy. It's built partly underground, which makes it a secure place to be at this dangerous time. Why is the idea of Alex living with other children so impossible to you?'

'To plunge a seven-year-old who's never been to school before into a strict boarding convent is unforgivable. The Mother Superior complained to me that you hadn't mentioned Alex has a bed-wetting problem.'

'She hasn't. Is that why they wanted her to leave?'

'Partly. They said she was disobedient and sullen.'

'I hoped that boarding school would teach her to stop daydreaming and help her to get on with other people.'

'It's probably done the opposite. She's a very anxious child and I'm not surprised. The Mother Superior seems to have very little understanding of young children. The whole atmosphere of the place struck me as oppressive. Why don't you admit it Sheena, you sent her to the convent partly so you could be free to go out with Basil every evening? It was convenient not to have a child hanging around you.'

Sheena's voice is now slightly raised in anger. 'I sent her to St. Mary's because I was going to be out at work all day, and because she needs to mix with other children.'

'Didn't it strike you that a school that only allows you to see your seven-year-old daughter once a term isn't satisfactory?'

'Basil says it's a deliberate policy. Children settle down much better if they don't see their parents too often.'

'At this stage Alex needs an ordinary day school.'

'Well, you find her one.'

'There's no need for her to go to school until September. As you know, I'll be here on leave for a fortnight. When we go back to Kirkuk we'll find a day school for her.'

'What kind of school would we find in Kirkuk?'

'There are perfectly good primary schools. Iraqi children have to be educated. And there's a school that teaches in English and Arabic.'

'No school in Kirkuk could possibly be suitable. People would think we were mad. Alex might well be the only British child of school age in Kirkuk.' Then Sheena says, lowering her voice again, 'In any case, Giles, I've decided not to come back to Iraq. It can't be much of a surprise to you. You know how much I hated K3. Even living in Jerusalem has been more interesting than being stuck in the desert.'

'So what are you going to do?' Giles's voice is suddenly flat and weary.

After a long pause Sheena says, almost whispering, 'Actually I'm going to Beirut with Basil. Now the Vichy government's been sent packing he can return permanently to his apartment near the American University. He knows one of the doctors at the University Hospital, who might be able to get me a job there as a nursing tutor. It would be well paid. We need the money if Alex is to go to boarding school in England. I'd be a fool to turn down such an opportunity.'

Another pause and then Giles asks 'Does this mean our marriage is over?'

'Perhaps, until the end of the war, anyway. You can't pretend we've ever been happy together. We've nothing in common except a child. Basil and I are going to try living together.'

'How are people going to regard that?'

'Beirut is a very cosmopolitan place, not like K3 where you can't sneeze without someone disapproving.'

'And what about Alex?'

'She'll have to come with me. You can hardly take her to Kirkuk on your own. There's a good American school she can attend in Beirut.'

'On Basil's recommendation, no doubt?'

'Yes, he knows Beirut very well. He has a large, two-storey apartment with a cook and a maid, so there will be someone to look after Alex when she comes home from school.'

'And how do I fit in with this plan of yours? Alex is my daughter too.'

'I know, Giles, but I don't see how you could have her in Kirkuk, even for holidays. On your own you won't be entitled to a bungalow. You'll get a tiny one-bedroom flat, no place for a child. You'd have to have a living-in maid. Basil suggests that you spend all your leave in Beirut with us. You should be able to get Christmas, and a few weeks in the summer holidays.'

'How generous of Basil!'

'Basil is generous, extremely generous, and he doesn't want to be on bad terms with you any more than I do.'

'And I suppose when the war's over you'll go to the States with him?'

'How can we look that far ahead?'

'You seem to forget that I love you and I love Alex. For me it isn't just a question of returning to Kirkuk and getting on with my job.'

'Giles, I'm trying to be practical and calm about everything. I don't want us to get angry and emotional and part as enemies. I'm very fond of you. We must remain on good terms. I'd like you and Basil to become friends. We mustn't row in front of Alex. In fact I don't want her to know we might be separating permanently. I shall tell her we'll be living apart because Kirkuk isn't a suitable place for a wife and child.'

'It would be far better for Alex if we were to stay together.'

'I'm sorry, Giles, I've made up my mind.'

'I find it hard to believe you're really serious about Basil. You hardly know him. You're infatuated because he's got money and connections and can give you a good time.'

'That's nonsense. I'll be earning my own money as I always have done. You can think what you like about Basil, but I'm going to Beirut with him in a couple of weeks.'

Sheena gets up. 'I must go now. I've got to get up early. I'll ring you at the weekend.'

The door opens quietly and then shuts.

Chapter Twelve

Alex wants to leap out of bed and comfort her father; she wants to ask so many questions, but daren't, since she's been eavesdropping. Giles sits for so long without moving that she becomes frightened. She emerges slowly from under the sheet and notices her father's face is glistening with tears. This is shocking and painful to Alex. Zilpha has told her that men hardly ever cry. Alex has never even heard her mother crying. How could Sheena prefer Mr Carrington? She can't imagine anything more dreadful happening. But it can't be true. She's overheard her parents having many quarrels at K3, and the next day they've carried on as though nothing has happened.

In the morning Giles is his usual cheerful self, saying they'll spend a few days exploring Jerusalem. What passed between her parents in the bedroom must have been a bad dream.

They set out early from the hostel each morning, catching a bus to the end of King David Street, and then walking along pavements doused in water against the heat. It's just cool enough to ramble round the Old City, over the lion-coloured ramparts and through the souks. They always see a middle-aged man in a dusty three-piece suit sweeping his shop front to lay out his wares. Gold fillings glint in his mouth as he grins at Alex. By mid-morning they're ready to sit under an umbrella at a pavement café to drink iced tomato juice through two straws. British trucks pass by at intervals. The heat increases, and with it the smells: burning charcoal, raw meat, garlic, new bread, cardamom-scented coffee and overripe fruit. Once, two bearded men in spectacles pass by, wearing long black silken coats, baggy black trousers and white stockings. Black corkscrew curls hang on each side of their tall black hats.

'Aren't they hot in those clothes?' asks Alex.

'They're what are known as Orthodox Jews, who live very strict, uncomfortable lives for religious reasons. It's hard to understand why.'

At the end of a week Alex's impression of Jerusalem is of a huge, noisy jumble of people and animals, of churches, mosques, synagogues, convents and monasteries, all crowded beside or above narrow cobbled streets.

One afternoon, when they climb up to the Temple Mount, Giles points out that here at least they are probably walking up the original steps. The Old City seems to be given over entirely to religion. The Christian churches are crammed full of gold statues, wax flowers, pictures of saints, dolls clad in silver, shot silk and tinsel, wrought iron lamps and boxes of bones. The atmosphere is overlaid with the sickly smell of stale incense and attar of roses. Every altar is covered with guttering candles and gilt icons with penetrating eyes. Women in black are kneeling in prayer, making it hard to get close to an altar. Even at her tender age Alex is aware that here is a glut of religious symbols to deaden rather than elevate the mind. She's always glad when they leave a church to emerge in the open air.

'We're walking down the Via Dolorosa now, Alex', says Giles. 'That's Latin for *Street of Sorrows.* It's the route Jesus is said to have followed on his way to death.' Then they climb many wide steps where sacks of millet, cucumbers, melons and artichokes are laid out for sale, and enter the Church of the Holy Sepulchre, which is hemmed in by other buildings.

'Each Christian sect has its own time for worship in this church', explains Giles. 'So there's always some kind of service going on. Sadly the different sects spend a lot of time fighting over their rights here. They're not very nice to each other.' To Alex it seems to be a confusion of chapels, pillars, tombs and gloomy passages where lamps burn night and day in dusty niches, and bats swoop above dripping candles amid clouds of blue incense.

They eventually pick their way out between groups of black-bearded priests in mildewed cassocks and tall black hats, glad to leave behind the chanting, whispering and sighing. Giles mutters that the whole experience is a mockery of religion. Alex isn't quite sure what he means, but is glad he doesn't like the atmosphere any more than she does. People are still pushing their way into the church, and she wonders if they all come away as disappointed as she is. The souvenir stalls outside the church are more interesting, with their olive-stone rosaries, silver crosses and marquetry boxes, but her father walks away, saying everything is wickedly overpriced.

They emerge into a sunny square where Alex begs to be allowed to buy lemonade from a street vendor dispensing the lurid over-sweet drink from two ornately decorated brass urns. Giles hurries her onto a bus, saying the lemonade won't quench her thirst and the little cups hanging on the urn might not be clean.

One morning, as he promised, Giles hires a car to drive to Galilee to try and locate Zilpha. They drive along a valley enclosed by brown hills. Cactus plants line the dusty white road among tumbled rocks, and brown hawks hang in the clear air waiting to drop like stones on their prey. After climbing for some time they enter a hot, dry little village clinging to the hillside. 'This is Kafr Kenna, the Cana in the Bible' says Giles.

'Where Jesus changed the water into wine?'

'Yes.' She looks around, hoping for some further miracle, but can only see a woman pounding chick peas in a mortar.

They drive on to Zilpha's village of Al Naher. Alex can hardly contain her excitement. At last she'll see Zilpha and the family she's heard so much about. They are to look out for two identical yellow houses with balconies. Giles is disturbed to see that several houses in the village have been reduced to rubble. Alex shouts, 'Look, is that the house?' But when they pull up alongside a shabby two-storey building with yellow stucco peeling off the walls, they see that one of the two houses is no longer there. Tufts of green are already showing among the blackened stones scattered over the site where the house once stood. Two children and a woman are hanging over the balcony railings of the remaining house. Giles greets them and then

125

asks after Zilpha. Alex is sure that these must be Zilpha's relations, and that she herself will appear on the balcony at any moment. But the woman shouts down in English that the house next door was destroyed by Jewish terrorists, and Zilpha and her family have gone to Beirut. She doesn't know the address.

This news is a great blow. Having found the village, Alex was certain they'd find Zilpha. Now her beloved nanny seems to have slipped out of her life for ever. As they leave the village Giles tries to console his tearful daughter. But crying won't bring Zilpha back, and she retreats into a gloomy silence.

'Let's go and have lunch by the sea', suggests Giles. From the road they can see the thirteen-mile long strip of water called the Sea of Galilee a thousand feet below. As they descend the air becomes hotter and they glimpse the dazzling flat white roofs of Tiberias. Bananas and sugar cane grow along the shore and they can see a group of the familiar Bedouin tents, this time made of dark brown hessian. The town of Tiberias which had appeared so romantic from a distance turns out to be a shabby, squalid place, smelling of rancid onions. The main road runs alongside the sea past open-air cafés where men sit playing tric-trac under striped awnings. At one of these cafés Giles orders bread and hummus – and felafel, a mixture of butter beans, red onions, garlic and cumin, made into fried cakes. They look out from under a shady awning at the quivering heat hanging over the light green water. Up above a gang of sparrows twitter in the eucalyptus trees. To the west lie greenish mountains, but to the east only barren cliffs. And northward rises the shining white ridge of Mount Hermon.

'Why is that mountain white?' asks Alex

'Because it's always covered with snow.' Alex's idea of snow is what happens to the tiny freezing compartment in the fridge when it needs defrosting. In this hot dry landscape she can scarcely believe in snow.

'That particular mountain is actually in Lebanon. *Lebanon* means white, from the Arabic word *laban. Labneh* comes from the same word.'

They sit in silence for a while. Then Giles says, 'Before we go back to Jerusalem I must tell you our future plans. I have to return to Kirkuk in two days' time, but I'm afraid I won't be able to take you with me after all.' In spite of the conversation Alex has overheard in the bedroom the news comes as a shock. She's becoming used to her father's presence and can't accept that he will disappear again so soon. She stares at him blankly as he goes on to tell her of Sheena's plans to live in Beirut. 'You'll be living for the time being with Mr Carrington in his large apartment near the sea. I'll come and see you in August and at Christmas and when I get leave next year.'

'Why can't I come to Kirkuk?' Alex says obstinately.

'Because I shall only have a small one-bedroomed flat and the schools in Kirkuk aren't as good as the one you'll be able to attend in Beirut.'

'I could sleep on a camp bed like I'm doing now. I don't want to live with Mr Carrington. I don't like him!'

'You'll like him when you get to know him.'

'I won't! I won't!' Alex bursts into tears and everyone in the café looks towards their table. 'I don't want Sheena to marry Mr Carrington!' Alex wails.

Giles looks stricken. 'She isn't going to marry him. She's married to me. These arrangements are because of the war. Lots of people have to live in difficult circumstances in wartime. Lebanon is a better place to live in than Iraq at the moment. You must be brave.'

Before returning to Jerusalem, they visit Bethlehem. They're no longer in the mood for sightseeing, but Giles feels this may be the last chance Alex will have of seeing the place. He tells her that Bethlehem – *Beit Lahm* in Arabic – means the place of food. No one is really sure where Jesus was born. Alex believes firmly what Zilpha has told her, that Jesus was born in Bethlehem, in a stable with donkeys and lambs and sweet-scented hay, while angels in gold and white sang songs in the background under a brilliant star.

After driving along squalid narrow streets, they enter the Chapel of the Nativity, with a marble floor and walls, and lit by many lamps. It's hung about with velvet and brocade, and decorated with a mass of icons and fake jewels. People are pushing each other to get in, and the stench of hot humanity is sickening. A large fourteen-pointed silver star has been let into a recess in the wall. Underneath it is a marble manger, marking the exact spot, so the guide tells them, where Jesus was born. Jesus is represented by a wax doll lying in the manger. Alex wonders why all the pictures in books are so mistaken, and can't wait to get outside.

'I'm sorry we came', says Giles wryly. 'It isn't what we imagined.' They drive the six miles to Jerusalem almost in silence. After supper Giles has to go and meet Sheena in town. Alex must go to bed and she can call the warden if she needs anything.

As soon as her father has gone, Alex finds his diary again and reads the last entry: *July 3. Sheena came to the hostel tonight and told me she's going to live with Basil in Beirut. Such a shock. I can hardly believe it. The idea of living without Sheena and Alex is shattering. So ironic that I was the one to suggest to Basil he visit Sheena at K3. I fear so much for Alex's future. She's had enough disruption.*

Alex stares at the words for a long time. There's no avoiding Sheena's decision, she thinks. There never is.

On Giles's last day they visit the Dome of the Rock in Jerusalem, also known as the Mosque of Omar. 'This isn't an ordinary mosque', says Giles. 'It's an especially holy place to the Muslims. And they believe Muhammad was taken up to heaven from here.'

'Who took him up?'

'I don't know how it happened. I only know that the Jews and the Muslims are always quarrelling over the Holy

Places in Jerusalem. It would have been more convenient if Muhammad had been taken up from Mecca.'

Alex expects the mosque to be yet another holy place overcrowded with people and ornaments. She is pleasantly surprised, when they have taken off their shoes and padded quietly across blue and white porcelain tiles, to find what a spacious, simple and uncluttered building it is. Shafts of sunlight pierce the stained glass, casting dancing spots of vivid red and blue on the columns of porphyry and the richly patterned Turkish carpets. It's very peaceful and awe-inspiring inside the Dome of the Rock.

Coming out, they are overwhelmed by the blistering heat and make for a shady garden café with a fountain playing in the middle. Two ladies are standing beside a nearby table saying goodbye. One leaves the café, and the other sits down again. It is Leila! Alex hardly recognises her, she looks so old and stricken.

After affectionate greetings and astonishment that they should be meeting in Jerusalem, Leila comes to sit with them. In a subdued tone she explains how difficult it became living in Baghdad with hostile youths parading the streets. She escaped just before the pro-Nazis took over, and was now about to go to Lebanon to stay with relatives. Her house must have been looted, and she's decided not to return to Baghdad. 'Christian and Jews will always be suspect, whoever rules the country', she says bitterly, and then asks, 'So what happened to you in Iraq?'

'Sheena and Alex were flown out from Habbaniya in April, just in time before Raschid's coup. I was put under house arrest in Kirkuk – nothing too drastic, thank heaven – and was freed at the beginning of June. I arrived here a fortnight ago. I'm returning to Kirkuk tomorrow morning.'

'At one point there was a rumour here that Habbaniya had been taken over by the Iraqi army.'

'No, it wasn't. A large number of Iraqi troops was sent, with artillery and modern aircraft to seize Habbaniya, but they met with severe resistance in a five-day siege. It was an extraordinary victory. You probably know that Habbaniya is a non-operational airfield. It's mostly a flying school for about a thousand cadets. There were only thirty-nine qualified pilots and some Assyrian military units to protect the place, plus nine thousand civilians. They had to make do with seventy-four ancient aircraft and nine obsolete biplane fighters. Three thousand bombs were dropped, and a hundred and sixteen rounds of ammunition were fired, but at the cost of a quarter of the pilots' lives and the loss of twenty-two aircraft. An Anglo-Indian force had arrived at Basra, but couldn't get to Habbaniya owing to the floods. Unfortunately the Allies are very hard pressed at the moment, and presumably it wasn't expected that Raschid would be successful.'

'So how was Raschid ousted?'

'A British overland force, mainly consisting of a cavalry regiment acting as a police force here, was sent, together with the Arab Legion. But motorised transport was in such short supply that it didn't set out till May 11th, five days after the RAF victory at Habbaniya. It was pathetically under-equipped, with no tanks, heavy armour or anti-aircraft guns, travelling mostly in old buses and lorries with only six World War One armoured cars. Being a cavalry regiment, few of the men knew how to drive, and the Morris army lorries had solid rubber tyres left over from the last war! It sounds laughable until you think of that appalling journey of over six hundred miles in 118° Fahrenheit, moving at fifteen miles an hour. It was an astonishing feat.'

'How on earth did they hope to defeat the huge Iraqi army?' asks Leila.

'I don't know what they hoped, but they had an incredible stroke of luck. A relief column sent ahead, led by a chap called Kingstone, reached the fort of Khaan Nuqta. The Iraqi garrison fled in panic, without neutralising the telephone switchboard. So an interpreter was able to monitor the Iraqi military movements, and to spread false intelligence about fifty British tanks being on their way, with an Allied force of sixty thousand coming close behind! This story was actually swallowed by the Iraqi military, and Raschid fled.'

Giles is smiling, and Alex wants to ask questions. But Leila, looking very unhappy, bursts out, 'Giles, I've just been hearing about the horrors which have taken place in Baghdad. My friend Fahima, who left just now, is a Jewish lady who fled from Baghdad in June, after being hidden during the pogrom by her Muslim neighbours.'

'What pogrom?' asks Giles.

'Haven't you heard what happened to the Jews?'

'No, I haven't.'

'During May, while Raschid was in power, the radio was constantly broadcasting propaganda against the Jews, and people were told the Allies were on the verge of defeat. Bands of men were entering the Jewish areas, looting, raping and even killing. The Jewish hospital was seized, schools were closed, and shops raided.'

'In Kirkuk we heard nothing about the Jewish situation.'

'It was very bad', continues Leila, 'Then suddenly Fahima heard that Raschid had fled because British forces had reached the outskirts of Baghdad, and an armistice had been signed. On Sunday, June the first, the Regent was to arrive, and Fahima went with her Jewish friends to welcome him. They all assumed, of course, that following the armistice British forces had entered Baghdad and restored law and order, and that the Iraqi army had been disbanded. She returned home at two in the afternoon and heard shooting. By the evening the news had gone round that Iraqi soldiers had started a fight with a group of Jews on Al-Khurr Bridge. In no time anti-Jewish violence had spread everywhere. One of my closest friends was murdered.'

Leila glances at Alex, and says, 'I won't go into detail. You can imagine what happened.'

'Yes, I can.'

'But Giles, the dreadful thing is, that the pogrom need not have happened. I can't understand it. Raschid had fled, the pro-British government was being set up, and British troops were stationed outside Baghdad. Why didn't they occupy the city and make sure that all those who had supported Raschid, didn't go on the rampage? Why did they allow the soldiers to keep their weapons?'

'As far as I can see, Leila – and I may be wrong – it must have been because Cornwallis, the Ambassador, was anxious at all costs to keep the British military well in the background outside Baghdad, to reassure the Regent's government and the Iraqis that we had no intention of becoming an army of occupation. As Raschid had fled, perhaps it seemed to him there was no need to enter the city. It's also possible that he thought all the British subjects under house arrest would be killed if British troops entered Baghdad.'

'And that would have included you', says Leila.

'It would, and we were expecting it.'

'Seven hundred murdered Jews, as compared to – how many British subjects?'

'I don't know. Possibly more than seven hundred. It's terrible, Leila, what choices have to be made in wartime.'

Leila takes out her pen and a scrap of paper, saying, 'There's so much more we need to talk about, Giles. But I have to rush now. Here's my address in Beirut. You might be able to write. One day perhaps we'll meet again.' She kisses Alex and Giles, with tears in her eyes, and walks away quickly.

They return to the hostel and sit in glum silence at supper. At bedtime Giles says, 'In the morning, Basil and Sheena will be collecting you to drive to Beirut. I shall be flying to Baghdad.'

During the night Alex wakes to hear her father moaning with pain. She hears him rise and open a drawer, hears the click of pills in a bottle, the swallowing of water.

He's quiet for a short time. Then he starts to pace the room in extreme discomfort. Alex lies rigid with consternation at the sounds he's making. She's never witnessed an adult in pain before. 'What's wrong?' she whispers.

'I have a stomach ulcer.' He's gasping by now, and she can hardly bear to listen, and to be unable to help. After half an hour doubled up over the bed in agony, the pain subsides. 'Don't worry, Alex. I'll be all right in the morning. You go to sleep.'

But Alex, whose nervous system has shared every stab of her father's pain, is too troubled to sleep. Together father and daughter lie awake till dawn, each visualising their bleak future apart.

Chapter Thirteen

Alex meets her mother and Basil outside the hostel half an hour after her father has left for Kirkuk, promising he'll write to her very often. Claude, who is to drive them to Beirut, flicks fine white dust off the Buick with a large feather duster. Alex sits by the window, her nose squashed against the glass. Sheena, in a white pleated crepe dress, sits in the middle looking radiantly happy. Her voice when she speaks to her daughter is soft and pleasant, and she laughs a lot. This is a Sheena Alex hasn't often experienced.

'For the rest of the summer', Sheena informs Alex, 'We're going to stay in a villa Basil has rented in the mountains above Beirut. Most people go to the mountains in the summer, as it's so hot in the town. You won't be going to school until nearly the end of September so you'll be having a lovely long holiday!' Alex is relieved. School doesn't bear thinking about yet.

After living in the desert and then coming to the dusty aridity of early summer in Jerusalem, Alex finds most of the hundred-kilometre coastal drive from Tel Aviv to Beirut

133

unexpectedly beautiful. Engrossed in the wonder of watching the dark green water dashing its white spray high against the rocky shore, her unhappiness at parting from her father is numbed a little.

They have to stop at the customs post at Nakoura, a bare, treeless place where the heat beats down remorselessly on the car roof and melts the asphalt on the road. A couple wait patiently beside their vegetable cart laden with marrows and huge tomatoes which are beginning to split in the sun.

'What's the hold-up?' asks Sheena with her usual impatience.

'They're checking travellers carefully, trying to prevent terrorists and refugees entering Lebanon', says Basil. The customs men look a ferocious unsmiling lot, and Alex is taken aback when one of them suddenly grins disarmingly and offers her a humbug out of a paper bag.

At length they move on to Adloun, and then Saida. The names are written up on signs at the approach to the towns. At Saida they see the long arched causeway leading out to a castle which seems to float on the sea. 'This is the Sidon of the Bible, of course', says Basil, 'And that's the Crusader castle, Qal'at Al Bahr, which means Fortress of the Sea.' Giles, no doubt, would have stopped to explore this castle, but Alex is glad, today, that she doesn't have to walk about in the heat.

Now they're driving along a flat shoreline and Alex is mesmerised by the repeated movement of the long foam-encrusted waves rolling lazily up and down the hard white sand. They pass a group of children selling baskets of large crimson cherries by the roadside. Basil won't stop to buy any, he says the kids charge far too much. When Alex looks eastwards out of the opposite window she can see a long mountain range with patches of snow still clinging to the shaded hollows. This is more interesting than driving in the desert.

Nearer Beirut the road turns inland for a while towards the small town of Damour, separated from the sea by a level plain of mulberry trees. Then it plunges on through a large pine forest to Khalde. 'The famous umbrella pines of Beirut', says Basil. 'They're planning to cut down much of the forest to build a new international airport. Over there is the golf course.' Alex thinks the pine trees look like giant toadstools with their smooth curved tops.

'We'll approach Beirut through Raouché, along the Corniche and the North Coast Road', Basil instructs Claude. Honking the horn, the chauffeur shoots along several side streets and comes out at the start of a wide straight three-mile boulevard fringed with palms. 'Slow down along here', shouts Basil, 'We want to look at the view.' Just off the coast they can see several rocky islets, one of which forms an archway through which, Basil tells them, a few intrepid water-skiers have been known to ski. 'The rocks are known as Pigeons' Grotto. The Lebanese love to parade along this Corniche in the evenings and on Sundays. Any excuse to gossip and show off their clothes.'

Later as they turn right along the North Coast Road Basil launches into a description of Beirut for Sheena's benefit. 'You'll notice how many of the streets have French names, even Laval and Pétain. French culture has gained enormous influence here. It surprises me that the Lebanese want to have their capital city commemorate First World War generals like Weygand and Giraud. Even their flag is the Tricolour with a cedar tree superimposed.. There's a French university, St. Joseph, run by Jesuits, where so many of the Maronite politicians were educated. Emile Eddé, a rabid Francophile, has dominated the government since 1936. He despises anything to do with Islam.'

'Has the French influence been a good thing?' asks Sheena.

'Yes and no. It's turned the town into a fashionable cosmopolitan place which will probably end up as the banking centre of the Middle East. But it's done nothing to address the poverty and corruption of the country as a whole. No taxation results in no public spending. There's much unrest among the Islamic groups. The government, which constitutionally has to have a Christian President, a Sunni Muslim Prime Minister and a Shia Muslim President of the Chamber of Deputies, is always divided. Very little gets done. They spend most of the time drinking sweet coffee and insulting one another. All they understand is making a profit, and if anything goes drastically wrong they can always blame the Palestinian refugees.'

'One would have thought the French government would have insisted on efficiency.'

'Yes, one would think so. But in fact they've done nothing to tackle the basic problems. There are still no traffic or building regulations. The most hideous blocks of flats, designed by unqualified architects, are spreading in every direction. And the Vichy government's been inculcating fascist ideas among the established leading Christian families. Pierre Gemayel has even formed a fascist party, known as the Phalange.'

'It sounds dreadful. How do people put up with it?'

'Fortunately there are various foreign groups and individuals who've put money into providing essential services, such as schools and hospitals. The American University and its teaching hospital where you're going to work, is excellent. The trouble is, the British should never have agreed to the French Mandate. It's going to cause a serious civil war one day. Yet Beirut's still an interesting and beautiful town to live in.'

'This part of Beirut certainly isn't spoilt.'

'No, this area's been lucky so far.'

Claude is driving round the small promontory of Minet al Hosn where Ottoman houses grace the area with their old Venetian-style stone arched windows and red tiled roofs. Basil remarks, 'Can you imagine anyone pulling down one of these exquisite houses to build a modern concrete excrescence? Concrete becomes an oven in summer. They soon discovered that in the modern Tel Aviv.'

They move out of the residential area into the fashionable quarter of hotels and night clubs, passing the Vendôme and the Excelsior. Basil says, 'I thought we'd spend a night at my favourite hotel, the St. George. It's cooler than my apartment at this time of year. We'll have lunch there and a swim, and then I'll take you to the medical school to meet Dr. Davis.'

Alex likes the idea of a swim, and soon she catches glimpses of vivid blue sea between the pink and white blocks of flats, the villas and the trees of sycamore and pine. The Buick turns left down a long street at the end of which stands Beirut's most famous hotel, balanced hugely and squarely on the tip of a spur of land curving round a small deep water harbour, sheltered by a rocky breakwater. On one side of the three-storeyed building sweeps a wide semi-circular paved terrace overlooking the sea.

Alex's room in the hotel is pale blue with a white divan bed kept cool by an overhead fan. Her balcony door is open. She goes out to watch the skiers skimming over the water and the glistening naked brown bodies of a group of small boys diving expertly off a high rock which they share with a crowd of noisy, jostling gulls. She can hardly wait to get into the sea herself.

Basil wears bright yellow swimming trunks. Alex has never seen a man swimming in any colour but black or navy blue. His legs are covered with pale ginger hairs. He uses the low, springy diving platform at the end of the breakwater, diving heavily but neatly into the turquoise water. Alex jumps in several times from this platform, but is too scared to try diving. The sea is like warm syrup, silky and buoyant, and she floats with ease. Sheena never dives or jumps. She wears a rubber cap to protect her from earache and getting her hair wet. She swims a strong, awkward-looking breast stroke with her head held high in the air.

After their swim they sit on the terrace. Basil and Sheena sip tumblers of cloudy white arak. The table is covered with mezze – small bowls of smoked fish, vegetables, nuts, pickles and spicy meat balls. 'What's this?' asks Sheena, sniffing at a bowl of something fishy.

'Octopus, I think. They do a lot of octopus spearing around these waters.' Alex avoids the octopus.

The waiter will only speak in French, which irritates Basil. 'They used to speak perfect English here before the war. The Vichy must have put a stop to that, but it's ridiculous to keep it up now.'

'Don't worry', says Sheena, 'They'll switch to English when the hotel fills up with British servicemen on leave.'

After lunch Alex is sent to rest. She lies on the white bed, lulled by the most soothing sound in the world, that of the sea washing up against the rocks and receding with a soft sucking swish. How lovely it would be to live with Giles and Sheena and Zilpha in a house by the sea!

At five it's cooler and Claude drives them to the university, first along a shabby coastal strip where old men in slippers sit on their crumbling doorsteps enjoying the cool of early evening; then up a wide road where he skilfully negotiates the chaotic traffic, including the swaying, ramshackle trams which come hurtling down the slope from the university. 'This traffic is a nightmare', grumbles Basil. 'Everyone wants a large American car and there are no parking restrictions. Lunchtime is the worst because the Lebanese insist on going home for their meal and a siesta.'

Alex notes the name of the road, *Rue Georges Picot.* 'Who's Georges Picot?' she asks Sheena, pronouncing the *'t'.* Basil answers her question. 'Georges Picot is a French politician. I daresay the name will be changed to that of a Lebanese politician when Emile Eddé goes.'

They pass tall houses with double-arched windows of lead tracery, and iron balconies supported by graceful stone columns, and porticoed villas with embossed iron doors. Then a row of shops with faded awnings, from behind which looms a block of unfinished flats with ugly reinforcing rods protruding from the sandstone. At intervals along the street stand policemen outside old Turkish sentry boxes. Finally they reach the university gates.

'We'll drive right through the campus before going to the medical school', Basil instructs Claude. 'So Mrs Kinley can see the grounds before it gets dark.' The extensive campus covers some seventy acres of high ground overlooking the sea. Mature trees – ilex, eucalyptus, araucaria, carob, acacia and the ubiquitous palm and fir – tower over the tall, dignified buildings, with battlements and rows of narrow windows in which lights are already appearing. The imposing facade of the main building boasts a clock tower, installed in 1873, some years after the university was founded by an American named Bliss. 'He was a missionary, I believe', says Basil.

When Claude parks outside the medical school Sheena says to Alex 'We're going in to see Dr. Davis. You wait here with Claude.'

After the noisy clangour of the streets the campus is very subdued, almost hushed. The chauffeur sits on the running board of the Buick and lights up a Lucky Strike cigarette. 'My mother smokes those and Du Maurier', Alex announces. 'She drops the ash and it burns tiny round holes in our carpets. She says she doesn't drop any ash, it's my father who makes the holes.' Claude laughs and pulls out a newspaper called *L'Orient*. Alex is impressed that he can read French. Soon the light begins to fail and Claude puts away his paper and produces a bag of unshelled pistachio nuts. 'Your camel will enjoy eating the shells', he says seriously. But when Soda is placed in front of a mounting pile of shells he doesn't seem interested. Alex thinks how boring a chauffeur's life must be, always waiting outside buildings for your boss.

Basil returns with Sheena who's talking avidly about the conditions in the hospital.

'Dr. Davis says they're desperately short of supplies. It was difficult obtaining anything under the Vichy. The government was always accusing the university of harbouring spies!'

'If we join the war' says Basil, 'Our boys will need to use the hospital. They'll find a way of sending out medical supplies, don't worry.'

At night the St. George Hotel, ablaze with lights, resembles a great floating liner. Sheena takes her daughter up to her room on the first floor. Alex sits on the bed and watches her mother change into evening clothes – crisp white lace and the three-stranded necklace of pearls Giles gave her. She twists her hair into a chignon and sticks a large white gardenia into it. Basil disappears into the adjoining bathroom and later emerges looking cool and dapper in a pale green shirt with pristine white jacket and white bow tie. Alex notes the knife-sharp creases in his oyster-grey trousers. As always, he smells of cologne. It's strange to see him in her mother's bedroom.

'A waiter has brought milk and sandwiches to your room. You must go to bed after your supper', Sheena tells Alex.

'Can't I have supper with you?'

'No, darling. You know it's only grownups at dinner time.'

Basil calls Alex out onto the balcony, saying 'Look, we'll be sitting at a table down there on the terrace. You'll be able to wave to us so you won't be lonely.' She's so much in awe of Basil that she can only nod her agreement. Inside she is bitterly jealous.

Alex hangs over the balcony, waiting to catch sight of Sheena among the guests. In a moment she appears with Basil, and Alex has to admit they make an elegant couple.

They sit down at a table near the balcony. Sheena waves and shouts 'Hello, darling!' and then turns her attention to the menu. Waiters in white move deftly among the tables under the strings of coloured lights. A basket of little biscuits and a plate of glistening black caviar surrounded with chopped ice and lemon wedges is placed in front of Basil and Sheena. A bottle of champagne in a bucket of ice is brought by another smiling waiter. Alex's eyes are fixed on her mother's every movement, as the caviar is taken away and other dishes are brought. There's a delicious smell of spicy roast chicken. Then Basil says something to Sheena and she looks up at Alex and says very firmly, 'Into bed now, darling'.

Reluctantly Alex obeys and falls asleep immediately. Later she wakes to hear the rhythmic strains of a dance band. The dance floor in the centre of the terrace is crowded with couples dancing to a slow, sensual tune. A sultry looking woman in a skin-tight black gown is crooning in front of the band. Alex can only make out the two title words of the song, *'Stormy weather'.* She's never heard a live band before and finds it thrilling. She recalls her parents dancing a slow foxtrot to a scratchy gramophone record in the living room at K3. Sheena wasn't wearing the same look on her face as she has now, dancing close to Basil. They seem utterly absorbed in one another. Sheena's head is resting on Basil's shoulder, and his lips are touching her hair. Alex would like to have shouted down, 'Leave my mother alone! You're not my father!'

Becoming aware that people are staring up at her, she retreats hastily. She goes back to sleep listening to the sound of the music intermingled with the constant slow pounding of the sea against the breakwater.

At breakfast Sheena tells Alex their plans for the rest of the summer. 'Today we're going to drive up to a village in the mountains called Beit Mery. We'll have a week's holiday with you, before I start my job at the hospital. Basil will be working in Beirut too. It's only sixteen kilometres away so we won't be far. Basil's maid, Georgette, will be in the villa to look after you when I'm not there. And your father will be coming to stay for a few weeks.'

The thought of a stranger looking after her doesn't appeal to Alex. She longs for Zilpha. 'I don't want to be left with the maid', she mutters.

'It'll be just the same as being left with Zilpha. Do take that sulky look off your face. And put that grubby camel under the table. It's about time you threw it away.'

Claude is ready to drive them to Beit Mery straight after breakfast. On their way they stop at Basil's apartment to pick up some provisions. Alex is told to wait in the garden. 'Abby, my cook, will keep us talking for ever if we take the kid up', says Basil. 'She misses Sally-Ann and is looking forward to seeing Alex.'

Alex stares up at the three-storey salmon pink block which is to be her future home. The front garden is paved with tiny black tiles interspersed with tall dark fir trees and cacti. Tangled strands of jasmine and bougainvillaea clamber up the three balconies. The possibilities of playing in this garden seem limited. Eventually Claude reappears staggering along with two heavy boxes, followed by Basil carrying a carton of bottles and a large shiny black camera, and Sheena carrying two holdalls.

Driving out of Beirut is a slow business. Now and again Claude spurts dangerously along a street, but mostly he has to crawl along, squashed between large American cars – Pontiac, Cadillac and Dodge. Alex can read their names in large chrome letters on the back of the dusty vehicles. The road runs along the tramlines, then skirts the town centre until they reach a stone bridge over the Beirut River. Soon after crossing the bridge they turn right and drive down a boulevard of acacia trees beside vegetable fields, banana palms and small riverside cafés under vine-clad pergolas which gradually peter out into date and citrus groves in the foothills of the mountains. The road starts to wind upwards, not too steeply at first, into higher orchards of apple, cherry, plum and pear. Claude overtakes a couple of shabby taxis laden with small furniture, household goods and even a crate of hens.

'Locals who can afford it rent unfurnished summer houses in the mountains', says Basil. 'Fortunately our villa is pretty well equipped. Georgette came up yesterday by taxi to get the place in order.'

Six kilometres from Beirut they pass through the village of Mukalles, where the river valley is crossed by the remains of a Roman aqueduct. Each village in the mountains is dominated by a church with an open belfry surmounted by a cross.

'These mountain villages behind Beirut are all Maronite Christian so they tend to attract Europeans more than the Muslim villages where the locals can sometimes be rather hostile.'

The raucous blare of Arabic music hits them as they reach each habitation, and then fades as they leave it behind. Orange trees and willows and bamboo provide shade at ramshackle outdoor cafés. In one of these Alex catches sight of two fair-skinned children with blonde, almost white hair. Sheena remarks on this with surprise, and Basil explains one does occasionally see the odd blonde or redhead among the Arabs, probably as a result of foreign invasions.

'We're coming into Beit Mery now.'

'It's very pretty' says Sheena.

'Yes', continues Basil. 'You'd never guess how much violent bloodshed there's been in this village. In the last century the Maronites tried to expel the Druze minority. Feuds between the Christians and the Druze sect continue to this day. Over there you can see Deir el-Qalaa, which means Fortress Monastery. There's an eighteenth century church up there too, built on the site of a Roman temple. There was probably a Phoenician temple before that. You get a magnificent view of Beirut from the monastery. And that enormous palace of a building is the Grand Hotel. We might dine there tonight. The food's excellent.'

Alex peers out of the car window and is impressed by the gleaming white edifice with a crenellated parapet. Rows of arched windows are spaced round the first two storeys and rectangular windows round the two storeys above.

Claude turns the Buick down a stony track with gullies on either side, hooting at a couple of scraggy black goats to shift out of the way. He pulls up outside two identical white villas in adjoining gardens. Each house has a wide verandah with a main balcony directly above. The garden consists of rough grass between clumps of flowering bushes. 'Our landlord lives next door, a Frenchman named Durand. His family spend most of the summer here. Madame Durand is half Lebanese and speaks very little English. They've a large family of six kids. Alex might like to play with the younger ones, twin girls and a boy.'

Alex's heart sinks. She doesn't want to play with the children next door. Why do all grownups assume she'll want to play with any child of her own age?

They climb out of the car into the dazzling sunshine, but a fresh mountain breeze makes the heat tolerable. Cicadas are chorusing faintly from the steep wooded slopes behind the villa, and the warm scent of pine resin hangs in the air. Further up the track a mule is rolling in the dust. The boxes of provisions are unloaded. In the top one Alex can see tins of corned beef and tunny fish and Kraft cheese. The crate of bottles contains gin, whisky and Dubonnet.

She walks to the edge of the track and looks down the terraced hillsides – tier upon tier of vineyards, almost all the way down to Beirut, beyond which the distant sea shimmers, luminous at the horizon. It's a view she is never going to forget.

Chapter Fourteen

Georgette runs down the steps to help carry up the luggage. She's a grinning, self-confident girl with short black hair, large white teeth and eyes like shiny black buttons. 'Good morning, Mr Carrington', she says cheerfully.

'Georgette, this is Mrs Kinley and her daughter, Alex.'

'Good morning, Mrs Kinley!' There's just a hint of insolence in the maid's bright tone. Her black eyes are taking in every detail of Sheena. She barely gives Alex a glance, and the child guesses immediately that here is one Arab who doesn't dote on children. Georgette picks up one of the boxes and staggers up the steps, chattering loudly to Claude in Arabic.

Alex follows the adults up onto the verandah. Two vivid blue plumbago plants in large greeny-brown terracotta urns stand on either side of the double door into the villa. The shutters are wide open, allowing the sun to glare mercilessly onto the black and white tiled floor of the living room. Several rolled up rugs and a pile of cushions stand against the whitewashed wall. Georgette hasn't yet removed broom, dustpan and brush. A flit-gun lies on the table and there's a strong smell of dust.

'This is the worst time of year for flies, one has to keep at them night and day', remarks Basil. 'The house is somewhat primitive, but quite comfortable in its way. You have to bring what you need. I'm afraid none of these holiday villas has carpets or curtains or upholstered chairs. But it's cooler without, and of course material doesn't last well through the cold, damp winters when the villas are empty. There's no fridge, just an ice box. A block of ice is delivered each day.'

Compared to the opulence of the St. George Hotel the villa looks very bare: in the living room cane tables and chairs, a cupboard, a standard lamp and three pictures of birds; in Alex's bedroom a chest of drawers, a chair and a narrow iron bedstead. Clothes are to be hung from a row of hooks on the wall. A knotted mosquito net hangs above the pillow and a small rug lies beside the bed. A miniature balcony gives Alex a good view into the adjoining garden, where she can see a cushioned swing bed shaded by a striped awning. The shutters are slightly open, but otherwise there seems to be no sign of life next door. Alex wishes the French family were not in residence. Sheena and Basil are to use the largest bedroom with the balcony over the verandah. There are two guest rooms and Georgette sleeps in a room not much bigger than a cupboard next to the kitchen.

While Sheena and Basil are having a rest after lunch Alex tiptoes out of her room and descends the stairs into the living room. She slips out of the half-open door onto the verandah and down the stone steps into the garden. A hedge of rhododendrons and myrtle separates the two villas. Beyond a windbreak of oleander Alex discovers a secluded concrete patch with a washing line strung across it between two posts. Just here she could sit, undetected by anyone in either of the two houses. If she takes care to keep out of sight on this further side of the villa, perhaps the French children might be avoided. Over a low stone wall running along the back of the villas Alex can see a tempting path leading up into the pine forest. She perches on the wall and begins to plan a make-believe game.

At four o'clock the house next door comes to life. Alex hears laughter and voices in the garden, sounding raucous and alien since the family are speaking in French mixed with words of Arabic. Twice Alex hears someone exclaim 'Merde!' From her balcony she watches the neighbours, taking care not to be seen herself. She notes two little girls of about her own age. But even if she wanted to play with them, how would she understand their language?

In the living room Sheena and Basil are about to drink a jug of iced tea. 'Would you like to try some, Alex?' asks Basil. The tall glass of clear, golden liquid laced with sugar, cinnamon, ice and a piece of lemon, is surprisingly refreshing.

Basil sits in a large cane chair with his feet on a stool, smoking a Chesterfield cigarette. Alex looks at him and realises finally he's not a visitor who will go home. He's going to be with them every day as part of a new family unit created all too abruptly. She relinquishes the hope of waking one morning to find Basil departed and Giles returned.

In the late afternoon Basil asks Sheena and Alex to come into the garden to be photographed. Photography is his latest hobby. Sheena poses for him, looking charming on walls, on steps, under pine trees and leaning against one of the pots of plumbago on the verandah. He takes about thirty shots of Sheena and, as an afterthought, three quick snaps of Alex with her mother.

They all stand on the verandah to watch the sun set, a fiery orange disc balanced on the edge of the seascape round the promontory of Beirut. The rasp of cicadas gathers strength in the cool of the evening, and the pines sway slightly in a stronger mountain breeze. The green flash is vivid as the sun slips under the horizon.

'Lebanon is the most beautiful country', says Sheena. 'Even Mount Carmel isn't as lovely.'

Night falls quickly, and a mist comes rolling up out of the valley. In the darkness Alex is aware that Basil and Sheena are standing very close together, his arm around her shoulders. She feels excluded and resentful.

At bedtime Sheena comes up at last to see her daughter without Basil. She's changed into an off-the-shoulder green frock which matches her eyes. 'We'll be gone until about eleven', she says. 'Georgette will be here to keep you company.'

'Where are you going?'

'Out to dinner at the Grand Hotel.'

'Why can't I come?'

'Children don't go out to dinner at night.'

Alex hears the Buick's tyres crunching down the uneven track. Next door the French children are still up. It sounds as though a squabble is going on. Georgette is chatting to someone in Arabic. Alex goes to sleep, consoling herself with the thought that Beit Mery is infinitely preferable to the convent.

During the next few days Alex learns some of the details of the family next door. They have two maids who come to gossip with Georgette on the kitchen steps. Alex watches secretly from her balcony and notes that the two older French children look almost grownup. Philippe is sixteen, and Danielle a year younger. Twin girls, Giselle and Jeanne, are eight. The two youngest are Marie-Claire, aged six, and a boy of five called Raoul. Basil thinks Monsieur Durand might have been married twice.

Philippe is dark and good-looking, with enormous energy. Early each morning he sets off down the track wearing white shorts with a tennis racket over his shoulder. Danielle is also dark, a thin girl with a pretty face marred by a slight sharpness of feature. She obviously adores her elder brother. Most mornings Alex observes Madame Durand lying in the swing bed – a handsome plump woman whose podgy hands covered with sparkling rings are constantly flicking through the pages of glossy fashion magazines. Long, perfectly filed red fingernails flash in and out of a bowl of sugared almonds.

'That boy next door', remarks Sheena, 'Has perfectly charming manners! He even bows when we meet. So different from English boys of that age.'

'Yes', agrees Basil. 'He's a clever kid too, doing very well at the French Lycée in Beirut, studying for the Baccalaureate. He's already a juvenile tennis star, and plays in the tournaments at Broummana.'

'You must go round and meet the little girls next door', Sheena keeps urging her daughter. 'Madame Durand says you're very welcome. If you don't make friends you're going to be very bored next week on your own.'

'I don't want to. I can't understand what they're saying.'

'You'd soon learn. It would be useful if you picked up some French.'

Basil's cook, Abla, has had to stay behind in Beirut to look after his apartment. Since Georgette is only capable of a little basic cooking Sheena and Basil eat their main meal out each day. Basil says the Lebanese have superb restaurants, providing a combination of French and Arab dishes. Basil drives Sheena and Alex around the mountain villages – Baabdat, Houmanna, Sofar, Shemlan, Dour Shouair – showing them the beauty spots and sampling the grandiose hotels. At Zahle she wishes they could lunch in one of the cool riverside cafés; but Basil insists on taking them to hotels, sometimes the Shalimar or the Semiramis; more often the Regent, or the Palace.

The Palace Hotel is particularly impressive, a gargantuan white four-storeyed building on the crest of a steep hill, its grand facade decorated with delicate wrought iron balconies burgeoning with boxes of brilliant geraniums and asters. Rich Lebanese chattering in French occupy the little round tables on the terrace. An extensive mezze is served with the drinks. Twenty or more shell-shaped white dishes filled with various cooked and raw marinated vegetables, nuts, smoked fish, spicy dips, meat balls, caviar and other delicacies Alex has never tasted before.

The swimming pool is a turquoise crescent surrounded with dwarf palms against a background of limes and pomegranates. Alex takes a dip with Basil and Sheena, but the water is too crammed with bodies for pleasant swimming. Unlike the European women in cotton frocks, the Lebanese ladies tend to wear tight-fitting black dresses with chunky gold jewellery in spite of the heat. The children are overdressed too, the girls in organdie frocks, white sandals and knee-length socks, with enormous bows in their black hair; the boys in long-sleeved white shirts and velvet waistcoats. Alex is the only child in shorts.

'Amazing how they dress their kids', says Sheena.

'Showing off their parents' wealth. To them a kid in shorts looks no better than a beggar.'

At the end of their week's holiday Basil and Sheena rise early and gulp down their coffee as the sun rises. Alex gets up in time to watch them drive away, the Buick disappearing into a thin blue mist hovering over the valley. She hears the sound of the car taking the first and second hairpin bends.

Her mother has explained the weekly routine. On Monday and Wednesday evenings she and Basil will return to sleep at Beit Mery. Tuesday and Thursday nights they will stay in Beirut. On Fridays they'll return by teatime for the weekend. Georgette will have Wednesday and Friday evenings off, and part of Sunday.

So far Georgette has hardly spoken to Alex, and she dreads being left alone with the surly maid. In the kitchen she finds her usual bowl of corn flakes and plate of fruit. Georgette is eating Arab bread dipped in condensed milk. 'Can I have some bread and milk?' asks Alex.

'No, you have what your mother told me to give you.'

Alex spends the rest of the morning in the garden keeping out of sight of the Durands. At midday Georgette calls her to eat an omelette and salad, and then orders her to take an afternoon rest. Lying on her bed without anything new to read is an agony to Alex. She has already exhausted the few magazines lying around the villa with strange names like *Life, Harper's Bazaar, Colliers, Movie Magazine.* At the bottom of a cupboard in her bedroom she finds a few copies of a newspaper called *Le Nouveau Temps,* which she can't read. She stands on her balcony and feels the heavy stillness of the hot afternoon weighing on the villa. The occasional faint drumming of cicadas intensifies the lethargy.

When she ventures downstairs Georgette is no longer in the kitchen. From the verandah she sees the maid coming out of the next door villa. 'Madame Durand invites you to play with Giselle and Jeanne', Georgette shouts to Alex, who immediately escapes to her secret place in the garden. For a while she amuses herself collecting fallen pine cones and arranging them in a pattern on the concrete. Some of the cones have small, cream-coloured nuts embedded between the hard woody sections. They have a delicate flavour, nutty but quite different from walnuts, peanuts or pistachios. Alex extracts a small pile of these pine nuts and eats them slowly, savouring them one by one.

She remains outside till sunset and then watches for the green flash as the sun sinks into the sea. Standing alone in the short-lived dusk she becomes vaguely aware for the first time in her life of a beauty not merely pretty, but moving, even rather sad. She remains motionless, gazing at the terraced mountain slopes turning a dark shadowy purple beneath the opalescent sky. The cicadas suddenly take new heart, and the whole mountain-side comes alive with their dry, crackling hum. Listening to the gentle soughing of the pines her mind drifts into the daydreaming state which helped her to pass the long nights at the convent.

Georgette's strident voice breaks the spell. 'Alex, time to come in for supper!' The inevitable bowl of corn flakes, this time mixed with sliced banana, is waiting on the kitchen table. At bedtime Alex stands in her pyjamas on the front balcony waiting for her mother's return. Next door the downstairs rooms are all lit up and someone is playing a dance tune on the piano. Every time the headlights of a car sweep up the last bend into Beit Mery her hopes rise. At last the Buick turns up the track and Alex flees to her bedroom.

In a while Sheena comes to say goodnight in a housecoat with her hair loose. Alex is enthralled yet again by her beauty. After the long day spent alone, she wants to tell her about discovering the pine nuts, but Sheena isn't in a receptive mood. 'Did you play with the girls next door?'

she asks, and is exasperated when Alex shakes her head obstinately.

'They're going to think you very rude if you don't.'

'They'll think I'm ugly in my glasses.'

'Of course they won't. Did you get on all right with Georgette?'

'She gave me my breakfast and my lunch and my supper.'

After the Buick has gone the next morning, Georgette announces 'We're going to the shops to buy vegetables', and hands Alex a wicker basket. They walk in silence along the track to the village, passing a shabby old woman collecting brushwood, whom the maid ignores. Alex notices how many of the doors, window frames and corners of buildings are painted a bright blue. A man in baggy pantaloons and a long striped shirt is putting up his awning and opening his faded blue shutters. His shop sells everything, from caviar to cheap canvas shoes hanging up by their laces. A girl sets up wooden planks outside a bakery and lays out egg pies and sweet pastries. Two women, balancing baskets of fruit on their heads, lift down their loads and proceed to spread their wares onto flat cartons. Alex watches in disgust as a mangy-looking mongrel pees copiously over a giant water-melon. A group of small Arab boys come hurtling down the road spinning large hoops with great expertise.

The shopkeeper encourages Alex to sample an unfamiliar fruit with sweet juicy orange-coloured flesh called an achidinia. No fruit has ever tasted so delicious, but the maid will only buy green peas, sweet potatoes, cherries, bananas and rice.

Georgette gives Alex the task of shelling a pile of pea pods. Alex remembers how often she used to sit with Zilpha shelling peas or stringing green beans. It's difficult to resist popping a few peas into her mouth. Suddenly without warning Georgette leans over and smacks her hand hard, saying 'Bad girl! Not to eat!' Alex is astounded and jumps up, threatening 'I'll tell my mother!'. Never in her life has she been smacked by anyone but Sheena, and that only when Giles wasn't present. Her father has definite views on smacking, and it would never have occurred to Zilpha to strike a child.

But the maid replies confidently, 'No you won't! I'm in charge of you while your mother is away.'

Alex retires to her room feeling not only humiliated but hotly resentful. A slight reprimand would have been quite sufficient.

Chapter Fifteen

Only nine o'clock. In the garden Alex wonders what to do. Then she becomes aware of someone calling, 'Giselle! Giselle!' Suddenly a battered old tennis ball sails over the hedge and falls at Alex's feet. There is a shuffling in the hedge as Giselle scrambles through the foliage.

'Pardon!' she says, with an engaging smile.

Alex holds out the ball to the intruder, a small sallow-skinned girl with hazel eyes and long brown hair tied back in a pony tail.

'Je m'appelle Giselle.' She puts out her hand and Alex places the ball in it. 'Merci.' They stare curiously at each other, and then the French girl disappears back into the hedge.

Alex feels a stab of disappointment. A few minutes later the ball comes over the hedge again. Laughter is heard. Surely this time the ball has been thrown over deliberately. She picks it up and throws it back. It appears again and Alex catches it. Then Giselle shouts 'Viens jouer avec nous!', and Alex pushes her way through the hedge.

'Bonjour! Bonjour!' Giselle, Jeanne and the two youngest children, Marie-Claire and Raoul, cluster round Alex. She senses genuine friendliness behind the French chatter and is happy enough to join in when Jeanne spaces the children out in a circle and they begin to throw a rubber ring. Raoul is the first to drop it and Marie-Claire squeaks 'Maladroit!' He retrieves the ring and aims it low over the ground to Alex, who just manages to catch it.

'Bravo! Bien jouer!' The game proceeds and as Alex catches the ring each time the children keep shouting 'Bravo!' She feels a warm glow of pride and liking for them. How easy it's been, after all, to make friends with the Durands, in spite of the language barrier. Already she's guessing at some of the French words.

When they've had enough of this game, Marie-Claire takes Alex by the hand and leads her up the verandah steps. 'Viens!' She pulls her to a room strewn with toys. The other children follow and clamour for Alex's attention the whole morning. Raoul wants her to play with his train but the twins insist that she look at their dolls. Finally they drag her off like a captured prize to Madame Durand, who's lying as usual on her swing bed. At close quarters Alex detects a dark fuzz on her upper lip and on her bare legs. Three rows of large pearls glisten above her ample bosom. She smiles, saying with a strong French accent 'It is good you come to play'. Then she bellows an order in French towards the open window. In a few moments a maid staggers across the grass bearing a huge jug of lemonade on a tray, together with glasses and a plate of guava jam tartlets.

With these new friends Alex's morning passes all too fast. Language is hardly a necessity for the games they play. Giselle's comments are all too obvious. Alex picks up phrases such as *'les grandes vacances'* and *'J'ai faim'*, and Raoul's constant wail, *'Ce n'est pas juste!'*.

At midday Madame Durand sends Jeanne to tell Georgette that Alex is staying to lunch. A spotless white cloth is thrown over the garden table under a fig tree. Two more chairs are lugged out of the house by Marie-Claire and Raoul. Salad and bread, fruit and cheese appear. Jeanne enjoys telling Alex the name of each fruit in French – *l'abricot, la banane, la pêche.....* the names are so close to the English there's no trouble in remembering them. They are far easier to pronounce than the Arabic words Saeb used to teach her.

Halfway through the meal Philippe and Danielle join the party. Alex becomes aware of the great admiration the whole family feel for the eldest son. They all want to sit next to Philippe, they ply him with food, they adore it when he teases them. Madame Durand's calculating eyes soften when she looks at her first-born. Alex feels only shyness as Philippe's dark eyes examine her too closely for comfort. He peels a banana for her and offers it with a little bow and an irresistible smile. Is he laughing at her? She isn't sure, yet she begins to fall under the spell of his charm. She gathers he has to study every morning after his early game of tennis. He has difficult exams to pass.

Alex returns home reluctantly for her afternoon rest, hardly able to wait for four o'clock, when she's been asked to visit the Durands again. At teatime the children devour thick slices of fresh white bread with squares of dark chocolate. 'C'est le goûter – petits pains au chocolat' explains Giselle, handing Alex a sample. It seems an odd but pleasant combination.

They decide to play hide and seek – *le cache-cache.* Philippe and Danielle delight the children by agreeing to join in. Danielle takes Alex by the hand and shows her the best places to hide. The game eventually spreads into the next door garden and the excitement is at its height when Georgette comes out and tells Alex it's time for bed. 'Quel dommage!' cry the twins. 'A demain, n'est ce pas?' Raoul gives Alex a big kiss and the girls follow suit leaving her feeling quite heady with social success. Unexpectedly life has become very sweet.

The following days pass in a ceaseless round of pleasure. Alex learns more French, she's taught to make pine needle baskets, and is introduced to interesting new food. She joins the Durand family in all their holiday pursuits, including a picnic organised by Danielle. She plays games of make-believe with the younger children in the large garden shed which Raoul calls *La Retraite*. There's a notice on the door in childish letters: *Defense d'entrer sous peine de mort!* Sheena is pleased that her daughter is happily and safely occupied, and even Georgette is less sharp now that she doesn't have to keep an eye on her charge all day.

On Friday evening Monsieur Durand arrives home from Beirut for the weekend and Sheena warns Alex 'You'd better not go next door on Saturdays and Sundays. The family won't want you all the time.'

'But Giselle's asked me to come every day.'

'Maybe she has, but we can't expect Madame Durand to feed and entertain you at weekends.'

'She does want to see me at weekends. She said so!' insists Alex, becoming unreasonable in her disappointment, so passionate is her devotion to the Durand family. But it's useless trying to argue with her mother. Alex gathers from certain remarks Sheena makes to Basil that she doesn't much care for Madame Durand and is amused at her child's lavish praise of the woman. All very confusing considering her mother was so anxious for Alex to make friends with the family in the first place.

At weekends Basil prepares a drink called Pimms – tall glasses of brown liquid filled with borage, slices of cucumber and orange, cherries and chunks of ice. Alex is permitted a small tumbler of the exotic drink. Sheena tries a glassful but much prefers her favourite Cyprus brandy. She and Basil spend much of their time sleeping after the tiring week in town. They rise around ten and return to their bedroom at two. Only at night do they come alive as Alex is getting ready for bed. Georgette lights mosquito coils and candles in glass lamps. But in spite of the acrid smoke from the coils there are always moths fluttering whitely around the candle flames. In bed Alex listens for the car tyres crunching down the track as Basil drives her mother out to dine and dance at one of the hotels. Then

Georgette turns on loud Arabic music on the wireless and sings along with it in her harsh high-pitched voice.

On Sunday morning the church bell starts tolling early. Alex watches the Durands getting into their huge Mercedes to go to Mass, and wishes she could join them. How hateful these Sunday mornings are, waiting for the house to stir! Sometimes out of boredom she's even driven to seek out Georgette in the kitchen. The maid is usually sitting at the table flicking through a pile of French magazines the maids next door have passed on to her. Alex boasts that she's learning French, she knows the months and the days of the week. She wants to look at the magazines but Georgette snatches them away. The maid never chats or smiles. But she shrieks with laughter when gossiping with the Durand maids. When Basil and Sheena are at the villa Georgette asks Alex to do things in a pleasant voice, but when they are alone together her tone becomes peremptory. There's a frightening quality in the maid's seething resentment at having to look after Alex.

Breakfast is at eleven on Sundays – 'brunch' Basil calls it. He consumes a pile of waffles with maple syrup, followed by fried ham and eggs. With envy Alex watches the Durands eating lunch in the garden, always starting with *le potage* out of an earthenware pot. With both sets of grandparents they make twelve at table – a noisy, bantering meal with Philippe the centre of attention. Sunday afternoons are as bad as the mornings. Within the half-closed shutters the house sinks into a deadly gloom. Even the fans seem to whirr round more slowly. Alex lies on her bed staring at the cracks in the ceiling, trying to pass the time by telling herself stories out loud. If only she had some new books to read! She's exhausted the few books saved from K3. She almost knows *The Wind in the Willows* by heart.

One morning when Alex slips through the hedge she finds the Durand girls filling pine baskets with anemones and threading necklaces of jasmine for their mother. It's her birthday and Philippe is taking a day off from his studies. He's lying on the grass trying to read, but Raoul pummels him to get up and play. Finally Philippe rises, growling like a bear, and charges at his brother. Raoul flees screaming with delicious fear as the older boy chases him round the garden. When Philippe catches the child he collapses with helpless laughter on the ground, rubbing his tummy and shouting 'J'ai mal au ventre!' Alex turns this new phrase over in her mind. Raoul is the easiest of the Durands to understand, his words are so often demonstrated with actions.

Madame Durand suggests that Philippe and Danielle take the children for a walk before it gets too hot. They troop in single file along a path through the pine forest, and then clamber down the low stony walls of several vine terraces. The grapes are beginning to turn a pale golden colour on long green stems trailing close above the ground. Danielle instructs them to leave the fruit alone, it isn't ripe. It will give them tummy ache.

Soon they are walking alongside an orchard of peach trees. There are no houses in sight. The luscious peaches hang temptingly just out of Philippe's reach – velvety yellow orbs flushed with pink and covered with a soft bloom. The children clamber onto the orchard wall to rest.

Philippe whispers something to Danielle. She nods and her brother jumps down off the wall into the orchard. He looks at Alex with a charming smile, and says 'Viens avec moi', as he holds out his hand to help her down. Then he explains with gestures that she's the tallest of the younger children. If he lifts her onto the lowest branch of a peach tree she'll be able to climb further up it to reach the fruit. Alex is flattered at being chosen for the task, especially as Raoul is clamouring 'Je veux cueillir les pêches!'

'Shh.... tais-toi!' hisses Danielle.

Philippe hoists Alex up, cupping his large strong hands under her bottom until she gets a grip on the branch.

The children stand under the tree while Danielle keeps a look-out. Alex climbs to the next branch, from where she can easily reach a dozen large ripe peaches. She tosses each one down into waiting hands. The foliage almost knocks her glasses off as she stretches to pick more of the fruit. Suddenly in the distance she hears the jangle of goat bells and catches sight of a herd of the animals descending the mountain side followed by their goatherd.

Within seconds Philippe has ducked the children flat on their stomachs behind the orchard wall. Her heart pounding, Alex climbs further up, hoping the leaves will conceal her. She watches with relief as the man leads his herd along one of the terraces and out of sight. The sound of goat bells grows fainter and Philippe stands up and comes back under the tree.

Alex discovers that climbing down a tree is harder than going up. Constantly catching her frock on twigs and wishing she was wearing shorts, she eases herself down until she's perched on the lowest branch. The hard uneven ground looks a long way down. Soothingly Philippe tells her to let go, he'll catch her safely. She must hurry, as they don't want to get caught in the orchard with the peaches. 'Vite! Vite!' he keeps saying. Alex jumps and falls clumsily into his arms. He clutches her tightly, his left hand supporting her shoulders, his right hand under her thighs. Adjusting himself to her weight he carries Alex across the orchard and stands her on the wall while he climbs over it himself. Danielle and the other children are already scrambling up the terraces almost out of sight. To her great surprise Philippe picks her up again, indicating that she should put her arms around his neck. He starts walking slowly towards the vineyards. Embarrassed at being carried like a baby, she wants to tell him she'd rather walk, that she can run fast to catch up with the others. But her French isn't up to it and she's afraid of offending him.

Alex's short frock is bunched up around her waist. As the boy moves, even more slowly now because of her weight, he contrives to work his fingers under her thin pants into the folds of skin. A painful spasm of shock and guilt which she barely understands convulses her body. Philippe's face is close to hers, grinning and watching her reaction. She can smell his sweat and struggles vigorously to be put down. The boy lets her go and she dashes ahead, meeting Danielle who's come back to find them. 'Lambin! Slow-coach!' she shouts at her brother as she takes Alex's hand.

When they reach the house Philippe disappears indoors, much to Alex's relief. Danielle leads the rest of them to the garden shed to devour their booty. The twins treat Alex as a heroine, showering praise on her as their teeth sink into the fruit, and peach juice runs down their chins. But Alex has little appetite for the plunder. She's thinking of Philippe's strange behaviour, which at a stroke has changed her relationship with the Durand family. She's on guard now, anxious not to lose her friends, but suspicious too.

Perhaps after all it was an unintentional action on Philippe's part. It all happened so quickly. Did it happen? By the end of the day Alex has pushed the incident to the back of her mind, has almost persuaded herself it never happened, that nothing has altered the friendship.

For the next three days Philippe doesn't appear to play with the children. Giselle and Jeanne can talk of nothing but their forthcoming birthday. Danielle shows them how to make paper hats and to blow up balloons.

Sheena brings home a large flat box from Beirut. 'I've bought you a frock for the birthday party. I do hope it's going to fit.'

With delight Alex lifts from its layer of tissue paper a flouncy white organdie frock embroidered with sprigs of pink roses. It fits her perfectly. 'There's a pair of frilly pants and a petticoat to match' says Sheena. Alex is overwhelmed with the gift. How wonderful of her mother. Life is very sweet. She can hardly wait for the twins' birthday.

Since Sheena is in Beirut on the day of the party it's Georgette who helps Alex get ready. She ties two big white bows into the child's hair and buttons up her frock. Her new socks are dazzling white against her deeply tanned legs. Alex regards herself critically in the mirror. Her thin elongated body, plain face and eyes behind the ugly spectacle frames aren't the ideal background for such pretty clothes. She removes the offending glasses. What luck that her mother's not at home to make her wear them!

The party starts after lunch. Alex approaches the Durands' verandah self-consciously clutching parcels for Giselle and Jeanne. She hears unfamiliar voices and for a moment wants to run away. But Danielle comes out and exclaims 'Comme tu es jolie!' and kisses her. She ushers Alex into the living room where the guests are being organised to play games. Besides Alex there are six children ranged between five and eight. They begin with a version of Blind Man's Buff and Alex is relieved to see there's no sign of Philippe.

The maids carry a wooden ice cream churn out under the trees onto the dappled grass and begin winding the handle to whip up the smooth pale yellow mixture in the gleaming metal cylinder surrounded with chunks of ice. There are crisp *langue-de-chat* biscuits to nibble with the ice cream piled into glass bowls with blue stems. Surprisingly there's no birthday cake, no candles to blow out.

After the refreshments the children are suddenly at a loss; they are very hot, and Danielle is tired of organising games. Raoul starts to squabble with a boy of his own age. Madame Durand shouts at him, tears follow, and it seems the party will turn into a disaster. Then Philippe joins the children and suddenly the mood changes. Everyone but Alex becomes alert and anxious to attract his attention. The youngest children want to be growled at, to be chased and caught and lifted up high in his arms. Soon the villa echoes with excited screams of pleasure.

Presently Philippe grows bored with this pastime. He and Danielle go into a corner to confer. Alex has a sudden foreboding. Philippe is looking at her as a cat might regard a cornered mouse. She has an urge to run home but knows it's impossible. Sheena has told her on no account must she leave the party without thanking her hostess for a lovely time. And Madame Durand is nowhere in sight.

'A La Retraite!' commands Philippe loudly, and all the children follow him down the verandah steps.

'Viens, Alex!', and Giselle grasps her hand and pulls her along. When they reach the shed Philippe tells Raoul he's to stand guard outside to warn them if any grownups approach. The rest of the party move into the shed and Philippe bolts the door.

'We're going to pretend this is a hospital ward. We're going to play at being doctors and nurses and patients', Danielle explains. Philippe then allocates a role to each child. Alex doesn't understand everything he says, but one thing is clear. She's going to be the first patient undergoing an operation and Philippe is going to be the surgeon. Danielle has spread an old rug over a wide bench and this is to be the operating table.

'No!' says Alex. 'Je ne veux pas.'

But Danielle hugs her and gives her a kiss and promises it won't hurt. 'It's only a game' she whispers, 'Not a real hospital.' The children are quiet now and twelve pairs of eyes are staring at Alex. She knows instinctively that if she moves toward the door she'll be restrained. There's no escape.

Giselle and Jeanne undo the buttons of Alex's party frock and in a moment she is lying on the rug in her petticoat and pants. The children gather closer. It seems they've forgotten their medical roles; they are only interested in what Philippe is going to do. Danielle lays a hanky over Alex's nose and mouth. 'Take deep breaths and you'll soon be asleep' she instructs her. She holds the patient's hand and strokes her forehead. In spite of soothing words Alex is so tense with fear she's unable to move. She hears a nervous giggle. Then there's a dead silence as Philippe proceeds to ease her frilly pants down over her knees and ankles. She tries to sit up but is pushed back firmly by Danielle. Philippe forces her legs apart and she sees his dark eyes glittering above her with a strange greedy expression. Giselle holds one leg and Jeanne the other. Alex can feel the intense curiosity and excitement of the spectators.

Alex is saved by Raoul's warning voice outside the shed. Madame Durand is calling for Philippe. He unbolts the door and strides off. Everyone runs out of the shed except Danielle, who hurriedly helps Alex to put on her frock.

Alex dashes out of the shed and through the hedge, tearing her frock slightly as she goes.. On reaching her room she collapses onto the bed, and suddenly realises her frilly pants have been left behind.

When it's quite dark Alex remembers that Basil and Sheena aren't returning home this evening. She changes into her pyjamas and falls into an exhausted sleep. In her dream a grinning Philippe and Danielle are pulling her along a corridor to some fresh horror. Once she wakes bathed in sweat to hear cats crying below the window and wonders how she's going to explain the loss of her pants and the tear in her new frock.

Chapter Sixteen

How to avoid the Durand family becomes Alex's main preoccupation. The villa next door, once so pleasant and welcoming, has assumed an aspect of horror. The friends she trusted and who provided such wonderful daily entertainment have banded together against her. She wanders around the house now with nothing to do. Several times a day Georgette exclaims irritably, 'Go and play next door!'

Alex spends a few days indoors, only occasionally creeping out to her secret place in the garden, hoping not to be observed. One day at dusk, feeling slightly sick, she risks going out onto the main balcony for some air, and to watch for the Buick coming up the mountain. She keeps an eye on the balcony and verandah next door. If anyone appears she will duck down quickly behind the balustrade. At the moment all seems quiet.

Suddenly an object zooms through the air from the direction of the Durand's villa, narrowly missing Alex. The missile consists of her frilly pants wrapped round an enormous pine cone and tied with string. She hears stifled giggles and sees two faces rising up from behind the balustrade of the next door balcony. Crimson with embarrassment Alex picks up the cone and scurries indoors, pursued now by hoots of laughter. 'Bonsoir, Alex! Viens jouer avec nous demain!' shrieks Giselle.

Alex sits trembling on her bed. How could she have been so foolish as to go onto the balcony? How can friends change into frightening enemies so quickly? Even scathing Tony Hotchkiss at K3 was at least consistent in his contempt for her, and occasionally she had the advantage over him.

At last she hears the car coming along the track, and then two unfamiliar American voices. Basil has brought guests to Beit Mery.

'Alex, where are you? Come down and say hello!' Sheena's voice sounds particularly bright and cheerful. Reluctantly the child goes downstairs and into the living room, dreading having to meet the strangers. A man and a woman are sitting on the settee, drinking gin and lime. There is a festive feeling in the room.

'Alex, come and meet Mr and Mrs Fielding', Basil says genially, 'Our guests for the weekend.'

'Oh, Sheena, you never told us! What a darling little girl!' exclaims Mrs Fielding. Alex senses immediately that this American lady is faking. 'Hi, honey!' she gushes, 'If your Mommie had only told us about you I'd have brought some candy. Do you like candy?'

Faced with the bright smile and appraising glance Alex is convulsed with shyness and her mother has to prompt her: 'Well, what d'you say?' In her confusion Alex's reply comes out surprisingly deep for a seven-year-old. The Fieldings bursts into laughter and Alex runs out of the room in tears.

Her mother follows her angrily upstairs. 'Why are you behaving in this ridiculous way? The Fieldings want to talk to you.'

'I don't want to see them; they laughed at me!'

'Oh, for goodness' sake, child, they weren't laughing in a nasty way. They were just a little amused.' Sheena looks at Alex, frowning. 'You're very flushed. Are you feeling all right?'

'No.'

'Have you been playing with the Durands today?'

'I don't like them any more.'

'You really are in a difficult mood. You must be sickening for something. You'd better go straight to bed. Perhaps you'll feel better in the morning.'

Alex curls up on her bed in stubborn misery, listening to the intermittent bursts of laughter down below. Her eyes are aching and her nose is running.

The weekend passes at its usual slow pace. The grownups sleep till eleven, take a prolonged brunch, and then return to their rooms to rest until after three, when they go for a short drive. Alex accompanies them, sitting on the back seat in between the Fieldings, silent unless spoken to.

On Monday Alex wakes feeling distinctly feverish. Her pyjamas are sticking to her skin and she feels too weak to get up when Georgette shouts that breakfast is ready. The maid comes up to the bedroom and exclaims in Arabic on seeing Alex's face covered in a red rash. When she returns with a drink she says 'I've telephoned your mother at the hospital. She thinks you have the measles and must be kept quiet in bed in a dark room.'

For the first week of her illness Alex is only vaguely aware of what's going on around her in the shuttered room. She's suffering from nausea, a dry cough and a hot, itching body. Sometimes she hears her mother's voice, sometimes Georgette's. Once she hears a strange male voice with a foreign accent, saying 'Yes, an unusually severe case for a child.' She ceases to distinguish between day and night. Shadowy figures come and go. Someone bathes her eyes with a cold solution. Her mind drifts from dream to uneasy dream. Once she seems to be in a deep dark hole, unable to climb out. People are peering down at her, laughing and pointing.

Then one day she hears her father's voice. He's bringing her soup, scrambled egg and labneh, feeding her with a spoon. He's gently sponging her burning limbs with cold water. She believes it to be a lovely dream, but when she wakes three times in the night, and there he is, still sitting in a chair by her bed, she realises it's no dream. Giles really has come to take care of her.

The day arrives at last when her body feels cool and her head clear. 'What time is it?' she asks her father. Her voice sounds normal, her throat no longer hurts.

Giles opens the shutters wide. 'Nearly time for the sun to get up.' He inserts a thermometer under her tongue and checks it. 'I think you could get up for a short while. Some fresh air might do you good.' He wraps Alex in a blanket and carries her out to the balcony. The mountain air is sweetly sharp, smelling of resin, bracken and drying grapes.

Giles perches his daughter on the wide balustrade, keeping his arms firmly round her. She leans her head against the smooth silk of his dressing gown, breathing in the familiar scent of coal tar soap, tobacco and peppermint. A single bright star is pulsating high above the pink blush creeping up from behind the dark outline of the mountain at the rear of the villa.

'That's the morning star we call Venus. D'you remember the stories I read to you at K3 about Venus?'

'Yes, she was the goddess of beauty. But in Greece they called her Aphrodite. I like that name better than Venus.'

They remain silent for a while, listening to the birds and watching ribbons of pink and orange cloud drifting across the eastern sky. After her long incarceration in semi-darkness, the sunrise comes afresh as an astonishing miracle. She would like to sit here for ever, basking in the pleasant warmth.

'How long have I been ill?'

'Nearly two weeks. You've had rather a bad attack of measles, but you'll soon be better.'

'When did you come?'

'Eight days ago. I'll be staying another two weeks before I have to return to Kirkuk.'

So he hasn't come to stay for good. The thought of parting yet again stirs up the old anxiety and mars the perfection of this moment of recovery.

'What happened to the little prince?' Alex asks suddenly.

Giles looks puzzled. 'What prince?'

'Prince Feisal, who's going to be King.'

'Oh, he's still in Baghdad, with his uncle, Prince Abdullah.'

'What about K3?'

'The houses are being repaired and people will be living there again soon.'

'Can we go back?'

'No. My job is now based on Kirkuk and soon I may have to move to Basra.'

Although it's a Sunday, Giles and Alex have the villa to themselves. Georgette has been given the weekend off, and Sheena and Basil are staying in Beirut. Best of all, the Durands have already departed. Their house is shuttered up. There will no longer be any need to hide from their taunting laughter. With her father as companion, life at Beit Mery assumes an entirely new character, and Alex's recovery is swift.

By Tuesday she's strong enough to walk the mile to the local abbey which Giles says might be interesting to see at close quarters. They follow the track past several isolated houses and clumps of Judas trees until they reach the rocky plateau on which the monastic house is built, its weathered cloisters carried on pointed Arab arches. Standing on the west side of the abbey it is possible to see the whole valley of the Beirut River.

'This mountain we're on now is called Jebel Sannine, and the abbey is known in Arabic as Deir el-Qalaa, which simply means Abbey of the Castle.'

'Where's the castle?' asks Alex.

'There was probably a castle nearby once. Before the abbey was built there used to be a Roman temple on this site, and before that a Phoenician one.'

'I know. Mr Carrington told us.'

'What else did he tell you?'

'Nothing. He doesn't like looking at old buildings.'

'You'll notice', continues Giles, 'As you see more of Lebanon, that there's a castle, a monastery, a church, a shrine or a tomb built at the top of nearly every hill.'

The abbey is constructed of huge, rugged stones. Groups of holm oaks and bushes of scented broom cluster outside the massive walls, and high above in the thin blue air a bird of prey is riding effortlessly on the back of a gentle wind.

'What sort of bird is that?' asks Alex.

'Some kind of hawk, probably a buzzard, but it could be a kestrel or a falcon.'

As they watch the bird, a door in the abbey wall opens and a short, stocky monk with jet-black hair, dressed in a blue robe emerges and greets them with a wide smile, beckoning them inside. They enter by a low, arched iron door leading into stone-flagged passages with vaulted recesses. They pass through several whitewashed rooms, sparsely furnished, delightfully cool and peaceful. Somewhere in the depths of the abbey can be heard a repetitive chanting, which becomes louder and more insistent as they approach the entrance to the abbey chapel. They peer down the shadowy single nave overhung with heavy vaulting, at a group of monks singing in perfect harmony. After listening for a while they are led to a room full of trestle tables and benches which reminds Alex of the refectory at the convent. Here their guide sits them down and offers glasses of mulberry juice and a bowl of giant walnuts glazed in honey. Alex tries to recall the Arabic word for walnut, but can only remember *assal* for honey.

'Yes, we have beehives', nods the monk.

In his usual stilted Arabic Giles asks questions about the abbey. Once, apparently, the monks grew mulberries in great quantities, and laid them in dark rooms for the silkworms to devour. But the silk trade declined and now they only have a few trees. Instead they grow barley and vegetables, and keep goats and rabbits. They make noodles and labneh and mountain bread to sell locally.

After Giles and Alex have sampled a few walnuts they are taken out to a small enclosed garden haphazardly planted with pink marguerites, orange marigolds, zinnias and antirrhinums. In the middle stands a dovecote inhabited by plump white birds cooing to one another. Beyond the garden grows a miniature orchard of apricot and plum trees. Unearthing a basket from amongst a pile of garden utensils, the monk fills it with velvety apricots for them to take home.

'Mish-mish', says Giles. 'A lovely name for apricots.'

Alex thinks how pleasant it would be to have a little house up here. But as they say goodbye at the abbey door the monk emphasises how cold it is on the mountain in winter, how the biting winds make it a torment to venture outside. He points to the oaks and sycamores which lean towards the ground as the result of gale-force battering.

'Come again one day', says the monk in English as he closes the door.

Giles and Alex walk out onto a large flat ledge of rock jutting out from the hillside to look at the view. Alex is intrigued by a lone, incredibly twisted olive tree growing out at right angles to the rock.

'It's amazing how deep and tough the roots of an olive tree are. You'd never think one could survive, growing out of that barren rock', say Giles. They climb down the steep incline to examine it more closely, and see that the base of the thickened bent trunk contains a hollow just big enough for Alex to sit in. Giles tests the tree for strength, and finds it firm enough to take his daughter's weight. He eases Alex into the hollow and props himself up against the hillside under the tree.

Just out of reach a piece of scarlet material is tied to a branch. 'What's that for?' asks Alex.

Her father explains that some old trees are thought to be sacred and to have special powers of healing. 'You'll often find a snippet of a sick person's clothing attached to a branch in the hope of its effecting a cure. In many Christian places of worship there are superstitious customs dating back many centuries before Jesus was born. That bit of cloth might be a pagan custom left over from the time when there was a temple here to the goddess, Astarte.'

'Does she cure sick people?'

'That's the belief. When the Christians began to settle in this part of Lebanon they tried to persuade the people to build shrines to Jesus and his mother, Mary, instead of to the pagan god and goddess. But it was hard changing the old ways. Most people began to light candles in the shrines thinking that Mary was just another name for Astarte.'

'Was Astarte a beautiful goddess?'

'The most beautiful of them all! She was the equivalent of the Greek Aphrodite and the Roman Venus we were talking about. Astarte was also the goddess of fertility. Fertility means all living things growing in abundance.'

'Did she marry a god?'

'Yes, she was married to Ares, the god of war, but she also fell in love with a mortal, a prince called Adonis.'

'What happened to Adonis?' Alex's interest is aroused by the beautiful goddess, but Giles says it's too long a story to relate now. They ought to be getting home, or she will become over-tired.

'I'm not a bit tired! Please tell me now!'

'All right, very quickly then. There are many different versions of this story, but roughly it goes like this:

'When the Phoenicians lived in Lebanon thousands of years ago, they worshipped Astarte and built temples to her all over the mountains. The Phoenician King Cinyrus lived in a town on the coast called Byblos, which we'll visit soon. He had a beautiful daughter called Myrrha. In fact she was so lovely that her mother, the queen, went round boasting that her daughter was more beautiful than Astarte.'

'What was the queen's name?'

'I've forgotten. Anyway, Astarte was very angry and decided to revenge herself on the Princess Myrrha. As a punishment she made the princess fall in love with her own father.' Giles pauses for a moment as his daughter ponders over this statement.

'How could she fall in love with an old man?'

Giles laughs, saying 'Normally she wouldn't have done, but Astarte put a spell on her; and of course it caused great problems. It was against the law for a daughter to marry her father. Everybody would have thought it very shameful.'

'Why?'

'Because if a girl marries a father or a son or a brother, sometimes even a cousin, there's a good chance of their children being born with something wrong with them. But this princess couldn't help falling in love with her father, and soon she found she was going to have a child. She was so frightened that she ran away to the mountains. But the goddess Astarte saw her and turned her into a tree.'

'What kind of tree?'

'A tree that became known as a myrrh tree in memory of the princess, a kind of gum tree. A sticky substance called resin oozes out of the bark, and it is said that these drops of resin are Myrrha's tears. Inside the tree her child went on growing, and one day a beautiful baby boy burst out of the trunk. Astarte took care of him and gave him the name Adonis, which means *Lord*. And when he grew up into a strong handsome young man, she fell in love with him and they spent all their time wandering through the forests of Lebanon together. This angered Astarte's husband, Ares, the god of war, and he decided to get rid of his rival. He changed himself into a ferocious wild boar, and when Adonis was out hunting one autumn day, the boar attacked him and wounded him fatally in the thigh. Astarte carried Adonis to her secret grotto high in the mountain-side where an ice-cold spring gushes out from a dark cave.'

'Couldn't she cure him with her magic?'

'Apparently not. The wound was fatal and he died in her arms as she tried to kiss him better. From then on the grotto was known as *Aphaca,* which means kiss. Next summer I'll take you there.'

'Why not this summer?'

'Because you're not yet strong enough for a long trip in the heat.'

'Is that the end of the story?'

'Not quite. Astarte carried the body of Adonis to the underworld and gave him to Persephone, the goddess who rules over the dead.'

'I know about Persephone', Alex interrupts eagerly. 'She was captured by Hades and taken to the underworld to be his wife. Her mother, the goddess Demeter, searched and searched for her daughter until she found her. Zeus said Persephone could only go back to Demeter if she hadn't eaten any food in the land of the dead. But Persephone had eaten seven pomegranate seeds. So Hades decided she had to spend the winter months of each year with him.'

'That's right. And oddly enough, the story of Adonis and Astarte turns out to be rather like the story of Persephone in its ending. Astarte begged Persephone to allow Adonis to come alive and spend the spring and summer with her. Persephone took pity on Adonis, and agreed to let him come to life each spring; but every autumn he would be killed again by a wild boar. So throughout the winter Astarte mourns her lover and then welcomes him back in the spring and spends the summer wandering in the forest with the handsome youth who never grows old.'

'Does anyone ever see them?' asks Alex hopefully.

'I don't know.'

'If we go to the secret grotto we might see them.'

'Maybe.'

'Does Adonis know he's going to be killed again in the autumn?'

'I expect he does. If you think about it, we all know we're going to die one day, but we still enjoy life and don't worry about dying.'

'I hope he didn't know because it would spoil his time with Astarte. I don't like the end of the story. I don't want him to keep on getting killed.'

'It's a sad story, but remember it's only a legend. It didn't really happen. But the strange thing is, the same legend crops up in different countries, only with different names. In Iraq it's the goddess Ishtar falling in love with the half-god Tammuz – and in Egypt you have the goddess Isis falling in love with Osiris. You see, people believed in a goddess of fertility who was responsible for making the crops grow each spring. Some years there were droughts and people would starve, so they assumed the goddess was angry with them. They thought that if they sacrificed a handsome young man to the goddess she would be pleased and make the crops grow well the following year. In some places they even sacrificed their king after he'd ruled for a number of years. And they would spread his ashes over the soil.'

'If I'd been the king, I'd have run away.'

'So would I! But as time went on, the people here decided human sacrifice wasn't necessary. So instead of killing someone they simply made a wax image of Adonis with a wound in his thigh, which they carried to Aphaca. Even today some people carry on the custom in these mountains.'

Thinking of Adonis with a wound in his thigh reminds Alex of Jesus who came back from the dead with a wound in his side. But the story of Jesus is true and he didn't have to keep dying each autumn. And yet Zilpha used to say Jesus died every Good Friday.

Giles says they must go home now, so Alex can rest. But she's reluctant to leave. She's enjoying sitting in the tree hollow watching the red votive rag dangling from the twisted olive branch.

'Can we come here again?' she asks.

'Of course we can.'

'This tree could be our secret tree. Shall we promise never to tell anyone about it? Not even Sheena?' Giles solemnly agrees.

'I'm going to tie a ribbon to the branch.' Alex pulls off one of her blue ribbons and attaches it to the tree.

'Can we come back next week and see if it's still here?'

'Yes, we'll do that.'

'Astarte might stop me from ever being ill again.'

'It would be nice to think so.'

Giles takes his daughter's hand and they walk back to the villa.

Chapter Seventeen

Alex swiftly regains her former energy, and her father has to hurry to keep up with her on their walks. They explore all the paths leading from plot to plot among the terraces and woodlands between Beit Mery and Broummana, and come to know all the landmarks including the sheepfolds built of stones and the isolated cemetery full of cupboard-like tombs. They discover a miniature waterfall tumbling into a clear pool in which long-stemmed watercress grows. Giles tells Alex about the inefficient system of cultivation in the mountains whereby each farmer divides his land up into small plots fairly between his sons, some on fertile and some on stony ground. His sons will later divide it again, with the result that a man will have to waste much of his effort cultivating small plots at different altitudes.

Alex insists on visiting their 'secret tree' again to make sure her ribbon's still there. People begin to greet them warmly in the village. Soon Alex feels as though she's lived in these mountains for years. Giles rises some mornings while the dew is still on the flowers, and takes Alex to buy fruit and vegetables before the sun shrivels them. They watch a wizened old lady baking mountain bread outside the back of her house, intrigued to see how her gnarled brown fingers pull out the paper-thin dough to fit the curved iron plate placed over a fire of brushwood. Within minutes the bread, crisp at the edges and mottled with dark brown spots, is ready to peel off the iron and roll up. Several times the old lady makes Alex a small roll of bread to eat on the spot. It's the best she's ever tasted.

In the evenings Giles allows Alex to stay up till ten, provided she's rested during the afternoon. They have supper together on the verandah – bread, tomatoes, goats' cheese, olives and an aubergine paste called mouttabal, followed by the first of the season's grapes and a bowl of plump yellowy-green figs with sweet deep red flesh. As darkness falls, pinpoints of light pop out up and down the mountain slopes from secluded habitations one would never notice during the day.

By the light of a kerosene lamp they play cards, or Giles reads to Alex from a thick well-thumbed anthology of poetry. It's the first time she's listened to poems written for grownups as well as children. She likes the sad story poems best, in particular *The Lady of Shalott* and *The Forsaken Merman.*

Giles suggests she write a poem herself, but Alex would rather write a story. 'You could try both. And you could write me a letter. You'll be going to school soon, and I'd like to hear all about it. I'll reply and tell you what I'm doing in Iraq. I'll leave you some writing paper and some envelopes already addressed and stamped, so all you'll have to do is to ask Mr Carrington to post them.'

The idea of writing letters to her father appeals to Alex, and to receive letters from him in return will be exciting. She plans to start a letter even before he's gone.

Basil and Sheena remain in Beirut. Georgette cleans the villa but otherwise keeps out of their way. She never smiles at Giles the way she smiles at Basil. She stares at him sullenly when he asks her to do anything. Alex says she hates the maid, and Giles laughs. 'What's she done to deserve your hatred? Hating people probably hurts you more than it does them. Don't compare Georgette with Zilpha. Zilpha is a very special person. Georgette's just a young girl who wants some fun. She's probably had a hard life and it's lonely for her here.' Alex knows he's right but she still hates Georgette.

Two days before Giles is due to return to Kirkuk he asks Alex if she'd like to go on a trip to see the Roman ruins at Baalbek. It would mean staying the night at a pension. After Babylon she fears Baalbek may turn out to be disappointing too.

'There are well-preserved buildings left standing at Baalbek', Giles assures her, guessing her thoughts. 'I promise you'll find it quite interesting.'

They travel to the ancient city in a large blue taxi driven by Fouad, a friendly man who speaks English and knows the mountains well. He tells them anecdotes about each village on the way, and bemoans the fact that many of the higher villages are becoming deserted because so many Lebanese people are emigrating to the States.

They stop for lunch at Zahle, an immaculate small town built on two mountain slopes facing each other, between which flows a pretty river beside a boulevard of silvery-leafed poplars. A short way out of Zahle the whole of the Bekaa comes into sight, the ten mile wide fertile plain lying between the two parallel mountain ranges of Lebanon. They drive along a road lined with poplar and beech, through fields of wheat, maize, barley, peas and beans. Then come extensive vineyards. Hordes of women in long colourful dresses stoop over the crops and children sell huge sweet elongated apples.

'Very good soil in Bekaa' says Fouad. 'Three crops a year.'

Nearer Baalbek the fields give way to an expanse of tall dark green bushes.

'What are those?' asks Alex.

'Hashish', says Giles. 'It's used for various things, but mainly for people to smoke or chew. Too much can be dangerous. You can get addicted to it as people do to cigarettes. The body gets so used to hashish that it can't do without. It's what we call a drug.'

'Are you addicted to cigarettes?'

'I'm afraid so. They have a calming effect and help me to think.'

'Have you tried hashish?'

'I did try it once but it made me very sleepy. Better not to be addicted to any drug.'

'Could I get addicted to chocolate?'

'People do get addicted to chocolate, but it's easier to give up chocolate than cigarettes.'

'If I ate chocolate all day would I be addicted?'

'You'd be very sick and that might put you off eating it again. You should never have too much of anything.'

Alex thinks of pistachio ice cream. She's certain she could eat ice cream all day without becoming sick.

Butterflies are hovering over a patch of white poppies and Alex remembers Zilpha telling her that the Arabs extract the juice from poppies and then dry it to smoke.

'That's called opium', says Giles. 'It's more dangerous than hashish. Too much can kill you, but on the other hand it can also stop great pain. So the opium poppy is either good or bad, depending on how you use it.'

Alex finds it hard to believe that a flower can produce anything bad. 'Why do people smoke opium?'

'To feel happy and carefree for a short time. Then it wears off and you need to take more to keep feeling happy. If you stop taking it you begin to feel ill and all you can think of is getting your next dose.'

'Like a wicked magic spell?'

'Yes, exactly like that.'

Late in the afternoon they approach Baalbek and are immediately confronted by the six great golden-brown columns of the Temple of Jupiter built high up on the acropolis. 'Isn't that a wonderful sight?' says Giles, and Alex agrees.

The taxi driver takes them through the dusty modern town and stops outside the imposing Palmyra Hotel, right opposite the ruins, assuming they'll be staying here. Giles tells him they want a modest pension, and Fouad seems disappointed. But he drives them to a grey stone house with a garden beside the river, overhung with drooping willows.

They sit on a rickety verandah which leans precariously over the River Litani. To east and west they can see the snow-covered peaks. For supper they have stuffed vine leaves and a salad of raw broad beans in a garlic and lemon dressing. Alex tastes knafi for the first time, a delicious cheese-filled pastry in syrup, and mahmoul, a date and walnut cake.

Early the following morning they visit the Roman ruins. Giles points out that they called their city, Heliopolis – *City of the Sun.* The site is protected by a wall and fencing, and a notice informs visitors that the ruins are open from May 1st to October 31st. In a shed at the entrance they rouse a sleepy guide who tries to charge Giles two Lebanese pounds, but agrees on one pound when he realises they aren't American tourists. He complains that business has been very bad since the war started. 'It's not our war, but we have to suffer', he moans. Giles tells him to go back to sleep as they don't need a guide. They have a good book about Baalbek.

As always when visiting historical sites, Giles is anxious to convey to his daughter all the interesting facts relating to them, and something of the excitement he feels. Baalbek is one of the chief historical sites in the world, and he's been waiting for years to see it.

They start with the Temple of Jupiter. Only six of the fifty-four columns are still standing. There used to be nine until an earthquake felled three of them in 1759.

'For centuries', says Giles, 'The Arabs pinched the stones as they did at Babylon. Luckily Baalbek was enclosed and put under guard before all the buildings disappeared. Look at this Temple of Bacchus! It's beautifully preserved. D'you see how these huge blocks of stone stick together without the use of mortar? It's an amazing feat. They were brought from two quarries near

Baalbek, and the Romans who cut and then transported them on rollers carried out a task that would be hard to do even today, with trucks and modern machinery.'

They pass on to the exquisite circular Temple of Venus. Alex is intrigued by the carved Cupids gathering grapes into little stone baskets.

They gaze up at a colossal entablature decorated with heads of lions, bulls and eagles, and garlands of poppies, vines, acanthus and ivy. Giles points out the carved ropes which stand for friendship, and the chains which denote slavery.

But Alex soon becomes tired of her father's detailed examination of each building. Eventually he suggests that she sit and wait for him in the gigantic shadow of one of the columns. Seated alone among the towering pillars and the great chunks of marble and porphyry – some with trees growing out of them, some as large as a tramcar, she feels there's something fearful about such size. Why did the Romans want such huge temples? Behind the massive thrusting facades the sky seems candescent with pearl-white heat. She feels dizzy and crushed by the magnitude of the giant structures. A lizard the colour of ash crawls across a fallen statue – Alex wonders what it thinks as it looks up at the Temple of Bacchus. Her head begins to ache, and she's thankful when her father reappears.

'Well, do you think Baalbek is more interesting than Babylon?' asks Giles.

'Better than Babylon, but still a bit boring.'

Her father smiles wryly. 'You're just like your mother!'

Fouad takes them back to Beit Mery by a different route, retracing the road along the Bekaa Plain as far as Zahle, and then driving to Dhour Shouair at the foot of Mount Sannine. Here they get out of the taxi briefly to buy peaches from a roadside stall and to look at the giddy view down the valley of Nahr el Kelb, *the Dog River,* beyond which the sky melts into the sea.

'One day when I come to see you in the summer', promises Giles, 'We'll explore that river at its mouth, and then I'll tell you why it's called the Dog River.'

Most of the villages they pass through are picturesque in pink and amber, especially Chtaura with its silver birches, and Rikfaya, surrounded with thick woods of oak, tamarisk, plane, willow and maple.

In the car the scent of the fruit is tantalising. 'Can I have a peach now?'

'No, they must be washed first.' Alex remembers the peaches she pinched for the Durand children. No one suffered any ill effects, but she can't tell Giles. There was a time when she had no secrets from her father. Now the secrets are piling up – the dead djinn, her experiences at the convent, and the unpleasantness with the Durands. She's beginning to shoulder the small burdens of childhood which must never be told.

When at length they reach Beit Mery and turn down the track, Fouad finds he has to reverse back onto the road because of cars parked all the way to the villa.

'What a nuisance', says Giles as they walk along the track. 'I didn't expect Basil home this weekend. He must be having a lot of visitors.'

The living room is full of people, mostly Americans. Sheena moves quickly towards her husband. 'For God's sake, Giles', she hisses at him, 'Where on earth have you been?'

'To Baalbek. You didn't tell me you were having a party this weekend.'

'How could you take a sick child all the way to Baalbek of all places?'

'Baalbek didn't do her any harm.'

'Being dragged round ruins in the hot sun isn't the way to convalesce.'

'I'm not ill any more', Alex pipes up, anxious to defend her father.

But Sheena continues angrily, 'You look dreadful. You'd better go and tidy up before coming in here.' Some of the guests stare curiously as Giles takes his daughter's hand and leaves the room.

Alex is too tired to do anything but wash her face and fall into bed. She's vaguely aware of Georgette coming into her room with a tray of supper, which remains untouched. At six the next morning Giles comes in to say goodbye. Alex twines her arms tightly round his neck.

'Take me with you. I don't want to live with Mr Carrington in Beirut.'

'I'm sorry, sweetheart, it's not possible for you to come to Kirkuk. You'll soon be going to school, and you'll enjoy Beirut.'

'But why do we have to live with Mr Carrington?' Alex persists.

'Because at the moment your mother can't afford to rent a house in Beirut. We have to start saving up to replace things we lost at K3. Mr Carrington is very kind, having you to stay in his apartment rent free. You'll be in walking distance of your school and Sheena can walk to her job at the hospital.'

'Are you still married to Sheena?'

'Of course!'

Giles extricates himself with difficulty from his daughter's grasp. She runs out to the balcony to watch him putting his battered old revelation suitcase into the waiting taxi. When the car's out of sight she returns to bed and lies awake, staring at the cracks in the ceiling, too miserable to cry. Recurring separation from her father has become a bitter fact of life.

Chapter Eighteen

When Alex wakes on the last day of August the sun's streaming across her bed. The house is unbearably quiet.

The prospect of a long, tedious Sunday looms ahead. No one will stir for hours. She gets up and drifts aimlessly around the silent garden. Boredom intensifies, creating an aching lump in her stomach.

When Sheena finally rises just after eleven she's exceptionally solicitous, asking Alex questions about her health and her trip to Baalbek.

'You do look very thin, darling. What can Giles have been feeding you on?'

Now that her father's departed, Alex no longer feels on the wrong side. Sheena has brought her presents from Beirut. For a while she's diverted by yet another pretty frock, together with a Chinese fan and a gold bracelet with four charms hanging from it.

'Each birthday you shall have another charm to add to your bracelet. And if you're a good girl and rest properly this afternoon we'll take you out to dinner tonight. Would you like that?'

Alex nods vigorously, bowled over by Sheena's concern and generosity and glad to bask in her mother's unusual attention. Suddenly she seems the kindest, sweetest mother in the world. She's even agreed to let Alex take Soda out to dinner.

They drive to the Shalimar Hotel at Bamdat. Alex sits in the back of the Buick clutching Soda against her new frock. On the hotel terrace she sits demurely under the coloured lights, watching the dance band and the couples gliding across the gleaming marble floor. The beat of the music makes her long to try dancing herself. Why is it always only for grownups?

Between dances they are served with delicious food. The hotel is famous for its highly spiced spinach purée, but the sight of the shiny glutinous mess on the white plate turns her stomach. Spinach is the only vegetable she can't abide. Fortunately the waiter removes her plate discreetly. As the evening wears on Alex falls asleep on her chair and Soda slips onto the floor. Every now and then she wakes to watch Basil and Sheena dancing. At the end of the evening she stumbles, heavy-eyed, into the car, hearing her mother say anxiously, 'We really shouldn't have brought her.'

On Monday after Basil and Sheena have left for work Alex realises with horror that she's left Soda at The Shalimar. Life without her camel is unthinkable and she bursts into hysterical tears. Georgette screams at her not to be such a baby, Mr Carrington will get her toy back the next time he goes to the hotel. Alex mooches around miserably all day, convinced she'll never see Soda again. Her mother will have little sympathy, will be glad to be rid of the toy, will refuse to return to Bamdat until the weekend. When Sheena returns she says, 'It's high time you grew up and stopped being so dependent on a toy. You can't take a camel to school with you. It's just as well you left it behind.'

Alex hates her mother for saying it doesn't matter. Soda is her connection with Zilpha and Saeb and K3. All the week she keeps asking about the camel until at last Basil telephones the hotel. Alex stands behind him in a frenzy of anxiety, waiting for the verdict. The manager has to go and enquire. But no one has seen Soda. Alex turns and runs up the stairs to her bedroom. She'll not make a scene in front of Basil, but when Sheena comes to find her, Alex shouts 'You don't care that I've lost him! You didn't want me to find him! You wouldn't let Mr Carrington telephone straight away!'

Her mother says coldly, 'It's not our fault you left your camel. You're being utterly unreasonable about something quite unimportant. Basil says he'll buy you another toy camel in Beirut, but you'll have to earn it by not being sulky.' But Alex doesn't want another camel, she wants Soda. She's disgusted that Mr Carrington could for one moment believe that some other camel would do.

Towards the end of September Basil and Sheena prepare to vacate the villa. It's still very hot in Beirut but Alex must start school in two days' time. She stands around, getting in the way, wanting to leave Beit Mery but dreading the idea of settling down in yet another new place. All the way to Beirut she's silent. With every kilometre she's going further away from Soda. Georgette is sitting in the front of the car with Claude, chatting non-stop in Arabic, delighted to be returning to town.

When they reach Basil's apartment block, Sheena gives Alex a basket to carry, saying, 'Do take that disagreeable look off your face!' They go through a small wrought iron gate and mount the three steps up into the garden. Before going up to the apartment she takes a quick look at the back garden. Here, patches of brown grass have almost given up the struggle to grow under three towering black fir trees. There are no hidden corners to this garden, and after the heat of the long summer no colour, no variation. Not a place she fancies playing in.

Basil's apartment comprises two spacious floors at the top of the three-storey building, reached by a black marble stairway mottled with grey. At the open door stands a short, dumpy woman wearing a brown turban. Her starched, dazzling white apron contrasts vividly with her wrinkled brown face and drab brown skirt. She's grinning broadly, showing gaps between her front teeth.

'This is Abby', says Basil, as the cook draws the child into her arms and gives her a smacking kiss. The smell of garlic and something bitter she can't identify makes Alex recoil from this sudden embrace. Yet it's gratifying to find Abby's reception so welcoming.

'We do need a child here again, don't we, Mr Carrington? Someone to make ice cream and cookies for.' Abby regards Alex critically, saying, 'Smile, darling. Don't be shy with Abby. Sally-Ann was always smiling, always laughing. What an angel, that girl!'

Georgette comes up the stairs, and Abby immediately pounces on her, yelling in Arabic. They both disappear into the kitchen. Basil leads the way from the hall into a vast L-shaped room cooled by three overhead fans. On the near

185

side of a slab of grey marble forming a room divider, stretches a floor of pale cream marble flecked with pink and partially covered with silk Persian rugs in soft shades of pink, lilac, beige and blue. Two long sofas and four capacious armchairs upholstered in pale blue shantung fill the main part of the room, interspersed with small carved polygonal tables. In one corner stands a life-sized sculpture of a young gazelle in black basalt. Water colours of mountain scenery hang on the cream walls, and a basket of fresh pink roses graces a long glass-topped table. Beyond the room divider are two more intimate living areas. One has an open fireplace. A leather swivel-chair partners a large roll-top desk, and here the floor is entirely covered with a thick Turkey carpet. The second area, down two broad shallow steps is dominated by a white grand piano and stool, and a firm white leather settee. Basil notices Alex staring at a silver-framed photograph of an attractive little girl with curly fair hair propped on the piano. 'That's my little girl, Sally-Ann, who lives in the States.'

On top of the room divider, next to a large oval silver tray loaded with bottles and glass decanters, Alex notices another photograph, of a pleasant looking blonde woman with frizzy permed hair. Basil makes no comment on this photograph. He flings open double doors of polished wood to reveal the dining room. Alex glimpses a rosewood dining table and matching chairs cushioned in dark blue velvet, a long sideboard covered with silverware, a heavy candelabrum hanging from the ceiling, and a mass of blue flowers on a stand... She's never seen such opulence in a private home.

She turns back to the living room, as Sheena appears saying, 'Isn't this a lovely lounge, Alex?'

Sheena puts down her suitcase and walks out through yards of billowing white gossamer-thin curtains onto a generous balcony, followed by her daughter. Begonias and azaleas spill out of terracotta urns around them as they sit on the cushioned basket chairs. Basil has ordered Georgette to serve glasses of iced coffee. Alex is longing to see her bedroom, but Basil talks on and on to Sheena. It seems he's very pleased at the news that the Shah of Persia has abdicated and a government friendly to America has been installed. He talks about how the war is progressing and the need to supply Russia with oil. Alex senses that Sheena's only half listening, so she ventures to interrupt.

'Can I see my bedroom now?'

'Yes, let's go up.'

They mount another flight of marble stairs leading straight up from the lounge and through a sliding door to a thickly carpeted further flight. On the top floor a long rectangular hall gives onto a replica of the balcony below, four bedrooms and a bathroom. Sheena shows Alex into a room decorated with Walt Disney cartoon characters from *Snow White* on pale blue wallpaper. There are so many toys she can hardly take them all in... a piebald rocking horse with bright red saddle and bridle; a child's desk with chair attached; a wickerwork dolls' pram; an enormous china doll with fluffy blonde curls and round blue eyes that survey the room with a constant look of astonishment; a golliwog sporting an emerald and orange bow tie who lolls on a child-size basket chair with one slim black leg crossed over the other...

'What a wonderful room!' exclaims Sheena. 'You're a lucky girl. Sally-Ann had to leave her toys behind when she went to the States.' She opens a tall cupboard and a heap of smaller toys falls out onto the carpet. 'Basil says you may play with all these things.'

'Didn't she have a dolls' house?' asks Alex.

'Yes, but they gave it away.'

Sheena opens a long deep drawer at the foot of the wardrobe. 'Look, here are drawing books, and paints and games – just the kind of thing you like best.'

'There aren't any books.'

'I expect Sally-Ann took the books with her.'

Sheena points out the basket for dirty linen in the hall and then takes Alex onto the upper balcony, which is lined with green boxes of begonias, nasturtiums and geraniums. 'And out here you've even got a swing.' She sits for a moment on the thick polished wooden seat supported on heavy chains and sets the swing in gentle motion with her foot. 'I'd love to have had a swing like this when I was a little girl!'

At the other end of the balcony jasmine and morning glory trail in profusion across a green trellis, behind which a spindly iron staircase spirals its way up to the flat roof.

'Can we go up?' asks Alex.

'Yes, I suppose so.'

They step onto the dazzling white space of the roof-top. The glare is so intense it takes a few moments to focus. A substantial parapet runs round the edge. On one side stands a small whitewashed hut, from which two washing lines run across the roof to a couple of metal poles. The hut is empty but for a basket of clothes pegs and a pile of loose bricks. For no apparent reason the other side of the roof space has a square section enclosed by a four-feet high wall.

Basil comes up the spiral staircase to join them. 'There's a good view of Beirut from up here', he says, looking over the parapet. Even on tiptoe Alex can barely see over it, so Basil fetches three bricks for her to stand on and Sheena holds her hand to support her.

'Never, never climb onto this parapet', he warns. Alex finds the warning unnecessary. Looking down makes her feel dizzy.

'This part of Beirut is called Ain el Mreisse, one of the most pleasant residential areas. Over there is Ras Beirut and St. Dimitri. You can just see the coast road, the Corniche, which we drove along on our way up from Jerusalem. Look, Alex, there's the University campus and the hospital where your mother works.' He crosses to the other side of the roof. 'And from here you can just see the race-course, the Hippodrome.'

Between the apartment and the sea, clusters of red-roofed houses, white villas and stone mansions surrounded by clumps of trees and greenery and fields of vegetables spread over the promontory of West Beirut. East of Ain el Mreisse the town sprawls in a muddled conglomeration of old and modern buildings thrown together with no attempt at planning. Unsightly concrete blocks, mostly clad in scaffolding, and slum shanties of corrugated iron have begun to oust the graceful old Arab houses. Reinforced concrete doesn't match the Arab talent for building.

'It's a wicked shame', says Basil, 'The way successive governments have allowed such cheap ugly houses to go up. They don't even employ properly qualified architects. And the worst feature of building in the Middle East is the way a landlord will take years to finish a block of flats. People move into the ground floor with no water or electricity, and the landlord will wait for the rent to accumulate for years before he completes the next storey and provides basic facilities. In another twenty years I guess this beautiful town will be mutilated beyond repair.'

From the roof-top they can hear the steady rumble of traffic, the rattling of the trams and the honking of taxis.

'Can we go on a tram?' asks Alex.

'Oh yes, I always take a trolley car to go shopping. It's impossible to park in the centre of town.'

Alex directs questions at her mother which Basil answers. 'Sure, you may play in the garden... No, there aren't any children living in the downstairs apartment, just an elderly Arab couple... Yes, you may bring the dolls' pram onto the balcony...'

Basil goes down to the lounge while Sheena shows Alex her own bedroom. 'What a huge bed!' gasps the child, looking at the expanse of silky white and gold bedspread.

Sheena laughs. 'Yes, It's what Basil calls a king-size bed. He had it specially made.'

An array of cut glass bottles and pots is reflected in the glass-topped dressing table. Alex recognises her mother's large white jar of Pond's cold cream standing amongst them next to a giant bottle of Chanel No. 5. The furniture is white decorated with gold; there are several full length mirrors, and swathes of frilled net curtains brush the soft blue carpet. The room is fit for a princess, the perfect background to her mother's beauty.

'Will Giles sleep in this bed when he comes to see us?' asks Alex.

'No', replies Sheena curtly.

'Where does Mr Carrington sleep?'

'He has the room next to the bathroom. You must remember to knock before coming into our rooms...... Now quickly go and wash your hands before lunch.'

The new bar of pink soap sitting on the shiny pink washbasin is carved in the shape of a rose. It seems a pity to spoil it, so Alex uses an old piece of soap from the side of the bath.

A hollow clanging noise sounds from downstairs. 'That's the gong to tell us lunch is ready.'

They descend the first flight of stairs and go through the sliding door. Seen from above the lounge reminds Alex of a hotel foyer, the way the furniture is so perfectly arranged, with no papers or books or toys scattered about. It doesn't seem like a home.

In the dining room the immense oval table gleams under a white lace cloth. It can accommodate a dozen people with ease. The three of them sit down at one end of the table, at places laid with monogrammed cutlery and crisp white damask table napkins rolled up in silver rings. A platter of fruit graces the centre of the table, flanked by two tall silver candlesticks. Copper finger bowls similar to those Alex remembers at K3 stand by each place setting.

Georgette serves at table in a black dress, white apron and cap. Abby has prepared three courses to celebrate their return from the mountains. Her cooking is excellent but the food is unfamiliar to Alex and she isn't hungry.

'Try a little fried Maryland chicken', coaxes Basil, 'Abby has cooked it especially for you.'

There's a hatch from the dining room into the kitchen through which Abby shouts remarks in a gruff voice. Alex senses Sheena is irritated by the cook's familiarity, but Basil doesn't seem concerned. 'If Alex comes into the kitchen', says Abby, 'I'll find something good for her to eat.'

'Go and make friends with Abby, Alex', says Basil.

Alex slips down from her chair and goes into the kitchen.

'Try some of this.' Abby hands her a chunk of something yellow and sticky on a small plate. 'Go on, taste it. We call it halawi.' The grainy-textured sweetmeat, made from sesame paste, nuts and honey, melts deliciously in Alex's mouth. Abby herself is eating a plateful of haricot beans with olive oil and garlic. Alex watches her callused fingers shovelling the beans between her thin lips.

'How do you like the halawi?'

'It's lovely!'

Abby looks pleased and offers her another chunk. 'Mr Carrington says you've been ill. You're far too skinny. We'll have to fatten you up.' The cook stares closely at the child. 'What's wrong with your eyes? You've got a bit of a squint. Is that why you have to wear glasses?'

Alex is taken aback at this personal comment. 'I've got a lazy eye.'

'Glasses certainly don't improve your looks.' Alex scowls with embarrassment.

'Goodness, aren't you a miserable child. Haven't you got a smile for Abby?' But as always when requested to smile, Alex can give no more than a faint grimace.

'Why aren't you like Sally-Ann – chattering and laughing all day? You don't look like your mother at all. I was expecting a real beauty. You must take after your father. Sally-Ann looked like her mother, which was lucky for her.' Abby lowers her voice. 'No girl would want to look like Mr Carrington, bless his heart! But looks aren't everything. Take me, for instance.' And the cook cackles with laughter. 'Would you like half a pomegranate?' Abby slices the solid shiny fruit, revealing the glistening pink pulp and seeds. She places a bowl on the table and begins to spit her seeds into it.

Alex can't decide whether she likes Abby or not. Her blunt approach will take some getting used to.

Abby speaks to Georgette half in English and half in Arabic. The maid comes into the kitchen with a tray of dirty plates and whispers something to the cook. Alex has a feeling that Georgette is telling Abby unpleasant things about her. The cook pats her head in a kindly fashion and hands her a linen drying cloth. 'You can help dry these if you're very careful', she says, indicating a number of warm crystal glasses. 'Rub them gently till they sparkle.'

A steep fixed wooden ladder leads up from a corner of the large L-shaped kitchen to a wide open trap-door in the ceiling. Georgette begins to climb the rungs and when she's nearly reached the top Abby hands up her cardboard suitcase and a bag, and the maid heaves the luggage through the square hole.

'Is that where you sleep?' asks Alex.

'That's right, my darling. The servants' rooms are up there in the attic', returns the cook, with an edge to her voice which is lost on the child.

'It must be fun going to bed up a ladder.'

'Lots of fun – and even more fun when you've got swollen legs and an aching back.'

'Why don't you sleep in one of the bedrooms upstairs?'

'Because servants must sleep in servants' quarters. Haven't you learnt that yet?'

'My nanny, Zilpha, used to sleep in the bedroom next to mine at K3.' Abby grunts.

'Can I go up your ladder?'

'Maybe one day if I decide to invite you.'

'Did Sally-Ann get invited?'

'Of course she did. No one could refuse that child anything.' Alex feels downcast at these ever more glowing opinions of her predecessor.

The rest of the day Alex spends exploring Sally-Ann's bedroom, feeling like an intruder. Beneath the eiderdown scattered with rosebuds the sheets are pink edged with white lace. What luxury! She had never imagined sheets to be other than plain white linen. She can hardly wait for bedtime.

Alex rummages through all the cupboards and drawers, ending up with the long drawer at the foot of the wardrobe. Its contents interest her most, and she pulls everything out onto the floor: jigsaw puzzles, a pile of exercise books, paints and crayons, writing paper and envelopes decorated with teddy bears, a tin of barley sugar, a china tea set, dolls' clothes, drawing books, a skipping rope, a rubber ball and a packet of letters.

Feeling rather guilty she opens several of the airmail letters from the States. The pages are covered with tiny scrawly writing which she can barely decipher. All are signed *'Your loving Granny.'* Then she finds an unfinished letter written by Sally-Ann to her grandmother on lined paper in large childish print. *'Dear Granny, Thank you for your letter and for sending me the darling golliwog. I was top of my grade this year. I have started learning French. Soon I am going to a boarding school in Jerusalem for two terms, because Mom and Daddy are going to be moving about a lot next year...'* The letter ends with an ink blot, presumably the reason it was never sent. Alex's only attempts at letter writing have also been a few thank-you notes to her grandmothers – Sheena's mother in Scotland and Giles's mother in Liverpool. Perhaps when school starts she will be able to say she is top of her grade. A disturbing sensation comes over her that Sally-Ann is in the room watching her, and she replaces the letters hastily in the drawer.

She unpacks her bag and arranges her three books on a shelf, but they make no impact on Sally-Ann's room. She climbs onto the rocking horse, but her legs are too long to ride it comfortably. Picking up the golliwog she stares into its grinning face. Is it male or female? Something about its expression repels her, and she lets it drop back limply into its chair. Only when bedtime comes and she can slip between the beautiful pink sheets and switch on the pink bedside lamp, which casts a soft glow over the walls, does she begin to enjoy the room. Tomorrow she will rearrange everything to suit herself. The golliwog is too large to hide away in the cupboard. She will stand it in the corner beside the wardrobe, with its face to the wall.

When Alex awakes in the morning the seven dwarfs seem to be looking at her from all four walls. She suspects the wallpaper is too childish for a seven-year-old. Something more suited to a princess would be preferable. Getting up she tiptoes into the hall. Sheena's bedroom door is open. She will have gone to the hospital by now, but Mr Carrington might still be upstairs. She listens, but all is quiet.

On the balcony the swing hangs invitingly on its heavy chains. Alex sets it gently in motion, then sits on it and swings high enough to see over the balustrade into the garden. If someone were to push her even higher and if she were to let go of the chains, her body would sail up into the air, into the sky, and then drop.... She shudders at the thought and slackens the momentum. Over the balustrade she can just see an Arab girl using a rattan beater on a carpet hanging over a balcony on the opposite side of the road. She recalls that the girl who came to clean the bungalow at K3 used to beat all the rugs over the verandah railing each Monday morning. It always seemed pointless to Alex because the dust flew up in a cloud and then settled again on the rugs.

On her way downstairs Alex stops at the sliding door. How smoothly, how noiselessly, it moves along its oiled groove. She slides it back and forth a few times. Opening it a couple of inches enables her to observe much of the lounge below without being seen.

The smell of toast and coffee wafts up the stairs. In the kitchen Abby is preparing a breakfast tray for Basil. Georgette, bleary-eyed and sullen, carries the tray upstairs.

The clock on the kitchen wall strikes eight as Alex is eating her cornflakes. The maid is vacuuming the carpets in the lounge as Basil comes down in his office clothes – pale grey suit with broad-lapelled jacket, spotless white shirt with wide cuffs, dark tie held in place with a gold tie-pin. His face is shiny clean and he smells of his usual cologne. 'So long, Alex', he says cheerfully. 'See you later on. Abby and Georgette will take care of you.' The apartment door clicks shut. What a relief he has gone!

'Go and play upstairs now', commands the cook. 'We have work to do.' On her way up Alex stops to watch Georgette pushing the noisy, unwieldy vacuum cleaner up and down the last carpet. She shuts the sliding door and skips on up, glad to have the top floor entirely to herself to explore all the rooms at leisure.

She opens Basil's door slowly, half expecting to find him inside. But all she sees is a reflection of herself in a full-length mirror opposite the door. The atmosphere reeks of cologne and talcum powder. She glances at the single divan covered neatly with a black and white tartan rug which matches a black and white goats' hair rug on the parquet floor. The sheets and pillow case under the tartan rug are crisply smooth and unused. Basil must have slept in her mother's bed. The thought still disturbs her, though she's accepted that Basil has taken her father's place for the time being.

She notes the pristine blotter and silver inkwell on the desk, the tallboy, the bookcase full of Readers' Digest magazines, the purple silk dressing gown behind the door... She becomes daring and approaches the tallboy, fingering the silver-backed brushes and the snapshots of Sally-Ann in silver frames. In the top drawer she finds a box of Lucky Strike cigarettes, a packet of cigars, fine linen hankies, a wad of blue Lebanese hundred-lira notes and sealed packets of something she can't identify. In the next drawer socks and suspenders and underpants are laid in neat piles. She pulls out a *Time* magazine, then a *New Yorker* from the bookcase and replaces them. Her father once told her that only lazy people read nothing but magazines.

Alex moves on into her mother's room. The unmade bed gives the place an untidy look, so alien to Sheena. She picks up the flimsy pink dressing gown and holds it against herself. She smoothes the satin on the peach-coloured camiknickers lying on a chair. In a bedside drawer she finds an airmail letter. Some friend from England who writes in a large, clear hand. A couple of sentences catch her eye. *'We were so sorry to hear you were caught up in the crisis in Iraq, but are relieved to hear that Giles is now free. How lucky that you and he have found somewhere to live in Beirut near your work. You must be glad that Alex can start school at last.'* No mention of Basil.

The guest room next door isn't worth looking at. The smell of mothballs hovers over neat white twin beds and shiny white furniture.

The morning passes quickly with sorting and rearranging Sally-Ann's possessions. Sheena calls her down at lunchtime to have a hurried meal in the dining room – cold meat and salad and ice cream. Basil doesn't appear.

When Sheena comes home she says, 'You'll be starting school tomorrow.'

'Will it be like the convent?' Alex asks anxiously.

'No, It's an American school. You'll like it.'

Her mother takes her upstairs to try on new cotton frocks for school. For the first time she puts on a woollen cardigan and a jumper, which will be needed when the weather turns cold in December. It's impossible to imagine cold weather.

In the kitchen Abby and Georgette are eating tahina sauce on bread sprinkled with pomegranate and sumac seeds ground to a powder. Abby lets her taste a piece and she finds it delicious.

In bed that night she prepares herself for the worst.

Chapter Nineteen

At a quarter to eight in the morning Claude comes into the kitchen where Alex is finishing her breakfast.

'Hurry up, Alex, or we'll be late.'

She follows the chauffeur down to the car, and they set off with Alex sitting in the front seat for the first time, clutching her lunch basket. In a few minutes they pull up in front of a two-level modern building. Claude leads the way across a concrete playground relieved at one end by a square of grass, some swings, a slide and a few dusty palm trees. At the top of a long pole hangs the United States flag. Claude hands Alex over to the superintendent, Miss Carter – tall and bony in flat leather sandals and horn-rimmed spectacles perched on her shiny scrubbed nose. Her grey hair is drawn back into a tight bun just above her collar. Her gentle, slightly protruding grey eyes belie her forbidding appearance. Miss Carter is the epitome of strict but kindly spinsterhood.

With a smile she puts her hand on Alex's shoulder.

'We hope you're going to be very happy with us, Alex', she says in a soft American accent. 'We have five grades in the Junior School with about ten to twelve pupils in each grade so we're like one big family. You're the only new girl in Grade Two but you'll soon make friends. Mrs Kellaway will be teaching you most of the time.'

Mrs Kellaway turns out to be a plump, motherly, energetic little lady with a platform of a bust and a roll of thick dark hair arranged in bangs around her sprightly round face. Alex feels an immediate liking for her teacher, an instinctive trust that she's on the side of her pupils.

'Come and meet the children in your grade', she says, taking her charge by the hand. The moment Alex has been dreading is made almost tolerable by the warmth of Mrs Kellaway.

The teacher leads Alex into a large airy room furnished with child-sized long tables and benches. A blackboard runs round two of the walls. The other walls are ablaze with brightly coloured paintings and collages. On a table at one end of the room stand jars of flowers and twigs, and displays of shells and pebbles and other natural objects on trays. The children sitting on the benches stop chattering and eleven pairs of eyes stare at the new girl, who hangs more tightly onto Mrs Kellaway's hand.

'Children, this is Alex Kinley. What do we all say when a new pupil joins our grade?'

A chanting of voices takes Alex by surprise. 'Welcome, Alex, to our grade today, we hope you'll like us and want to stay!'

She blushes deeply as Mrs Kellaway adds 'Now who's going to look after Alex for a week until she settles in.' Every hand goes up, but the quickest belongs to the prettiest girl Alex has ever seen. 'Annabel will take care of you', says Mrs Kellaway. 'You may sit between Annabel and Bobbie.'

Annabel is the essence of American cuteness combined with a budding dark eastern beauty which sets her apart from the other children. Even at first acquaintance it's clear to Alex that this girl is superior to the rest of their grade. During her time at the American Community Junior School she'll never have reason to alter her first impression. Annabel's frocks are crisp and fresh, her curling dark hair glossy with health and care, her nails always clean, her smooth brown knees never grazed, her socks spotless, her smile eager, frequent and charming. She's the kind of daughter Sheena yearns to have. All morning Alex keeps

198

glancing with admiration at the tiny gold earrings Annabel wears, and the diamanté bobby pins glinting in her hair.

Annabel chatters away, she smiles and laughs and shows her charge where to find things. She whispers little snippets of gossip as though she's known Alex all her life. Mrs Kellaway announces the rest of the week will be spent dealing with the theme of the fall.

'In England they call this time of year the autumn, and in The States we call it the fall because all the leaves are falling.' They write about the fall and read poems describing trees turning red and yellow and orange...

By the time school finishes at three o'clock Alex is deeply absorbed in her new life and has become passionately attached to Annabel. With this confident attractive person by her side she loses a little of her own shyness. Bobbie sitting next to her and Jake sitting opposite ply her with questions about her home and family. Alex is evasive, determined not to mention Basil, whose position she can't explain. Bobbie's father is a doctor at the American University Hospital and his family have a house on the campus. Jake's widowed mother teaches English to Arab business men. Annabel's father is a professor at St Joseph's University. Alex tells them her father works for an oil company. It's a relief no one asks further questions. She feels ashamed of her unusual home situation.

Of the twelve children in her grade, eight are Americans, and the rest a mixture of nationalities, with Alex the only British child. Mrs Kellaway treats everyone as a proud citizen of the United States. Kindness, friendliness and honesty are her watchwords. She drills the grade in these virtues. No one must be left out or made to feel inferior.

At the end of the school day Alex is reluctant to go home. She's discovered the pleasure and stimulation of learning in a group of friendly children led by an enthusiastic teacher. She also gathers that every girl in the grade aspires to becoming Annabel's best friend.

Apparently this position is vacant, for the girl who enjoyed the privilege has just left the school and Annabel's looking for a replacement. Annabel seems to be impressed by the way she reads aloud, and by her drawings which are praised by Mrs Kellaway. Bobbie is a very slow reader, and is amazed at how quickly Alex can read a page. With a good-natured grin he tells his buddy, Jake, that Alex is too clever for Grade Two. She experiences a heady glow of success for the first time in her life.

Georgette is waiting at the school gate to escort Alex home. Alex notes the way carefully – along a stony lane, then left for a short distance along a tarmac road called Rue Jeanne d'Arc, turn right into a long dusty track that passes the back entrance to the University Hospital and brings her out onto a road a few yards from home.

Abby is about to make labneh in the kitchen. She tells Alex to find herself a cookie and a glass of lemonade. Alex opens the tall white door of the gigantic refrigerator and is amazed at the array of food inside it.

'Did you have a good day, honey?' Abby asks. Alex begins to describe her day at school, but Abby isn't really listening. She's concentrating on measuring a tablespoon of fresh labneh into a large earthenware bowl and boiling half a litre of milk in a pan.

Alex drifts into the lounge, wishing there was someone she could talk to about school. How large and silent the room seems at this time of day, and above all, how empty. Her exhilaration melts away. She picks up the framed photograph of Basil's daughter, wondering whether Sally-Ann liked the American school better than the convent. When she puts it down Sally-Ann's eyes appear to be following her, the smile becomes taunting.

Alex sits down on each of the armchairs in turn, spilling a few drops of her lemonade on the blue silk. She uses a lace doily to rub them off. Then very gingerly she opens the white grand piano and dares to play a single note, which lingers in the air. Georgette comes out of the kitchen, and she flees upstairs.

In the bedroom her mind is still engrossed by the idea of school. She roots out every doll and toy animal in Sally-Ann's cupboard and arranges them in a row sitting against the walls. She stands the blackboard on an easel and finds a box of chalks. By the time Sheena returns at half past four Alex has transformed herself into Mrs Kellaway and is reluctant to end her game.

Her mother says brightly, 'Hello darling, did you have a good day at school?' Alex launches into an enthusiastic description while watching Sheena taking off her veil and shaking out the glorious auburn hair which has been tied back in a tight chignon all day. Kicking off her sensible lace-up shoes her mother lies on the bed in her white silk slip and closes her eyes. Like Abby she only half listens to her daughter.

By the end of the week Alex is still obsessed with school. She's discovered the satisfaction of always being the first to put her hand up in answer to Mrs Kellaway's questions, and she laps up information about The States. Her imagination delights in the exotic-sounding names of American mountains and rivers and states – Appalachian, Susquehanna, Potomac, Mississippi, Indiana, Illinois, Ohio... In the book corner she discovers a series of graded readers with colourful pictures, describing the life of a typical middle class American family – mother, father, two children, a dog and a cat. Here is the perfect pattern of how a family should live. She gains the mistaken impression that all American families live well-off, comfortable, healthy secure lives in houses with pretty gardens in tree-lined streets. The grownups love to spend time with their children and never quarrel. There are no nannies or maids or cooks. Mother does all the cooking in a frilly apron over her pretty summer frock in a bright kitchen full of shining gadgets. There is no mention of war, no characters like Philippe Durand. American family life is idyllic.

American expressions creep into her vocabulary. She wants to wear *sneakers* and *bobbysox*, her torch becomes a *flashlight,* she walks along a *sidewalk,* the children wear *galoshes* in wet weather, will Sheena take her to the *movies?* Can she have a *soda-pop?* She's *gotten* a tummy-ache.

Alex walks to school each morning carrying her packet of peanut butter and jelly sandwiches in a satchel with some fruit. At the end of the school day she's been told to come straight home without dawdling. Some of the children go to play at each other's homes, but much to her relief she's not yet been asked. There would be no question of having anyone back to Basil's apartment. Her old fantasy world of princesses and fairies and magicians loses its appeal and is replaced with the bright orderly world of the American family. During the many hours Alex spends alone in her room or on the balcony, she plays the roles of Father, Mother and Teacher. Sally-Ann's china tea set and her miniature cooking utensils are filled with lemonade and milk and scraps of bread and cookies which Abby has given her. But her bedroom is no place to embark on a long term game of make-believe. Each morning while she's at school Georgette clears away the toys and scolds Alex for leaving food lying around to attract mice.

Then she has a brain-wave. Why not carry all her toys up onto the roof, into the secluded section behind the wall where they won't be seen by Georgette when she hangs out the washing? The autumn weather is pleasantly warm in the afternoon and no longer scorching at midday. She moves some of the bricks out of the hut and uses them to form boundaries to the rooms in her 'house' – a living room, a dining room, a kitchen, bathroom and two bedrooms. Furnishing these 'rooms' with make-believe objects gives her intense pleasure. She climbs the spiral staircase again and again, carrying up the necessary paraphernalia of her game. She becomes more daring after a while and even takes up a small table and a stool from the spare bedroom.

Soon any object in the apartment which might not be missed finds its way onto the roof. Her great fear is that Georgette will eventually discover her 'house'. But the days go by without the maid looking over the wall into Alex's secret domain. Shoeboxes serve as beds, with some of Basil's hankies as sheets. So absorbed does Alex become in this fantasy world that she finds it frustrating to be called down for supper at six.

Between having a bath and sitting down at the dressing table to fix her hair and apply her make-up, Sheena comes to kiss her daughter goodnight. She's always asking 'How are you getting on at school? Are you keeping up with the other children?' Within a few weeks Alex is able to tell her mother she is top of her grade.

Sheena has heard that American schools are way behind English schools, and says, 'If you're doing so well perhaps we'll ask Miss Carter to put you up into the next grade.' This is the last thing Alex wants. She's beginning to feel at home in her present grade. She plans to stop working so hard.

A definite pattern of life has established itself in Beirut. As a nursing tutor Sheena works from eight until four. Basil is usually out from just before nine until half past five. Every evening they go out or entertain friends at home. On Saturdays they walk down Riad Sohl, then left along Rue de Clemenceau to the tram stop outside the university gates, where an old man sits selling brushes and bunches of loofahs no one ever seems to buy.

At this point along its route the tram is never too crowded. But as the cream-and-chocolate painted vehicle clangs and rattles its way down Rue Georges Picot it fills up to capacity and soon there are youths hanging dangerously onto the back railings. Women with shopping baskets struggle to mount the steps and are often shooed back by the ticket collector.

This irritates Basil. 'You'd have thought the French government would have tackled the transport problem.

People get injured all the time on these damn trolley cars, but no one cares.'

Just before their stop Basil rises and starts to work his way down the aisle, with Sheena and Alex following behind. Facing them as they alight is a wide road called Bab Edriss. Here Basil goes off on his own, having arranged to meet later for an ice cream soda at the ABC department store.

Alex has never been shown a map of Beirut but after a few of these Saturday morning shopping expeditions she learns to recognise certain landmarks. Three tramlines converge on the Place des Canons at the centre of town. This huge rectangular space is flanked by dark yellow sooty French architecture and ornamented with flower beds and two fountains. On one side run three long balconies adorned with *Socony Vacuum* in large lettering.

The trams add their din to the high pitched screech of street vendors hawking all manner of wares. Alex is particularly intrigued by men carrying huge glass flasks on their shoulders. These flasks, full of lurid coloured drinks – mulberry and sorrel sherbet, liquorice, mint-flavoured labneh – are held together by wide leather straps with little metal cups attached.

'Can I have a drink in one of those cups?' she begs, but Sheena says, 'No.'

The fruit market, bus station, smart boutiques, patisseries and cafés are teeming with noisy, shoving humanity. Outside the cinemas – *Roxy, Odeon, Empire, Capitol* – colourful hoardings proclaim the week's entertainment. On one occasion Alex's attention is held by a glamorous picture of Hedy Lamarr wearing a daringly low-cut dress in a film entitled 'Ecstasy!' She stands admiring the film star's beauty until Sheena pulls her away saying it's not a suitable film for little girls. She promises to take Alex to the next Walt Disney movie.

Alex is anxious to buy some of the hot bread rings flavoured with dark thyme and olive oil, or one of the bags of hot *fistakiyyeh* – pistachio nuts – from the street stall, but her mother hurries her on to Spinney's, a grocery store for Europeans which stocks the kind of tinned food Alex is used to seeing in Abby's kitchen cupboard – processed cheese, condensed milk, tinned pineapple, corned beef and sardines among other things. Far more interesting is the food market behind its impressive, enormously high nineteenth century facade off Avenue Weygand. Here is a bewildering array of flowers, fruit and vegetables, carcases of meat dripping blood, fish in buckets of ice and tray upon tray of sweetmeats. Sheena will never buy food in the market. Georgette is sent to bring home chicken and lamb and such delicacies as walnuts in honey, tubs of dill cucumbers, pickled onions, bunches of fresh herbs – and the turbot, tuna fish and red mullet Basil's so fond of.

Sheena likes to spend time browsing in the souks between the Maarid and the Boorj tower where the taxis gather at their terminus. She leads Alex past the Shia boys pestering to shine shoes, past the wheelbarrows of melons, past an old Arab coffee house with white colonnades, past the Armenian watchmakers and gold dealers to the fabric shops where bales of silk and linen and cotton reach to the ceiling. Here Sheena will barter with her few Arabic phrases, *kâm?* – how much? – being the word Alex hears most.

Alex is accustomed to sit on a high wooden stool in her mother's favourite fabric shop while bale after bale of cloth is brought out for inspection. Once, after sitting for twenty minutes, she panics, having lost sight of Sheena among the people in the shop. Ten minutes later when her mother descends a dark little staircase at the back of the shop she finds her tearful daughter surrounded by a bevy of sympathetic and indignant Lebanese lady shoppers.

'You silly girl, I only went upstairs where they keep the damask. Come on, we must hurry or Basil will wonder what's happened to us.' She walks out briskly holding Alex's hand, followed by disapproving stares.

The ABC department store where they always meet Basil is painted inside and out in a harsh yellow ochre offset with brown. They sit at a table in the basement café to have ice cream sodas. Alex envies a child at the next table who's enjoying a knickerbocker glory, a concoction of ice cream, nuts, bananas, chocolate and whipped cream, in a tall glass topped with a cherry.

'Can I have one of those next time?' she begs, but Sheena says 'No, you'd be sick.'

Alex wants to chatter to her mother, but as usual is inhibited by Basil's presence. On weekdays in the apartment Sheena rarely has time to talk to her daughter, and when asked questions she usually replies, 'I'm busy just now, darling. Ask me another time.' Some subjects she refuses to discuss altogether, Zilpha being one. If only she could open the front door one morning and find Zilpha standing there!

Chapter Twenty

One Saturday morning on the way home in the tram, a young woman three seats in front turns round. Alex starts in astonishment exclaiming excitedly 'Look, there's Zilpha!' At the same moment Zilpha recognises Alex and gives a cry of delight. She rises and struggles past the standing passengers with a beaming smile to embrace Alex, saying, 'Sweetheart! Is it really you?' To Sheena she says 'I've been wondering and wondering what happened to you. Is Mr Kinley working in Beirut now?'

'No, he's in Kirkuk. I have a job at the American Hospital here.'

'I'm living with my great-aunt, just off this road at the next stop − a yellow house with bright blue shutters, you can't miss it.'

'And are you going to stay in Lebanon?'

'Yes. Our house in Galilee was burnt down by the Stern Gang', says Zilpha bitterly. I left, and now I can't go back. I'm a refugee dressmaker now.'

'We live in the tall pink house in Riad Sohl', says Alex eagerly. 'In the top apartment, up the black staircase.' What utter bliss if Basil were to get rid of Georgette and employ Zilpha instead! But one look at her mother's face tells her that Sheena has no wish to see Zilpha again.

When the tram stops Zilpha says, 'I'll come and visit you very soon.' She gets off and Alex watches her turning down a narrow lane. As the tram moves on she catches a brief glimpse of a yellow house with blue shutters. 'I saw the house!' she exclaims, 'We'll be able to go and see her, and she can come to see us!' The prospect fills her with delirious pleasure.

'How extraordinary!' Sheena says to Basil, 'Meeting her on the tram. She could become a nuisance. I don't really want to get involved with her again.'

'It's fortunate she has a relative in Beirut' comments Basil. 'Otherwise she might have ended up in one of the overcrowded refugee camps in Lebanon. They're beginning to cause quite a problem to the government.'

'Zilpha's going to come and visit us!' states Alex triumphantly.

'I rather hope she doesn't. It will be very awkward.'

'Why?'

'I've told you before. That part of your life is over. Zilpha isn't a friend of ours, she's a nanny.' But Alex is certain Zilpha will come.

Sundays in Beirut have a definite pattern, as they did in the mountain villa. Basil and Sheena don't rise until after ten. At half past nine Georgette takes up a pot of tea and a plate of buttered toast fingers. Abby gives Alex a round of Arabic bread filled with blackcurrant jam to keep her going until brunch at eleven. She pinches an egg-cup of sugar and a banana and flees to the roof 'house' where her 'children' are all tucked up in bed. Alex wakes them up, dresses and feeds them. She discusses with her imaginary husband what they will do this Sunday: take the children for a swim in the lake, or have a picnic in the forest?

At weekends Basil listens to classical music on his radiogram. He keeps a stack of heavy records in a special cupboard. Sheena doesn't care for classical music but Alex is fascinated by the sound of an orchestra, and learns the thrill of hearing a beautiful melody suddenly appearing in a concerto. Basil never speaks to Alex about the music, and she herself never dares to ask questions. He often mentions the Boston Symphony Orchestra to Sheena, saying it's the best in the world. Mrs Kellaway tells Alex Boston is in the States.

At half past twelve it's time to leave for the British Club situated on the coast opposite the St George Hotel. It's a place where people swim, sunbathe, play table tennis and dance. The upper storey of the club is at street level, with a lounge, reading room, library and office, all very bright and modern. The lower, old part of the building is dark, damp and smells of seaweed. The flagstones in the changing cubicles are slippery with green mould and the faded sailcloth curtains hanging from rusty rings are stiff with salt spray. The deep green water slaps gently against shiny stone steps. Two diving boards, one low and springy and one much higher, are covered in rope matting to stop people from slipping.

Alex enjoys swimming in the sea instead of in a pool. The buoyant water enables her to dog-paddle out to the sunbathing raft with very little effort. This anchored raft mounted on huge metal barrels is the size of a small room. There are two ladders to climb onto its surface. Alex loves lying on the thick rough matting peering over the edge at the dark water surging under the slimy green barrels and listening to the booming sound and the rattle and clank of the heavy chain. How terrifying to be sucked under those barrels and crushed by the chain! How lovely to be lying warm and dry on top of the heaving raft!

They share Sunday lunch at the club with friends of Basil's, sitting in their bathing costumes on damp benches at long trestle tables. They all talk and laugh loudly but Alex finds the conversation uninteresting. She never sees other children at the club. As lunch drags on she becomes bored and petulant and whispers to her mother, 'Why can't we go to the beach where my school friends go to swim?'

'I don't like beaches. There's so little shade, and you know I can't sit in the sun.'

'When are we going home?'

'When we've had our coffee.'

'Can I have some coffee.'

'No, It's not good for you.'

After several of these Sunday lunches at the club a lady remarks, 'For Pete's sake, Sheena, why on earth didn't you send your brat back to the UK when you had the chance?' Alex, quivering with dislike, watches her mother smile with apparent good nature. But she knows from the way Sheena's mouth stiffens and her eyes turn cold, that she's annoyed.

One of Basil's friends is a wiry. sharp-featured little New Zealander called Norman. People often gather to watch his perfect jack-knife and swallow dives from the high board. He drinks a great deal of beer and whenever he sees Alex he says 'Here comes our doggy-paddler!' Alex hates Norman.

One lunchtime he offers to teach her to do the crawl and to dive. Sheena's delighted and then furious when her daughter bursts into tears and refuses to be taught by Norman. In the changing cubicle Sheena rails at Alex for being such a silly coward. 'How rude you sounded. I'm utterly ashamed of you!' Alex feels utterly ashamed of herself. It would be lovely to be able to do a proper stroke and to dive – but she could never face being taught by Norman.

When they return to the apartment Sheena is still annoyed and Alex is sulking. Then to her delight she finds

Zilpha waiting in the kitchen and is overwhelmed with happiness. But her mother's mood doesn't change. Zilpha isn't invited to sit in the lounge and have a cup of tea. Alex doesn't mind. It means she can have Zilpha all to herself.

They sit at the kitchen table and Abby makes a pot of tea. Zilpha tells them she's to be married soon to a Lebanese Christian. The idea of Zilpha being married comes as an unpleasant surprise. But when she's asked to be bridesmaid her happiness returns. She can think of nothing more exciting and runs to tell her mother the good news. 'Can I? Please let me!'

'We'll see', says Sheena doubtfully. When it's time for Zilpha to leave Sheena comes to the door and says 'Congratulations! I hope you'll be very happy. I'll be in touch with you.'

Alex goes down to the garden gate to say goodbye to Zilpha. When she returns to the apartment one look at her mother's face tells her she's still annoyed. It comes as no surprise when Sheena says 'I'm afraid there can be no question of your being bridesmaid to Zilpha.'

Obstinately Alex argues. 'Why not? She promised to make me a frock. You won't even have to buy one.'

'That isn't the point. I don't want to discuss it. The answer is no, and that's that.'

Alex runs up to her room. For the first time in her life she experiences a consuming hatred for her mother. She climbs up to the roof and immerses herself in the game of make-believe. It's mid-October but the days are still warm and sunny. Basil has said the winter rains usually come at the beginning of December, so she feels no need to end her game yet.

Alex has a shock when she wakes one night to hear a clap of thunder. All is quiet for a few moments. She thinks it must have been a dream, when suddenly lightning streaks across the sky, followed by yet another great roll of thunder. She rises and walks to the window,. Again all is ominously silent. Then the sky is split open by forked light, revealing a lowering mass of angry cloud. If it rains, her 'house' on the roof will be soaked.

Taking her torch she climbs up the spiral staircase as the next bout of thunder rumbles above her. How is she going to take everything down in time? Exposed to the elements she begins to feel frightened. She starts to put some of the things into the roof hut. Then comes the threatened rain, falling at first in huge isolated drops and then sheeting down in a deluge. It's too late to drag everything under cover. She seizes two dolls and works her way gingerly down the glistening wet stairs. As she puts her foot on the last step she's horrified to see Basil standing at the balcony door.

'For Christ's sake, child, what are you doing out there?'

Alex comes in out of the deluge and stands dripping on the carpet, clutching the sodden dolls under her arm. 'I left my dolls on the roof. I didn't want them to get wet.'

Sheena emerges in her dressing gown, exclaiming at the sight of her bedraggled daughter.

'She left her dolls on the roof', explains Basil. 'It's an early freak storm.'

'You shouldn't have gone up in the dark. You could have fallen down the stairs', scolds Sheena. 'You'd better get out of those pyjamas. I'll find you some dry ones.'

Back in bed Alex listens to the rain coming down even more heavily. Everything outside will be soaked by now. She thinks with horror of the stool she's borrowed, of the rug and little table from the spare room, of the cushions and the pillow cases.

Alex lies awake until dawn, thinking there will be no possibility of bringing down the rest of the things before school. Her only hope is that Georgette won't go up and see them. But when she hurries home she finds everything from the roof laid out on the balcony in the sun. Georgette has looked over the wall for the first time! The maid comes upstairs yelling 'You're a bad, bad girl! It took all morning to carry down these things. Look at the velvet cushions! What will Mr Carrington say when he sees them? They're only good for the garbage can.'

But Georgette's anger is nothing compared to Sheena's. She comes storming into Alex's room, shouting, 'How could you be so stupid? You'd no right to take Basil's things up to the roof without permission! And how dared you go into his room and pinch hankies out of his drawer! I can hardly believe it! The cushions are ruined. So are the magazines and books and the stool and table. Why did you take things up to the roof? There's plenty of room to play down here!'

Her mother's tirade is justified and Alex is mortified. 'It's no good looking so defiant. You deserve a good smack bottom!' Alex flushes with shame at such a thought. At K3 her mother had several times smacked her in exasperated fury, but each time there had followed a row with Giles who maintained that no child should ever be disciplined with violence. On this point he would never give way to her mother.

'I thought it wouldn't rain till December. I meant to put everything back. They were only borrowed for a little while.'

'That's not the point. You should have asked permission. In any case furniture should never be left outside. Basil will be furious. I hope he gives you a good smacking!'

The idea of Basil chastising her is nightmarish.

'Before you go to bed you're to come and tell him how sorry you are. You must promise never to take any of his things without asking. And never to go into his room again.'

'I'm sorry, I am', the child protests. 'I don't want to say sorry to Mr Carrington. You tell him for me.' Alex dreads Basil's fury. Having so far been unable to form a relationship with him, she has an irrational fear of facing him with an apology.

'You'll say sorry to him yourself, my girl, or there'll be trouble. And you'll take that sulky look off your face when you do it!'

Alex sits by her window watching for the Buick and rehearsing over and over again the words she must say to Basil. There he is, walking up the garden path. Soon he will be in the bathroom taking a shower. She hears her mother coming upstairs and through the partly open door she watches Basil and Sheena going out on the balcony to inspect the damage. This is the moment when she should emerge and say the stiff sentences she has prepared. But she doesn't move. She would rather be punished than face Basil.

Sheena comes into her room and says ominously, 'Are you coming to apologise?'

'No, I can't!'

'Then you'll stay in your room until you do!'

On Saturday morning Alex dares not leave her room until she's heard Basil and Sheena departing on their usual shopping expedition. Then she moons about upstairs, weighed down with misery, boredom, regret and hunger. At one o'clock Georgette brings a lunch tray to her room – meat balls and mashed potato, tomato sauce and spinach, with rice pudding to follow. She still detests spinach, the more so because it's Basil's favourite and Abby is always cooking it for him. She pushes the slimy mess around her plate in disgust. Sheena has instructed Abby to make sure that her daughter eats up her meat and vegetables because since her illness she's become very thin. The only solution is to throw it out of the window, to fall among the shrubs unnoticed. Unfortunately it splatters on the window ledge of the apartment below. Someone, no doubt, will complain. There will be more trouble. She sees no end to it.

At five Sheena comes at last and says, 'Well, are you ready to say you're sorry?' Basil is standing at the door behind her mother and Alex bursts into hysterical tears.

'For goodness sake, Sheena, it doesn't matter' says Basil. 'She's had her punishment. Let's say no more about it.'

'Stop crying and wash your face before you come down to tea', says Sheena.

Downstairs Alex's tears begin to fall again over her toasted muffin, and when Basil pats her knee kindly she's too overwhelmed to finish her meal. She gets up and dashes back to her room.

She longs for Zilpha, who always knew how to deal with these mishaps, how to put everything right. If only she could go and live with Zilpha! How impossible to please her mother!

For the rest of the weekend Alex keeps out of Sheena's way. It's become rather too cold to swim, so Basil has suggested Sheena learn to play golf. He takes her off to the golf club after brunch, and the long afternoon stretches before Alex. She finds a piece of chalk and marks out squares on the balcony for a solitary game of hopscotch which the girls at school have taught her how to play.

Chapter Twenty-one

When Alex returns to school on Monday to find that Mrs Kellaway has pinned up one of her drawings on the wall her spirits begin to revive. And when Annabel beckons her into a corner of the playground at recess and whispers into her ear, would she like to be her best friend, life suddenly becomes radiant with pleasure. The incident at home pales into insignificance. To seal the friendship they must swap something precious to be given back only if they break the relationship. Annabel gives Alex a ring with a diamanté heart. Alex in return promises to bring her black cat brooch with the green eyes.

After school Alex is in no hurry to return home. The sky is a deathly grey and it's drizzling. She dawdles in her galoshes along the track behind the hospital, stepping in the puddles and thinking of Annabel – Annabel, her best friend!

She's about to pass the small gate at the back of the hospital when her mother emerges, carrying a black umbrella. 'Hello, darling!' Her anger seems to have disappeared. 'I'm coming home early today. You can share my umbrella.' They start walking slowly, pressed close together.

Alex asks 'D'you always come out of that gate?'

'Yes, it's the quickest way home.'

With great pride the child bursts out, 'Annabel Hitti has asked me to be her best friend!'

'That's good news.'

'Annabel's house is quite near the school. She's going to ask her mother if I can go there to play on Saturdays. Will you let me?'

'Yes, of course. Are you friendly with Bobbie Carson? His father's a doctor at the hospital.'

'Bobbie sits next to me at our table. He's nearly a year older than the rest of the class, but he can't read very well. His buddy's called Jake. They play around in class and don't get on with their sums.' Sheena laughs.

At home Alex and her mother have tea alone together for the first time since coming to Beirut. It's cosy and relaxed without Basil. Alex chatters freely about school life and for once her mother seems to be interested.

Going home the following afternoon is an anticlimax after the first whole day of being Annabel's best friend. She wanders upstairs into her mother's bedroom and picks up an airmail letter from the bedside table. It's from Sheena's sister, Alison. Sheena rarely talks about her family but Giles has told Alex the names of all the uncles and aunts she will meet one day in Scotland. Alison has married recently, and now she writes that she and Gordon have just bought a 'semi' for six hundred pounds. Alex guesses this must mean a house since Alison says it has a small garden which they have dug up to plant vegetables. They've spent ten pounds on an Anderson shelter, and Gordon has had to put his Austin car on blocks. It all sounds very strange. How difficult it is to picture Alison and Gordon and their wartime life.

Just before four it stops raining and the sun bursts out. Alex has a sudden idea. Why not go to meet her mother from the hospital? She tells Georgette, 'I'm going to wait for my mother outside the hospital. She asked me to come.'

'She didn't tell me', retorts the maid.

'I expect she forgot', lies Alex.

Opposite the hospital gate there's a gap in the hedge where a patch of smooth hardened earth over a bent tree root has already dried in the sun. It might have been made for Alex to sit on. She can perch here and see the hospital on one side and a field of emerald green anise behind the hedge. The recent rain has left a strong smell of damp dung, more pungent than the smell of dung in dry heat. Somewhere a clock strikes four. Sheena comes out twenty minutes later. She's surprised to see her daughter again. Alex can't divine whether she's pleased or not.

It becomes a daily ritual for Alex to meet her mother from work, even when it's raining. She becomes superstitious about never missing a day. Often she has to wait half an hour, but it's worth it to have Sheena to herself for a few minutes, to see her smile and apologise for being late.

'At school we're making animals out of pipe cleaners, and silver paper doilies, and witches' hats for our Halloween party!' says Alex excitedly. 'We're going to have three pumpkins with candles inside and we're dressing up. It's at seven o'clock, and parents are invited. Can you come?'

'I'm sorry, darling, I can't come at Halloween.' Alex isn't surprised. She has never expected her mother to participate in school activities.

After the thrill of her first Halloween party Alex looks forward to Thanksgiving Day on the fourth Thursday in

November. Mrs Kellaway asks, 'Who can tell Alex why we celebrate on Thanksgiving Day?'

To everyone's surprise, Bobbie shoots his hand up. 'Because of those people who sailed in the *Mayflower* to Massachusetts.'

'And what did they call themselves?'

'Pilgrims', interrupts Annabel smugly.

'That's right. A hundred people left England on September the 6th, 1620, because they weren't allowed to practice their Protestant religion. They landed at Plymouth Rock on December the 16th. A year later they celebrated with a special meal to thank God for bringing them to America, and for giving them their first harvest.' Mrs Kellaway goes on to tell the Grade, as she does each year, how fortunate they are to have ancestors who went to America and worked so hard to create the wonderful country it is today.

'We always have a lunch party at Thanksgiving', says Annabel. 'What do your family do?' Alex has no idea. The subject hasn't been mentioned. 'I suppose English people don't celebrate', Annabel adds with pity. 'I'll ask Mom if you can come to our party.'

Annabel's mother telephones the same evening. 'How nice that you've been invited to your friends for Thanksgiving', says Sheena. 'Basil will be having a party, but it will be an evening dinner, not for children.'

When Basil comes home, Sheena asks, 'Do you know Constance Hitti?'

'Vaguely. She's an American woman married to a Lebanese professor. She was partly brought up out here, the daughter of an American missionary. She's full of religion and good works, not your type at all', says Basil with a laugh. Alex is disappointed. It would have been lovely if her mother and Mrs Hitti could be friends. On the other hand she's reluctant for the Hittis to know that Basil isn't her father.

On Thanksgiving Day, a school holiday, Alex wakes early and goes down to the kitchen. Abby and Georgette have been up since four, preparing food for Basil's party. 'This year', grumbles Abby, 'We're feeding an army, British servicemen as well as his American friends!'

Two gigantic turkeys lie, naked and repulsive, on the kitchen table next to a basket of mullet. Alex shudders at the thought of handling the raw poultry and fish. Abby is making pastry for the pumpkin pie. Her wrinkled, leathery hands deftly manipulate the dough, and for the first time Alex notices the protruding blue veins on the cook's swollen legs, and wonders about her age.

'Are you very, very old?' she enquires curiously.

Abby gives a loud cackle. 'Of course, my darling! I'm a hundred and five years old!'

When Abby beats up the mixture of pumpkin, brown sugar, milk, minced ginger, egg, cinnamon and nutmeg to fill the pie she lets Alex try it. It has a very distinctive taste. Alex loves watching Abby cook – all the chopping and mixing, the colours and textures and scents, the moist pink meat worming its way out of the mincer, the egg whites transforming miraculously into stiff mountain peaks, the bread dough ballooning out of its bowl...

Later, when Alex announces Abby's great age with awe, Sheena replies, 'Don't be silly, Abby's only forty!' Forty isn't as impressive as a hundred and five but it's still quite old.

'I'm going to a better party', Alex tells the cook.

'No, you're not', retorts Abby. 'Mr Carrington gives the best parties in Beirut because I'm the best cook in town. He pays me the highest wages because he knows I'd pack my bags and be off to another family if he didn't.'

'D'you like working here?'

'Of course not! Would you like to get up at five and do my work? But Mr Carrington is generous enough. He doesn't ask where the left-over food goes.'

At midday Georgette is told to escort Alex to Annabel's house, as Claude has been given the day off. Listening through the hatch into the dining room Alex hears the maid complaining to Abby. 'Why do I have to take the kid? I've been up since four. I need a rest at lunchtime. If Mr Carrington wants a nursemaid he should pay me more!'

Annabel's house is half a mile beyond the school. Georgette accompanies Alex in sullen silence, only saying when they reach the gates, 'This is the house', and then hurrying away.

For a moment Alex panics and wants to run after the maid. Then she plucks up courage, opens the gate and walks up a long drive into a spacious shady garden dominated by date palms. Annabel is standing on the rickety wooden verandah that runs around the solid grey stone house.

'Hi, Alex!' she says breezily. 'I just love your frock. I haven't changed yet. We're still getting ready. Lunch probably won't be until two.'

A number of folding wooden chairs are piled up on the verandah. 'I've got to put these in the dining room. Twenty people have got to be fitted around our table. You and I will have to share the long piano stool.'

As they pick up a chair each, two identical small boys appear and stare at Alex. 'This is Alexandria, my best friend', announces Annabel solemnly.

'Alexandria!' they repeat together, spinning out each syllable and giggling as they scamper off among the trees.

'Those are my kid brothers, Jimmy and Konrad. I hate little boys, don't you?' Alex agrees fervently.

The house, with its delicate fretwork shutters, and rooms built round a high-ceilinged central hall with cream mouldings and a terra cotta tiled floor, is typically Lebanese. The girls are reflected in two long ornate gilt mirrors as they walk through the hall. The living and dining rooms are linked by a wide arched entrance with interior windows on each side surmounted by three smaller arched windows. The furnishings in the living room – large brass trays on legs inlaid with ivory, Persian rugs, climbing plants, blue pottery, leather pouffes in rust and cream, a damascene bowl – are vaguely reminiscent of Leila's house in Baghdad. For all its apparent grandeur, it has an air of shabbiness about it. The old damask-covered sofa is sagging a little, the paintwork is cracking, the glass chandeliers are coated with yellow dust and the carpets are faded and threadbare.

The long dining table is covered with a linen cloth patterned with the stars and stripes of the American flag. Miniature flags stick up out of posies of red, white and blue anemones down the centre, alternating with bowls of candy and sugared almonds. A stalk of maize with its silken tassel lies beside each place to symbolise the harvest. Mrs Hitti enters the room looking hot and bothered wearing navy blue slacks and a red pinafore apron with her hair tied up in a red scarf. She places dishes of cranberry sauce on the table and then kisses Alex warmly. 'My goodness, look at the time! We must go and change before the guests arrive.' She hurries away. Already Alex has decided Mrs Hitti is a friendly person.

Annabel takes Alex upstairs. Her bedroom isn't a childish room like Sally-Ann's. No toys or Disney characters on the walls – only a tall dark wardrobe, a high white bed and a marble washstand with a large white bowl and jug standing on it. Unframed pictures of flowers and animals adorn the white walls.

'D'you want to see my jewels?' asks Annabel, taking a sandalwood box out of a drawer in the wardrobe. Inside are gold bangles, a pearl pendant, a filigree bracelet, an amber necklace, a pair of small gold earrings and at least a dozen rings. 'I love jewels', she says, fingering her treasures. 'Have you got any?'

'No, not real jewels.' Alex remembers her tin box full of Sheena's discarded trinkets and wonders whether it's still hidden under the stone on top of her 'castle' in the desert.

Hanging on the back of a chair is a pink and white gingham frock trimmed with broderie anglaise. Annabel slips this on and ties a white satin ribbon into her thick dark curls with expert fingers. She puts her arm round Alex's waist and they go down to lunch.

'That's my father' whispers Annabel as a distinguished looking man with a mass of curly black hair takes the head of the table and says a long prayer of thanks. Alex sits shyly on her end of the piano stool and listens to snatches of conversation. The men burst into deep hearty laughter at frequent intervals and the ladies have loud penetrating voices.

'Who's Annabel's little friend?'

'I don't know, I've never seen her here before.'

'Such a shame, a child of that age having to wear those ugly spectacles!'

'Doesn't Annabel look pretty. What a beauty she's growing up to be!' Alex accepts this remark as entirely justified. Annabel is perfect in every way.

The children sit patiently throughout the lengthy meal of soup followed by roast turkey, sweet potatoes, cranberry sauce, pumpkin pie and ice cream. Surprisingly Mrs Hitti does her own cooking. A maid serves the food and clears away the dishes with the help of Annabel and Alex. After lunch Alex is taken round the garden, a large area of grass and trees and overgrown flowering shrubs – a paradise for children. 'Mom likes a garden to look wild. She doesn't like tidy flower beds', explains Annabel. By the time they've explored the garden it's nearly five and the guests are beginning to leave.

Alex walks with Annabel to the gate, but Georgette isn't waiting outside. Half an hour later she still hasn't arrived. Mrs Hitti doesn't seem perturbed, and offers to drive Alex home. Annabel insists on coming and Alex hopes Mrs Hitti won't want to come in and meet Basil and Sheena. Fortunately when they reach the apartment Annabel's mother doesn't get out of the car.

'Now you know where we live you must come and play with Annabel next Saturday', she says cheerfully.

Alex goes straight to the kitchen where Abby's putting the finishing touches to the dinner.

'Hello, did you have a good time?'

'Yes, I did. My friend's mother had to bring me home because Georgette didn't come to fetch me.'

Abby shouts up the ladder to the maid. 'You stupid girl! You forgot to fetch Alex. Mrs Kinley will be mad!'

'I don't care what she says!' Georgette yells from her room.

'You will care if Mr Carrington decides not to give you that rise at Christmas.'

Georgette's face suddenly appears at the open trap door, glaring down at Alex with intense dislike and then retreating.

'Can I do some cooking?' Alex asks Abby.

'Yes, you can fill these eggplants with that tomato stuffing, and then put a little grated cheese on top of each one.'

As the child laboriously performs this task the cook sits on a low stool beside the large ice cream bucket, to undertake the arm-aching job of turning the handle and bringing the ice cream in its central cylinder surrounded with packed ice to a perfect smooth finish. Alex, watching her, recalls Zilpha making ice cream in a similar but much smaller bucket.

Sheena comes into the kitchen, asking, 'Did you enjoy the party?'

'Yes, it was lovely and Mrs Hitti wants me to go and play with Annabel on Saturday. I know the way now, so I can go by myself.'

'All right – but you'll have to take care crossing the road.'

Later, in bed, Alex goes over the day's events as she listens to the guests arriving for the party and hears the strains of Basil's dance records drifting up through the half-open sliding door.

Chapter Twenty-two

On a late afternoon in early December Alex experiences a twinge or two of toothache for the first time. To begin with it's bearable and she continues to chew her anchovy toast carefully as she sits with Basil and Sheena in front of the first log fire of the winter.

Basil turns on the wireless to listen to the news bulletin. Since coming to Beirut Alex has ceased to take in news of the war. Without her father to explain what's happening she's lost interest. But today her attention is caught by the repeated use of the words *Pearl Harbour,* which conjure up the vision of a blue bay full of little boats encrusted with pearls. The reality, she gathers from Basil's reaction to the bulletin, is that the United States have finally joined the Allies owing to the Japanese having attacked Pearl Harbour.

'Thank God we're in this war officially at last', he says. 'Now we should be able to get it over with quickly.'

The solemn voice on the wireless continues to give details of the conflict in various parts of the world. Alex stops listening as her toothache is getting worse. During the night Sheena gives her aspirin to ease the pain.

'You'll have to miss school and see a dentist in the morning', she says, kissing her daughter's swollen cheek. Alex lies awake most of the night, dreading the thought of anyone touching her aching tooth.

An appointment is made for ten o'clock to see Basil's dentist, a Mr Khadduri on Avenue Clemenceau. Sheena is taking the morning off work and comes down to breakfast in a brown jersey skirt and a soft blue cashmere sweater. Georgette brings in a large brown envelope which Sheena hands to her daughter. Inside is a large photograph of Zilpha and her husband on their wedding day. There she is, smiling out at Alex in a long trailing white dress with a garland of white flowers in her hair. Standing close to her, holding her hand, is a pleasant-looking, dark-haired man in a smart suit with a flower in his lapel. Alex is relieved to see there is no bridesmaid.

'I wanted so much to go to her wedding', she says wistfully.

'I'm sorry', says Sheena, 'But it was quite impossible. You couldn't have gone on your own, and I certainly couldn't have gone.' Alex can't see why not, but there's no point in arguing.

It's raining as they leave the apartment. The tram's crowded with people smelling of damp clothes. As they rattle down Rue Georges Picot Alex watches out, as always, for Zilpha's lane and the yellow house with the blue shutters.

The dentist's waiting room is grey and high-ceilinged, gloomy with a strong odour of disinfectant. The chairs are hard and the French magazines old and tattered. Sheena searches for an English magazine and finds an out of date *Vogue.* Two people waiting with them stare into space with gloomy faces as the high-pitched whine of the drill plays on all their nerves. The very sound of this machine is enough to intensify the pain.

'It's going to hurt, I know it is!' she whispers fiercely to her mother, but Sheena assures her, 'It won't hurt much, and as soon as he's put in a filling the pain in your tooth will disappear. Try and be a brave girl. If you're good and don't make a fuss I'll buy you something nice on the way home.'

As soon as Alex is seated in the large, adjustable dentist's chair she begins to sweat with terror at the mere sight of the instruments – the drill hanging overhead like some lethal folding insect, the white circular tray gleaming with a row of long pointed tools. In a white bucket Alex catches sight of a bloodied wad of cotton wool.

Mr Khadduri, a bulky man in a starched white coat, and bald but for a few strands of black oiled hair lying across his shiny brown skull, takes a small mirror and begins to probe her tooth with one of the sharp instruments. Then he pulls down the drill and fits a new head into it.

'This may hurt a little', he says. But he lies, for nothing in her life so far has prepared her for the horror of the relentless drill – its insistent buzz, its penetrating needle seeking out the tender inflamed nerve and dwelling on it until Alex feels as though her eyes are starting out of her head. The blood drains from her hands, leaving her white fingers clutching at the worn leather arms of the chair like a drowning person. Every nerve in her thin body is taut with agony. There's no escape, for the dentist's massive arms and huge face are swamping her as his eyes stare with concentration on the task of working in her small mouth, keeping his monstrous machine within the tiny hole in the miniature tooth. Now she can smell stale garlic and a wave of nausea compounds her pain and the aching discomfort of her jaws.

'Take a little rest now', says Mr Khadduri. Her mouth collapses shut with overwhelming relief. But almost immediately the dentist swings the ruthless machine down over her face again. Sheena, who's sitting in a corner of the room, says 'Good girl, it won't be long now.' Alex grips the chair and the torture resumes, but this time she squirms and pulls away as the sweat trickles down her back. Mr Khadduri remonstrates, 'You must sit still, or we shall never finish.'

By the time the filling is in place and Alex has rinsed her swollen mouth, trailing threads of bloody unswallowed saliva from the white cup, she's almost unable to stand. She hasn't been a good patient. Mr Khadduri must think she's a baby. But at least Sheena is smiling at her, showing her row of even white teeth.

They step out of the dark corridor into a miracle of sunshine after three days of continuous rain. This morning Alex has learnt the true meaning of pain – not mere discomfort or nagging ache, but the explosion within the brain. In future she will never read or hear about someone else's pain without relating it to her experiences in Mr Khadduri's surgery. And something else she has learnt – that grownups always say it won't hurt much when they know it will. It would seem that pain must be inflicted in the cause of health, and henceforth the smiling face above the white coat combined with the smell of ether and disinfectant will always trigger pain in her imagination.

'You said it wouldn't hurt much', Alex bursts out accusingly as Sheena hurries her along the wet pavement.

'It doesn't always hurt. You must have very sensitive teeth, like your father.'

'Has Mr Khadduri done your teeth?'

'No, I've never had anything done at the dentist. I'm lucky to have strong teeth.'

Alex is soon to discover that her own teeth are prone to decay and that the dentist always does hurt. Her fear starts at least two days before an appointment, leaving her exhausted long before she even climbs into the dental chair. Her mother must be quite unable to feel pain, otherwise how could she sit so calmly making trivial comments to her tormentor, even smiling. Alex gasps and fidgets and sometimes pulls away from the instruments, and the process of drilling takes longer and longer as she has to be given more rests. She can feel Sheena's impatience, and Mr Khadduri makes it plain he thinks she could try harder to be brave.

After a second visit to the dentist Alex waits to cross Rue Clemenceau with her mother. In her dazed state she steps too soon into the road and Sheena yanks her back just in time as a Pontiac flashes past hooting madly.

Alex begins to cry. 'I feel sick!'

'You'll soon be home and then you can lie down.'

'You promised to buy me something nice last time we went to the dentist but you never did.'

Sheena buys her a bag of toffees. 'But you're not to eat any of them today. Today only labneh and mashed banana.'

After lunch Alex feels better. Sheena returns to the hospital and Abby and Georgette retire to their rooms. The apartment looks grey and cheerless, smelling of brasso and furniture polish. Alex goes upstairs and looks at Zilpha's wedding photograph. She longs to see her, to tell her about the dentist, about Annabel and school. She pores over every detail of the bride with her radiant smile. Did she ever look as happy at K3? Suddenly an idea occurs to her. Why not visit Zilpha this afternoon? She could run there and back without anyone knowing. Two tram stops away isn't far, it must be within easy walking distance in this winter weather. Abby and Georgette will think she's playing in her room.

With infinite stealth she goes downstairs and eases open the main door, slips through and clicks it shut. She listens for a few seconds and then dashes lightly down the stairs. Five minutes later she is half skipping, half running, past the University gates and alongside the tramlines down Rue Georges Picot. Twenty minutes later, breathless and triumphant, she's knocking on Zilpha's door.

Zilpha herself opens it, and for a moment it's like being back at K3. After the hugs and kisses Alex launches into a description of her ordeal at the dentist. Zilpha listens, but is more worried about Alex coming alone down the busy main road.

'Did your mother bring you?'

'She let me come alone.' And when Zilpha looks doubtful, Alex adds 'I go to school alone and to my friend's house.'

It is only then that Alex notices an old lady with a glazed look in her eyes sitting in the corner. Her lined hands dotted with dark brown liver spots are clutching a large grey tin on her lap. She gives a low moan from time to time and stares straight in front of her without looking at Alex.

'That's my great-aunt', says Zilpha. 'She's rather deaf and she doesn't always remember where she is. She's thinking all the time about her home in Palestine, and her husband, who died some years ago. She fled to Beirut to live with her daughter, my cousin, who's now emigrated to the States.'

'Why does she keep that tin on her lap?'

'She's kept it with her ever since leaving Galilee. She even takes it to bed with her. It contains the door key and the deeds of her house.'

'What are deeds?'

'The documents proving that my uncle bought the house.'

Zilpha puts her arm round the old lady and says loudly, 'Show Alex what's in your tin, Aunty.' The eyes in their sunken sockets kindle like the revived embers of a fire as she opens the tin. On top of a pile of papers lies a pale brown British passport. She mutters something in Arabic to her niece.

'She's asking how many days until we return to Galilee. I can't tell her she'll probably never see her village again. Her house was blown up before ours by the Jews.'

The tiny living room is crammed with furniture, the focal point being an enormous Singer treadle sewing machine. They sit on a backless wooden sofa with carved arm rests and cushions covered with floral cretonne. No curtains at the window, but there is a patterned rug hanging across one wall and a camel hair rug on the tiled floor. Family photographs in elaborate frames, each one on a crocheted mat, jostle one another on the sideboard. Two narrow glass doors reinforced with wrought iron bars lead onto a small back yard draped with washing on two clothes lines. A bale of cotton in kingfisher blue is partially unravelled across a high-backed rocking chair of polished wood with a cane seat. A half finished red dress is tacked onto a headless tailor's dummy.

'Can I see your wedding dress?' Alex begs. Zilpha takes her into the bedroom and opens the lid of a large Druze chest raised on blocks. She lifts out the white silk dress and a garland of silk orange blossom. Beneath is a black silk dress.

'D'you want to see my trousseau?' She lays the contents of the chest on the high brass bedstead – a brown dress beautifully embroidered in red and gold, petticoats edged with intricate crochet work, lace doilies and mats and embroidered sheets and pillowcases. Alex is enthralled by a silk bag made out of a remnant of the wedding dress and covered with tiny seed pearls and gold sequins. In the bag are grains of rice and orange pips.

'Our guests threw rice and orange seeds over us, in the hope that we'll be blessed with children', explains Zilpha. Now you must have something nice to eat.'

Alex is taken into a small kitchen where glass jars full of home-made pickled vegetables – beetroot, onion, cucumber, egg-plant and pepper stand on a shelf. Zilpha boils milk with molasses and cuts a slice of semolina cake.

In her delight at being reunited with her beloved nanny, Alex is in no hurry to go.

'Your mother will be worried about you', says Zilpha. 'I'd better take you home.'

'I don't want to go home. I wish I could live with you here.'

Zilpha laughs. 'You'd find it very uncomfortable in this tiny house after Mr Carrington's large apartment. And in a few months there will be a baby as well.'

A baby! Alex is stunned, unable to visualise Zilpha with a baby. She feels sick with jealousy. 'You'll love the baby better than me!'

Zilpha regards her with a sad smile. 'Perhaps I will. It has to be like that. Your mother loves you best.'

'No, she doesn't!' Alex blurts out passionately. 'She doesn't love me or Giles. She only loves Mr Carrington.'

'Of course your mother loves you!'

Alex drinks the flavoured milk and struggles to eat the semolina cake on the good side of her mouth. Then Zilpha walks her back to within a few yards of Basil's apartment.

'Can I come and visit you again?' says Alex as Zilpha hugs her goodbye.

'Yes, but you must promise to ask your mother first.'

But Alex knows her mother would never let her walk down the Rue Georges Picot on her own.

Alex runs round the back of the apartment block and climbs up the fire escape to the kitchen. Georgette is peeling potatoes, and when the child knocks on the glass pane she barks 'Where have you been?'

The answer comes without hesitation. 'Playing ball in the garden.' Georgette grunts but asks no further questions.

Abby descends the ladder from the attic room, dressed only, to Alex's astonishment, in navy bloomers. Her pendulous brown breasts hang almost to her waist, and her thin grey hair straggles loose across her bony brown shoulders. Alex is shocked at her lack of inhibition. Zilpha would never have behaved so immodestly. She was always emphatic that undressing was a private matter.

'Mr Carrington might come and see you!' she gasps.

Abby laughs coarsely. 'What do I care? Let him see me.' She piles her loose flesh into a bust bodice, then pulls on a skirt and a crumpled blouse from the ironing basket. She twists her hair into the usual bun on the back of her head. Alex is half repelled, half fascinated, by Abby's ugliness and her daring.

When Sheena comes home from work Alex says she's been resting and that her tooth feels better. She's sorry she didn't manage to meet her mother at the hospital gate.

'It's getting much too cold and damp for you to hang about waiting. You'd better not come again until the spring', suggests her mother. So now Alex will be free to visit Zilpha after school, and when the Christmas vacation starts there will be even more opportunity.

Two days later after school Alex dashes down to Avenue Bliss, past the University gates and starts down Rue Georges Picot. She stops for breath and notes that a few feet ahead the pavement is being dug up. It's cordoned off with rope. She waits for three cars to swoop by and then crosses the road to walk on the right hand side. When she reaches the tram stop almost opposite Zilpha's lane she waits again while more cars whizz in both directions. A tram lumbers to a halt beside her, and for a moment it looks as though the road is clear of moving traffic. In her eagerness to reach her destination Alex runs out in front of the stationary tram without stopping, just as a Cadillac overtakes and swerves with a screech of brakes, barely avoiding hitting her. Swept off her feet, Alex tumbles hard onto the tarmac, breaking her glasses, grazing her face and hands and slightly gashing one of her knees. Several male passers-by gather round her as the driver of the Cadillac gets out of his car and crosses the road, cursing her furiously in Arabic. In fright Alex gets up, and one of the onlookers starts remonstrating with her.

The driver gets back into his car and the passers-by move on, leaving Alex alone on the pavement. A line of blood trickles down from her right knee onto her white sock. Tearful and humiliated, she waits until the road is completely clear, and then limps across and down the lane to Zilpha's house.

The shutters are tightly closed and her frantic knocking at the door brings no response. Refusing to believe there's nobody at home, she bangs her fists on the door until a woman standing on a nearby roof shouts, 'No good knocking. They've gone to visit relatives at Jounie. They'll be back on Sunday.'

Sunday! She could just as well have said next year. Alex begins to weep with disappointment and pain as she retraces her steps. Now it seems a long way and her legs are aching by the time she mounts the stairs to the apartment. Instead of Georgette it's Sheena who opens the door. She takes in the bleeding knees and the broken glasses in her daughter's hand.

'My God, what's happened to you?'

'I went for a walk and fell over.'

'Where did you go for a walk?'

'Down Avenue Bliss.'

'But you know you're meant to come straight home if you're not playing at Annabel's house.'

'Why can't I go for a walk?'

Sheena takes Alex up to the bathroom to clean up. She paints iodine on the gashed knee before putting on lint and a large square of plaster.

'You'd better get your spare glasses. These will have to go to the optician's. And if you want to go for a walk', says Sheena, 'Georgette can take you to the University campus once a week.' Alex is horrified. The last thing she wants is a weekly walk with Georgette.

However, Sheena is determined on the idea of a walk. Her daughter needs more fresh air and exercise, she spends too much time playing indoors. She would have a better appetite after a brisk walk. So the next day when Alex returns from school, Georgette announces sharply, 'Your mother says I must take you for a walk.' She pulls off her apron and picks up a large basket with a napkin over its contents. Alex wants to refuse, but Georgette's tone frightens her. She follows the maid downstairs, but it soon becomes obvious they're not bound for the University campus.

'Where are we going?' demands Alex.

'To visit my family in Ras Beirut.' She takes the child's hand firmly and pulls her along at a fast pace. Alex is outraged that Georgette isn't following Sheena's instructions. At the same time she's curious to see the maid's house and family.

They quickly move out of the leafy residential area of Ain el Mreisse into drab dusty streets of rutted asphalt between blocks of hideous concrete tenements where lines of washing flutter from every narrow balcony. They cut through a small garden enclosed by stern iron railings on which a notice in French reads *Jardin Publique.* Miniature palms and cypresses together with mimosa and heliotrope are struggling to grow out of the hard dun-coloured ground. A garden seat with peeling green paint under a layer of grey dust hardly invites one to sit down. It is the ugliest garden Alex has ever seen.

They cross a very wide road called *Rue Madame Curie.* 'Who's Madame Curie?' asks Alex, and isn't surprised when Georgette snaps 'How should I know?' They walk beside a high faded yellow wall and then turn down a track with an evil-smelling gutter running down the middle. On each side are squalid wooden shacks with corrugated iron roofs. In a yard two elderly men are sitting beside a stinking oil stove playing *shesh-besh* – backgammon. The stench of decaying matter rises from piles of garbage and pools of stagnant water. Two pye-dogs are fighting over what might be a dead rat. Alex shudders.

Suddenly out of the door of one of the shacks runs a young girl in a ragged dress, shrieking wildly. She is pursued and caught and held by a large bearded man who proceeds to whack her with a leather belt. Georgette stops to watch, and in a few seconds a group of women gather, chattering excitedly to one another but making no attempt to intervene.

This first witnessing of physical cruelty to a human being is painful in the extreme to Alex. Her heart begins to pound. This is even worse than the dentist. With horror she sees blood running down the girl's back, staining her skimpy cotton garment. Her agonised high pitched shriek splits Alex's mind in two.

'Tell him to stop!' she bursts out. But Georgette only pulls her away and hurries on down the track. Alex shouts 'Why didn't you help the girl?'

'Don't be stupid! It's none of our business. Her father beats her because she's bad.'

'What's she done?'

'She didn't tell me', sneers Georgette. Alex lags behind the maid, still hearing the cries in her mind.

They reach an ugly block of flats six storeys high, and Georgette says, with a threat in her voice, 'This is where my family lives. If you sit quiet and promise to say nothing to your mother about coming here, I'll buy you some k'ak bsim-bsum on the way home.' Alex is somewhat mollified by this offer. She's been longing to try these sesame rings fried in a mixture of thyme and sumac which look like crisp doughnuts and smell so tantalising.

The stairs up to the fifth floor are chipped and lacking a banister. There are dark stains on the clay-coloured walls and the stench of urine and orange peel pervades. The door is opened by a harassed looking woman who resembles Georgette. Alex is surprised to see the maid kissing her mother on both cheeks. She'd not judged the girl capable of affection.

Alex sits on a horsehair sofa and surveys the dismally poor surroundings. The concrete floor is bare of any kind of covering, a naked electric bulb hangs from the cracked ceiling and three tattered paper carnations in a dirty glass jar stand on a table. An old woman swathed in thick black clothes huddles at the other end of the sofa. She leans towards Alex and prods her arm, muttering incomprehensible words. A door opens and three young girls tumble into the room and rush at Georgette to see what she's brought in her basket. The maid takes out packets of food – cheese, fruit and cakes, even a bowl of cooked rice. The children grab the cakes and start cramming them into their mouths.

Alex watches, feeling uneasy, guilty and revolted. The girl being beaten so harshly, and these starving sisters of Georgette all engender contradictory feelings in her – a choking, stifling pity, together with a desperate longing to escape for ever from the crude and cruel reality of these lives.

A young woman comes into the flat carrying a child. Alex can't tell whether it's a boy or a girl. She puts it down and it crawls across the floor, then pulls itself up and attempts to walk, encouraged by its mother. Everyone claps and kisses it, even Georgette. Soon the girls are squabbling – or maybe it's simply their way of communicating. Someone is spooning rice between the old woman's toothless gums. Alex wants to visit the toilet and is shown into a space no bigger than a cupboard. The toilet has no seat and the chain won't pull. A sheaf of newspaper is threaded onto a rusty wire attached to a nail in the wall.

It's drizzling when they set off for home. Passing the shacks Alex wonders what the poor beaten girl is doing now. Perhaps she's dying. When they arrive home and begin to climb the stairs, Georgette stops and grips Alex's arm hard. 'Remember', she hisses, 'You're not to tell your mother where you've been today or something very bad will happen to you. D'you understand?'

Georgette's fingers press so painfully into her thin arm that Alex promises not to tell.

'You didn't buy me any k'ak bsim-bsum.'

'Maybe next time, when it isn't raining. Just remember, you've been for a walk to the campus.'

Chapter Twenty-three

Only two weeks to Christmas and yet a gloom seems to hang over everyone. Even Mrs Kellaway is not her usual cheerful self. As the children make cards and decorations at school she tells them the news is bad. In spite of America joining the allies there's no end of the war in sight. They must remember that Christmas isn't going to be any fun for the soldiers and airmen and sailors. America will certainly win the war, she says, but in the meantime a great many men will die. The children are so lucky not to be suffering hardship in Beirut.

It rains heavily most days and in the school cloakroom stand four pairs of galoshes – three black pairs belonging to Bobbie, Jake and Alex, and a neat little scarlet pair which are Annabel's. They are the only pupils in Grade Two who live near enough to walk to school.

One afternoon Bobbie walks part of the way home with Alex in silence, kicking up the water in the puddles. When he leaves her, he grins and says 'So long, see you tomorrow.' She feels nervous with Bobbie. Annabel is always telling her he's rough and rude and dirty and hasn't any brains. He often sticks his tongue out at Annabel behind her back. He and Jake are slow at reading but they know everything there is to know about fighter planes. Their conversation is full of Mustangs, Messerschmitts, Super-Fortresses, Liberators and Lightnings. They can look up at a speck in the sky and say exactly what kind of plane it is.

Sheena doesn't ask Alex about her walks with Georgette. Her hospital work and various other commitments occupy all her thoughts. The second time the maid takes Alex to her family home she tips soap, talcum powder, toilet rolls, lipsticks, hankies and a box of starch onto the table from her basket. Alex is in two minds about these items pinched from Basil's apartment. Zilpha would never have stolen in any circumstances. If Georgette had been a pleasant, kind person, the child could more easily have condoned her taking things to give to her poverty-stricken family. But Georgette is hard and unpleasant, and self-righteously Alex condemns her as a thief.

On this occasion Georgette quarrels with one of her young sisters and ends by slapping her across the face. Alex watches the girl's cheek go white and then dark red but she doesn't cry. The females are all frightened of Georgette as well as being dependent on her. There seem to be no men in the family. After observing the maid in action within her own family, Alex knows she will never dare tell tales to Sheena. On the way home she does venture to accuse Georgette of pinching her mother's lipsticks, but Georgette laughs jeeringly. 'Mr Carrington will buy her some more. He'll buy her anything.'

Alex's first term ends a week before Christmas with a party in the classroom. Every pupil brings a plate of food and Mrs Kellaway provides lemonade. Abby grumbles at having to bake cookies for Alex. There's too much cooking to be done at this time of year. Once vacation commences during the cold grey days of December, Alex is so bored it almost feels like being ill. Sheena says she mustn't hang round Abby, but Alex can't help being drawn towards the cook who, in spite of her sharp tongue, is kindly and tolerant at heart. When Georgette is with Abby they talk in Arabic, often mentioning American names and laughing crudely. The maid will say 'Shush!' to Abby when she realises Alex is trying to pick up what they're saying.

'Why don't you speak in English?' asks Alex.

'Because, darling, we're talking about sex and rude things little girls mustn't know about.'

Involuntarily Alex's thoughts travel back to Philippe. He wanted the children at the party to participate in 'rude' things. Surely this isn't what Abby and Georgette are discussing. Or perhaps it is. She finds it an uncomfortable mystery.

When Georgette is out of the room Abby seems to be a nicer person, with a genuine love of children. Most of all, she loves telling Alex about Sally-Ann. 'Mr and Mrs Carrington adored that girl; she could do no wrong. She was spoilt, of course, but kept her sweet nature. On her last birthday in Beirut her mother gave a party at the St Simon beach. In those days, before the war, there were lots of

American children living here. Mr Carrington hired a small truck and took about twenty kids and all the food to the beach, even buckets of ice cream. Sally-Ann was only nine, but already the boys were after her, trying to kiss her behind the sand dunes. My, she was a lovely girl!'

Alex is sure she wouldn't like Sally-Ann.

When Abby isn't rhapsodising about Sally-Ann she will sometimes describe her own childhood with four sisters and two brothers. 'My family are not Lebanese, we are Armenians from Turkey.'

'Why did you come to Lebanon?' asks Alex.

'We didn't want to come. We were forced to leave Kharput, where we lived. During the last war the Turks massacred one million of us Armenians. Some were killed in Turkey, the rest were killed or died on the forced marches.'

Alex is shocked. 'Why did they kill the Armenians?'

'Because we are cleverer than they are, because we work hard – and because we are Christians. My family were forced to leave in July 1915, when I was fourteen. I was the only one of the family left alive when we reached Aleppo in Syria. And that wasn't the first massacre. They tried to exterminate us before that. When I was only twelve I was made to watch my brother of seventeen being hanged by the Turks. These Jews think they are the only ones being massacred, that the Nazis are the most terrible monsters the world has seen. They should have been in Armenia during the last war to see evil at its worst!'

Alex stares at Abby with new eyes in fascinated horror, aware that the cook is relating experiences which Giles and Sheena wouldn't dream of telling a child.

'Oh, yes', continues Abby, 'Many were hanged or shot – some were beheaded.'

Hanged! Beheaded! Such barbarities surely belong only to long-ago history. Giles has told her that in Britain murderers are sometimes hanged in prison, but he's against it. To Alex such cruelty is inconceivable.

'Was your brother hanged in prison?'

'No, darling, he was hanged in the street, and left there to rot. My mother went mad. She never spoke another word from that day. I had to take care of my sisters.'

Alex is distressed to see tears in Abby's eyes. It's beyond the child's imagination to visualise such a hideous event. From that moment Abby ceases to be merely Basil's cook. She becomes a heroine who's brought Alex into contact with the blood-chilling experiences of thousands of real people. Amazing that Abby has actually seen innocent people being hanged, and has yet survived to joke and laugh and enjoy her food.

'People shouldn't kill each other', Alex ventures feebly.

Abby snorts. 'You'll soon learn that the story of the world is the story of killing.'

'Are all Turks wicked?'

'All the Turks are Muslims and all Muslims are wicked devils', Abby declares firmly. Alex thinks of Mustapha at K3 and decides that what Abby says about Muslims isn't entirely true.

Two days before Christmas an enormous fir tree is delivered and set up next to the staircase in the lounge. Alex begs to be allowed to help decorate it but Sheena says no, Basil doesn't want any of his beautiful decorations to get broken.

'When will Giles arrive?' Alex keeps asking.

'Early Christmas morning.'

The child wanders round the apartment in a haze of happiness, trying to picture her father's face, planning what to tell him. She wants to buy him a present, but Sheena says the nice card she made at school will be quite enough. But it's not enough. Alex wants to wrap up a whole pile of presents for him and for her mother, tied up with pretty red ribbon.

'Why can't Giles come on Christmas Eve?'

'Because Basil always gives a big party on Christmas Eve.'

239

Alex is disappointed, knowing she'll be sent upstairs early instead of joining in the excitement of the last minute preparations.

'Can't Giles come to the party?'

'He doesn't want to come. He doesn't know any of the guests.'

'He could come and stay upstairs with me', Alex protests.

'Don't be silly, darling, of course he can't. You've got to go to sleep, otherwise Santa Claus won't fill your stocking.'

'How does Santa Claus know I'm in Beirut and not at K3?'

'Santa Claus knows everything.'

'Does he know as much as God?'

'I expect so.'

It's an uncomfortable idea to think that God and Santa Claus are watching her all the time. Alex would prefer her thoughts to be private, and the more she tries to think good thoughts suitable for God's inspection, the harder it is to stop her mind being filled with bad and guilty thoughts. Zilpha used to say feeling guilty is a good thing because it means you're sorry for being bad. Sometimes Alex feels guilty for not being sorry that she's bad. It becomes very complicated.

On Christmas Eve Basil finishes work at lunchtime, and after a short rest he decorates the tree. He has to use a step ladder, and allows Alex to hand him up the shiny balls and bells and tinsel. Several of Basil's records in brown cardboard covers are lying on the carpet. He comes down the ladder and shows Alex how to put on a record of the ballet, *Swan Lake,* placing the heavy needle carefully so as not to damage the disc. She's enraptured by the music, the flood of sensuous rhythmic sound. But the record is over almost as soon as it's begun. She's allowed to put on the second side, but then Basil says that's enough music for today.

Later in bed Alex can't stop thinking about the ballet music. If only she could have a gramophone of her own in the bedroom and listen to it all day! If only Mr Carrington would allow her to play his records whenever she liked! But Sheena has warned her never to touch Basil's record collection. He hates anyone handling them, they get scratched so easily.

It's impossible to sleep. The party starts downstairs and she recognises some of the Basil's familiar dance tunes – *Pretty Lady Waltz, Smoke Gets in Your Eyes, Sentimental Journey...* After two hours of wakefulness she creeps down to the sliding door and opens it a couple of inches. She can see the crowd of animated grownups dancing and drinking and talking so loudly she can hardly hear the music. It's too chilly to watch for long so she returns to bed. resolving to stay awake until Santa Claus arrives. Eventually the hall clock strikes three. Surely he'll come soon.

The sound of water running in the bathroom indicates that Basil and Sheena are at last on their way to bed. A moment later her door opens very slowly and Alex holds her breath. A shape enters, carrying something which crackles. Her heart seems to miss a beat as she strains to see Santa Claus from under the bedclothes, not daring to move a muscle in case he should decide to go away without filling her stocking. Her toe feels something heavy being laid on the bed. Then the shape retreats hurriedly from the room. A light goes on in the hall and Alex hears a giggle outside the door, and her mother's voice saying in a loud whisper 'Did you pick up the empty stocking?'

Someone comes back into the room, and in the shaft of light from the hall she recognises Basil. Once again he goes out and this time shuts the door. More giggles and then all is quiet.

Alex is outraged that Santa Claus has turned out to be Mr Carrington. Surely it couldn't have been him; and yet it looked like him. She will be much too shy to question him

241

at breakfast. But Giles will be able to tell her. She's almost reluctant to get up and examine the stocking, half hoping that the real Santa Claus may yet arrive.

When the door bell goes at nine o'clock Basil and Sheena are still in bed, and Abby and Georgette have left to visit their own families. Alex runs to open the door to her father, who looks unfamiliar in flannels and a tweed jacket. He's carrying a large parcel under one arm, and a basket covered with a cloth under the other. For the first time Alex feels a certain reserve, not knowing what to say and yet longing to say everything at once. He follows her into the lounge and puts down the parcel and the basket. Georgette has cleared away the dirty glasses but the air is stuffy and the smell of stale tobacco and alcohol lingers. Outside, the sky is overcast. Alex switches on the electric fire and the Christmas tree lights, and suddenly the room looks festive.

'Santa Claus didn't come to fill my stocking. It was Mr Carrington!' Alex tells her father indignantly.

'So you've found out at last!'

'Why didn't Santa Claus come?'

'Because I'm afraid Santa Claus isn't a real person. It's just a fairy tale we all believe in as small children and then grow out of.'

Discovering Santa Claus is a fairy tale comes as a blow but Basil taking his place is worse.

Then Alex becomes aware that something alive is moving about in the basket Giles has placed on the floor. He removes the cover and a chestnut brown puppy, not much bigger than a man's fist, with a shiny black snub nose, climbs out, stretches its legs and makes a tiny puddle on the carpet.

'Quick, fetch a cloth from the kitchen', says Giles. He scrubs away at the wet patch while Alex, laughing with delight, kneels down and gathers the dazed animal into her arms.

'It's your Christmas present', says Giles, 'If Basil will allow you to keep her here. You're going to have to house-train her for a few weeks, which means taking her out into the garden or onto the balcony at regular intervals, starting early in the morning.'

'What kind of dog is it?'

'It's a miniature dachshund.' The tiny creature has settled itself in her arms. Every other gift she's ever received, even the dolls' house, pales into insignificance compared to this one.

'Sheena will say I can't keep it!'

'It's a big responsibility, looking after a dog. You'll have to prove that you're prepared to train and feed it and clear up any mess it makes and stop it chewing things like slippers. I shall have to persuade your mother you're sensible enough to do all that. And of course, while you're at school one of the servants must be willing to help.'

'What's the puppy's name?' asks Alex.

'A man in Baghdad who's writing a book about Egyptian history sold her to me. He called each of the four pups in the litter after an Egyptian king or queen. Hatshepsut is this one's name, Hatty for short. But if you don't like it you can choose another name.' But Alex likes the idea of an Egyptian queen, and they agree to keep the name Hatty. Fortunately Basil finds Hatty very cute, and says he'll bribe Abby and Georgette to help train her while Alex is at school.

'What about food?' asks Sheena.

'For a while she'll need scrambled egg, baby porridge and milk. Later she'll go on to minced meat and rice and vegetables and cod liver oil.'

It's an unusual but exciting day for Alex. Basil opens bottles of champagne and they eat cold turkey and salad and trifle left over from the party at lunch.

From time to time Giles and Alex carry the pup down to the garden and stand around in the cold waiting for her to perform. At six Abby and Georgette return. The maid makes it clear she dislikes dogs. But Abby is enthralled with the dachshund and promises to help look after her.

Suddenly it's bedtime again, and Giles brings the pup upstairs in her basket. He watches his daughter unwrap the large parcel of books he has brought her. 'They're not new, I'm afraid. A lady in Kirkuk gave them to me. Some of them might not be suitable until you're older.' But Alex is delighted. Now there are books to read she won't be bored at home. She lays them out on the bed: *Treasure Island, What Katy Did, Little Women, Peacock Pie, Bambi, The Railway Children, The Secret Garden...* The books are old and shabby, but the titles look promising.

Sheena comes into the room and sits on the bed. Suddenly it seems they are a family again. The child recounts to her father how they met Zilpha on the tram. 'She asked me to be her bridesmaid but Sheena wouldn't let me', says Alex reproachfully.

'Alex must understand that Zilpha has a new life and we can't be part of it. It's better to make a clean break.'

'Maybe you're right', agrees Giles.

'How's life in Kirkuk?' asks Sheena.

'As you can imagine, it gets tedious living alone in a tiny flat. Apart from drinking at the club and watching the odd film, there's very little to do in the evenings. I read a great deal.'

'It sounds dreadful.'

'How's your job?'

'Interesting, but damned hard work. The wards are overflowing and we're trying to train Lebanese nurses in months rather than years.'

'Are you satisfied with Alex's school?'

'She likes it, but I suspect they don't work the kids very hard. Instead of proper lessons they seem to do what the teacher feels like teaching.'

'We do have proper lessons!' protests Alex. 'Mrs Kellaway is teaching us about the Civil War in the States and I can draw a map of America.'

'So you're happy, then, in Beirut?' says Giles at last.

'Yes, very happy', replies Sheena, and gets up abruptly. 'I must go down now. Some friends are dropping in for a drink.'

'What, on Christmas Day!' Giles says in annoyance.

'We had friends in on Christmas Day at K3. Anyway, we've said all there is to say.'

Sheena bends over and kisses Alex lightly on the cheek. Then she goes, leaving a strong whiff of perfume in the air.

'Are you going to sleep in the guest room?' asks Alex.

'No, I'm staying in a nearby pension run by a very nice Lebanese lady.'

Alex is amazed. 'Why can't you sleep here?'

'You'll understand when you're older.'

'Aren't you married to Sheena any more?'

'Yes, of course I am. But in wartime life is often disrupted. It will all work out once the war is over.' But how will it work out? She hates the uncertainty.

Giles picks up Hatty and takes her onto the balcony. After some time he returns and says, 'Don't forget to put her out the minute you wake up.' As soon as her father has gone Alex lifts Hatty onto her bed and the pup curls up in her arms. At dawn it's drizzling and Hatty stands shivering outside, refusing to oblige. Back in the bedroom she immediately wets the carpet. Alex hurries to the bathroom and seizes the nearest flannel.

On Boxing Day Abby and Georgette are given the whole day off. Basil and Sheena go out to lunch, and Giles cooks bacon and eggs for Alex and himself. The rain eventually ceases and a little watery sunshine appears, creating a great double rainbow in vivid arcs of orange, magenta, apple green and violet. It's the first rainbow Alex has ever seen.

At K3 Boxing Day was a holiday for everyone. Not so in Beirut. The trams are running as usual and the shops are open. Giles suggests they visit the bookshops in Hamra Street and in Avenue des Français. It sounds a good idea, but in the event it turns out a disappointment for Alex. Nearly all the books are in French and they don't look like genuine books. They resemble thick pamphlets bound in grey or buff-coloured paper covers, and some have uncut pages. They don't have the lovely smell of a new book. They search in three bookshops but find nothing of interest to Alex. However, her father does buy her a large box of Caran d'Ache, the best coloured pencils. Before returning home he wants to visit the National Archaeological Museum. She might have guessed her father would be bound to find a church or a castle or a museum to look at. The very name, *National Archaeological Museum*, sounds forbidding.

The neo-classical building is vast and gloomy, particularly the dingy basement full of cold statues and sarcophagi. On the ground floor are endless displays of weapons, mosaics and pottery standing on plinths or in glass cases. To Alex all the objects seem lifeless and uninteresting. She sits on a step with Hatty while her father reads the inscriptions beside the exhibits. He tells her that the name, *Beirut,* possibly derives from the Phoenician *Beroth,* City of Wells of Sweet Water. 'And it's interesting to know that the emperor Alexander Severus came from Lebanon and founded a school of law at Beirut.'

But Alex isn't listening. They step out into the wintry sunshine again, and Giles takes her to *Le Crémier* for an ice cream as a reward for being patient.

Chapter Twenty-four

Having a dog to care for softens the usual misery of her father's departure, and the rest of the vacation is occupied almost entirely with looking after Hatty – taking her down to the garden, cajoling her to eat, and making sure she doesn't chew the rugs. Even so, Alex needs more diversion, and one afternoon she goes down to the lounge in search of inspiration.

For a while she amuses herself picking out tunes with one finger on the grand piano, songs she's learnt at school. Then she stands on the leather sofa and sings all the verses of *Clementine,* which her father taught her at K3, drawing out the final refrain with such sadness that tears come into her eyes. She has a great longing for music, for movement, for some means of expressing all that she feels. Perhaps she will risk playing a record. Why not? She knows how to handle the gramophone. Abby is having her usual afternoon nap and Georgette is in her room. With mounting excitement she opens the polished cabinet and pulls out the *Swan Lake* records. It's hard work winding up the handle, but soon the room is filled with the ravishing music. Spontaneously Alex starts to dance, leaping lightly on and off the chairs and sofas with flowing repetitive movements.

All too soon the record comes to an end and she has to wind up the gramophone again. She's about to play the third record when Georgette appears and says she shouldn't be touching the gramophone. In frustration Alex finds herself protesting that Mr Carrington said she could use it. The maid gives her a suspicious look and walks out. It's becoming obvious to Alex that to tell a lie is the only way of keeping out of trouble. Will Georgette tell tales on her? Possibly not, since Alex herself has kept silent about the visits to the maid's family.

Now she has discovered the exhilaration of ballet music, the temptation to put on the records is too great to resist. During the next three days she works her way through other ballets, but *Swan Lake* remains her favourite. She makes up a fairy story to fit the music and begins to co-ordinate her movements. But her luck is too good to last. One afternoon as she's winding up the gramophone Basil appears. Alex leaps away from the instrument in guilty fright as he says acidly, 'Alex, I didn't give you permission to play my records.' He puts *Swan Lake* away and shuts down the lid of the gramophone firmly.

'If you'd waited until the weekend I would have played the records for you. You must learn to do as you're told.' He reprimands her calmly but Alex can feel his suppressed anger. She slinks off upstairs, embarrassed and disappointed. Dancing to the records has become a passion and she can think of no other pastime as interesting. The Christmas tree has been taken down and Sheena is irritable and preoccupied with news of the war in the Far East. Now the bulletins are concerned more with Malaya and Singapore than North Africa. Basil says the Japs are having it all their own way in the Pacific and he doubts Singapore will be able to hold out.

It's a relief when school begins again. The new term starts with an assembly in the hall. The superintendent begins with the traditional solemn words, 'In the year of our Lord one thousand, nine hundred and forty-two, and of the Independence of the United States the one hundred and sixty-sixth, I ask you all to remember the soldiers, sailors and airmen who are suffering for the cause of our freedom...' By the time Miss Carter has finished her address Alex feels very proud and very American.

In the classroom Mrs Kellaway draws a sketch map of the Far East on the blackboard to show the children how close Japan is to the States. Jake whispers to Alex that the Japs are cannibals and eat their prisoners of war. He's glad he hasn't got a father who might have had to fight the Japs.

'My father isn't fighting', says Bobbie. 'Doctors are too important to be soldiers.'

'Don't be silly', scoffs Annabel, 'There are lots of doctors in the forces.'

Mrs Kellaway reads poems by American poets to her grade. She has a pleasant, sonorous voice, and knows how to make the most of dramatic or amusing poems. Annabel and Alex are enthralled by her rendering of Edgar Allan Poe's *Annabel Lee.* The teacher asks Alex if she's read any British poems. She brings Walter de la Mare's *Peacock Pie* to school, and Mrs Kellaway reads some of the book to her pupils. Bobbie and Jake spoil the lesson by sniggering at these charming verses. But Mrs Kellaway is not daunted. 'Will anyone recite a poem to us?' she asks, and Alex offers to recite some of *Hiawatha.* Amazed at her own temerity she finds herself standing up in front of the grade. The lines come easily at first, but suddenly she catches sight of all the faces riveted on her and takes fright. Her memory fails and she stands awkward and silent. Mrs Kellaway starts to clap and all the children join her.

'That was good – very good indeed – and very brave to be the first to do it.' She then suggests that each child should learn a poem to recite, however short. Even Bobbie, who regards all poetry as 'sissy' is persuaded to try. He manages to memorise a limerick, and when his turn comes he delivers it in a rush, blushing to the roots of his platinum hair.

Mrs Kellaway starts reading aloud a chapter or two a day of *Anne of Green Gables,* a novel set in Prince Edward Island.

'Can anyone tell me where Prince Edward Island is?' Annabel and Alex shoot up their hands simultaneously. They admire the confident and clever brave young heroine.

'D'you think I'm rather like Anne Shirley?' asks Annabel.

'Oh, yes!', says Alex.

Alex is now in the habit of going to play at the Hitti's every Saturday. For the rest of January it rains heavily and the girls spend their time indoors, dressing up and acting stories in which Annabel plays the beautiful princess and the good fairy while Alex plays all the wicked, ugly roles, which she's realised are much the most interesting to act. When they aren't dressing up Annabel likes to play board games or to sit and discuss the other girls in the grade, listing them in order of preference. The boys are ignored. Dirty, rude and stupid continues to be Annabel's opinion of boys. But secretly Alex thinks the boys have more fun than the girls. At the moment Bobbie and Jake are in competition with one another as to who can climb the most trees on the University campus. Alex suggests she and Annabel might try climbing a tree in the garden, but her friend says no, it would be dangerous.

In February the rain stops at last and there's a feeling of spring in the air. Alex hears her mother telling Basil in shocked tones that Singapore has fallen to the Japanese. Sheena is particularly upset by this news since she has friends in Singapore. 'What will happen to them?' she asks.

'They'll be put into a concentration camp', Basil tells her, 'And, knowing the Japs, they'll be starved and tortured.' Sheena notices her daughter standing at the door and gives Basil a warning look.

Alex imagines a cold, dank dungeon and a diet of bread and water. 'Are there any kind Japs?' she asks. 'I doubt it', replies Sheena bitterly.

Much to her surprise as Alex is walking home from school one afternoon, Bobbie and Jake catch up with her, asking whether she'd like to join them in a secret adventure. Flattered at being asked, Alex agrees without considering what she might be letting herself in for. 'How long will it take?'

'Not long.'

'I'm meant to go straight home after school.'

'Well, don't come if you're afraid.'

Alex dreads being thought a sissy. It might be worth risking trouble in order to take part in an adventure with the boys.

'Come on, we know a short cut to Avenue Bliss.' They start running and Alex follows them down an alleyway leading to the wide main road with the campus on one side and a series of small shops on the other.

Bobbie and Jake stop outside a shop selling cigarettes and confectionery.

'Got any piastres?' Jake asks Alex.

'No.'

'Well, take these, and when we go inside ask for a hundred grammes of peppermints. The old lady in there speaks English.' Alex has never bought anything in a shop before, but the boys don't give her a chance to hesitate. 'Go on, she won't bite you!' urges Bobbie.

She enters the dark little shop followed by the boys. Behind the counter rise shelves filled with large jars of sticky sweets. Boxes of chocolates and candy and chocolate bars are displayed on a shelf opposite the counter. A tiny wizened old woman in black gets up from a chair and peers at Alex short-sightedly.

'I want some peppermints, please – a hundred grammes.'

The woman has to climb onto her chair to reach the jar of peppermints. Behind Alex the boys seem to be looking round the shop. When the sweets have been weighed and slipped into a twist of paper Alex puts her coins on the counter and watches them being scooped up into the wrinkled brown hand.

The children leave the shop and cross the road. Alex hands the peppermints to Bobbie. 'Why did you want me to buy them for you?'

He grins. 'You'll see. Come on, let's go to my house.'

'How far is it?'

'It's on the campus. Only a few minutes.'

Alex knows she should return home but curiosity overcomes her anxiety.

The Carsons live in a square white house with emerald green shutters and a bright red roof set amongst trees on a slope overlooking the sea – a beautiful site that fills Alex with envy. Bobbie leads them down to a grassy promontory at the bottom of the terraced garden. They sit in a row on a damp wooden seat. From the pockets of their shorts the boys produce between them three Kit-Kat bars and three bars of Cadbury's milk chocolate.

Alex is amazed. 'When did you buy them?'

'We pinched them while you were buying the peppermints.'

'That's stealing!'

'What if it is? The chocolate in that shop is old stock from before the war. The old woman will never sell it so we might as well take it.' Jake puts a bar into Alex's hand. The boys start eating, and she can't resist joining them. The Kit Kat tastes musty but none the less delicious. The fact that it's stolen adds to the pleasure.

'Do you often pinch sweets?' Alex enquires with a mixture of admiration and disapproval.

'Quite often', admits Bobbie.

'Does your mother know?'

Bobbie doubles up with laughter. 'Of course not! It's our secret, and you must never tell anyone, not even Annabel. Annabel would go and tell Mrs Kellaway because she's a sneak.'

'She's not!'

'Yes, she is, she's sneaked on me before!' insists Bobbie.

The boys escort Alex to the campus gate and watch her cross the road. 'Ask your mother if you can come to our house after school tomorrow', Bobbie shouts after her. She walks home with a glow of pride mixed with guilt at having been chosen to be the boys' companion in petty crime.

Sheena is pleased that her daughter's made friends with Bobbie Carson and agrees to allow her to walk to his house after school. Mrs Carson is a pleasant, homely woman whose main task seems to lie in dispensing home made cookies and lemonade to her son and his friends. Bobbie has an eighteen year old sister, Karen-Sue, who's studying at the University. Whenever he brings his friends to the house she picks up her books and retires to her room.

'Karen-Sue has to work all the time because she's so dumb', chants her brother loudly. 'She's just flunked her first exam.' Alex feels sorry for Karen-Sue.

During Alex's first visit Dr. Carson comes into the house through the back door and says hello to the children in the kitchen. When he goes into the hall Alex hears him say to his wife, 'Is that the Kinley kid?'

'Yes.'

'She's nothing like her mother. Sheena Kinley's a real stunner!'

'Bobbie says Alex is very clever at school.'

'Good. Let's hope she influences Bobbie to do some work.'

Bobbie escorts Alex all over the University campus, along the cinder paths, showing it off as though he owned the place. 'That's the main building', he says, pointing to the imposing columns, the clock tower, the walls covered with pink and red creepers, the neat flower beds just coming into bloom with azaleas. Alex has already discovered that Bobbie is always on the lookout for mischief, often teasing and playing tricks on people. Alex likes him because he makes her laugh and he's good-natured.

One afternoon he and Jake take her into the University museum to look at the stuffed whale and the gigantic model of a dinosaur until they're chased out by the curator. Then they hang around the back entrance to the medical school close to the Carson's house, in the hope, Bobbie tells her, of seeing a corpse. He regales Alex with the gruesome details of dissection, assuring her that the bodies are dug up at dead of night from the local graveyard.

'If we watch this door we might see them bring a dead body in or out.' She lies hidden in the shrubbery with Bobby and Jake, waiting in fearful anticipation in case Bobbie is telling the truth for once. Presently they see two men in white coats wheeling a hospital trolley out of a side door. Under a white sheet lies a body, covered except for the feet. To the children's surprise the men park the trolley alongside the wall and disappear back into the building.

'There you are!' whispers Bobbie triumphantly. 'Didn't I tell you? That's a corpse under there which they're going to dissect.'

'Is it really dead?' asks Alex in awe.

'Of course it's dead. Lift the sheet and you'll see its dead face.'

A chill overtakes Alex. She has a feeling that if she were to look under the sheet she might see the eyeless face of the dead djinn.

'I dare you to touch its feet', Bobbie says to Jake.

'I will if you do it first', replies his friend.

Bobbie dashes towards the trolley, puts out his hand and briefly tickles one of the waxen yellow feet. Alex half expects the corpse to sit up in annoyance, but it lies motionless, quite dead. Jake follows Bobbie's example and then it's Alex's turn. She moves slowly, terrified that someone will appear and yet hoping they will.

'Go on, just give its foot a tickle', urges Bobbie. Her index finger barely touches one of the feet when Jake hisses 'Quick! Someone's coming!' She darts back into the shrubbery and then the children race away with pounding hearts and collapse on the grass outside Bobbie's house. Here they roll about with relief, giggling helplessly.

'How about pinching more chocolate?' suggests Jake.

'OK.' agrees Bobbie, and they both look at Alex, who says hurriedly, 'I've got to go home now.' She suspects the boys have continued their shoplifting expeditions and instinct tells her that soon they'll get caught. She experiences a blurring of morality for the first time. There's a limit to the amount of danger she wishes to share with Bobbie and Jake.

Her fears prove to be well-founded, for the following morning Mrs Kellaway with a very grave expression asks Bobbie and Jake to go and see the superintendent. Alex expects to be summoned at any minute, but nothing happens. The boys don't return, and at recess Annabel says smugly, 'I bet they've been expelled.'

'What for?'

'They've done something dreadful. I'm not allowed to tell', she whispers. Does Annabel know about the shoplifting, or is she just pretending? Alex's mind is in confusion between her loyalty to Annabel the ideal, and Bobbie the rogue. Bobbie turns up to school again the next day with his usual grin and an added air of bravado. Alex is grateful that the boys haven't implicated her, and she wants to know what's happened to them. But they ignore her, and Bobbie stops asking her to his house.

Sheena's birthday falls on the third Saturday in February, and Alex is anxious to buy her a present. But how to do it, since she doesn't receive pocket money? She rehearses in her mind asking Basil to give her some money and suggest what she might buy. But the days pass, and still she can't bring herself to mention the subject. At K3 Alex had accepted her mother's view that there's no point in a child giving presents to a parent. But now at school she's discovered that all the children in her grade buy Christmas and birthday presents for their parents. During his last visit her father had mentioned that it was high time Alex learnt how to use money, but Sheena disagreed. 'I don't want her handling this filthy local money. Besides, we buy her everything she needs.'

When Alex comes down to breakfast on her mother's birthday she's mortified to see that Basil has placed two beautifully wrapped parcels by Sheena's plate while she herself has only a home-made card to offer. Her mother drools over the card and kisses her, but this only accentuates the feeling that she's being treated as a baby. Basil's presents consist of a diamond brooch and a silk stole. Alex looks on with misery, jealous that Basil is able to bring Sheena such delight. Later in the day a parcel is delivered from Giles – a soft Gabistan rug similar to the one he bought with Alex in Kirkuk.

After lunch Sheena changes into what she calls an afternoon frock which matches her new silk stole. Basil is taking her to a tea dance at the Phoenicia Hotel. Alex has been asked to join them, but she doesn't relish the thought of sitting in a ballroom watching her mother dance yet again with Basil. It's a relief when Mrs Hitti rings to ask if she may come to tea with Annabel.

During her afternoon with the Hittis Alex doesn't mention her mother's birthday. They would be amazed that she hasn't been able to give her mother a present, or had a family birthday tea. Alex can't face the idea of Annabel's pitying contempt.

Chapter Twenty-five

In March, during the delicious days of early spring, Ain Mreisse appears to be buried in a foam of apricot and orange blossom. The sun is warm on Alex's back as she walks home from school. Mrs Kellaway takes her grade on nature walks in the university campus, and the children pick flowers to press in their exercise books. Bobbie and Jake hate these expeditions. The two boys are becoming harder for Mrs Kellaway to control. Yet Bobbie has such a winning smile and contrite manner that he's hardly ever punished for being lazy and disruptive.

The children are warned that a school photograph is to be taken. Everyone must come to school looking smart and tidy. Annabel turns up in a red tartan frock with a white piqué collar, wearing red shoes and a red bow in her hair. Bobbie has forgotten about the photograph.

'You look a real mess, Bobbie Carson!' scolds Annabel. 'You're going to spoil it.' But when the children each receive a copy to take home, Bobbie's seraphic smile makes up for his untidy appearance. Annabel and Alex are sitting in the front row holding hands – Annabel looking so pretty, and Alex so plain in comparison. But at least everyone can see Annabel is her best friend.

One warm afternoon Alex is taken aback when Bobbie, who's ignored her since the chocolate incident, approaches her and says, 'Do you want to come swimming with us?'

'When?'

'Now, of course.'

'I haven't had permission.'

Alex is flattered at being asked to join the boys again and agrees to go. They race down the alley leading to Avenue Bliss and cross the road to the campus.

'Where are we going to swim?'

'Off the rocks below the tennis courts.'

'Isn't it dangerous there?'

'Yes, but we've found a pool which is safe.'

'Does your mother know?'

'Of course not! She'd say it was much too dangerous.'

They leap down the many steps leading to the tennis courts, run along a path overlooking the baseball ground, descend more steps and then cross the busy coastal Rue de Paris. The deep green sea water whips treacherously against the rocks and retreats with an ominous sucking noise. Not an obvious place for swimming, but further along the coast the boys have discovered a small pool sheltered from the full force of the water by a curved finger of rock. To swim more than half a dozen strokes in any direction would be impossible, but it looks safe and invitingly cool. Bobbie and Jake discard their shirts and shorts immediately and slide carefully into the sea. Alex hesitates, shy of appearing in her pants.

'Come on, hurry up!' shouts Bobbie, splashing water at her. She slips out of her cotton frock and wraps her glasses in it. Then she lets herself gingerly into the cold water. She can feel the strong undercurrent trying to pull her beyond the safety of the enclosed pool, and she has to cling to the rocks. Bobbie shows off, pretending he's going to swim out to sea and then returning at the last minute. They sit on a rock drying themselves in the sun and watching the glistening spray leaping over the barrier into their pool.

Jake says threateningly, 'You've got to swear not to tell Annabel about this place.'

'Of course I won't.'

'You did tell her about us pinching chocolate.'

'I never did!' Alex insists vehemently, on the verge of tears.

'Then who was it?' demands Bobbie.

'Someone must have seen you in the shop.'

'OK, I believe you.'

Far out on the horizon they can just make out a grey ship. 'I guess that might be a German battleship', says Jake.

'Don't be an idiot', replies Bobbie. 'We wouldn't let a German ship get that close.'

The boys start talking about ships and planes. 'When I grow up', Jake boasts to Alex, 'I'm going to be a pilot in the US. Air Force and wear a uniform with stars and bars.'

'I'd rather be a paratrooper', says Bobbie, 'And get dropped behind the enemy lines like you see in the movies.'

Alex isn't interested in their conversation. She's wishing the boys liked Annabel. 'Do you go to church on Sunday?' she asks Bobbie suddenly.

'No, never.'

'Annabel does. She says it's fun.'

'She would! My father says Mrs Hitti's a boring do-gooder.'

'Why is it boring to do good?'

Bobbie hesitates and then evades the question. 'Mrs Hitti thinks she's better than anyone else, that's why.'

Secretly Alex wishes she could go to the American Mission Church with the Hittis. She knows Mrs Kellaway attends the same church.

The children dress and return to Bobbie's house where they find Karen-Sue sunbathing on the lawn amidst beds of blue alkanet flowers with white centres. Bobbie picks up a handful of gravel and sprinkles it over her back. She leaps to her feet in annoyance, but the children have already fled into the house.

As Alex's eighth birthday approaches Sheena asks, 'D'you want to have a birthday party?' For a moment the idea of a party sounds exciting. But then she shrinks from the idea. Her friends mustn't see her mother with Basil. Seeing her daughter's reluctance Sheena says, 'Would you prefer to have Annabel to tea and then we could take you to see *Snow White* at the cinema?'

'Will Mr Carrington come too?'

'No, he certainly won't want to see *Snow White*.'

She'd like to have asked Bobbie and Jake as well, but the boys only enjoy Tarzan films and they would annoy Annabel.

On April 29th Alex panics as she walks home from school with her friend. What will she think of Abby and Georgette? Will Sheena be nice to her? Will Basil appear and make some tactless remark? She needn't have worried. Annabel, looking charming in a new frock, chats without reserve to Sheena and to Abby. They are both entranced with her. Basil doesn't appear, and the film is the best they've ever seen. Annabel identifies herself with Snow White, and at school the next day imitates the Disney-American accent. The idea of a wicked stepmother intrigues her. 'Will I meet your stepfather the next time I come to visit you?' she asks Alex.

'I haven't got a stepfather.'

'Mom said Mr Carrington is your stepfather.'

Alex blushes with confusion. She hates to think of Mrs Hitti discussing Sheena's affairs. Divorce is something Alex knows nothing about. Annabel however continues to be intrigued by her friend's background. Changing husbands seems to her like changing your best friend.

As summer approaches Alex sees very little of her mother. Basil and Sheena go swimming or play golf every weekend while Alex spends Saturdays and Sunday afternoons with the Hitti family. On Saturdays Mrs Hitti piles the four children together with a picnic basket into her old Packard and drives to the St Simon beach beyond Pigeon Grotto. This is much more fun than going to the club. After swimming Annabel and Alex bury themselves up to the neck in the soft white sand or play leapfrog on the hard-packed strand.

Lunch is always the same, bought from a small beach café – an enormous platter of creamy hummus glistening with olive oil and dotted with whole yellow chick peas and red cayenne. The children are allowed a round of Arab bread each to tear into pieces and dip into the hummus. They finish off with fruit and cookies, and lemonade to drink. Annabel wears a blue and white floral swimming costume with a short pleated skirt attached. Her swimming cap is blue and white to match. All the children on the beach have colourful swim suits, but when Alex grumbles about her own plain costume, Sheena says it's ridiculous for a child to wear a fancy costume with a skirt. 'You can swim far better in a plain suit without a skirt.'

Mrs Hitti sits under the thatched awning of the café and chats to her friends, including several ladies who speak to her in French. The Lebanese women are divided into two kinds – those in modern dress who go swimming, and the ones in traditional costume who never enter the water. The latter sit huddled together on the sand wearing headscarves with brightly coloured frilled trousers showing under striped skirts. Some wear one blue bead on a strand around their foreheads, reminding Alex of the Bedouin women outside K3.

One Saturday at St Simon Alex hears Mrs Hitti talking to a grey-haired Englishwoman in a plain linen dress, a straw sun hat and flat brown sandals. She's governess to a little boy, a slight dark-skinned child with jet black hair and dark liquid eyes. Annabel bounces up to him in her usual friendly manner.

'Hi, what's your name?'

The boy is tongue-tied at first, not knowing whether he should speak to strangers.

'Don't be shy, Feisal, you can make friends with the little girls.'

'Come on, I'll race you!' shouts Annabel. The boy darts like quicksilver across the sand, beating both girls into the water where they start to splash each other.

'D'you live in Beirut?' asks Annabel.

'No, I live in Baghdad.'

'I've been to Baghdad', Alex says boastfully.

The boy looks unbelieving. 'I've never seen you there.'

Annabel wants to know how old he is.

'I was eight on the second of May.'

'I was eight in October, and Alex was eight in April, so you're the baby of us three.'

'I'm not a baby, I'm the King of Iraq!'

For a moment Annabel is at a loss for words. Then she scoffs, 'You don't look like a king. Where's your crown?'

Feisal flushes with annoyance and waves his hand towards the beach. 'See those men in sunhats and dark glasses sitting behind my governess? They are my bodyguards. They carry guns all the time and will shoot anyone who tries to hurt me – or if anyone is rude to me!'

The girls are startled and impressed by this information. 'Do you cut off people's heads if they disobey you?' Alex enquires.

Feisal grins widely. 'I order my soldiers to do it.'

'You're telling fibs', accuses Annabel.

'I'm not!'.

'You are!'

'I'm not! Come to Baghdad and see what happens to you!'

'I don't want to come to Baghdad.'

But Feisal quickly tires of this conversation. 'Race you to that rock!' he shouts, and cuts through the water at great speed with an expert crawl stroke. The girls are left far behind.

Annabel wants Feisal to share their picnic but he refuses politely. Later Mrs Hitti tells the children Feisal is going to be sent to Harrow as soon as the war is over. 'Poor kid!' she says. 'He's going to be so homesick and unhappy. Boarding schools are not much better than prisons.'

The girls go swimming with Feisal on subsequent occasions but out of the water he becomes too polite and oddly formal. He's unwilling to answer questions about his life in Iraq and he's aware of his dignity as a king and as a male. Alex feels sorry for him.

Mrs Hitti asks Alex if she would like to attend the American Mission Church with her family on Sunday mornings. 'We can pick you up on our way if your mother will allow you to come.' When Sheena is asked she laughs and says to Basil, 'I see Mrs Hitti is determined to make a Christian out of my little heathen!'

The service takes place in a cool, simple building near the Maronite Cathedral on Derb el Kebire – a service in Arabic at nine and one in English at eleven. The whitewashed room with small high windows is furnished with wooden benches and a lectern standing on a low platform at one end. The congregation consists mainly of middle-aged and elderly American ladies who sing hymns in high quavering voices. A stocky smiling man with short spiky hair and thick glasses gives a long address standing behind the lectern. In a soft persuasive voice he calls on everyone to repent of their sins. Alex is sure he's looking directly at her and feels guilty. But Annabel isn't listening. She has a packet of Rowntree's fruit gums and passes one to Alex every few minutes. Eventually a green gum rolls off the bench and Mrs Hitti gives the girls a whispered reprimand.

After the service everyone assembles in a small adjoining room to take coffee and cake. An overpowering smell of stale cologne, face powder and straw hat pervades the atmosphere. Annabel, Alex and the twins are the only children present. Alex doesn't enjoy the service, but it's better than being at home with nothing to do, and after church there's the pleasure of having Sunday lunch in the Hittis' garden under the trees – invariably roast chicken stuffed with pine nuts and raisins, followed by lemon meringue pie. The girls take off their church frocks and Annabel lends Alex a pair of shorts to play in.

During the summer term Mrs Kellaway announces that a new girl called Naomi will be joining their grade. With her mother and grandmother Naomi has escaped from a country called Czechoslovakia which has been occupied by the Nazis. Her father is dead, her brother has disappeared, and now she and her mother are refugees who've suffered a great deal. She writes the words *Czech* and *refugee* on the blackboard. 'I want you all to be especially kind and welcoming to Naomi when she comes tomorrow. She may not speak much English, so be patient and help her to learn it.'

Annabel is greatly excited by the news and spends recess discussing how they can make the poor little refugee happy. 'I shall bring her some candy and one of my best toys', she announces grandly, and the other girls determine to do the same. Naomi turns out to be small and neat with short dark curly hair and a pasty complexion. She says very little, but smiles all the time, showing a row of teeth that seem too big for her thin face. She wears a shabby brown dress and a pair of heavy lace-up shoes a size too large. Bobbie whispers to Jake that Naomi looks like Minnie Mouse in those shoes. Annabel tells him sharply that if he really wants to know, he's the ugliest boy she's ever seen.

After school when Naomi has gone, Bobbie declares he doesn't like her. Alex jumps to her defence. 'You've got to be nice to her. My father told me refugees have an awful time. They live in damp cellars with nothing to eat and often the soldiers come in the middle of the night and shoot them.'

The children find Naomi can speak quite good English, although her pronunciation is strange. She's certainly not the frightened little waif they'd been expecting. Her round black eyes dart about taking in everything, and her shyness quickly disappears. She asks Mrs Kellaway questions in a loud, confident voice.

'Isn't she brave?' Annabel whispers to Alex. 'She hasn't cried at all.' But Alex thinks why should the Czech girl cry when everyone is being so nice to her?

'I'm going to ask if she can come and play with us at my house. We can let her decide what game to play.'

Annabel discovers that Naomi and her mother live quite close to the school in a cramped rented flat on the ground floor of an ugly concrete block. They have no garden, only a narrow balcony overlooking the street. During recess one morning Bobbie can't resist asking Naomi, 'Where did you get those funny shoes?' The children are so accustomed to Bobbie being rude that they're surprised when the new girl flushes red with anger and flings herself at Bobbie, scratching his face and knocking him to the ground. He gets up and grins, pretending not to care. After a week Alex begins to suspect that Mrs Kellaway may not like Naomi either. She makes such an effort to be kind while the Czech girl persists in asking her questions she can't answer. Gradually Naomi manages to change the casual, easy-going atmosphere of Grade Two into one of tension.

All the girls want to please Naomi and to be her friend. Naomi, however, decides that Annabel is to be her 'best friend' and to Alex's consternation Annabel is only too glad to oblige. She even allows the new girl to make all the decisions in their relationship. It's astonishing how swiftly Naomi extends her English vocabulary, how easily she becomes the leader in and out of the classroom. She's so bright that all the respect the pupils once gave to Alex is transferred to the newcomer. Naomi is particularly quick at arithmetic which Alex finds hard. Only Bobbie and Jake remain indifferent.

Alex is worried that Naomi will oust her in Annabel's affection and the weekend invitations to the Hitti's house will come to an end. In fact Naomi is anxious that they should remain a threesome, while making it clear that Alex is only there on sufferance to help out with their games, to run errands and to play the unpopular parts when they act improvised plays. The Czech girl's personality is so powerful that when she's being pleasant Alex finds herself succumbing to her will. Yet Naomi can become unpleasant, even sly, in a moment, and it's galling that Annabel will not hear a word against her.

One Sunday afternoon, when Annabel and Naomi spend the afternoon whispering secrets to one another, Alex decides she's had enough, and goes home. In school the next day Naomi makes her pay dearly for her rebellion. In her subtle way she turns the whole grade against Alex, with the exception of Bobbie and Jake. The only consolation is that Mrs Kellaway suspects what Naomi is about and remains Alex's firm ally. 'You mustn't let Naomi upset you, Alex', she advises her quietly. 'She won't be here for long. Her mother is hoping to move to Palestine soon. So don't let your work deteriorate. When you concentrate you can be just as clever as Naomi.' Alex knows this isn't true, but Mrs Kellaway is comforting. Her misery lies mainly in the fact that Annabel will no longer stand up for her against Naomi. She's too lazy and too spoilt to bother, and enjoys having two girls vying for her favours. Annabel resembles Sheena in the way she never has to struggle for affection or admiration.

Without the stimulation and security of Annabel's friendship, Alex becomes withdrawn and lonely. One Saturday she gets up early and hurries to the Hittis' house hoping to catch Annabel on her own. As she enters the gate she passes Mr Hitti driving out.

'Hello, young lady! I'm afraid Annabel's gone to spend the day with her little Jewish friend. She'll be sorry to have missed you.'

Alex takes this stroke of bad luck as an omen and gives up the battle to keep Annabel's friendship.

Chapter Twenty-six

On Monday Annabel arrives at school before Naomi and says earnestly to Alex, 'Sorry I wasn't home on Saturday. Naomi invited me to lunch and tea and told me lots more about her life in Czechoslovakia. Just think, they lived in a cellar with rats and no fire or bathroom or stove to cook on. The whole family had to share one mattress. And now her mother is so poor they don't have nice things to eat, and Naomi hasn't got any pretty clothes. She really is so brave. When you come to our house next Saturday we're going to play at being refugees.'

When Naomi enters the classroom Alex notices she's wearing a pair of red and white sandals and a red poplin dress that once belonged to Annabel. Naomi sees the recognition in Alex's eyes, but her smile never falters. During recess she whispers to Alex, 'Come over here, I've got something to give you.' She holds out her hand and on her palm Alex sees the black cat brooch with green eyes.

'Annabel says you can have this back. She's my best friend now and we don't want you playing with us at weekends. You've got to give back Annabel's ring because she's promised it to me.'

Alex flushes with anger and humiliation in the face of Naomi's blatant triumph. 'No, I won't give back the ring! And I don't want the brooch!' she replies, moving away quickly.

When Alex stops spending her weekends with the Hittis Sheena suggests she come to the club to swim. Her daughter agrees for want of anything better to do. The place is more crowded than ever with young servicemen on leave, and they all seem to know Sheena. They greet her with loud voices, teasing and plying her with drinks.

As they emerge from the changing cubicles the small, sharp-featured man called Norman who had offered to teach Alex to swim properly, leaps up to offer his deck chair to her mother.

'The brat will have to sit on the floor.' He smirks down at Alex. 'Ready for a swimming lesson yet, ducky?'

'No!'

When Norman goes to the bar, Sheena says angrily, 'How could you be so rude?'

'He called me a brat!'

'He was only joking. All children are brats to him.'

Alex stands watching Norman swallow-diving off the high board, followed by several tanned young men who jump in with much splashing and laughter. Jumping in seems to be a possibility and Alex makes a decision. During a lull she makes her way boldly to the end of the rope-covered board and looks down. Her stomach lurches as she sees the water so far below. Impossible to jump from this height, and yet maybe she could. She imagines plunging like a heavy stone to the bottom of the sea and not being able to reach the surface in time. But there is no going back now and she braces herself to jump. But as she waits a few seconds for a swimmer below to move out of the way, Norman runs lightly up behind her and pushes her off.

There's a rush of air. Her body grows rigid as the sea leaps upwards and she hits the surface with a resounding and painful belly-flop, narrowly missing the swimmer. She goes under and eventually struggles to the surface, spluttering with mouthfuls of salt water.

Someone shouts 'Damn silly kid! You should look before you jump!'

Alex climbs the steps feeling sick and dizzy, and making her way back to Sheena she bursts into tears.

Her mother, who hasn't noticed the incident, demands irritably, 'For Christ's sake, what's wrong with you now?'

'Norman pushed me when I was going to jump by myself!' Alex sobs. Everyone stares at her with disapproval.

'If you don't stop that noise you'll get a good smack!'

Alex continues to sob with self-pity, outraged that no one is offering sympathy for the trick Norman has played on her. Sheena leaps up and hustles the child back to the changing cubicle. Here she gives her a hard slap across the back of her legs, saying furiously, 'If you insist on behaving like a spoilt two-year-old you're going to be treated like one!'

Basil drives home early, looking none too pleased. Alex rushes up to her room and clutches Hatty to her for comfort, almost squeezing the breath out of the dog. Later, driven by a gnawing hunger, she creeps down as far as the sliding door. She hears Basil saying, 'I can't stand kids who have tantrums for no good reason. Alex needs discipline. You let her get away with far too much!'

'I didn't want to take her to the club. It isn't a suitable place for children. But I can't leave her alone all day. What did you do with your daughter at weekends?'

We took her everywhere with us. All our friends adored Sally-Ann.'

'Well, how lucky to have such an engaging child!' retorts Sheena sharply.

There's a long silence. Alex wonders what's happening, but dare not slide the door open too far. Then Basil says, 'I'm sorry, honey. I don't mean to boast about my kid. At home I hardly notice Alex. It's just a pity she makes some kind of scene every time we take her out. What do you say we ask Abby to occupy her in the kitchen for a couple of hours while we slip back to the club?'

'Abby's having her rest.'

'Don't worry, I can get round Abby!'

Basil and Sheena depart and Abby, grumbling in a good-natured way, descends from her room to make pastry. Alex watches the deft brown fingers lightly bringing the flour and butter together into a springy lump of dough. She pushes a portion in front of Alex and shows her how to cut out rounds for jam tarts. The task is absorbing and therapeutic.

When the tarts are in the oven Alex asks if she might see the rooms in the attic.

'No!' grunts Abby. 'There's nothing to see.'

'Oh, please let me!' the child begs.

'Oh very well, up you go.'

Alex climbs the ladder and finds herself on a small landing with three doors. Abby directs her into a tiny whitewashed room with a strip of frayed matting on the floor, lying beside an iron bedstead covered with a grey blanket. Three hooks on the wall hold Abby's few clothes. A battered tin trunk acts as her table. Two pieces of broken mirror are propped on a shelf beside a jam jar of fake lilies.

Alex peers through the dirty window down to the garden far below, and notices that the fire escape doesn't reach up to the servants' attic.

'Can I see Georgette's room?'

Abby opens another door and Alex glances into a second bleak little room. On a shelf stands a bottle of cheap scent and a large white comb full of tangled black hairs. On the wall is pasted a photograph of a young man. The third door leads into a toilet containing a badly stained lavatory bowl with no seat. Alex shudders as she catches sight of a large cockroach picking its way across the uneven floorboards.

These rooms disturb Alex deeply. For the first time she feels intense pity even for Georgette. She remembers that Zilpha's room at K3 was furnished in the same way as her own. 'Has Mr Carrington been up here?' she asks.

Abby screeches with laughter. 'Of course not. He can't be bothered with servants' rooms.'

'Wouldn't he let you buy a carpet and curtains and proper furniture?'

'He would, but we can't afford such things. Georgette and I have families to support.'

Alex descends the ladder carefully, glad to be in the kitchen again. 'Where's your bath?' she asks Abby.

'No bath. We wash at the kitchen sink.'

'Why don't you use our bath upstairs?'

The cook gives her a searching look and then laughs. 'Mr Carrington wouldn't like us to contaminate his bath.'

Alex contemplates this statement and then says, 'Are you married?'

'I am, but my husband ran off and left me with three children to bring up.'

'Three children! When do you see them?'

'On my days off. They live at Bachoura, two tram-rides away.'

'Who looks after them?'

'The eldest is sixteen. He's a golf caddy at weekends, and a shoe-shine boy during the week. He looks after the other two.'

'Why don't they come and visit you here?'

'Mr Carrington doesn't like relations hanging around the kitchen.'

'Mr Carrington isn't kind at all.'

'He's better than most employers. He's polite and he pays more than the French or the British. That's enough questions for now. You take Hatty down to the garden.'

Outside, the freshness of spring has long passed. The palms and shrubs in the garden look tired and dusty, and the tiled paving is burning to the touch. Alex thinks constantly of Annabel and feels wicked for wishing Naomi had never escaped from Czechoslovakia. Then she notices a child she's never seen before, sitting on the downstairs verandah – a girl younger than herself, with olive skin and black hair. Alex smiles, assuming she will speak Arabic or French, and is surprised when she calls out to her in English, 'What's your name? Come and see my doll.'

Alex mounts the three steps up to the verandah and takes the rag doll which the girl holds out to her. It's a faded, grubby-looking toy, but Alex says it's pretty. 'I'm called Alex, and I live upstairs.'

'My name is Nadya', the child announces. 'I'm seven years old. We came to Beirut yesterday to live with my aunt and uncle. Have you got a doll?'

'Yes, lots of dolls.'

'In Haifa I had three dolls but I had to leave two of them when we ran away.'

'Why did you run away?'

'Some men came and set fire to our house.'

'Why did they?'

'We are Palestinians.'

Full of sympathy, Alex wonders what she can do to make up for Nadya losing her home. 'I'll go and fetch my dolls. We can play a game.' Suddenly the future seems brighter. Alex makes three journeys from her bedroom, bringing down the dolls and the soft toys. Nadya's mother comes out through tinkling bead curtains onto the verandah and stares vaguely at Alex as though her mind is on other matters. Alex suggests they might construct a house if Nadya could procure a few chairs and a blanket or two. Nadya is delighted. She flits in and out, fetching chairs, a shawl, a blanket, a bedspread and some cardboard boxes. In no time they construct a tent-like house and start playing with the dolls. When Sheena and Basil return from the club Alex waves and asks if she may stay with Nadya till suppertime.

When Alex returns to the apartment she hears Sheena asking Basil, 'Where have that family downstairs come from?'

'They're a family of Palestinian refugees, relatives of the couple already living there. There's seven of them crowded into that apartment now. I guess the landlord will complain.'

'Poor devils', comments Sheena. 'Where can they go, with no job and no possessions?'

'God only knows', replies Basil. 'More families arrive in Lebanon every day. Those with relatives are the lucky ones. The rest have to go to refugee camps.'

'Those camps look appalling. I don't know how the people manage to exist.'

During the next few days, when Alex meets Nadya's brothers and sisters and sees how little they possess, she determines to remedy the situation. She goes through all Sally-Ann's toys deciding she can do without most of them. She realises she's growing out of toys. On Sunday morning, while Basil and Sheena are still in bed Alex carries the toys to the downstairs verandah. Nadya and the other children are delighted and Alex feels a self-righteous glow of satisfaction.

'You can keep the toys. I don't want any of them back', she insists, and when Nadya looks uncertain adds 'My mother wants you to have them.' The girls play together until Alex has to go up for brunch.

'I'll come back this afternoon', she says happily.

Later, as Basil and Sheena are about to depart for the golf club, the doorbell rings. A shrill female voice is demanding to speak to Sheena. Alex follows her mother to the door and sees Nadya's mother standing by a pile of toys. She proceeds to toss them into the hall, shouting, 'We Palestinians don't need your charity! We need our country, our homes! You British allowed the Jews to throw us out of Palestine and now you think you can throw us scraps of charity!'

Sheena tries to speak but the woman continues with her torrent of accusation. 'Our beautiful stone house was burnt by terrorists. We fled with nothing. My husband will never teach again – and you think we should be grateful for toys! Help us get those Jews out of Haifa and then we'll be grateful!' Sheena eventually shuts the door on the agitated mother without saying anything in reply.

Alex flees upstairs but her mother calls her down immediately. 'How dared you give away Sally-Ann's toys?'

'I thought they were my toys now and I don't need them any more. The children downstairs haven't got any toys.'

'You'd no right to give them away without asking Basil. You'd better take them all upstairs and then you can go straight to bed!'

Bursting with indignation Alex makes the necessary journeys with armfuls of toys. It is amazing that her mother can't see how good were her motives. On her final trip up she pulls the sliding door almost but not quite shut and listens.

'You're too hard on the kid', says Basil. 'She was trying to be kind.'

'It's easy to be kind with other people's possessions.'

'I'll go down later and try to explain that it was Alex's idea.'

'She must be stupid to imagine we sent Alex down with all those things.'

'She's obviously in no fit state to think rationally.'

Nearly every day Alex sees Nadya on her verandah. They smile and wave to each other but dare not speak. It's bitterly disappointing. At school Naomi is still flaunting her relationship with Annabel and loses no opportunity of making Alex look foolish. It becomes difficult to concentrate on her work, even painting, which she enjoys most. Her pictures are no longer put up on the wall. Her time is spent daydreaming about what might have been.

One blazing hot afternoon Alex returns to the apartment and lolls idly on the swing. Hatty, feeling the heat too, doesn't want to chase her ball around the balcony. Alex gets up and wanders through the bedrooms, examining everything. Nothing interesting catches her eye. Downstairs in the lounge she's once more tempted by the gramophone. Basil is away for a night on business, so there's no fear of sudden discovery. Just one record, before Sheena returns! On her hands and knees she pulls out the heavy leather record cases – Tchaikovsky, Brahms, Beethoven, Haydn, Mozart – such strange names! She can hardly wait to try one. She winds up the instrument, inserts a new needle and puts on the first record of a

Brahms symphony. The music, crackling a little, fills the room with its glorious melody. It sounds familiar. Basil has played it a few times. She listens to both sides. Then Hatty begins to bark. Worried that someone might be coming up the stairs, Alex hurriedly snatches the record off the turntable and it comes apart in two pieces. In a panic she stuffs them both into the brown cardboard sleeve, replaces it in the leather case and dashes up the stairs. She pulls the sliding door across as Sheena comes into the lounge.

Alex waits in agony for the breakage to be discovered. It's almost a relief when two days later her mother comes storming into her room at bedtime, shrill with anger. 'You've been playing with Basil's records again!' And before the child has time to reply Sheena yanks her out of bed and starts to smack her hard across the backside, shouting, 'You've ruined one of Basil's favourite symphonies and he can't get a replacement here in wartime. If you can't stop meddling with other people's things you'll have to be locked in your room after school. Why can't you do as you're told? You've got a dog and a swing and lots of toys, yet you can't be trusted to behave properly....' Suddenly she stops smacking her daughter and says grimly, 'Now get back into bed and don't ever touch Basil's things again!' Sheena leaves the room, banging the door as she sweeps out.

At first Alex is too shocked to cry. A swipe across the legs is one thing, but a real hiding is humiliating beyond belief. Hatty, who had crept under the bed during Sheena's raging, now comes out and nuzzles up to her mistress in apparent sympathy. She clutches the dog, feeling angry and defiant.

After a while she gets up and runs down to the sliding door, goes through it and shouts over the banister to Sheena and Basil, who are sitting on the sofa, 'I'll tell Giles you hit me! He said you must never smack children. It doesn't do them any good. They just grow up and hit their own children!' To her surprise Basil laughs, and then her mother joins in. To be laughed at is the ultimate humiliation and Alex retreats to bed to cry herself to sleep.

Alex begins to experience an anxiety akin to despair. Nothing is going well at home or at school. Mrs Kellaway scolds her for not paying attention, and she doesn't know what to do with the hours she has to spend alone in the apartment.

One afternoon her room is oppressively warm and she goes into Basil's room to turn on the large ceiling fan. The photograph of Sally-Ann seems to mock her, so she plonks it face down, hating this pretty child who seems to cope so well with life. As always, everything in Basil's room is very neat. Nothing catches her eye, and in any case she must be extra vigilant in not disturbing his possessions. She rights the photograph and is about to leave the room when she catches sight of something glinting on top of the wardrobe. Standing on a chair she can just reach a large flat box which she lifts down carefully. It's a giant-sized box of chocolates with a shiny gold lid. She lays it on the carpet and gazes wide-eyed at the row upon row of silky dark chocolates. With relief she notes that half a dozen are missing from their crinkly papers. Maybe she could just take one without fear of detection.

Fudge and nuts! Her favourite filling! Having tasted one chocolate Alex throws aside all caution. She's already sunk so low in her mother's esteem that she has ceased to care. It seems impossible to please her so she may as well be wicked. She stuffs another chocolate into her mouth and replaces the box exactly as she found it. The taste of the chocolate is an extraordinary comfort and she feels much better.

The next day Alex believes herself to be alone upstairs, and her mind returns to the box of chocolates on Basil's wardrobe. If he has eaten some more, then perhaps she could risk another couple herself. It's worth having a look. She opens Basil's door and carries a chair over to the wardrobe. The box is still there. Kneeling on the carpet she's about to lift off the golden lid when the door leading to the bathroom opens and Alex leaps to her feet in consternation.

Basil is standing naked in the doorway with his bathrobe over his arm. They both remain transfixed for what seems like minutes. He takes in Alex's flushed face, the chair by the wardrobe, the box on the carpet. She takes in the stocky pink legs covered with ginger hairs, the fleshy white shoulders, the damp hair on his chest and the genitals hanging from the hairy ginger patch beneath his protruding belly.

Basil's metallic blue eyes gaze at the terrified child with cold fury. Alex feels as if she's been caught at murder itself. She dashes out of the room and into her own and flings herself on the bed. Nothing worse could ever happen to her. She must leave the apartment and never come back! But where can she go? She lies in a cold sweat until she hears Basil's car driving away. For the rest of the day she waits for the storm to break, but nothing is said, either that evening or during the next few days. During this time she keeps out of Basil's way, dreading she might meet him alone on the stairs or in the garden. On Saturday Sheena says 'We're going shopping as usual, and then on to lunch with some friends who live just outside Beirut. You may come if you like.' Alex declines, and Sheena promises to be back about five.

It would seem Basil isn't going to raise the chocolate incident. She's immensely relieved, but at the same time uneasy and wary. An already difficult relationship has now become an impossible one. She will certainly never enter his room again.

Chapter Twenty-seven

Alex is glad to have a whole day without fear of interruption. Once Georgette has cleaned the bedrooms and bathroom she's unlikely to come upstairs again. To celebrate her freedom Alex jumps onto her mother's bed and lies there with Hatty, planning a new game. It would be fun to dress Hatty in dolls' clothes. She returns to her room to find a frilly bonnet and a button-through doll's dress. The dog lies compliantly on her back to have the dress buttoned up after her paws have been pushed through the sleeves. Alex squeals with laughter at the sight of Hatty, who makes no attempt to rid herself of the clothes. She curls up on the bed and watches Alex effecting her own transformation.

Alex has decided to play at being Sheena. Now she can dress up in her mother's clothes without fear of interruption. She takes off her shorts and shirt, and secures her plaits on top of her head with bobby pins. She puts on Sheena's best house-coat of pink satin with silver embroidery, and slips into her white satin court shoes. Seating herself at the dressing table she removes her glasses and with passable expertise, the result of watching her mother for years, applies rouge, powder, lipstick and eye make-up. A quick dab of perfume behind each ear and she's ready. She holds the folds of the housecoat up in front and lets the back trail across the floor as she totters up and down in front of the long mirror. She's pleased with the result. Surely she bears some resemblance to her mother.

'I'm going to a dance tonight, darling', says Alex. 'You'll have to be a good girl and put out your light at half past seven.' She tucks the bemused animal between the sheets and kisses her lovingly.

It takes her a while to decide on the silver lamé evening dress from among her favourites. With difficulty she adjusts it to her figure with the help of a belt and then finds necklace and earrings to match. She pirouettes around the bedroom and across the hall, and attempts to copy some of her mother's expressions. Something is missing – the cigarette in a long black holder. There is a sealed box of du Maurier cigarettes in a drawer which Alex dares not open. She'll have to pretend with an eyebrow pencil.

At this point Hatty decides she's had enough and leaps down from the bed. Alex heaves the reluctant dog back onto the bed and tucks her up. 'If you're very, very good I'll read you a story.' While she goes to fetch a book, the dog struggles off the bed again. Alex catches her and once more tucks her tightly between the sheets. 'You're a very disobedient little girl and you don't deserve a story!'

Hatty stays put for a few minutes as Alex waltzes around the room. The dog senses her elation, and this time leaps off the bed and jumps up at the child, barking and tearing threads out of the silver lamé dress with her sharp little claws.

This time Alex flies into a rage of frustration, part real and part a simulation of her mother's recent anger. She seizes Hatty and smacks her, shouting, 'You're sulky and lazy and rude and dirty – you've been spoilt by your father and I want nothing more to do with you!' The dog jumps out of her grasp and slinks under the bed. Immediately Alex is overcome with painful remorse. She coaxes her pet out from under the bed and gathers it into her arms, exclaiming 'Hatty, dear little Hatty, I didn't mean to hurt you. I'll never hurt you again, ever!' Reassured by this new tone of voice Hatty relaxes and licks Alex's face. In return Alex covers the silky head with kisses. She wallows in the reconciliation, gaining satisfaction in having the power to determine the dog's happiness. 'I love you, I love you, I love you!' she murmurs, over and over again.

This solitary little drama has a cathartic effect on Alex. Feeling happier than she's done for a long time she undresses the dog and taking off the silver lamé dress, she hangs it among Sheena's many evening dresses. Sooner or later the damage will be discovered and there will be more trouble. But that will be another day.

Since Christmas Giles has written to his daughter several times but hasn't received a reply. She's started half a dozen letters, getting as far as *Dear Giles,...* and then being unable to continue. She wants to tell him all her woes, but how to express herself in words? She hasn't seen him for nearly six months. How can he understand her frustrations and failures? He's too far away to affect her life.

But after restoring Sheena's bedroom to rights Alex suddenly feels inspired to write to her father. She'll send him a chatty letter presenting herself in a cheerful light.

Dear Giles, Mr Carrington has rented a bigger villa for our summer vacation at Broummana. He's going to have lots of visitors. Hatty doesn't piddle on the carpet any more, but she did chew up one of my slippers and a corner of the rug in the hall. Abby has shown me how to make jam tarts. Mrs Kellaway gives us a spelling test every week and I've had ten out of ten every time. Bobbie and Jake are my friends at school. They are rather naughty boys but I like them because they make me laugh. Mr Carrington says he will teach Sheena to drive and will buy her a car if she learns. I still hate spinach and okra, they are so slimy. Write soon. Lots of love, Alex.

Towards the end of June Alex becomes aware of another crisis point in the endless war. The talk on the wireless refers once more to Egypt and North Africa. Will Cairo fall to the Germans now that a town called Tobruk has been taken? Basil doubts whether Mr Churchill will remain the leader in Britain. His tone of voice when he mentions Churchill is slightly disparaging, which annoys Sheena. At school Mrs Kellaway doesn't mention the Western Desert. She only talks about America's part in the war, and Alex identifies herself strongly with the American view.

The heat in Beirut is becoming unbearable. Only a few more days until the long vacation. Naomi informs Alex with great satisfaction that she's been invited to spend a month with Annabel at her uncle's house in the mountains. Mrs Kellaway hears Bobbie announcing loudly, 'Naomi and

Annabel are a couple of twerps. Who'd want to spend two months with them?' and chides him for being spiteful.

'I think you should apologise.'

'Sorry, Naomi and Annabel!' intones the boy insincerely. The teacher is relieved term is coming to an end; the atmosphere in Grade Two is far from friendly.

It's wonderful to leave the sticky humidity of Beirut and to head for the mountains. Claude negotiates the hairpin bends with his usual reckless skill, and in forty-five minutes the Buick is drawing up outside the holiday villa. The house is much grander than the one at Beit Mery, with a white balustrade running round the flat roof. Every bedroom has its own balcony.

The extensive garden is steeply terraced both behind and in front of the house, with a wide verandah at one side, paved in black and white marble. A bright blue umbrella is perched above a marble-topped garden table and wooden garden chairs. This is a place full of possibilities, thinks Alex, as she explores the lawns, paved areas, flower beds and shrubberies all connected by numerous stone steps and wind-breaks, and dotted with statues. Here at last is a real garden where she can play hidden away from adult view. Best of all, the house is isolated, standing on its own above the village.

They sit on the shady front verandah to eat a picnic lunch. All around them crown daisies, peonies, pelargoniums, aloes, convolvulus, marigolds, are spilling out of stone urns. Hatty is confused by the sudden freedom to run loose in this vast space, and to begin with she follows Alex closely around the house, sniffing all the rooms. Entering the main bedroom Alex catches a glimpse of Basil and Sheena on the balcony – a fleeting impression of two bodies in a close embrace which part hastily at her approach. She looks at the huge double bed and asks 'Who's going to have this room?'

'I am', replies her mother. 'You're to sleep in the little room next to the small bathroom.'

During Basil and Sheena's two week vacation Alex is content to occupy herself while they entertain friends and go out for drives. In such a large house it's easy to avoid Basil most of the time. At the end of the fortnight Sheena says, 'We'll be driving down to Beirut each morning as we did last summer. It will be the same routine. Georgette will look after you on Tuesday and Thursday nights.'

Alex still hates being left in the care of the maid. In Sheena's absence she's apt to bully in a subtle manner, and will sometimes give Hatty a kick. When Alex threatens to tell Sheena, Georgette replies, 'I can tell her bad things about you. Keep your mouth shut and do what I tell you. Mr Carrington would never believe anything you say. He doesn't like you.'

Left on her own, Alex finds plenty to explore around Broummana. Every morning she follows yet another well-trodden goat track into vineyards of ripening grapes, and orchards of pomegranate and mulberry. The parching heat is alleviated by numerous streams trickling down the mountain. On each excursion she comes across shabby little flat-roofed houses, and often watches children playing from a distance. Once she comes upon a more substantial house with a bright red tiled roof and some attempt at a garden. By mid-afternoon her enthusiasm for exploring wilts; heat and loneliness combine to produce a paralysing stupor. For hours she lies on the grass under a tree, thinking that after all, it would be nice if she could join a group of children in their games. She wonders what it would be like to belong to a Lebanese family. But her Arabic is scanty and she's no idea how to approach local children. Few of the mountain people speak more than a word or two of English. Alex wonders what Annabel and Naomi are doing at this minute.

As her father's three weeks' leave approaches, Alex is almost sick with excitement and apprehension. Will he be the same as he was at Christmas? Will she recognise him? Will Sheena tell him all the bad things she's done? She sits on the bed Georgette has made up for him with starched linen sheets. This time tomorrow the room will be filled with the smell of tobacco, coal tar soap and mints. The thought of rising each morning to have breakfast with Giles while they plan what to do is intoxicating.

When Alex sees an unfamiliar car stopping outside the villa and watches Giles coming up the terrace steps in white aertex shirt and khaki shorts she is overcome with shyness and escapes to her room. Her father bounds upstairs to find her, calling her name, and immediately all is well, he hasn't changed at all. He looks and smells just the same. His moustache is still stained with nicotine and it still tickles her cheek as he kisses her. It's pure bliss to be with him.

After lunch Giles gives Alex sugared almonds in a wooden box with a mosaic pattern on the lid. He produces a Shani pomegranate as big as a football. 'These Syrian pomegranates are meant to be the sweetest in the Middle East', says Giles. 'I thought we'd celebrate my coming to Broummana by sharing this one. Did you know this village was once called Beit Rummana? *Beit,* as you know, means place, or house, and *Rummana* was the Assyrian god of storms. His emblem is a pomegranate; so Broummana means *Place of the Pomegranate.'* Giles cuts the fruit in quarters and they bite into the sweet fleshy seeds until the juice runs down their chins.

Giles has managed to procure a map of Lebanon, and for the first time Alex is able to see where Broummana is in relation to Beirut. She traces the road up through Beit Mery and her father points out the two long mountain chains which make up the country with the Bekaa plain in between. 'D'you remember we crossed the Bekaa last summer when we went to Baalbek? I've hired a car, an old Humber, so tomorrow we could drive up to Aphaca to Astarte's Grotto at the source of the Adonis River up here – look, it's called the Ibrahim River on the map – would you like that?'

'Yes.'

'And on the way I'd like to have a look round the ruins at Byblos, down here on the coast.'

'Do we have to see the ruins?'

'We'll make a bargain, shall we? We'll go to Byblos for me, and we'll take a boat trip on an underground lake at Jei'ita, for you. How about that?'

'Can we take Hatty?'

'Yes, why not?'

The pleasure of being with her father far outweighs her reluctance to visit yet more ruins. She still enjoys the feeling of conspiracy as she and Giles rise well before dawn and creep out of the villa before anyone else is stirring.

At this hour a thin cobweb mist fills the valley and there's a moist freshness to the mountains as though they have been dipped in icy water. They drive in a leisurely way to join the coast road at Jaideh, just north of Beirut. As they move on up the coast, orange and banana groves stretch away into the darkness on their right, and on their left they can make out the white rectangular salt pans cut into the rock. The sun is about to burst forth from behind the mountain as they reach a narrow point where a steep headland overhangs the road. Giles stops and they get out of the car. It's quiet but for the sound of surf breaking on rocks.

'This pass where we're standing, Alex, is famous in history. Before the modern road was built, and now the recent railway line, the headland used to plunge straight into the sea. Until the Romans laid a road everyone had to negotiate this pass along a very narrow track, and an army could easily be ambushed. Up there on top of the cliff is a large square white stone which used to act as a plinth, so legend has it, for the statue of a wolf. This statue was said to howl whenever an army was approaching.'

'Did it really howl?', asks Alex in amazement.

'I shouldn't think so. Someone probably heard a real wolf howling. Anyway, when the Turks ruled Lebanon they are said to have thrown the statue into the sea.'

'Why?'

'Because Muslims aren't allowed to have statues of animals or people.'

They drive on a little way up the steep mountain corridor down which the Dog River flows amongst boulders to the sea. 'The Greeks called it the Lycus River. Lycus means dog or wolf. In Arabic it's the Nahr el-Kelb.'

On the edge of the coast runs the newly constructed railway line, bridging the Dog River at the widest part of its mouth. Further up river is a stone bridge carrying the modern road , and beyond that the ancient cobbled Arab bridge, with three graceful arches. Giles stops on the north bank of the river and they get out once more to look at some of the inscriptions carved into the rock face – each one commemorating a victory or the invasion of a foreign army. The first one, written on two columns, goes back as far as King Nebuchadnezzar, describing his invasion in 587 BC. Giles produces a notebook in which he has written down a translation of the king's cuneiform inscription: *I cut through steep mountains, I split rocks, opened passages and constructed a straight road for the transportation of cedars.*

'Did he do all that by himself?' asks Alex.

'No, It's just a way of saying he got his many slaves to do it.'

There are seventeen inscriptions altogether. Another one, written in Latin, records Marcus Aurelius Caracalla's commemoration of the valour of the Third Gaul Division. The name of the Division is chiselled out with a hammer. The two most recent inscriptions commemorate the invasion of Syria in 1918 and the Allied capture of Damascus in 1941. 'So, if we'd been here last year we might have seen the troops driving across the bridge in their Jeeps', says Giles.

They walk up the river to stand on the old Arab bridge. Above the lemon trees they can see woodlands of sweet chestnut, maple, walnut and almond. Below them, swifts are twittering in the spray of the river, and above a waterfall gushes down the ravine. Giles remains motionless on the bridge for so long that Alex wonders if they will ever move on. She tugs at his hand and he comes out of his reverie and walks back with her to the car.

By the time they have reached the Bay of Jounieh the sun has become very warm. The sea washes up and down the beach in a slow, lazy rhythm. A string of camels is humphing its way along the edge of the sand.

'We can swim here if you like', says Giles. ' the most beautiful bay in Lebanon.' A beach of pure white sand is backed by a handful of small houses. A dog barks at Hatty as they walk past a fisherman mending his nets, and they wade into the warm water until it becomes deep enough to start swimming. Eventually they turn and tread water for a few minutes, gazing at the backdrop of towering mountains surrounding the arc of the bay.

After their swim Giles hands Alex a ham sandwich and a beaker of cold milk. Hatty, who has been sitting patiently on the beach, is given a dog biscuit and some water. 'We'll have to hurry with our breakfast because we've still got to drive eighteen kilometres to Byblos.'

Hoping to instil a sense of awe into his daughter, Giles says, 'Byblos is said to be the most ancient city in the world. People lived here seven thousand years ago. It was a great religious centre where the yearly celebration of the Festival of Adonis attracted thousands of worshippers. It was also an important trading centre. Ships used to take papyrus to other Mediterranean ports and cedars were floated from here to Egypt. The first olive tree was shipped to Greece from Byblos, and the Greeks called their books *Byblia,* after the city that sent them paper. We got our word 'book' from the word *byblia.* Examples have been found at Byblos of the first Arabic alphabet. The Egyptians used to call Lebanon 'The Land of the Gods' because it was such a rich and beautiful country; and in fact the Arab name for Byblos is Jbeil, which means *Land of the god.'* Alex is only half concentrating, but she likes the idea of the cedars being floated over the waves to Egypt.

When they reach the town they drive past the miniature harbour, only twenty yards across and wander over the ruined ramparts of a Crusader castle. They look into the Church of St John, built in yellow stone with colonnaded windows and domed baptistery. 'There's a complete mixture of architecture here', explains Giles. 'Not much of the Phoenician to be seen, but plenty of Greek, Roman and Crusader. Look at the slices of Roman column embedded in that wall!' But Alex prefers jumping from stone to stone in the cool sea breeze, and watching the lizards scurrying for safety.

Giles heaves open a great wooden door and they peer into a room with holes in the roof through which shafts of sunlight pick out dusty corners. Everywhere thistles and tall pink and mauve hollyhocks thrust towards the sky from between the broken ramparts. They move on to the remains of a temple of Astarte almost buried in elder flowers, thyme and cistus.

'What did all the people do at the religious festivals?' asks Alex.

'After drinking plenty of wine they danced and sang to flutes in honour of Astarte. In the autumn they would wail and beat their breasts because Adonis was dead. The priests and priestesses of these ancient temples would tell the people that they were guarding the secrets of the goddess.'

'What were the secrets?'

'No one knows. They were probably just pretending so they could keep their power over the people. They also insisted someone must be sacrificed each year, saying the goddess demanded it. It was thought that if you sprinkled blood or ashes on the soil the crops would grow well the following spring.'

'You told me about that last summer', says Alex. 'You said they sacrificed their kings in Byblos. It sounds horrible.'

'It was. The priests encouraged the idea that the king must be killed, because their kings were half-gods who would come to life again like Adonis.'

'He should have run away.'

'They would probably have hunted him down and dragged him back to the temple.'

They reach an amphitheatre with its horseshoe of stone seats and tiny pedimented niches. In the first tier of seats are the holes into which wooden lances were stuck to hold up an awning against the sun. On the wide cobbled orchestra below the seats the head of Bacchus can be seen in a mosaic. 'Bacchus is the Roman version of the Greek god, Dionysus. Now he was another god who was said to die each year and to return in the spring', says Giles.

Marguerites are growing out of every cranny between the seats. Alex picks a bunch of these large daisy-like flowers as she listens to her father eulogising over the ancient city where so many nations and generations have fused over the centuries. By now the heat is rebounding from the rocks, in spite of the sea breeze.

'If you look carefully in that shallow water you might come across a Phoenician gold coin', he tells Alex.

She stares hard into the limpid green water, hoping to see the glint of gold amongst the rippling, eroded Greek and Roman columns which have toppled into the sea; but she can see only pebbles and sand.

Chapter Twenty-eight

They walk back to the sizzling car in the midday sun. Burning stones beneath their sandals throw the heat back into their faces.

'Are we going to Astarte's Grotto now?'

'Yes', says Giles. 'Up to Aphaca. It will be a cool place to have lunch.'

Not until they've retraced their route back to the mouth of the Adonis River and started driving inland, bumping slowly up the steep valley towards the village of Majdal, does the air become fresher. The scent of pine and fig is overwhelming in the sun. They pass neat little villages with red-roofed houses set amidst mulberry trees until they reach a desolate high land spiked with white limestone.

When the road comes to an end Giles stops to consult his map. They step out of the car into a wild landscape with no sign of habitation. Alex looks down the rock faces on each side of the chasm descending to surging water crashing over boulders on the river bed. She wonders how any car could have driven up so steep a terrain. Trees of juniper and oak and the dusty, leathery foliage of oleander crowd thickly around them as they take a track which Giles hopes will be the right one. They walk along a ridge above the river until the road loses sight of the sea and the valley seems to gather round them. Crickets rasp and streams splash down.

All at once they come across the ruins of a miniature temple – merely four columns and a sanctuary wall with the remnants of another wall encircling it. They sit in its shade to eat the last of the melting cheese sandwiches and squashy bananas, Giles turns over the pages of his guide book, saying, 'This temple is apparently dedicated to Astarte, but there's another one next to the grotto.'

Giles takes his daughter's hand as the path is leading dangerously close to the edge of the gorge. In a few moments the way ends in a group of small cypress trees growing round the entrance to the grotto set into the cliff face. Out of the cave bursts the river descending by cascades into green frothy pools. A second ruined temple filled with flowers stands guard over the grotto. A fig tree grows out of the crumbling walls around it. Pieces of faded material hang from every branch.

'Look!' exclaims Alex. 'That's like our fig tree at Beit Mery!'

'Yes, sick people obviously come all this way for a cure. And yet it's not a place where you'd expect to meet anyone.' He stops speaking for a moment before saying quietly, 'I feel as though we're the first two people to have set foot here for centuries.'

'It is very lonely', agrees Alex.

'It says in this guide book that a procession of mountain people climbs up here every Good Friday carrying an effigy of Jesus with a gash in his side and lay him in a tomb in the temple. That's probably why there are the remains of so many votive candles on that ledge beside the cave.'

They sit for a long time, mesmerised by the continual roaring of water plummeting from the grotto entrance. It is a truly awesome spot, and both father and daughter are affected by its strange atmosphere. 'Anything could happen here', murmurs Giles, quoting something he's read, *Nothing ends but sinks underground, awaiting its time'*. He becomes abstracted until his daughter takes his hand and begs him to tell her the story of Adonis again. All the while he's speaking she's looking round hopefully for a glimpse of the beautiful goddess.

'If we'd come in the spring', says Giles, 'We'd have seen the water running red. People used to think it was the blood of the dying Adonis.'

'Why is it red?'

'When the spring rains start they carry the red soil down the river and it discolours the water. It's the iron oxide in the clay.'

Science has provided the reason, but Alex is disappointed. She would rather the river was running red with the blood of Adonis. Grownups are too concerned with finding a rational explanation for legends. 'At the end of the fourth century', continues Giles, 'The cult of Adonis was stopped, but it went on secretly while pretending to be a Christian cult. The old idea of the life force in the earth dying each year and then rising again fitted in quite easily with the death of Jesus and his rising again. They turned the goddess Astarte into the Virgin Mary.'

'But it's not the same story', objects Alex. 'Astarte fell in love with Adonis.'

'Yes, she did. But she also brought him up, so she was a mother and a lover. I don't think the people worried about the details. The important thing was that they'd always worshipped the goddess of fertility, and it didn't really matter to them whether she was called Astarte or Mary.'

But Alex isn't satisfied. The vivid image in her mind of Adonis and Astarte bears no resemblance to her idea of Jesus and his mother, Mary. In Giles's guide book Alex finds photographs of paintings and carvings of a woman cradling the body of a dying young man bleeding from a gash in his side. One of them obviously depicts Mary and Jesus. The others, partly destroyed or faded over the centuries, are less definite; yet each one shows the image of a woman weeping over a dying or a dead man. The simple sad story has now become muddled and blurred, and she's puzzled by the strange mixture of beliefs.

'D'you remember what Aphaca means?' asks Giles.

'Yes, it means a kiss. Astarte tried to kiss Adonis better.' The word reminds her of another image and she says abruptly, 'I saw Mr Carrington kissing Sheena on the balcony.'

Alex sees the pain in her father's eyes, and wishes she hadn't told him as he says quietly, 'A difficult time for us all, having to be separated. It will sort itself out in the end.'

Alex isn't convinced.

'Mr Carrington is taking Sheena away from us. I hate him!'

'You don't really understand the situation. And you must stop calling Basil *Mr Carrington.*'

'I don't call him anything. I don't speak to him much.'

'That's not very friendly. He likes children.'

'Only pretty children like Sally-Ann. He thinks I'm a nuisance.'

'How do you know?'

'I've heard him talking to Sheena.'

'You really must stop this habit of eavesdropping, Alex. People who eavesdrop always hear bad of themselves.'

'I don't care!'

Giles makes an attempt to reassure his daughter, but she knows he's not telling her the truth.

'We'd better go down now if you want to have your boat trip at Jei'ita.'

By the time they reach the car Alex and Hatty are tired, and they fall asleep at once as the car winds its way slowly back towards the coast. They wake with a start when Giles stops at Jei'ita, and parks under a tree four miles from the mouth of the Dog River. The heat of the day has passed and the sun hangs low in the sky.

'We'll leave Hatty in the car. It would be difficult keeping her still in a small boat.'

They are the only visitors to the underground caves in which it's said the Dog River has its source. A tall, taciturn man with a deathly pale face paddles a flat barge over a smooth underground lake of velvety blackness through a stone arch into what seems to be the womb of the earth. The rock formations, fashioned over centuries by rain seeping into cretaceous limestone, resemble organ pipes, giant shells, spires and gargoyles. Subtle lighting above and below the water brings out every detail of the astonishing array of stalactites and stalagmites, and sinister shadows hover over smooth opaline surfaces. Delicate strands of stone hang like necklaces from a roof seemingly studded with pearls. The boat glides through cavern after cavern, each one glowing weirdly in pink and yellow and beige, like rooms in a glittering fairy castle. Alex trails her fingers in the ice-cold lake and shivers, listening to the water dripping for ever into the silent rocks.

Stalactites hang above them and sometimes they feel the boat scraping against a rock. Strange noises similar to the sound of a xylophone reverberate round the caverns behind the constant sound of dripping water.

'You couldn't come here in the winter', says Giles, 'Because the water rises too high and it would be freezing cold. This kind of subterranean lake must have given people the idea of Hades.'

Alex has a frightening vision of dead people swimming for ever in the smooth slippery black water. 'How far do we go on this lake?' she asks her father.

'About four miles in a boat. Then it becomes too narrow.' As Giles speaks the boatman is turning to travel back to the entrance, and soon they are emerging into the fading afternoon light.

'We shall see the sun set over the sea if we're lucky', says Giles as they drive back towards Beirut. As the sun lowers itself from behind bars of pink cloud the sea darkens under a scattering of gold flecks. On the salt pans, women who have been stooping for hours stand and stretch, their hair caked with brine and their skin burnt the colour of dark leather. Then suddenly the blood-red sphere squats on the horizon and gradually disappears.

'Did you see the green flash?' asks Alex.

'No', replies Giles. 'I had to keep my eye on the road!'

It's dark by the time they reach Broummana. Alex is so tired she can barely drag her feet up the many steps to the verandah. Basil and Sheena are having a light supper on a trolley in the living room.

'Where on earth have you been?' asks Sheena.

'Byblos and the grotto at Aphaca. Then on the way home we visited the caves at Jei'ita.'

'All in one day? No wonder Alex is exhausted.'

Georgette brings more food and Giles describes the places they have seen. Basil attempts a polite interest but he has no background knowledge of the history and mythology of the Mediterranean. He sees little point in walking round a ruined city. The conversation moves on to a discussion about the war and Alex is sent to bed. By the time Giles goes up to say goodnight she's asleep fully dressed on top of the bedspread. He shuts the door without disturbing her.

Chapter Twenty-nine

Giles spends the remaining days of his holiday almost entirely with his daughter. He joins Basil and Sheena for dinner but doesn't accompany them when they go out. He reads to Alex and they play board games. He gets out the old atlas he takes everywhere with him and tells her about the war. Things aren't going well in North Africa. 'Everyone's worried about Rommel capturing Cairo.'

'If he does capture Cairo he could march round the corner to Palestine', says Alex. It looks very close on the map.

'It would be a disaster, but I don't think it will happen. They've recently appointed a new commander of the Eighth Army called Montgomery, and American troops are going to be sent to help the Allies.' They listen to the bulletins on the wireless, and once more Alex begins to take an interest in the progress of the war.

They walk down to Beit Mery to visit their fig tree at the abbey. The fragment of red cloth is still tied to the branch, but Alex's hair ribbon has gone, much to her disappointment.

'I expect somebody pinched it', says Giles. 'There are some very poor people living in the mountains.'

They discover a short cut from Broummana to the abbey, bypassing Beit Mery. Halfway down the path it's possible to see the fig tree in the distance.

'D'you think it will still be here when I'm grown up?'

'I see no reason why not.'

'I'll come and see it when I'm an old lady.'

'Maybe you will.'

One evening Basil and Sheena return at midnight to find Giles and Alex still up playing cards. Sheena remonstrates with Giles, but he's unrepentant.

'What does it matter what time she goes to bed in the vacation? Why don't you stay in and play games with her as I do? When did you last spend some time with her alone?'

Sheena gives Giles a withering look and walks out of the room banging the door. Alex is glad that her father has at last scored over his wife.

Surprisingly, after Giles's departure Sheena stops insisting on Alex's going to bed early. She buys her daughter a box of paints, and Basil provides a large packet of thick paper. One Sunday she teaches Alex to knit. Knitting becomes a craze. She makes a blanket for Hatty's basket and then starts on a scarf.

But during the day it's too hot to knit. Alex paces round the garden aimlessly with Hatty at her heels. One Monday afternoon she's desperate for company, and she's drawn towards the village by the sound of a tolling bell. She walks along the main road with Hatty on a lead, and finds herself being swept along by a funeral crowd of wailing, shrieking people, all dressed in black, some of them clapping their hands on their knees. With difficulty she manages to extricate herself from the pressing mass and turns down an alleyway. When the procession has passed Alex takes the dog to the village fountain to drink.

Three bare-bottomed toddlers are playing in the water. When they see Hatty they point and laugh, and start throwing water at the dog. Alex pulls Hatty away, wishing she'd never ventured into the village. However, even this unsatisfactory encounter with people is better than seeing nobody.

She walks back through some vineyards towards a house she has often seen in the distance but never dared to approach, for there are always children working or playing nearby. This house is more substantial than most, being built of large hand cut blocks of stone. An outside stairway leads up to an unfinished upper storey. The roof frame of rough timber is still exposed. Bags of cement and piles of stones and red tiles lie in the yard, next to clay water pots and a number of whitewashed petrol cans in which rosemary, basil and marjoram are growing.

Alex comes near enough to the house to see several fat brown hens pecking away at the ground, and a woman thumping dough on a tray. On a domed circle of black iron bread shaped like a giant pancake is browning over a charcoal fire. The smell is tantalising. Khubz, thinks Alex, the Arab bread she much prefers to the white loaves from Spinneys. She moves nearer and watches a man in baggy black trousers and a braided waistcoat come out of a door. He puts on a keffiyeh and secures it with black cords. In a moment he's surrounded by goats, pushing and nudging. As Alex moves even nearer, to watch a tiny kid feeding from its mother's teat, she is noticed by the man, who grins and waves at her. She turns and flees up the mountain-side towards the villa.

Early next day the house draws her back like a magnet. She spends all morning watching the comings and goings from a hideout. There is always some member of the clan, milking a goat, filling up the panniers, sharpening a sickle, carrying a water jug indoors...

Behind the house out of the stony hillside bursts a spring which has been diverted into a makeshift pipe. Two boys ride off together on one mule and return later with baskets of white rocks gathered from the outcrops of limestone dotting the vineyards. They use these to repair one of the terrace walls. A girl of about nine or ten staggers home with a sack of kindling wood on her back. Below the house, men are ploughing a field with yoked oxen. Everyone is fully occupied and there is plenty of chatter and laughter and quarrelling. One could never be bored in such a family. Alex wants to meet them, but can't bring herself to come out from behind her rock.

A delicious spicy smell wafts up from the house, and reluctantly Alex makes her way home for the glass of milk, fruit and a sandwich which Georgette leaves on the table for her each day. She's been told not to feed Hatty, but she can't resist giving the dog half her sandwich. Watching an animal eat is a pleasure.

In the afternoon she sits under the trees digging pine nuts out of a pile of cones. So absorbed is she in this task that she fails to notice a group of children gathered behind her. By the time she becomes aware of her audience it's too late to run away. The children are staring at Hatty with delight. She runs towards them, enjoying their gasps of admiration and allows herself to be fondled. There are six children between the ages of four and ten, all barefooted with lustrous black eyes. The three boys wear faded shorts, and the three girls shapeless cotton dresses with tiny gold rings in their pierced lobes and gold bangles round their skinny wrists. To Alex's amazement two of the girls have squints.

The children have gathered two baskets of pine-nut cones between them. They point to Alex's pile of nuts, saying, 'Snoober! Snoober!' One of the girls picks up Hatty, and Alex recognises her as the girl from the house who was gathering kindling wood during the morning. Without protest the dachshund is passed round the group, none too gently. Then the children lose interest in the dog and two of the girls take Alex by the hands and pull her along towards their home. The hens run squawking to take cover when Hatty runs into the yard. The boys disappear behind the house and a woman appears at the door and yells something at the girls. Seeing a stranger she smiles and says 'Ahlan wa sahlan.' Alex recognises the words of welcome, and knows she must be polite and stay.

The girls enter the house pulling Alex along with them. The ground floor consists of two large rooms with hard floors of packed clay over which goat's hair rugs are scattered. One of the rooms serving as kitchen and store cupboard is crammed with sacks of nuts, wheat, corn, sweet potatoes, rice and charcoal. In a corner is a brass brazier next to an iron stove. A kerosene lamp perches on a wooden crate. Baskets of figs and strings of onions hang from the ceiling. A crock of dried milk and one of labneh stand on a table where two women are shelling walnuts, their hands stained dark brown from the juice.

In the second room on a backless wooden sofa pushed against the wall and spread with cushions in bright cretonne, sits an old lady. She's engrossed in her crochet work, peering at it through spectacles on the end of her nose. A vast cupboard, a table, two benches, two cane chairs, jars of paper flowers, a small plaster statue of the Virgin painted bright blue and a number of family photographs retouched with sepia complete the furnishings. The windows are shuttered, with no curtains.

A woman who seems to be the mother of the house offers a cup of dark brown liquid. Alex has never really liked liquorice, but she remembers Zilpha telling her how one must never refuse refreshment in an Arab house. The three daughters are not given liquorice juice. They drink water in enamel mugs filled from an earthenware pitcher. Hatty licks up a few drops of water spilt on the floor, but Alex dare not ask for water for the dog. Dogs can fend for themselves. Hatty starts to sniff behind the sacks on the floor round a wooden cradle on rockers. A baby lies on it under gauze netting into which a line of blue beads has been sewn. As Alex bends to pull the dog away her nostrils fill with the dusty smell of wheat.

The three girls are called Sania, Rabiha and Sulafa. Sania, the eldest, leads Alex up the outside stairway to the upper rooms still open to the sky under the roof frame, but already used by the family while the warm weather lasts. Mattresses and quilts are stacked against the walls. When the tiles are put in place the roof will be sloping. Tacked onto the building is a small storehouse with a flat roof, on which pans of tomatoes, figs, apricots, peppers, coriander, mint, walnuts and quinces are drying in the sun. Leftover grapes have been put into two crocks with vinegar and yeast.

They go downstairs again and Sania offers Hatty a ripe fig, but she won't eat it. She needs a drink and must be taken home. Alex wants to say 'Thank you' but is too shy to try her Arabic. all she manages is 'Bye-bye' in English. The girls grin and chant 'Bye-bye' and 'Bukra' and Alex feels a glow of pleasure. She may get to know these friendly children tomorrow. She gathers they want her to bring her 'kelb' again. As she is walking away she remembers an Arab phrase, and turns to shout it back to the children – 'Bukra, ensh'Allah' – 'if God wills'.

Early the following morning Alex is taken aback to see the three girls appear outside the wall of the villa. They stand calling to Hatty, who runs to be stroked. The youngest girl, Sulafa, has picked a bunch of bugloss, campion and poppies for Alex.

In their harsh little tones they insist on Alex and Hatty going with them. When they reach the vineyard near their house Alex is handed a basket to help pick grapes. She's always wanted to pick fruit off the vine, and for a while she enjoys this task, pushing a few of the heavy purple grapes into her mouth as she walks along the terrace. But very quickly it becomes back-breaking, boring work. The vines run low over the ground and her legs begin to ache. Picking fruit in quantity is far from the pleasant occupation it looks from a distance. She fills her first basket long after the other girls have finished their second, and is shown how to empty it into one of the enormous panniers the mules will carry back to the house.

With another basket filled, a large blister appears on her thumb. The sun beats down relentlessly. Alex wanders away from the pickers and lies down with Hatty on the stony ground in the shade of a wall. Face down, she observes hundreds of ants scurrying to and fro carrying tiny burdens on their backs. She shuts her eyes and dozes for a while. When she wakes the pickers have gone. But they can be seen in the distance leading the heavily laden mules down the hill. Disappointed, Alex is about to go home when Sania looks back in her direction and beckons her to follow.

When they reach the house two women unload the panniers and put the grapes into boxes which they place on the back of a small dilapidated lorry. Alex knows she should be returning to the villa by now, but the Lebanese family want her to stay and share their meal. They sit tightly packed round the scrubbed wooden table and eat bowls of something called *kishk,* a mixture of burghul and labneh eaten hot with a salad of raw onions, cream cheese, okras and crushed basil. It doesn't look appetising but it tastes wonderful. The girls' mother, who says her name is Tamam Fahiliya, is pleased that Alex likes her food, and refills her bowl.

Alex visits the Fahiliya family every day, and watches their daily routine. She recalls Arabic words Saeb taught her, and by the end of a week she can speak enough basic Arabic to get by. In particular she learns words to do with food – she loves the sound of *sfoof,* for a cake made with semolina; *badinjan*, for eggplant; *banadoura* for tomato; *mdardara* for lentil. She relishes the interesting highly spiced dishes Tamam prepares. She samples a variation of yakhne made with dried tomatoes and peppers, and she develops a passion for knafi, a cheese-filled pastry with syrup poured over it. The only food she dislikes is a gelatinous soup made of sheep's feet. She has to drink goat's milk to help it down.

Alex feels most content when she isn't just standing around watching the busy family. She helps the girls collect pine cones and pick figs. She learns how to beat the rugs with a rattan carpet beater, and most skilful of all, to peel an orange in one long curl to be dried as a firelighter. She discovers that most of Tamam's meals are based on burghul, and all the baking, apart from the mountain bread, has to be done at the bakery in the village. There's no oven inside the house.

Georgette, aware that Alex has made friends with the Fahiliya family, ceases to bother whether she returns home at lunchtime. She continues to leave the glass of milk and the plate of sandwiches usually made with bright orange tinned Kraft cheese on the table. Alex takes to saving the sandwiches for her friends to feed to the hens. Often when Alex comes home on the days when her mother remains in Beirut Georgette is absent, sometimes not returning until after dark, by which time Alex is beginning to feel anxious. The villa suddenly seems large and empty. The first time Alex is left alone after dusk she threatens to tell Sheena. 'If you do', retorts Georgette sharply, 'I'll tell your mother you spend your days with the Fahiliyas. She'll stop you going.'

'Why will she?'

'Because those children aren't good enough for you to play with.'

Alex isn't sure what she means and doesn't know whether to believe Georgette. But she does know Sheena would have wanted her to ask permission to visit the Lebanese family. Her mother might decide to visit the family herself to find out what the children are like. Instinctively she knows this wouldn't be a good idea. Mrs Fahiliya wouldn't want to be vetted. It becomes an unspoken deal between the maid and herself that neither of them should bother with what the other is doing.

Sometimes Alex accompanies Sania to the shops. Shopping has to be done daily as the family has no refrigerator and no cupboard stacked with tinned food. Sania has to buy items such as soap, matches, lye water and kerosene as well as food. Often she buys a small bag of aniseed balls to share with the other children. Alex dislikes aniseed and wishes she had money to buy the peppermints she can see in a tall glass jar.

Once all three sisters go to the village to buy ice cream as a treat. Rabiha decides she would rather have a chunk of water melon which is offered to her at the end of a knife. Alex is pleased but embarrassed when Sania buys her an ice cream too. As the children sit on a wall licking their ices they see Georgette coming out of a shop with two soldiers in uniform. The maid notices Alex but doesn't speak. That evening when Alex is in bed she hears voices coming from the kitchen. She creeps downstairs and beyond the open door she can see the same two uniformed men drinking arak. Georgette is flushed and laughs loudly. Alex scurries away without being detected.

One morning Georgette announces she will be out until teatime.

'Where are you going?'

'To visit a friend.'

Alex is pleased to be rid of the maid and at the same time uneasy. Later she will go and find her friends, but just now she has a slight stomach ache and doesn't feel like walking in the sun.

An hour later, as she and Hatty lie half asleep on the grass watching a sparrow take a dust bath, she hears a giggle close to her ear and sits up with a start. Her friends are sitting round her. They want to see inside the villa. Alex leads them up the verandah steps into the living room, and then into all the other rooms. She feels proud and rather superior as the girls exclaim at the space, the furniture, the many clothes in Sheena's wardrobe, the bottles on the silver tray, the packets of food in the tall refrigerator, the bathroom... And this is nothing, she thinks, compared to the luxury of Basil's apartment in Beirut.

The visitors must be offered something to eat, so Alex searches for food and drink which Georgette will not miss. She opens three small bottles of ginger beer and spreads some bread with Hartley's fig jam. It doesn't seem sufficient after all the food she has consumed at their house. Perhaps a tin of something to take home? She chooses a tin of peaches, a tin of pineapple chunks, a tin of sardines and a jar of marmalade. These gifts are accepted with animated thanks from Sania. Alex enjoys being a benefactor and wonders whether she might find something else to give the girls.

Sheena still keeps a wooden box of fake jewellery which she hardly ever wears, an assortment of earrings and beads she's picked up in the bazaars. Alex extracts a pair of earrings, a necklace and a ring. Sania removes the gold rings from her ears and tries on the fake diamanté earrings in front of the mirror. With cries of admiration Rabiha and Sulafa demand to try them on as well. Alex rummages through the box and manages to find two more pairs of earrings. She longs to give the sisters more gifts just to hear their gasps of delight. As a final gesture she sprays each girl lavishly with Chanel perfume.

Suddenly the girls become tired of the villa and go racing out into the sunshine again, much to Alex's relief. The onus of playing hostess to these children is becoming too much for her. And there is always the possibility that Georgette might change her mind and return home early. Alex is ambivalent about her friends She relies on them for company but finds it hard to follow what they're saying, especially when they're quarrelling. In spite of having learnt some basic Arabic she still feels very much an outsider. The girls seem to respect her, yet they often whisper to each other and laugh, making her feel uncomfortable. Most days from early morning until dusk the girls are kept doing jobs to help their parents. Alex is sure they think her lazy and spoilt. None of them has ever possessed a toy bought from a shop, yet they are never bored. The boys play with home-made hoops and catapults, the girls with home-made rag dolls. When the children have a free hour Alex shows them how to play hopscotch. She brings her skipping rope and her rubber ball, which one of the boys immediately loses.

Alex discovers that the end of the grape harvest is an occasion for a celebration among the mountain people. The children tell her a sheep will be roasted on Thursday night. There will be singing and dancing all night long in the village. Alex is invited to join in the festivities and to spend the night with the family. Basil and Sheena will be in Beirut that night and Alex wonders if Georgette will allow her to go. At first the maid says no, her mother would never want her to be out all night. Later she relents and allows Alex to go on the understanding that on no account is Sheena to be told.

Behind the Fahiliyas' house a lamb has been roasting all day, buried in hot embers in a hole in the ground. Now it's deliciously tender and ready to fall apart. Outside the house a white cloth covers a trestle table laden with large platters of rice fried with pine kernels, onion and garlic, surrounded with small dishes of labneh, sliced cucumber and dill. They sit on rough benches under a pale mauve sky and eat the rice and lamb with rolled up mountain bread. Soon Alex is so full she can hardly stand. When it's dark and the feast cleared away she's ready for sleep. But now it's time to make their way to the village for the music and dancing.

The night is clear and fresh, the stars so large and bright that the road to Broummana glimmers palely as the party walks to the large open-air café. In daylight this café looks shabby and run-down, but after dark comes alive with strings of coloured lights, and loud music. Dancers appear in elaborate costumes − flounced skirts of gauzy multicoloured material worn over red pantaloons with bluey-grey stoles and orange waistbands. The men carry knives at their belts. The women jangle as they move, their arms adorned with bangles and bracelets from which hang gold coins.

Sania leads them into a crowd sitting around a huge bonfire in the centre of the village. Vendors are moving amongst the people, some selling *mahmoul*, hot nuts and halawi, others *furuq mishwi*, pieces of chicken grilled over charcoal. The flames light up the many faces and it strikes Alex that Basil is quite wrong in his assertion that 'All Arabs look the same'.

Alex is wide awake now. It seems the whole village is out on the streets. Mothers have brought their babies strapped to their backs. Arabic music, loud and insistent, issues from half a dozen instrumentalists and singers. Mrs Fahiliya gives the girls cane syrup to sip and tells them to remain sitting by the bonfire while she and her husband go off to join the dancing. Alex wishes she could get up and join in too. It looks simple enough – the swaying and clapping of hands and weaving in and out. Children always get excluded from the dancing.

It's nearly two o'clock by the time the Fahiliya family starts for home. On each side of the road the glow-worms form a shimmering necklace of light in the dry grass. The old grandmother is cradling the screeching baby in her arms. Alex has still not worked out who the baby belongs to, since there are several young women in and around the house. Mrs Fahiliya yells at her children to get to bed quickly. Alex follows them outside and finds herself in a queue for the toilet shed a few yards from the house. Sania places a torch lamp on the hard mud floor. Alex is dismayed at the primitive arrangements – two wooden boards laid on either side of a deep hole – and almost wishes she was back at the villa. Sheena would certainly not approve.

Picking up the torch, Sania leads them to the water pipe from the spring. When she's washed her hands Alex has to dry them on her dress. Upstairs in the children's bedroom she helps to lay out the mattresses they are to share. They lie down without undressing, crowded close together under faded quilts, since the night air has become chilly.

Alex is unable to sleep in these unfamiliar surroundings. She gazes up at the immensity of the starry sky through the rafter frame and remembers the first time she slept looking up at the stars from the Mother Superior's roof terrace in Jerusalem. Towards dawn she dozes off, and wakes abruptly to find the sky has lightened to a translucent grey with a hint of the pink sunrise to come. The early morning, with its elusive scents and sounds, transports her into a mysterious dreamlike state only to be experienced when sleeping out of doors. Her nostrils pick up the scent of oranges, and she notices a string tied across one end of the room on which long curling orange rinds have been hung to dry. She would like to lie here for ever, savouring the sharp contrast between the cosy warmth under the quilt and the exhilarating spiky morning air.

A few minutes later, however, the household starts coming to life. The mattresses are rolled up for the day, the stove is lit and the goats are milked in the yard. Breakfast consists of a cup of foaming warm goat's milk and a bowl of burghul with either labneh or honey. But no one sits down to this meal. The children are washing and changing their clothes and starting on the various jobs assigned to each of them. Alex slips away unnoticed back to the villa to find Hatty and enjoy the luxury of a bathroom.

She's surprised to find Georgette talking to a man in the kitchen. 'Did you have fun last night in the village?' he asks Alex genially. 'We saw you sitting by the bonfire.'

'Yes' replies Alex, and hurries upstairs. But almost immediately she comes down again and listens outside the kitchen door.

'Will the kid tell her mother, d'you think?' Alex hears the man say.

'No, she won't', returns the maid.

'Are you sure?'

'Quite sure. She knows what she'll get if she does!'

Chapter Thirty

Alex asks her mother if she may accompany the Fahiliya family to church on Sunday. Sheena looks doubtful. 'How did you get to know the family?'

'I met three of the children in the woods.'

'Well, I suppose you can go to church with them.'

Alex changes into her party frock and ties clean white bows onto her plaits.

'Why are you dressed for a party?' asks her mother.

'Because Sania and her sisters always wear their best frocks to church.'

'You won't understand a word of the service.'

'I don't mind.'

When the church bell starts to ring Alex walks to the church and waits outside. A priest in black with a long black beard and a tall chimney hat glances at her in surprise and opens the church door. People start going in, each one turning to stare curiously at the English girl. Alex finds the Arab habit of unabashed staring hard to cope with.

Inside, the church has dazzling whitewashed walls and high arched windows, under which candles flicker in niches beside vases of paper flowers and plaster statues painted in silver and gold and the ubiquitous blue. No seats – only a glittering altar at the far end, before which the priest stands chanting away in a strange Arab liturgy. Every now and then a bell tinkles and wisps of smoke waft over the heads of the congregation. The bread dipped in wine is handed out over a white cloth. There's a strong smell of something, not unpleasant, but which makes Alex's eyes prickle and water. She is reminded of mass at the convent. She notices that the men stand at the front and the women at the back. A few elderly people are seated in high-backed chairs. Several toddlers dash to and fro between their parents. It's irksome having to stand. The American Mission Church where everyone sits down between the hymns is much more comfortable. Nevertheless she finds the atmosphere awe-inspiring. This is the kind of service Zilpha has often described to her.

Before leaving the church the Fahiliya children each place twenty-five piastres on a plate beneath a statue of the Virgin. Outside, Sania makes admiring remarks about Alex's frock, and she in turn praises Sania's pink poplin dress trimmed with white lace, although it's bursting at the seams. Rabiha and Sulafa are wearing blue organdie with many frills.

She slips off home and finds Basil and her mother having brunch. 'You'd better take off that party frock before you spoil it', Sheena advises.

'Did you enjoy the service?' asks Basil.

'I didn't like having to stand all the time.'

'Is it a Roman Catholic church?' Sheena asks Basil.

'No, Maronite. But they're united with Rome. They have a Patriarch of Antioch who lives in a monastery somewhere on Mount Lebanon.'

'What language do they use?'

'Syriac, I expect. There are lots of shrines in these mountains, some inscribed in Syriac, some in Latin.'

'Are the Druzes Christians?'

'They're an offshoot from the Muslims, with a dash of Christianity. A guy called Darazi compiled a book of doctrines which they keep secret. They have no mosques or prayers. It's all very mysterious. They believe in reincarnation and predestination.'

Alex is intrigued and would like to know more about the Druzes. Her father will be able to tell her.

When Alex next visits Sania's family, the day before she's due to return to Beirut, all the furniture is standing outside the house. Mr Fahiliya has re-clayed the ground floor inside and two women are rubbing it smooth with flat stones. Mrs Fahiliya is beating the rugs, and she shoos the children away from the dust. The boys are chattering excitedly. Sania takes Alex's hand and pulls her along, saying everyone must go to the village. Something of interest is obviously afoot, since people are gathering on the edge of Broummana. Standing at the back of the crowd, Alex can't see what she's been brought to witness, but can hear the agonised bellowing of an animal. The sound freezes her blood and she senses something terrible is going to happen. She wants to run away, but the children are pushing her forward, eager to reach the front of the excited onlookers.

In a moment they emerge in the front row, and Alex sees the animal, a young steer lying on its back on a concrete slab with runnels on each side leading to a drain. Its hooves are tied together and a man in a striped apron is sharpening a knife. Alex glances at the faces of some boys opposite and sees the same expression as she saw on the faces of the children when they were playing 'hospital' in the Durands' den. Her stomach heaves, but there's no chance of escape. She's hemmed in on every side.

The terrified creature is fully aware when the knife descends to slit its smooth white throat. Blood spurts in the air and a gout of red splashes over the feet of a little boy who's come too close. Alex watches with horror as the boy dabs his fingers in the blood and then licks them.

The horrors multiply. Alex seems to hear the steer's agony above the cheers of the crowd even after the wretched animal's abdomen has been cut open and a heap of steaming purple entrails slops out into the thick pool of blood on the concrete. The sight of this slaughtered flesh triggers deep fear and revulsion in Alex. She feels an explosion in her head, a wild hatred of these people who are laughing and enjoying the spectacle of an animal in pain. She had no idea such quantities of blood could flow from one body. The stench, and the flies glistening black on the heaving mass of raw flesh is more than she can stomach.

Frantic now, Alex worms her way through the crowd and escapes into the pine woods. Here she kneels on the ground and vomits, and then vomits again – her body retching, her skin pouring with sweat. Later she hears many voices going past down the hill, and then all is quiet. She walks home without seeing her friends again.

Two days later Alex is back in Beirut, preparing to return to school. To her immense relief she finds that Naomi has left for good. To think of never seeing that taunting, grinning face again! Mrs Kellaway tells her that Naomi's mother has moved to Jerusalem. Alex expects Annabel to be desolate, but she seems quite cheerful.

'I never really liked Naomi', she states blithely. 'She was much too bossy. Mom hated having her to stay. She likes you far better, and so do I.'

Alex is astonished. 'Then why did you let her be your best friend?'

'I felt sorry for her. She seemed nice at first', Annabel says vaguely. She takes it for granted that Alex will resume her role of 'best friend'. Alex can't resist Annabel's charm, but her trust in the girl has gone.

Annabel will be nine years old on October 23rd. She spends much of the school day planning her party and making a list of the guests. There had been no eighth birthday party the previous year, as Mrs Hitti was ill. This year's celebration will make up for the loss. Bobbie and Jake have no chance of being invited. They despise Alex for giving in to Annabel so soon after Naomi's departure. They hardly speak to her now. Alex regrets losing their friendship, but Annabel is the one she likes best.

Sheena has had a new party frock made for her daughter. In front of the long mirror in her mother's room Alex tries on the light green velvet frock trimmed with broderie anglaise. Without her glasses and with her hair unplaited she looks almost passable, but certainly not the attractive child Sheena would like.

At Annabel's party there are several children Alex has never seen before – the daughters of Mrs Hitti's Lebanese friends. They are cheerful little girls who twitter away like birds without constraint, making admiring comments about the clothes and the furniture. Then Alex notices two familiar faces and recognises Giselle and Jeanne Durand. Annabel whispers that her mother insisted on inviting the twins. She herself didn't really want them to come because they only speak French. The twins stare at Alex and nudge each other. But as Annabel's special friend Alex can afford to stare back and then to ignore them.

At the end of the party Alex stays on for a while and Annabel takes her upstairs to her bedroom. They pass the half-open door of Mrs Hitti's room. She's sitting with her feet up, listening to the wireless.

'Mom's always listening to news about the war', says Annabel. 'I hate the war. It's so boring and just goes on and on.'

'So do I', agrees Alex.

Annabel shuts her door and says, 'If you take your shoes off I'll paint your toenails red!' Alex is thrilled with this idea, but when the task is completed she wonders how she's going to keep it a secret from her mother. 'You have got big feet!' Annabel comments.

Now when Sheena comes home from the hospital she no longer takes a rest. She changes out of her uniform and goes out. Someone picks her up at the gate in a car. She often doesn't return until late at night. She begins to look tired and becomes irritable.

Late one evening when Alex is reading in her room she hears loud voices in the lounge, and slips down the stairs to the sliding door. Opening it an inch, she listens to Basil and Sheena's voices raised in anger.

'You haven't spent an evening with me for two weeks', Basil is complaining. 'Are you the only woman in Beirut who can run the club for those servicemen? There must be a dozen others who'd be glad to take a turn in the evenings!'

'I was elected by the committee to look after the servicemen. There are so many things to organise and I can't do them in the daytime.'

'You could have a rota. They can't expect you to work every night after a tiring day at the hospital.'

'I shall arrange to have weekends off soon.'

'Weekends! And what am I expected to do on weekdays?'

'Come with me and help.'

'And watch all those kids in uniform fawning around you? No thank you!'

'You sound jealous. You ought to be glad I'm doing something for the forces.'

'Of course I'm not jealous. I just hate to see you getting run down.'

'You want me at home to entertain your friends! Well, the boys at the club need me more. You've got a cook and a maid to help you here!'

Sheena mounts the stairs quickly and Alex only just manages to flee out of sight as her mother slides open the door. A moment later Basil comes up and knocks on the bedroom door. Sheena shouts 'Go away! I want to get some sleep!' This is the first time Alex has heard them quarrel. She's glad. It fills her with the hope that Sheena will leave Basil. But the next day they are being nice to each other again.

In November comes the exciting news that the Eighth Army has won the Battle of el Alamein. Rommel has been defeated at last. Cairo and the Middle East have been saved. The church bells are ringing in Britain for the first time since the war started. Sheena organises two celebration parties in Basil's apartment for American, British, Australian and New Zealand servicemen. These events are riotous affairs, with much laughter and jazzy records playing until three in the morning.

On one occasion when Alex is kept awake by the popular tune of *Chattanooga Choo-Choo* played over several times she goes down to the sliding door to see what's going on. She observes Sheena through a haze of cigarette smoke, sitting on the marble room divider in between two men who have their arms around her. She can't see Basil anywhere. So absorbed is she in watching her mother in this unusual role that she doesn't notice a guest has come halfway up the stairs. The door slides back abruptly, nearly knocking her over. A man grins down at her. 'Well, well, young lady! Don't be shy! Come on down and join the party!' And before she can make her escape the man lifts her in his arms, and carries her down the stairs into the noisy throng.

'Hey, folks!' shouts the man. 'Look what I found upstairs!'

He puts her down, and everyone turns to inspect Alex standing in her pyjamas, her face burning with embarrassment.

'Is that Sheena's kid?' someone asks in a slurred voice.

'Sheena's kid? Never! It must be Basil's!' And everyone laughs. Then a woman in powder-blue crepe de chine puts her plump arm around Alex, saying, 'Don't you take any notice of these drunks, honey. You come with me and I'll fix you some ice cream.' She propels Alex into the dining room, but supper has been cleared away. So she proceeds to the kitchen.

'Ice cream for the little girl', she says in an unsteady voice.

Georgette regards them with contempt. 'No ice cream left' she says sourly.

'Did you hear that, honey? No ice cream! Let's go find a drink.'

On the way back to the lounge Alex wriggles out of the woman's grasp and dashes upstairs.

When she comes down for breakfast she finds Georgette clearing away the usual dirty glasses and overflowing ashtrays. She can see several cigarette ends stubbed into the carpet and wonders if Sheena will be angry. In the kitchen Abby and the maid start to squabble. The cook wants to move her afternoon off to Wednesday, which is Georgette's afternoon off, but the maid refuses to swap. 'I have to visit my mother on Wednesdays' shrieks Georgette, 'Because that's the day my married sister visits, and I want to see her.'

Basil appears and tells the maid she'll have to change her day to Thursday. Abby has been with him much longer and has the right to change her day once in a while. And they can't both have Wednesday because someone has to be in the apartment when Alex returns from school.

But Georgette has other ideas and the following Wednesday she waits outside the school for Alex. Since their return from the mountains the maid hasn't taken Alex on a so-called 'walk' to visit her family. Sheena has told her it's no longer necessary for Alex to be taken for a walk once a week.

'We're going to visit my family', announces Georgette.

'I don't want to go. I'll tell my mother you took the afternoon off when Mr Carrington said you must stay at home for when I come back.'

Georgette grasps her roughly by the arm. 'No, you will not. You'll keep your mouth shut. I know all the bad things you've done.'

'What bad things?'

'Things you don't want your mother to know.'

Alex is suddenly afraid. How much does Georgette know about her? Is she spying secretly all the time? Her mind races to and fro, trying to remember the times she has been disobedient, has told lies, even the wicked thoughts she's harboured.

Alex drags her feet and sulks all the way to Georgette's home. As they near the block of flats it begins to drizzle. Up above, Georgette's sister is taking in a sheet from the washing line strung across the balcony. She hangs over the railing and waves. Behind her comes running the toddler who was just learning to walk when Alex first came to the flat. He clings onto the iron railings of the balcony, pulling at them and shouting down to his aunt.

Suddenly two of the railings give way and the child plunges through the gap with a high-pitched scream, falling swiftly, head down, onto the concrete pavement. He lands with a sickening thud a few inches from Alex's feet.

The mother up above stares down, mouth wide open, eyes transfixed with disbelief. Georgette and Alex stand frozen with shock. The small body lies so still, a shapeless heap with a smashed bloodied head. The little feet are bare, and Alex notices the perfection of the tiny brown toes and pink nails. From above come wails of pure primeval agony. Alex shuts her eyes tightly as Georgette picks up the body and disappears up the stairs, leaving her basket on the pavement. Under the napkin Alex glimpses the remains of a pumpkin pie. She lifts the basket and climbs the stairs in a daze, her legs heavy as lumps of clay.

Inside, the flat is full of lamenting females. The mother is sitting on the floor, rocking to and fro as she clutches the dead child, wrapped in a linen cloth, to her breast. The grandmother lies on the settee as though in a coma. The balcony door has been closed and the atmosphere is stifling in spite of its being a cool December day. The wailing rises and falls, repeating itself in a dirge-like chant. Alex's head begins to swim as she sits down in a corner and breathes in the stale odours of cooking and cheap cologne. Eventually Georgette wrenches the child from his mother and carries him into another room. A woman leaves the flat and two men enter it. An argument ensues and more people arrive, but Alex is unable to grasp what's happening.

Half an hour later Georgette emerges from the bedroom, her face streaked with tears. She takes Alex's hand and they descend the stairs and walk home in silence. It's the first and only time Alex is glad of her touch.

Sheena is standing at the door of the apartment. 'Where have you been?' she demands, not noticing bloodstains on Georgette's black dress.

'Alex wanted to go for a walk on the campus', mutters Georgette, and Alex doesn't deny it. She's desperate to pour out the shocking events of the afternoon. But the moment has passed and she goes to her room in silence.

The harrowing experience affects Alex deeply. To think that an active child should be so vulnerable, that in seconds it could fall and lie like a crushed insect on the pavement. How can such vibrant life leave the body so quickly, so mysteriously? Alex leans against the stone balustrade of the upstairs balcony and thinks – *If I were to fall, my body would lie dead on those black tiles down there. If I stood on a chair and leaned too far over the balustrade I could leave this world in a few seconds.* She draws back hurriedly, her heart thumping.

Two days later, when Alex returns from school Abby tells her Georgette has gone to a family funeral. Her nephew has died in an accident. Alex imagines the little corpse lying in a glass coffin like Snow White. She wishes she knew the child's name. When her mother comes to say goodnight on one of her rare evenings at home, her daughter suddenly dissolves into tears. Sheena is sympathetic at first, but soon becomes irritated when Alex refuses to say why she's upset.

'Has Mrs Kellaway been cross with you?'

'No.'

'Well, cheer up then. Have a good sleep, and you'll feel better in the morning.' She brushes Alex's wet cheek with her lips.

Now that Naomi has departed, Alex resumes her visits to the Hitti household and joins the family each Sunday morning to go to church. The service is still tedious, but she and Annabel are made much of by the friendly American ladies. And there's always lemonade and cakes. Annabel asks if she may come and play at Basil's apartment.

315

Flustered by this sudden request, Alex says 'There isn't anywhere to play. We don't have a proper garden to ourselves.'

'I don't mind. We can play inside.'

Alex imagines introducing her friend to Basil.

'I can't invite you. Mr Carrington wouldn't let me', lies Alex.

'Why not?'

'He doesn't like children.'

Annabel is intrigued. She can't imagine an adult not being charmed by her. Mr Carrington would be a challenge. 'Is he nasty to you?'

'Yes.'

'What does he do to you?' asks Annabel, wide-eyed with curiosity.

Alex warms to the fantasy of Basil as a wicked stepfather. 'He never lets me have any fun. He makes me go for walks with his horrid maid who smacks me.'

'Does he smack you himself?'

Alex hesitates and then lies again. 'Sometimes he does.'

'Why does your mother let him?'

'Because she's frightened of him.' Alex is beginning to enjoy herself in this role of victim, but she can see it might have repercussions. 'You must promise not to tell anyone about Mr Carrington', she warns Annabel, 'Not even your mother.'

Annabel is full of sympathy. 'You poor thing! How awful to have a wicked stepfather.'

'When the war ends my real father is going to come and take me away to England.'

'When the war ends, we're going to the States', announces Annabel.

Alex envies her friend. Mrs Kellaway makes America sound the best and the most beautiful country in the world – much better than wartime Britain.

In spite of her promise Alex is sure Annabel has mentioned Mr Carrington to her mother. Mrs Hitti starts to ask questions about Alex's home life, and worries that Sheena and Basil have no religion and spend so little time with Alex.

At school Mrs Kellaway has been rehearsing her pupils for a nativity play. Mrs Hitti, who drives Alex home after the performance, says she and Annabel were by far the best. Their words were the clearest. Alex climbs the stairs in a glow of achievement, wishing that Giles and Sheena had been present with the other parents. The lounge is in darkness. Abby is in her room. Georgette is reading at the kitchen table. 'Your supper is under that plate', she remarks, barely looking up from her magazine.

'I was in a play', the child proclaims proudly as she eats her egg sandwiches.

But the maid seems not to hear. 'Hurry up with your supper. It's long past your bedtime.'

Chapter Thirty-one

Alex is overjoyed when Sheena informs her that on his next visit her father will be arriving in time for the Christmas Eve party, and will be sleeping at Basil's apartment.

The seven-foot tree blazes with light, tinsel and shiny baubles. Abby and Sheena are putting the finishing touches to an extravagant buffet supper.

When Giles comes up to her room, Alex says 'Can I come to the party? I don't have to go to bed till late now.'

But Giles thinks not. 'You'll have to ask your mother.'

When Sheena comes up to dress for the party Giles says to her, 'I hope Basil won't object, but I've asked a friend of mine, Daoud, a Palestinian from Kirkuk, to come tonight. His family's in a refugee camp. He's no home to go to over Christmas. So I brought him to Beirut. He's staying at the pension I stayed at last year.'

'Oh, Giles, how could you? He won't enjoy our kind of party and there are already far too many guests.'

'I don't suppose he'll stay long. I don't like to think of him sitting in his room alone all evening.'

But Sheena isn't satisfied. 'A Palestinian refugee isn't going to go down well with Basil's Jewish friends.'

'You used to sympathise with the Palestinians when we lived in Haifa.'

'Of course I'm sorry for them. But I don't want your friend to spoil the party.'

Sheena says Alex may come downstairs for a while until the guests have arrived. In the lounge Basil is sorting out records to play during the evening. He starts with a tune called *Lullaby of Broadway.* 'Hi there, Giles!' he says. 'Let me fix you a drink.'

Giles finishes a neat whisky as the door bell rings and the first few guests come spilling across the marble floor. The ladies hand their stoles, sequinned jackets or fox furs to a hired waiter wearing black with a bow tie. An overpowering scent of French perfume wafts across the room.

A log fire burns in the fireplace. The glow of several table lamps and the tree lights gives the room a warm, welcoming feel quite distinct from its usual daytime emptiness. From behind the Christmas tree Alex admires the lovely frocks in taffeta, silk, satin and fine wool. She is longing for Sheena to come down the stairs. She's had an outfit especially made for this party which Alex hasn't seen. She hopes it's a proper ball gown like a princess! What a disappointment when the sliding door opens and Sheena appears wearing a close-fitting black dress with long tight sleeves! A diamond necklace sparkles round her white neck, matching a diamond clasp in her hair. She descends the stairs slowly, while *Lady, Be Good* is being played.

As Giles looks up at his wife coming down, Alex sees the familiar adoring expression on his face. It gives her a stab of pain on his account, and on her own a stab of jealousy. Basil moves towards Sheena and takes her hand. How can she allow herself to walk by his side smiling at the guests with Giles looking on!

Alex can't bear to watch, and she darts from behind the tree, setting in motion several of the silver bells. She bounds up the stairs as the doorbell rings once more. Concealing herself behind the sliding door she waits to see who will come in. Her father greets a slight dark-haired man with a light brown skin and leads him over to meet Basil. This must be his Palestinian friend.

She goes to bed and much later wakes to the sound of raised voices down below. She listens, and then creeps down to the sliding door. She can see several guests, including her father, talking to the Palestinian man who's shouting and gesticulating wildly. It's hard to make out exactly what anyone is saying, but she catches the words *Israel, Palestine, homeland, Jews, Phalange, genocide* and *terrorist.* Giles is obviously trying to calm his friend down. The other guests are sitting around, looking on with embarrassment.

The room is dark except for the Christmas tree lights and one lamp. The usual fog of cigarette smoke pervades the atmosphere, so Alex can't see Daoud clearly. But she can hear how emotional he's become and feels frightened for him. Suddenly he makes a stiff bow towards Giles and rushes out of the room. Complete silence falls on the guests until a woman drawls, 'My God, Norman, it's three o'clock! We must go home!' In a few minutes the room empties except for Basil, Sheena and Giles.

Sheena bursts out furiously, 'How could you bring that little twerp to our party, Giles? From the moment he set foot in this room he killed it with all that self-pity and political argument!'

'Political argument! For heaven's sake, Sheena, Daoud's lost his home, his family and his country! The Jewish authorities allowed defoliant to be sprayed on his father's crops to force him into selling his farm. That's a human argument!'

'I don't care what it is, he shouldn't have been invited to our party. As a guest in our apartment he should have controlled his feelings.'

'It was a pity he got so emotional, but he was provoked several times by people who should know better. It's a very unsettling time for Palestinian refugees. You can't expect them not to get heated.'

'It's your fault for bringing the bloody man here!'

'I know, and I'm truly sorry. But I also think it's no bad thing for us to meet Palestinians and listen to their grievances.'

Basil says nothing, but he looks angry. Sheena gets up, saying, 'I suppose we'd better go to bed and sleep it off.'

When Alex wakes at seven her stocking is still empty. Indignantly she takes it with Hatty into the guest room where her father is sleeping soundly. For a few moments she lets him sleep on, thinking how young he looks, almost boyish. How different from the slightly harassed expression he wears during the day.

She puts her mouth close to his ear. 'Giles, wake up! It's Christmas Day and Santa Claus hasn't filled my stocking!'

He wakes instantly and sits up, saying, 'Oh, hell, I forgot all about it! It's in the wardrobe.' Alex takes out a bulging stocking and lays it on the bed with an exciting crackling noise. She opens the little parcels slowly, savouring each one. A tiny musical box which plays *Clementine* pleases her most.

'I'm going to make some tea', says Giles, and slips on the shabby brown dressing gown he used to wear at K3. Alex and Hatty slide into the still warm bed and curl up at the bottom. When Giles returns and sits on the hump Alex squeals with delight.

'Shh! You'll wake your mother.' He pulls up a chair and sips his tea, after taking some pills for his hangover. Alex props herself against his pillow, eating a piece of dry toast.

'Why do you drink whisky if it makes you sick?'

'It also makes me feel happy. It's only when I drink too much that I feel sick.'

'Did your friend drink too much last night?'

'No, he doesn't drink whisky.'

'Why did he get so upset at the party?'

'Alex, have you been eavesdropping again?'

'I couldn't help it. You woke me up making such a noise.'

'It's difficult to explain. The argument started when someone mentioned a group of Lebanese Christians who call themselves the Phalange. They want the Jews in Palestine to help them get rid of the Muslims in the Lebanon. Daoud himself is a Christian Arab but he was arguing that the Muslim Arabs haven't been treated fairly by the Western countries and by the Jews. He said the Palestinian Arabs have always tolerated the Jews in the past, and it's a crime that the Jews are now terrorising the Palestinians.'

'Is the Stern Gang still bombing and shooting the Palestinians?'

'Yes, only now it's run by a man called Shamir. Stern himself was shot dead in November. The Arabs who've stayed on in Palestine are trying to get their own back.'

Alex is silent for a moment and then says, 'What are we going to do this morning? Basil and Sheena won't be up for hours.'

'Shall we get dressed and go for a walk? And then call on Daoud? He'll be feeling lonely, all by himself on Christmas morning.'

Alex skips along the pavement holding her father's hand, asking him more questions about Daoud. 'Did the Jews take his home?'

'Yes, they did, though I don't know the full story. The trouble is, there just isn't enough land for all the Arabs and Jews in Palestine.'

'Can't they go to the friendly countries until the war ends, and then go back to their own countries?'

'A few will do that, of course, but most won't feel like going back to the place where they were treated so badly.'

Alex considers this statement, and comes to the firm conclusion that the Jews must share Palestine or get out. 'They shouldn't have made Zilpha or Daoud go. I don't like the Jews.'

Giles laughs. 'Now it's you being unreasonable. Most Jews are very good, peace-loving people who don't wish to hurt the Palestinians. It's only a few who behave badly.'

'If most of them are good, why don't they make the bad ones behave kindly?'

'Because the bad Jews have become the leaders and they have guns to make people do what they want.'

'Can't the good ones get guns too?'

Giles sighs. 'The difficulty is, Alex, that if you're trying to be fair and kind and unselfish you don't want to force anyone to do something by threatening him with a gun.'

They turn into Avenue Clemenceau and stop outside the pension. Giles rings the bell, and a large, genial-looking female proprietor opens the door.

'Happy Christmas, Mr Kinley! Come in, come in! And this is your little girl!' She plants a kiss on Alex's forehead and ushers them into a living room. Daoud appears looking tired and solemn. He's full of apologies for his outburst at the party. Giles smiles and pats him on the shoulder saying it doesn't matter, everyone had had too much to drink.

Daoud agrees to come for a walk. Alex soon warms to him because he talks naturally to her, asking questions about Hatty and school and Christmas. He stops looking

322

solemn and laughs a great deal. Alex holds hands with Giles and with Daoud and pulls them along to the campus. The university is closed for the day and there are few people about. The sea is a sulky grey under heavy low cloud.

'Where are your family spending Christmas?' Alex asks Daoud.

'In Jordan', he replies, 'In a refugee camp. My mother and three sisters and my grandparents.'

'Why don't you go to visit them?'

'Because you have to have a special visa to get into Jordan, In wartime it's difficult to get one.'

'Will you see them after he war?'

'I hope so.'

'Will they have a Christmas tree and presents in the camp?'

'No. Most of the refugees are Muslims.'

It starts to drizzle, so they hurry back to Daoud's pension. The proprietor offers them cakes and coffee, and then they leave, Giles promising to return during the evening. On their way home Alex asks, 'Will Daoud have turkey and ice cream?'

'No, but he won't mind. He prefers Arab food.'

'I do too.'

They stroll along in silence for a while. Then Alex ventures to ask, 'When the war ends and Mr Carrington goes back to the States, will you live with Sheena again?'

Her father hesitates. 'I expect so.'

'Why can't you be certain?' she urges relentlessly.

'I am certain', he says shortly.

There are other things she needs to say. She wants to tell Giles about the child who fell from the balcony and about Georgette's threats. But she's afraid her father might confront the maid and later she might take revenge. It's safer to keep quiet.

As they go up the stairs to Basil's apartment Giles says, 'It's Christmas day and we must all be good-tempered and kind to one another. Do you promise to try?' Alex promises, but inside she knows nothing is solved.

Basil is amiable at lunch. The disturbance at his party isn't mentioned. Sheena is very bright, almost too cheerful, asking her daughter questions as though she were a toddler. Year after year, thinks Alex, she never changes the way she speaks to me. Doesn't she realise I can understand grownup conversation? And can't she see I've grown out of dolls? Sheena has given her a large sophisticated doll this Christmas, beautifully dressed, wearing a hat, boots and gloves, and carrying a parasol.

She admires the doll, but feels disappointed. She was hoping to receive a gold signet ring like the one Annabel wears. When Alex opens Basil's present it turns out to be an enormous box of chocolates tied with a huge red ribbon. He grins at her and she blushes, hardly knowing how to stammer out her thanks.

After lunch Sheena retires to rest and Basil goes out. Giles helps Alex to put together a jigsaw puzzle of the pyramids of Egypt. 'Have you seen them?' she asks.

'Only from a distance. Your mother didn't want to go when we lived in Cairo. I'll take you to see them one day.'

In the evening when Giles reminds Alex he's going to spend an hour with Daoud, she asks, 'Has Daoud had any presents?'

'I don't expect so.'

'You can take him my box of chocolates', suggests Alex in a fit of generosity. 'And tell him I sent them.'

'I'm sure he'll be very touched.'

To part with Basil's chocolates in a good cause salves her conscience.

On Boxing Day Giles suggests a long walk to the lighthouse. Alex, who's become restless listening to the polite conversation between Basil and her father, is glad to get out of the apartment. She knows Basil and Sheena will be relieved when Giles has gone.

They walk along Hamra Street, and Giles buys two enormous milles feuilles from the Bros Hallab cakeshop. Under the tall evergreens and the high university buildings the campus seems dark and gloomy in the cloudy December weather. But as they pass the turn-off down to Bobbie's house the clouds part to reveal clear blue cavities and Alex begins to enjoy the walk. Giles wants to visit the Nami Jafet Memorial Library, but he finds it locked. So they move on towards the tennis courts where Alex shows her father the secluded seat where she used to sit with Bobbie and Jake.

They sit down now for a few minutes to watch the greyish-green waves pounding against the rocks below the baseball ground. To stare at the sea in good or bad weather is always exhilarating. Behind them the snow-covered Sannine mountain range is bathed in heavy cloud, its lower slopes below the snow line streaked with the full spectrum of rock colours. Hatty is beginning to shiver, when suddenly the sun pierces through the clouds, flooding the wintry sea with light and allowing them to bask for a while under the illusion of warmth.

When they reach the black and white banded lighthouse which dwarfs the surrounding houses and palm trees, Alex announces she's learnt the French word for lighthouse – *la phare.*

'That's right', says Giles, 'But do you know the Arabic word – *manara?*'

'I do now!'

'How is your Arabic coming on? Do you talk to Abby and Georgette in Arabic?'

'Georgette never talks to me and Abby likes to speak in English.'

'Well, try and pick up as much as you can. It's easier to learn when you're young. I've been studying it for years and I still find it very hard to speak.'

Alex is tired after walking all the way to the lighthouse so they sit on a wall and eat the pastries before catching a tram home along Avenue Bliss. The problem of Alex's relationship with Basil is worrying Giles and he says seriously, 'It's a pity you dislike Basil. He would probably become fond of you if you were to talk to him the way you do to me.'

'But he isn't you. I don't know what to say. He doesn't like me.'

'What makes you think he doesn't like you?'

Alex thinks of the incident with the chocolates. 'I don't know', she lies.

'D'you think it's because you eavesdrop on him?'

'I don't eavesdrop!'

'Your mother says you do. You see, Alex, no one likes being spied on or listened to when they think they're alone or they're having a private conversation. You wouldn't like it yourself. And of course, when you eavesdrop, you probably hear things which upset you.'

Alex nods, but knows she will continue to eavesdrop. It's become an addiction. She will just have to be more careful not to be discovered.

When they enter the apartment they find a note on the table – *'Gone to The Normandy for lunch. Help yourself from the fridge.'* They devour turkey sandwiches and fruit, ravenous after their walk in the cold air.

'Shall we play some music?' says Giles.

'Mr Carrington doesn't like anyone touching his records', warns Alex.

'He doesn't like little girls who break his records!'

In a moment the room is filled with beautiful piano music. Giles tells her the name of the composer and the pianist.

When her father departs for Kirkuk the following morning Alex becomes almost hysterical. 'I don't want to live here! I want to come with you! I want it to be like K3.'

Giles tries to calm her down, but to no avail. 'I'll be back in the summer vacation for a whole fortnight. I'll write you lots of letters.' But nothing consoles his weeping daughter and he leaves hastily.

The same evening Sheena comes to kiss her goodnight. For the first time since coming to Beirut she sits on the bed to talk, and promises to take her to see the film *Pinocchio.*

'Just you and me?' asks the child.

'Yes.'

'Are you going to marry Basil?'

'No, of course not, we're just very fond of each other. And we want you to be happy with us.' She kisses Alex and gets up before her daughter can probe more deeply into the relationship.

During the night Alex gets up to go to the bathroom. Her room is bathed in a flood of stark, cold moonlight which streams across the hall when she opens her door. She sees a dark length of something lying across the floor. She stares at it for a moment and becomes convinced that it moved. It could only be a snake. Surely that slight bulge at one end must be its head. She is sure it moved again. In a panic she leaps across it and bursts into her mother's bedroom.

'Wake up, Sheena! There's a snake in the hall!.'

Seeing Basil's head emerging from beneath the sheet gives Alex a further shock. She's never seen them in the double bed together. She still has a vivid image of her father and mother in their bed at K3 sipping their morning tea.

Basil switches on the bedside light and Sheena's face appears on the further pillow.

'There can't be a snake in the hall', says Basil. He puts on a dressing gown and goes to investigate. Alex is impressed that he isn't frightened, and wonders how he'll kill it. He returns with a length of something dark in his hands, holding it out to her with a smile. The 'snake' is only Basil's long navy blue dressing gown cord. How could she have been so stupid?

Back in bed, Alex feels humiliated. She eventually falls asleep and dreams of Basil sipping tea in Sheena's bed. But some unidentifiable horror lurks within the dream and she wakes bathed in tears.

Chapter Thirty-two

Every two weeks Alex receives a letter from her father and she replies to each one. Sheena often asks to read Giles's letters, and at first Alex enjoys showing them to her, proud to be the one to whom her father writes. But soon she hopes Sheena will forget to ask. The correspondence has become a private matter.

The day after her ninth birthday Alex writes to Giles in the careful rounded print Mrs Kellaway has taught her:

Dear Giles, Thank you for the red leather bag you sent me for my birthday. It has a lovely smell. Sheena gave me some new shoes and Mr Carrington gave me a pen with a gold nib which I am trying out now. We went to see The Wizard of Oz which I enjoyed very much. Sheena still does her war work at the club most nights so I hardly ever see her. She looks rather tired. Annabel is still my best friend. She's growing her hair to reach below her waist. Mine never grows very long. I wish I had hair like hers. Mrs Kellaway took us on a nature walk through the campus last week to see the cherry and orange blossom and the wild flowers. Last Sunday after church Mrs Hitti drove us to Aley and let me take Hatty. I wish you could see the flowers in the mountains. We drove past orchards of gladioli. The yellow and blue irises are the prettiest. The snow is melting and streams are running everywhere. Next Saturday I am going to the beach for the first time this year. Mrs Hitti says Annabel and I can have a bowl of hummus each. We are just crazy for hummus but Mr Carrington doesn't like it. He's silly not liking Arab food.

This summer we are going to Broummana again. Hatty sends you a lick and a tail wag. Oceans of love from Alex.

The relationship with Basil doesn't improve. Alex has become a precocious nine-year-old, tall for her age, and seeming sullen and awkward to him. He can manage little more than polite questions and gleans nothing of her thoughts. Alone with him she's convulsed with shyness. She can only mumble a few words and escape quickly.

Frequently she overhears Basil and Sheena arguing with raised voices. These disputes give her a hope that Sheena will decide to leave Basil's apartment. One evening as she is playing patience in her room she hears them rowing in the bedroom and catches her own name. She tiptoes barefoot across the hall to listen.

'I tell you, Sheena, your kid's behaviour isn't normal', Basil is saying.

Alex is surprised to hear Sheena retort angrily, 'Oh, for God's sake, Basil, there's nothing wrong with my daughter, even if she isn't a charmer like your Sally-Ann.

'She's living in my home and making it very obvious she dislikes me for no good reason, though heaven knows I try to please her. She creeps around spying on us. The way she stares at me sometimes is quite unnerving. I can't stand much more.'

'Obviously she'll side with her father against you. She's made a hero of Giles because she sees so little of him. Once she goes to boarding school the problem will sort itself out.'

'If her attitude to me doesn't change pretty soon we may have to rethink our future.'

'I'll have a talk with her.'

Once when Alex returns home from school she overhears Abby and Georgette discussing Basil and Sheena. Abby is saying Mr Carrington should go back to his wife in the States. 'He was crazy to leave them for Mrs Kinley and her daughter.'

'I hate kids', remarks Georgette. 'I never want to have any.'

'Then you'd better keep away from men', Abby warns her sharply. 'You run after anything in trousers. You'll end up with a child before you find a husband! And if you don't watch out Mrs Kinley will catch you pinching her cosmetics and Mr Carrington will get rid of you.'

'Why should I care? He'll be going to the States soon, anyway. I'll find a GI to marry.'

Abby snorts. 'Who'd want to marry you?'

Later Alex asks 'What's a GI?' and Abby tells her it's an American soldier. GI stands for Government Issue. It's the uniform they wear. Beirut is full of GIs, and Mr Carrington invites the officers to his parties. You can tell them by the stars and bars on their uniforms.

The freshness of spring changes abruptly into the oppressive heat of summer. In the mornings Mrs Kellaway is busy and bright, but by midday she begins to wilt. She's informed her grade that America now leads the Allies, and soon they're going to clear the Germans out of Italy and get rid of Mussolini. A feeling of expectancy pervades the school. Things are going to change. The children talk constantly of what their parents are going to do when the war is over. Even the non-American pupils want to know everything about the States. Mrs Kellaway describes the pleasant American town where she grew up.

Annabel says excitedly, 'Just think, Alex, we might go to the States on the same boat!'

'I might not be going to the States.'

'But you told me your mother was going to marry Mr Carrington!'

Alex feels ashamed and confused. It's impossible to explain the situation to Annabel. 'I want my mother to go back to my father.'

'If you don't come to the States', says Annabel, 'We'll never see each other again. And we promised to be friends until death.'

'I'll write to you every day', Alex assures her friend.

'I hate writing letters.'

The future seems fraught with problems. But at least she has come top in the composition test. Bobbie is bottom as usual. Sometimes Alex is asked to help Bobbie with his spelling, but he can't concentrate for long. Alex is often surprised to find him staring across the table at Annabel. When she looks back at him and smiles he blushes deeply.

The school year ends, and during the drive up to Broummana Basil and Sheena talk about the recent Allied landing in Sicily and the hope that Mussolini will soon be overthrown.

'D'you think this might be our last summer in Lebanon?' asks Sheena. 'Could the war be over by Christmas?'

'I doubt it', replies Basil. 'The Germans won't give in as easily as the Italians.'

On arrival at the villa Georgette hurries around flinging open the shutters and snatching off the dust covers to shake over the balcony. Hatty trots from room to room sniffing the smells. The buoyant mountain air and the extraordinary beauty of the surroundings affects Alex more strongly than before. In the late afternoon she begins to explore the countryside further afield. Alex still hates being left with Georgette. The maid has discovered that life in the mountains is interesting after all. Two GIs call for her in a jeep every Tuesday and Thursday evening at eight. Usually Alex wakes up when the jeep returns and one of the soldiers escorts a giggling Georgette up the steps. Then she hears the jeep drive away, its brakes screeching as it takes the hairpin bends.

The GIs bring Georgette long boxes containing packets of Lucky Strike cigarettes and square boxes of candy. The maid doesn't smoke, but she can sell the cigarettes. One day Alex sees a cellophane packet on the kitchen table while Georgette is outside hanging up the washing. She pulls out two wispy pale brown nylon stockings. As she's trying to stuff them back Georgette returns and slaps her hand in fury. When she next goes out with her boyfriends she's wearing the nylons with their dark seams running up the backs of her shapely legs. The next day she lets out a howl of annoyance as a ladder shoots up her stocking.

'Those nylons don't last long', says Alex with satisfaction.

'My friend will buy me plenty more', comes the rejoinder.

Sheena won't wear nylon stockings. 'They ladder so quickly. I prefer silk stockings. Anyway, they look rather common.' Alex is never sure how her mother decides what is common and what is not.

Georgette never shares any of her candy, though once she grudgingly handed over some packets of fruit gums which her boyfriends brought for Alex.

'Where do you go in the jeep?' asks Alex.

'None of your business', snaps the maid.

Alex wishes she could go for a ride in a jeep – anything to ease the tedium of the long hot hours between eleven and four. After breakfast, time loses all significance as she drifts around the house and garden with Hatty. The days lack a focal point.

Alex wonders whether she should go down to Sania's house. It seems such a long time since last summer, the family might not remember her. Finally, boredom drives her to approach the house, which now boasts its new roof. She is surprised to hear a low wailing sound coming from inside. Sania appears in the yard and tells her in a solemn voice that their grandmother has died. She asks Alex to come in and see the body. With trepidation she follows the girl up the stairs into a darkened bedroom. Several women, including Mrs Fahiliya are sitting round the bed moaning and wailing. Incense is burning in a bowl, but it doesn't entirely disguise the sickly sweetish smell of death.

The corpse of the old lady hasn't been prettified in any way. The closed grey eyelids are sunk deep into the bony sockets, the shape of the skull stands out under the papery yellow skin, the grey lips hang open above the fallen jaw. Alex shivers with fear and revulsion and is glad when she can make her escape. Sania doesn't ask her to come again and the experience puts her off seeking out the family again.

One Tuesday Alex awakes during the night to a new fear. Something is lying on her bed, something alive and moving. She dives under the sheet for a moment, hoping that whatever it is will go away. All is silent, and she begins to think she must have been dreaming. She sits up and suddenly a living creature flies at her hair and brushes against her forehead, some horrible winged animal which falls back on the bed. Her eyes have become used to the dark and she can just make out the grotesque form of a large bat. She leaps out of bed and runs downstairs, shouting for Georgette.

No one comes and when Alex stands outside Georgette's room she has a feeling the maid isn't there. She opens the door and listens, then switches on the light. The blanket is smooth over the empty bed. Frightened at being alone so late in the house, Alex moves from room to room, switching on all the lights. She dare not return to her own room to see what's become of the bat. The silence, broken only by the constant throb of the cicadas, seems menacing. For an hour she sits in the kitchen wondering whether Georgette has gone for good. Then she hears the jeep stopping outside the villa. Relief and fury sweep over her. This time she will certainly tell Sheena what the maid has done.

Georgette enters the kitchen with a sheepish smile on her face, wearing a new pair of nylon stockings with flimsy high-heeled sandals. Alex gains an impression of scarlet lipstick, dangling diamanté earrings, bangles, a flushed face, and something very familiar about the dress which clings too tightly around the maid's hips. It is one of

Sheena's dresses. For the first time Alex feels she has the advantage over Georgette.

A lanky soldier in uniform stands behind the maid, grinning at Alex. 'Hi, kiddo! The name's Ed', he drawls. 'Sorry we're so late. The jeep broke down.'

But Alex isn't mollified. 'I'll tell my mother you left me alone at night and you pinched one of her dresses!' Alex shouts, trembling at her own daring. War is declared at last.

Georgette sits down, her black eyes wary, while her boyfriend cajoles, 'Look, kiddo, we didn't mean to be away more than an hour. You were sound asleep.'

'It isn't your evening off', persists Alex. 'You're not allowed to leave me alone at night.'

'But no harm has come to you, kiddo', continues the soldier, yawning. 'Here, I've brought you some chocolate.' He holds out a giant slab of milk chocolate. 'If you're a good girl and keep quiet I'll bring you a slab every time I come.' Alex has never seen such a large bar of chocolate.

Ed's casual friendliness is reassuring. In his presence Georgette will make an effort to appear pleasant. A new unspoken deal is made.

'You'd better go back to bed', says Georgette.

'I can't. There's something horrible in my room.'

Ed laughs. 'Don't worry, kiddo, whatever it is, Uncle Ed will get rid of it for you.' He and Georgette go up the stairs followed by Alex. When they turn on the bedroom light she sees something black-winged and monstrous still lying on her sheet. When Ed moves towards it the bat flies up and swoops across the ceiling.

'It's only a bat', says Ed. He picks up a chair and swings it round, and the bat dives out of the window. 'There you are. That's got rid of it. Bats won't hurt you, but they sure are ugly fellers.'

Alex gets into bed and the boyfriend pats her forehead and switches off the light. 'So long, kiddo!' and they go downstairs. Alex listens for the jeep but hears nothing.

When she wakes again the sun is shining, and the giant slab of chocolate has begun to melt on her bedside table.

Chapter Thirty-three

The following Tuesday at dusk Alex hears the jeep again, stopping outside the villa. She listens to Georgette and Ed arguing in the kitchen. He's saying 'We could take the kid with us. Why not? She'd enjoy the ride. Throw in a few pillows and let her sleep in the back.'

'No', Georgette replies. 'I don't want her hanging around us. She'll tell her mother in the end, and I'll lose my job.'

'She won't. She's too darn scared of you! I bet she'll keep her mouth shut for the candy. Aw, come on, Georgie, she's not a bad kid, and it's going to be a swell dance tonight. If we take Alex we needn't be back till dawn.' He coaxes Georgette into relenting.

Alex sprints up the stairs as Ed comes out of the kitchen shouting 'How'd you like a ride in my jeep, kiddo?'

Alex is tempted by the ride but not with Georgette. Yet she dreads they might leave her alone all night. 'I don't want you to go', she says warily.

'We'll take you to a café, kiddo, and buy you an ice cream. And I've got some chocolate bars for you in the jeep.' Alex gives in to his friendly manner. Even Georgette is smiling.

At nine o'clock as Alex is clambering into the jeep Ed warns, 'Remember, this trip is our secret, never to be told to anyone.' She sits squashed between Georgette and Ed. He drives too fast round the bends but it feels safe in the solid heavy vehicle. She enjoys the ride despite being almost suffocated by the smell of Georgette's cheap perfume, and being bitten by midges. It's exhilarating to watch the white road rushing towards them in the powerful headlights.

'Where are we going?'

'To a village called Bhanniss', Ed tells her. The name sounds familiar, one of the many places Basil has driven to at weekends. They pull up outside a crowded outdoor café with rustic tables and chairs around a dance floor. Someone is playing a battered-looking accordion under an acacia tree. Ed parks the jeep in a field adjoining the café and Georgette climbs into the back to arrange pillows and blankets into a bed for Alex.

'What about my ice cream?' says Alex.

'Ed will bring it to the jeep.'

'Oh, let the kid stay up for a while', says Ed.

'No. There aren't any children here. People might ask questions. She'll be quite safe in the jeep.'

Ed brings Alex a bowl of chocolate ice cream and a tall glass of lemonade. From the back of the jeep she can see Georgette sitting at a table, tapping her feet to the music.

'You go to sleep, kiddo. We'll just have a few dances and then we'll head for home.' His tone is so reassuring, that Alex feels no fear at being left. For some while she enjoys hanging over the back, listening to the loud music and watching the people in the café. Several other jeeps arrive and a crowd of GIs spill out under the coloured bulbs strung over the entrance gate. Now there are far more men than women in the café.

Georgette looks elated, almost pretty, her black eyes sparkling as she dances with Ed and then with several other soldiers. Between dances Ed sits and tosses back glass after glass of arak.

When Alex lies down on the pillow the café disappears and all she can see is an immense velvet-soft sky pinpricked with stars. The music accelerates, mixed with raucous laughter and the occasional shriek. Eventually she drifts off to sleep, only to wake with a start. The music has ceased. She can hear voices and the clink of bottles. There is a strong smell of fried chicken and garlic. She has an urgent need to go to the toilet.

She climbs out of the back of the jeep with difficulty, falling heavily onto the grass. Ed and Georgette are nowhere to be seen. Panic seizes her. She dare not walk into the café among the strangers to ask for a toilet, yet she must relieve herself quickly. The only solution is to get into the forest. She runs down the road beyond the few houses and plunges into a clump of fir trees just in time. For a few moments she remains hidden in the dry undergrowth, listening. An owl hoots but otherwise all is quiet. She's about to walk back to the café when a vehicle sweeps down the hill and she crouches to avoid the headlights. She wonders whether she will be able to walk up the road without being seen. More headlights loom out of the darkness. She guesses that people are leaving the café. She has a sudden overwhelming fear that Ed might have gone too.

She runs back up the road, her heart beating wildly. The jeep is no longer parked in the field. Surely they can't have gone without her? But they have, assuming her to be asleep in the back. Her absence might not be discovered until they reach the villa.

As she hovers outside the now deserted café wondering what to do, a man comes out of the house to clear the tables. Alex steps out of the darkness and he regards her with astonishment. He turns and calls a name, 'Muna, Muna', and a woman appears.

'What you do here at night?' she asks. Alex bursts into tears and the woman puts a comforting arm around her. Her kindly gesture makes Alex cry even harder, and it is some while before she can make herself understood.

'Where you live?'

'Broummana.'

'Broummana not far. Your friends come back soon. You come into house.' They escort Alex into a tiny kitchen and hand her a glass of mulberry juice. For an hour she sits and watches the couple washing plates and glasses. They keep patting her head and saying that her friends will come.

It's two o'clock and the proprietor and his wife want to go to bed. They take Alex into a back room and turn on a naked light bulb. Three pairs of blinking dark eyes stare at her with amazement. The mother says something and the youngest child obediently gets out of the double bed.

'You take her place', the mother says to Alex. 'She sleep with us.'

Alex is saved from the embarrassment of having to get into bed with these children by the arrival of a car. The father goes to the door, and to her consternation and relief she hears Basil's voice. Why has he returned to the villa a day early? How is she going to explain what's happened? What will Georgette already have told him? Whatever transpires, Basil will be sure to think she's behaved badly.

She need not have worried, for Basil is full of kindly concern. 'Well, young lady, thank heaven you're safe and sound. You seem to have had quite an adventure.' Thanking the couple for looking after her, he hands them some money, and opens the car door for Alex. She climbs in with tears pricking her eyelids and Basil lends her one of his huge monogrammed hankies.

He tells Alex they decided to return to the villa in the early hours because Sheena hasn't been feeling well, and couldn't sleep in the heat of Beirut. They were horrified to find the house empty and were about to ring the police when the maid and her boyfriend turned up. 'Georgette said you were asleep in the back of the jeep. She couldn't understand why you weren't there. What happened to you?'

'I got out of the jeep while they were in the café to go to the toilet and they went home without me.'

'What a fright you must have had. We must be thankful it's all turned out OK. Georgette will be leaving later today so I'll have to find a new maid. But as your father's arriving tomorrow there's no urgency.' Alex had completely forgotten her father was coming the next day.

This thought, and the news that Georgette has been sacked cheers Alex immensely.

'Has Georgette taken you out at night before?'

'No, but she often left me alone in the house at night.'

'Why on earth didn't you tell us?'

'I don't know', she mutters feebly.

'You could have saved yourself, and us, a lot of worry.'

Sheena is waiting up in her dressing gown when they reach the villa. She looks feverish and distraught. 'You'd better go straight to bed', she says.

Alex sleeps soundly until after nine, when she comes down and hears Basil remonstrating with Georgette in the living room. Alex is amazed to hear the maid sobbing. Her tin trunk lies open on the rug. A pile of linen – sheets, pillowcases and towels – is spread out on a chair. Tins of food lie scattered on the floor.

'I could call the police and have you locked up for being a thief', Basil says sternly. 'As it is you're extremely lucky that I'm going to pay you for this week and send you home in a taxi. Now shut your trunk and get out!'

As she leaves the room Georgette gives Alex a look of pure hatred. It should have been a moment of triumph, but all she feels is unease, even guilt. She watches from the top balcony as Georgette departs, and wonders what the next maid will be like.

Sheena stays in bed all of Wednesday. When Giles arrives on Thursday morning she gets up to cook an omelette and make a salad. It's the first time since leaving K3 that the three of them have had a meal alone together as though they were still a family. Alex stares at her father, hardly able to believe he has actually come. He seems thinner than he was at Christmas and his smoking fingers are a brighter yellow. She is bursting with things to tell him, but they must wait. It's impossible to talk freely in front of Sheena. Giles remarks that Sheena herself looks thinner and very tired.

'It's not surprising', she answers. 'I'm run off my feet at the hospital.'

After the meal Alex sits reading a book called *Swallows and Amazons,* which Giles has brought. Inevitably her parents start a conversation that leads into an argument.

'Anything could have happened to her', says Giles. 'It was most unwise to leave her overnight with that maid.'

'How were we to know Georgette would turn out to be so irresponsible? She came with excellent references.'

'But not for looking after children. In future I trust either you or Basil will sleep here every night.'

'It will depend on who Basil finds to replace Georgette.'

'It would have to be someone like Zilpha, someone absolutely trustworthy. He won't find a maid like that in a hurry.'

'Don't worry, Alex will be looked after.'

'I'm still not happy about the situation. You should think about giving up your job and staying with Alex.'

'Oh, don't be ridiculous, Giles, I have to work! I don't want to be completely dependent on Basil.'

'I can let you have some money.'

'I don't want your money. You're making a fuss about nothing. Most Arab women dote on children. We'll find someone suitable for Alex. I'm going back to bed.'

'Before you go', says Giles, 'I must tell you I'm taking Alex on a trip to Palmyra tomorrow, staying in Tripoli on the way.'

Sheena is indignant. 'You grumble at me not being responsible, yet you can think of taking a child to Palmyra in August. No European goes there at this time of year if they can avoid it. She'll get heat stroke!'

'Alex has been used to desert heat.'

'I thought Palmyra was a German base.'

'Not any longer. Syria is an independent country now. It may be our only chance of visiting Palmyra. It's an ideal time, before they get it going as a tourist resort.'

'What possible interest could Alex have in Palmyra? It's for boring archaeologists, not for children.' Sheena's voice becomes shrill with irritation. 'She didn't like Babylon. Why should she like Palmyra?'

'There's no comparison. Much of Palmyra is still standing, and Alex is older now. There's plenty to look at.'

'You're going for your own selfish interest. You'll put the child off ruins and museums for ever. You should stay in the mountains where it's reasonably cool and look after her health.'

'I'm afraid it's already arranged. We'll visit Palmyra in the late afternoon and early morning so it won't be too hot.'

'And where will you spend the night?'

'At T4.'

'Is that near Palmyra?'

'Yes. Don't you ever look at a map?'

'Why should I? I don't want to see Palmyra.'

'I seem to remember your saying in Cairo that you couldn't wait to visit all these romantic places, Palmyra included.'

'They're not romantic when you get there. They're hot and dusty and fly-ridden and deadly dull. You're going to bore Alex just as you bore everyone else with your craze for ruins.'

'I'm going, nevertheless.'

'If Alex comes back with some illness, who's going to nurse her?'

'I shall, just as I did the summer before last. And when I've gone, you should give up your tutoring and take an interest in your daughter. You've got a rich partner. You don't need the money.'

'And how d'you think the hospital could carry on without me? There's no one else who could help train the local student nurses. And apart from nursing, there's my war work at the club, organising entertainment for the forces, listening to their problems until three in the morning. I often work an eighteen hour day.'

'You enjoy it, Sheena, why not admit it?'

Sheena gets up in fury. 'Why don't you go away and leave us alone? We get on perfectly well without you!' She becomes aware of Alex staring at her, and tries to control her anger. 'Where are you going to stay in Tripoli?'

'With Leila.'

'Leila?'

'I did mention at Christmas that she'd married a Scotsman, Tom Maxwell. He's recently retired to Tripoli from Baghdad. He's a lot older than Leila.'

'I suppose she got tired waiting for you!'

'Don't be silly, Sheena. You know I never had any designs on Leila. I just find her an interesting person to talk to.'

'And I suppose she finds you interesting too. So intellectual and well-read!'

'She appears to.'

Sheena flounces out of the room. Alex hopes her father has won this argument. She likes the idea of seeing Leila again. 'I do want to go to Palmyra', she says. 'I promise not to be bored.'

Chapter Thirty-four

The two of them leave for Tripoli early in the morning, wearing swimming costumes under their shorts, for Giles has promised to stop for a bathe at Jounieh. He also tells Alex to bring a coat and a jumper.

'What for?'

"You'll see.'

For Alex this period before dawn has become associated in her mind with setting out on an adventure with Giles. As they drive away from the villa in a hired car the familiar sweet freshness arises from the earth and the half-light seems full of mystery. They are conspirators travelling to a magic place.

On the outskirts of Jounieh they pass two donkeys heavily laden with panniers of vegetables for market. At this early hour no other cars pass, but the shopkeepers are already opening up their shutters. A strident cockerel perched on a gatepost is hailing the dawn.

'How far is it to Tripoli?'

'Another eighty kilometres. The road continues along the coast all the way.'

They pass through the village of Chekka and enter a short tunnel in the chalk cliff. At each end of the tunnel the olive trees are white with dust. Tripoli eventually comes into sight, its houses half submerged in orange groves, its roofs shimmering in the heat.

The town is dominated by a grim-looking castle with high walls and square towers – 'Built by a French Count, Raymond de St Giles', says Giles.

'Are we going to see the castle?'

'No, It's too hot, and anyway, I don't think they allow you to go inside. We'll drive through the town and up to the residential hill of Abu Samra where we're going to spend the night with Leila.'

As they work their way across Tell Square, flanked with cafés, hotels, taxi ranks and a clock tower, the usual sights and sounds of a busy eastern town bombard them from every side: rickety backfiring buses, honking taxis. rattling trams, vendors selling baskets of dried quinces, apricots and leafy oranges, urchins fighting and beggars picking lice from their bodies. And everywhere the overpowering smell of leather and spices, and *felafel* shops.

'Tripoli means three towns', says Giles. 'There used to be three separate walled quarters.'

The car bumps along narrow cobbled streets, then climbs up a winding road leading to a quiet area of pleasant substantial modern homes. They draw up outside a long white house with a curved verandah running all the way round. The walls are shrouded in a mass of overgrown jasmine, and the garden is a jungle of shrubs. At the back of the house a wide, flat plain of silver-green olive groves stretches into the foothills of the mountains, behind which tower the high rocky ridges of Mount Lebanon.

Leila opens the door and flings her arms round each of them, exclaiming at the sight of Hatty and dispelling Alex's shyness immediately. She hasn't changed. She still wears exotic clothes; this time a dark blue silky kaftan, with gold bracelets jangling at her wrists, and gold sandals criss-crossed down to her scarlet painted toenails. The same tortoiseshell comb with its row of seed pearls holds back her swathe of black hair.

'How strange to see you in a modern house' says Giles.

'Yes, I can't get used to it. My Baghdad junk wouldn't match this place.'

While they are drinking tea made in the old samovar, Leila explains that Tom, her husband, has to rest a lot. He'll see them later. Leila notices Alex eyeing a bowl of orange acadinias, her favourite fruit, and says she may help herself.

'Not too many', warns her father. 'You don't want tummy trouble at Palmyra.'

'Are you and Tom happy here?' asks Giles.

'I adore the sea, and it's a good climate. But all these houses in Abu Samra, and the other residential area on Tel Kubba, are too colonial for me, too clean and neat with little individuality. I can't observe the local life here as I did on my verandah overlooking the Tigris.'

Alex vividly recalls sitting on Leila's verandah and hearing about the corpse washed up against the muddy river bank. 'I like this house.'

Leila laughs. 'Of course you do, darling. No rats or cockroaches here!'

'And is your marriage working out well?' Giles continues as they move from the lunch table to sit on a calico-covered divan.

'Tom has to take life slowly, but I'm content. We enjoy things together when he's well. He writes his poems and I get on with my painting. Tom finds it hard to stop behaving as a European. His happiness used to lie in constant activity. I'm trying to show him that rest and contemplation can bring happiness too.' She stops and says, 'You must be bored, Alex. D'you want to go and explore the garden with your dear little dog?'

Is she trying to get rid of me? Alex wonders. 'No, I'd rather stay here with you.'

Leila smiles. 'I forget how quickly you're growing up. You can enjoy taking coffee with the grownups now.' She hands Alex a tiny cup of very sweet Turkish coffee and an almond cake. Alex senses that her father would talk to Leila about Sheena and Basil if they were alone. He would tell her all the details she herself would dearly like to know.

In the late afternoon Leila takes them round the garden. She has managed to clear part of it to create a herb garden. As she points out each plant – rosemary, lavender, sage, marjoram, spurge, thyme, basil, chicory – Alex is reminded of Zilpha's herb garden.

'Herbs have such lovely names, but they're not an impressive sight', remarks Leila. 'Soon I shall plant a rose garden, and then we shall have something beautiful to look at.'

'And are you enjoying the American Community School, Alex?' Leila asks.

'Yes..'

'It's shrunk to being a very small school, I'm afraid', says Giles. 'It was doing very well before the war, but now there are only a handful of American children, and Alex is the only English girl. The headmistress and Mrs Kellaway, an American widow, struggle, with the help of a few part time teachers, to educate an age range from seven to eleven. Sheena maintains the children do nothing but play. Alex may find it hard fitting in to the formality of an English school.'

'But you're happy at school', Leila says to Alex, 'That's the important thing. Learning all the facts will come in its own good time.'

'We don't just play! I've learnt lots of things!' says Alex indignantly, 'All about America. I know more about America than my mother. – Will you come to Palmyra with us?' she begs Leila.

'Goodness, no! Can you see me walking among the ruins? Archaeology isn't my idea of fun. You go with your father, and then come back and tell me all about it.'

Led by Hatty they stroll into a different part of the garden, amongst pepper trees, madonna lilies and tobacco flowers. A blue dragonfly alights on Leila's arm. As they go back to the house Tom comes out to meet them, walking slowly with the support of a stick. He has a shock of unruly white hair and a strong Scots accent. He grins at Alex and she likes him instantly.

They stand for a few moments to watch a subdued sunset beyond the orange groves. The horizon line appears unnaturally high on a motionless sea as the sun slips into it. Then they re-enter the house and Tom offers Giles a whisky.

'The doctor says he mustn't touch alcohol', says Leila, 'But Tom swears it's what keeps him alive.'

'The best discussions are to be had over a bottle of whisky', Tom says, winking at Alex. Then he asks Giles, 'What's Beirut like these days?'

'Too many cars, too many men in uniform, too many beggars and too many ugly blocks of flats going up all the time. You can just about see it was once an elegant and beautiful town.'

'I dislike its cosmopolitan atmosphere and the noise. Urban Arabs love noise. All those rich entrepreneurs gambling in flashy night-clubs, but underneath the glamour a creeping decay. I prefer primitive old Tripoli with its Muslim simplicity. And the mountains of course. Only there do you see the real Lebanon. You can see the sea from so many ridges, and round every corner there are surprises – shrines, hidden grottos, miniature water falls – yes, I love the mountains!'

After supper the adults sit on the verandah. No one suggests that Alex should go to bed. The conversation turns to religion. 'What I like about this country', says Tom, 'Is the way the ancient gods refused to be driven out by those arrogant crusaders and missionaries. Officially the Christians and Muslims are running the show, but every village superimposes its old mythology onto the new religion. The shrines to the mountain gods have never quite been obliterated by Christians setting up white statues of the Virgin. Behind her docile impassive stare you can usually detect the tantalising smile of Astarte. She'll always be waiting in the spring among the trees for her Adonis to rise again.'

'Don't listen to Tom', says Leila, smiling. 'He always sets out to shock our friends. He maintains that when I go to church that I'm going to propitiate the fun-loving heathen gods behind the respectability of Christianity!'

'The trouble with the many religions practised in this small country', continues Tom, 'is that they're becoming politicised. There was a time when persecution was rare. The Sunni, the Shi'ite, the Maronite, the Melchite, the Armenian, the Greek Orthodox, the Druze, the Jew and at least a dozen other sects... all rubbed along tolerably well most of the time. Now the Maronites are trying to turn Lebanon into a European colony, and old feuds are being resurrected.'

'How did the Maronites originate?' asks Giles.

'A group of Christians broke away from the Orthodox Church to follow St Maron, a Syrian hermit. They settled in Mount Lebanon and built monasteries in cliffs, inaccessible except on foot. On the 9th of February they celebrate his birth – or his death, I'm not sure which.'

Giles and Tom are soon deeply engrossed in a discussion about Mediterranean civilisation. 'Our Judaeo-Christian mind, which cherishes the immortality of the individual soul, has never come to terms with the eastern concept, which is more likely to regard man as a fragment of the whole, which at death is gathered into the cosmos', says Tom.

'I agree', replies Giles. 'All the signs of pre-Christian religion in Lebanon suggest that philosophical view. Presumably easterners don't value their own personalities as much as we do ours.'

'No, I suppose they don't. One sometimes envies them their detachment.'

Alex, sitting quietly on a stool with the dog on her knee, notes that the kind of conversation her father is now having with Tom and Leila is in marked contrast to those he has with Basil and Sheena. His face in the light of the oil lamp is animated. He talks with such enthusiasm.

'Are man's instincts to be trusted more than his reason?' Giles wonders. 'The instinct to fear the supernatural, to be in awe of the unknown, to believe in a personal God who intervenes in our lives, to worship and to pray – can this instinct be truer, more reliable than our reason which tells us we can't be sure of anything beyond this world? We can contemplate the mystery, we can marvel at the power of love, we can wish for paradise, but we can't know why we are here or what will become of us after death.'

Leila is not always in agreement with Giles and Tom. 'I feel it's better to trust our natural instinct, to have a strong faith in a good, personal God as an incentive to act against evil. You and Tom could so easily sail into the danger of being too tolerant of everything, including evil, because you think there are no definite moral answers.'

'I don't think we would', says Giles. 'Reason provides a good workaday guide to morals which can be adapted as circumstances change and knowledge increases. The alternative is a rigid moral law communicated miraculously to religious leaders. They often interpret it to suit their own ends, using it as a means of controlling people's minds.'

In a much vaguer way Alex's own childish thoughts on religion and morality echo the dilemma of her father and his friends. The tenets of the Greek Orthodox Church which Zilpha has drummed into her, combined with the Protestant zeal of Mrs Kellaway and Mrs Hitti, have impressed her at times as being the only truth. But her father's uncertainty, his reluctance to fall in with Christianity, has also influenced her mind. In the final count whatever Giles tells her seems the most reasonable.

To reach Palmyra they first drive north to the bustling, leafy town of Homs, where shabby houses cluster round a blue mosque and they have to swerve to avoid an emaciated dead dog lying in the road. They journey east between red fields and patches of vivid green, passing whitewashed houses, a goat tied to a post and a pair of yoked oxen pulling a cart. Soon all habitation peters out as they cross the desert under the burning white sky of midsummer. After two years in a fertile mountainous country the endless barren wadis growing nothing but thorns and dry woody herbs now seem oppressive.

By lunchtime they reach the compound of T4, another oil-pumping station. To Alex it seems smaller than K3, but Giles says it isn't. As she grows bigger, so places she's known earlier will shrink. She finds it uninteresting and unbearably hot even under the large fans in the rest house. The stench of oil is overpowering.

They are served a lunch of mashed potatoes, tinned peas and tinned frankfurters, followed by tinned peaches and watery custard. An acquaintance of Giles sits down at their table and asks if they have come from Beirut. 'I was thinking of taking a holiday there next week, but we'd heard there'd been anti-government riots after the elections.'

'There's very strong feeling against the Free French influence', says Giles. 'The elections were probably rigged. The Muslims want the Francophiles out and a completely independent republic. But no sign of that yet. You'll be safe enough if you steer clear of crowds.'

Giles borrows a small icebox from T4 and puts some blankets, a large canister of water and a box of provisions in the car, and they start across the desert again in the late afternoon. To Alex's great delight a gazelle appears and runs alongside the car. Giles puts on speed and still the graceful creature keeps pace until it eventually falls behind and gallops away across the scrub.

They begin to move along a curving valley undulating through low hills. Suddenly as they round a corner they glimpse a castle, and then beyond it the outline of the ancient city which seems to hang almost weightless under the hazy sunshine. At a distance it appears to be a city of walls and pillars entirely contained within a bank of dark green trees. But as they drive closer the pillars begin to detach themselves into separate groups reached by numerous narrow tracks.

As always, Giles can't resist giving her a few historical details. 'Palmyra was called *Tadmor* by the Arabs. It was already a town nineteen centuries before Jesus was born, because it was on the caravan route from Persia to the sea. Travelling miles across the desert was very dangerous in those days. Bandits would attack the caravans, and Palmyra provided a kind of police force to protect them. They had to pay quite a lot for what we would call a safe conduct from Iraq to Damascus. Then the Romans invaded Syria, but they found it very hard to keep control of Palmyra so far out in the desert. A famous Arab Queen, the beautiful Zenobia, refused to give in, and soldiers were sent to capture her. She was taken to Rome, so they say, and allowed to retire to a villa nearby.'

'Did she like it in Italy?'

'I expect she was glad to be alive. Italy is a lovely place, but I'm sure she must have missed the desert.'

They get out of the car and find themselves in a ghost town, standing in a vast area of broken walls and colonnades. The sense of space stretching in every direction is almost frightening. The eye is relieved only by the hills to the north which resemble immense static waves.

Alex is disappointed there's no river as there was at Baalbek, no café, no sign of human life at all. It's a relief when they do notice a Bedouin camp in the distance and a flock of flat-tailed sheep grazing outside the town.

'With no river, how d'you think they manage for water here?' Giles asks.

'I don't know.'

'Yes, you do. Just think.'

'From the sky?'

'Very little if anything from the sky.'

'From under the ground?'

'Yes, of course. It's an oasis. Palmyra water comes from a spring called Ein Efqa. We'll go and see it before walking through the ruins.'

Beneath a grove of palms at the bottom of a steep stone wall the spring issues forth from underground – a narrow clear stream between banks of vivid green moss, yellow lichen and angelica. A flight of wide shallow steps leads down beside green fronds and clumps of yellow iris into the water in which lie fragments of two fallen pillars amongst the water-grass. A couple of giant lizards are basking on the top step. They disappear like lightning when Hatty approaches.

The atmosphere is infected by the bad-egg smell of sulphur which Alex remembers from the Eternal Fires. 'It's a horrible smell', agrees Giles, 'But the spring is quite safe to drink from.' Alex cups her hands and tastes a few drops, while Hatty laps up the water.

They become aware of a shepherd grinning down at them from above the wall. He shouts 'Kef halak!' and Giles tells Alex to reply. She shouts back, 'El hamdu lillah taiyib!' *['Well, thank God!']*

'Neharak sa'id!' *[May your day be happy!]* The shepherd grins again and launches into mouthfuls of swift Arabic. Both Giles and Alex are flummoxed. 'Ana ma behkish Arabi', says Giles, but the man continues to address them for another few minutes before striding off through the palms.

'Come on', says Giles. 'We're going to walk through the Valley of the Tombs before it gets dark. Then we'll climb that little mound over there and watch the sun set.'

'Are we going back to T4 tonight?'

'No, I thought we'd have an adventure and spend the night at Palmyra.'

'The whole night?'

'Why not? Then we'll see the sunrise as well as the sunset, and we can explore the rest of the town in the cool of the early morning. Would you like to do that?'

Alex is intrigued by this unconventional idea. 'Sheena wouldn't want us to.'

'Then it'll have to be our secret.'

Chapter Thirty-five

Giles and Alex move slowly along the wide gently undulating floor of the Valley of Tombs. The ground is dotted with tall chimney-like constructions four or five storeys high, bathed in a weird red light from the declining sun. Nothing stirs.

'Are we the only people here?' whispers Alex.

'Probably the only visitors. A few Arabs live in these odd-looking tombs.'

As her father's speaking Alex catches sight of an old man on a donkey disappearing behind one of the tombs. A group of goats scampers off at their approach. these two signs of habitation do nothing to dispel the atmosphere of desolation.

'I'd hate to live in this spooky place', says Alex.

They return to the car, and after eating sandwiches and having a drink from the ice-box, Giles feeds Hatty and puts a Thermos in his rucksack with some grapes. He tells Alex to put on her jumper and coat, gives her a blanket to carry, and they climb the mound outside the city.

From their raised position they can now see the extensive dimensions of the ruined city spread out below them, backed by groves of date palms beneath a crimson sky splashed with streaks of violet. Golden masonry casts long shadows across an expanse of open ground littered with sections of pillar and chunks of stone.

'All that rubble was once covered with tall buildings', says Giles. But Alex finds it hard to imagine Palmyra as ever having been a city. For her the word *city* conjures up pictures of tarmacked streets, shops, blocks of flats and lines of cars. Then comes the moment they're waiting for. The sun, a deep red orb suspended between two chimney tombs, slips silently below the horizon. For the short period before darkness envelops the earth the stones still glow with light and then are thrown into dark relief against an eerie yellow sky. Nothing's prepared Alex for this unique sight. The night closes in swiftly, an almost tangible presence gathering around them. She dozes off under her blanket laid over a waterproof sheet and a thick rug.

She wakes later to find the scene transfigured by moonlight into an ethereal fairyland she will never forget. The temperature has dropped and a crystal-cold white light floods the city and intensifies the inky blackness billowing behind the moon-bleached stones.

'What time is it?' murmurs Alex, but Giles doesn't reply. He sits wrapped in a trance. She catches something of his mood, and together they gaze at the moonlit city until she loses all sense of reality.

Much later her father leads her back to the car in a daze. The moon is so bright that each blade of grass, every small stone is clearly defined. She sleeps soundly across the back seat only waking to feel the car moving and to hear the familiar sound of goat bells filtering into her consciousness. She sits up and finds herself in the midst of a dizzy world of pillars – thousands of white marble pillars, dark red granite pillars, honey-coloured limestone pillars – some in broken colonnades, some lying prone on the dark scrub and some sprouting upwards from the ground like dark sentinels against the palest pearl sky.

Giles stops the car near the great archway which Alex remembers seeing in a picture.

'This is the famous monumental arch that once gave onto a long colonnaded road. Try to imagine, Alex', says Giles in excitement, 'A long line of pillars and statues giving shade to the shops and houses on each side.'

But it's beyond the child's imagination to picture a standing, breathing city. As they plunge further in amongst the ruins the sun becomes hot on their backs and they observe a small snake wriggling out of a hole to bask in the warmth.

Giles consults his small dog-eared Baedeker guide as they go along, making remarks partly addressed to Alex and partly to himself. 'Mark Antony arrived here in 41 BC and found the city empty. The people had heard he was coming, and they packed up and fled. Even though they were living in a great city they still retained the habits of the nomad. They hadn't accumulated too many possessions.'

Thick slices of fluted columns lie amongst wild thyme, oleander and thistle. Upright pillars and stones rise to form precarious incomplete temples and porticoes, archways and walls. Massive paving slabs take them ever onwards past doorways leading into banks of earth, and steps ending in the air. Giles is intensely interested in the detail of carvings, in the times and dates and uses of each building.

Alex's impressions are more sketchy. It's just a jumble of pillars and stones and tombs in a golden space of ever-changing light and shade.

'These pillars originally had capitals of gilded bronze', says Giles. 'Think how they must have shone in the moonlight!'

They've now walked a fair distance with Hatty trotting behind. The sun has gained a hold on the land and the ground seems to move away into torrid shimmering nothingness under the steel-blue sky. Hatty is panting, and Alex is seized with an urgent thirst.

'We'll go back', says Giles. 'It's too hot to go on.'

The car bonnet is already sizzling, the leather seats are like oven shelves. They swallow lemonade and bathe their faces with water. As Giles drives away quickly to cool off the car, Alex looks back at the evanescent shapes of Palmyra in the heat haze and wonders if she'll ever return. She's beginning to experience an inexplicable sadness at leaving any place she may never see again.

Back at Broummana, they find Basil has hired a new maid called Janine, a timid young girl who knows very little English and poses no threat. She works hard and smiles whenever she sees Alex.

Basil and Sheena come and go as usual, but don't impinge on life at the villa. When her mother spends the night at Broummana Alex listens for any arguments between her and Giles. But it seems they're avoiding being alone together. At meal times everyone is very polite. One afternoon, however, Alex does overhear her father on the phone to Leila. *'She says she's going to the States with Basil... He's planning to get a divorce... Personally I think we could be reconciled... I'm not sure that Basil is making her happy... Perhaps no one ever will... But if Sheena wants to marry him I won't stand in her way... If only this war would end!... We're just marking time... It's not good for Alex...'* When Giles starts to talk of other matters Alex slips away.

All too soon there are only two days left of Giles's leave, and Alex wakes in the morning dreading the months ahead. At the end of his last day they revisit their 'secret' fig tree near the abbey. This time there are no pieces of cloth hanging on its battered branches and its leaves look small and undernourished.

'It's dying', says Alex despondently.

'No, it isn't. Next spring it'll revive, you'll see.'

'I won't see it in the spring!' Alex bursts out. 'You don't come to see me in the Easter vacation. I wish I belonged to a proper family like Annabel's with a father and a mother and a brother and a sister who all like each other and go out together. I wish I'd never been born!'

Giles, usually so calm, so slow to anger, grabs Alex by the arm, shouting 'Never say that again, d'you hear? Never! You were born because we wanted you. I wanted you more than anything I've ever wanted apart from your mother!' Alex is deeply impressed by the passion in his voice. Then he continues more quietly, 'You have to realise that very few people get everything they'd like from life. We both love you, we both want the best for you, but that doesn't mean you'll always be happy. When you grow up you'll look back and see that you learnt something from your parents' difficulties. You must learn to be a survivor. I'm learning it too.'

Listening to the sadness in his tone Alex forgets her own troubles in her fierce sympathy for him. 'D'you still love Sheena?' she asks.

'Yes. I always will.'

For some reason of her own, Hatty jumps onto Giles's knee and begins to lick his face. 'Hatty loves you. She's going to be so unhappy when we go to England and leave her behind.'

'We'll find her a good home with someone who loves dogs.'

'Is the war nearly ended?'

356

'It may well end next year. But we still have Japan to defeat. Soon it may be possible to travel to England by boat.'

After Giles's departure Sheena returns to the villa every night for the rest of the summer. She has to come by taxi on the days Basil stays in Beirut. He says it's high time she learnt to drive and then he'd buy her a car. Sheena says she hates the idea of driving in Beirut.

In September the dust sheets are put back over the furniture and the villa's locked up. They drive down to Beirut and Basil shows Janine round the apartment. In no time Abby is bossing the new maid about, delighted to have got rid of the obstinate and sullen Georgette. 'I told Mr Carrington she was a no-good girl', says Abby to Alex with satisfaction.

Life in Beirut resumes its normal routine. Alex spends every weekend with the Hittis. In addition to the Sunday morning service the girls go along to the Bible Study meetings on Sunday evenings. They're the only children at these gatherings. They find them boring, but the atmosphere is warm and friendly and the home-made doughnuts are exquisite.

One Sunday evening to her surprise Bobbie turns up at the Bible Study with his mother. His face is scrubbed clean and his sailor suit newly pressed. He sits opposite the girls, grinning sheepishly. Alex becomes aware that Bobbie is staring admiringly at Annabel in her frock of red velvet trimmed with cream lace.

'He's growing into quite a good-looking boy', Annabel says in exactly the same tone her mother uses. 'I might ask him to my party this year. I've decided to have boys from now on.'

At Annabel's tenth birthday party Mrs Hitti suggests they should play charades. There are plenty of old clothes and sheets and bedspreads in the cupboard upstairs. The children divide into two groups with Alex and Bobbie in Annabel's group. Bobbie is very shy about the idea of acting, but when they've decided on their word, Annabel says he'll make a very good maid dressed up in a skirt and apron with a large white handkerchief as a cap. Alex doesn't see why he can't act a male character, but Annabel insists it will be much funnier this way.

The children shriek with laughter when Bobbie appears and he immediately plays up to his role. Mrs Hitti presents him with a box of chocolates for being the best actor at the party. Next day at school Annabel confides to Alex, 'Bobbie has given me his box of chocolates with a note. He wants to date me!'

'What does that mean?'

'Oh, you are a baby, Alex! Fancy not knowing about dating! It means that Bobbie wants to marry me when we grow up.' She lowers her voice. 'I'll tell you something very, very secret. Bobbie kissed me in the cupboard at my party!'

It's impossible to imagine Bobbie in this romantic role. Alex is disturbed and quite jealous. 'D'you want to marry Bobbie?' she inquires.

Annabel looks arch. 'I might if I feel like it.'

The romance adds a new dimension to the girls' intimacy. Annabel can talk of little else. 'It would be lovely if Jake dated you and we could be a foursome', suggests Annabel kindly. To Alex the idea of Jake as a boyfriend is ludicrous. He's still a grubby kid with ink-stained fingers who can think of nothing but aeroplanes and guns and submarines.

Bobbie starts to walk Annabel home from school each day, and they don't want Alex tagging along behind. Mrs Hitti doesn't like Bobbie playing alone with her daughter. She wants Alex there as chaperone. Alex, however, isn't happy with this arrangement. 'I don't want to come to your house any more', she complains. 'Bobbie wants you to himself.'

Annabel puts on her cajoling voice. 'But you're our very best friend in all the world!' she gushes. 'Best friends are different from dates. Bobbie's always liked you.'

Alex is won over, but Annabel's no longer the same girl when Bobbie's with her. They hold hands and are always giggling and whispering secrets to one another. Alex despises Bobbie in his new role. She much prefers the boy who used to take her on risky expeditions. Annabel makes it clear that little boys grow up and fall in love with pretty girls. 'If you want a boy to date you, you'll have to take off those glasses and wear your hair loose.'

Alex tries out this advice in her bedroom but the face that looks out of the mirror is not pretty. Secretly she thinks the whole idea of dating is silly.

An uneasy tension has arisen in the classroom because of Bobbie and Annabel. Mrs Kellaway seems oblivious to what is going on, but all the children know what happens when Annabel disappears into the stationery cupboard with Bobbie. In a sense they are all envious of Annabel, but subconsciously they want to retain the easy, friendly rivalry between the boys and the girls.

One afternoon when Alex is on her own with Annabel in the bedroom the older girl surveys herself in the long mirror. 'D'you think I'm really pretty?' she asks.

'Yes!' Alex replies fervently. Then Annabel takes off her frock and her vest. In the mirror Alex watches as she shakes her mass of curls over her bare shoulders. She observes the two slight swellings surmounted by two delicate pink nipples on her smooth golden chest.

'I'll soon have to wear a bra', Annabel remarks casually. 'Bobbie is always asking to see my breasts, but he'll have to wait till they've grown a bit more.'

'Why does he want to see them?' asks Alex in amazement.

'All boys want to see a girl's breasts.'

'How silly', Alex declares vehemently. 'And kissing is silly too!'

'You're too young to understand', replies Annabel.

'Are you really going to marry Bobbie?'

This time Annabel says 'No, of course not. No one marries their first date. Look, Mom gave me these.' She floats a pair of filmy nylon stockings in front of Alex's face. 'I have to be very careful putting them on. If I catch my nail in them they'll ladder.'

'I know. Our maid used to wear them.'

Annabel draws the stockings carefully over her slender legs. Under her white lacy pants she's wearing a white lace suspender belt.

From now on Annabel's main concern is 'How do I look?' and Alex is always ready with the admiring answer. She wants to be Annabel's friend for ever, yet at the back of her mind is the creeping suspicion that there's little substance to the relationship.

Chapter Thirty-six

Lebanon becomes an independent republic on November 22nd and the streets are crowded with rejoicing people. The schools are shut and Alex stands with Basil and Sheena on the balcony watching the noisy celebrations. Sheena is irritated because she won't be able to get through the streets to the club. Alex is glad to be safely upstairs. The crowd below looks as if it could turn into a revolution at any moment.

'President Khoury's a capable guy', says Basil. 'And his financial adviser, Riad Sohl, is reliable from all accounts. But they're going to have one hell of a time dealing with all the problems of this country. As a Christian Khoury must curb the excesses of the Maronites, who regard themselves as the only civilised people in Lebanon. And the Palestinian refugee problem can only get worse.'

When the school vacation begins, Sheena tells her daughter, 'Your father isn't coming to spend Christmas in

Beirut this year. He'll be taking you to Tripoli to stay with Leila and her husband.'

Basil and Sheena decide to spend Christmas with friends at Aley. The day before Christmas Eve they depart, leaving parcels for Alex, wrapped in glittery silver and green paper and tied with red ribbon. She waits in the kitchen for her father to arrive.

'Where will you spend Christmas?' she asks Abby.

'Here, of course.'

'All by yourself?'

'I'll visit my family on Christmas Day.'

'Will you have a Christmas tree and presents?'

'Only rich people have those things.'

'Did you have presents when you were a little girl?'

Abby laughs. 'We were much too poor. But we did go to Midnight Mass and then we would have a special meal.'

Alex feels an intense sympathy for Abby who's lived such a hard life. She doesn't like to think of her all alone in the undecorated apartment on Christmas Eve. But in the excitement of going away with Giles she almost forgets to say goodbye.

The snow-covered Sannine looks its most beautiful at this time of year, but the villages they pass through on the way to Tripoli look drab and grey. Alex spends the journey watching the fierce winter waves pounding against the rocks, throwing white spray high in the air. Giles wraps a rug around her, for the car is draughty. He's wearing leather gloves. She herself has never worn gloves, apart from trying on Sheena's elbow-length white evening gloves.

'Will Leila have a Christmas tree?' asks Alex.

'I don't know what Leila will have. She's full of surprises. It's going to be an interesting Christmas.'

In Beirut the shops are decorated for Christmas, but Tripoli, being predominantly Muslim, doesn't encourage Christian trappings. Alex pities these people who are missing so much. Giles is amused at her consternation. 'Muslims do have their own festivals and celebrations', he assures her. But she can't imagine any festival as good as Christmas.

When they reach Leila's house at Abu Samra they find her outside loading cardboard boxes and a small fir tree into the back of a pick-up.

'What on earth are you doing?' asks Giles.

'Going to The Cedars above Bechare for Christmas. We only decided two days ago, so it's been a bit of a rush. Tom's rented a chalet. It was a sudden whim of his, to have a Scottish-type Christmas in the snow. We drove up yesterday with bedding and kitchen things.'

'Will Tom be warm enough up there?'

'Oh, yes, it'll be very cosy. It's a basic wooden hut, but there's a fireplace in each room and a pile of logs. We'll wrap Tom in rugs and sit him in front of the fire with his whisky bottle!'

After a quick lunch they set off across the orchards behind Abu Samra. Row after row of ashy-green trees grow out of the red earth scattered with stones. As they reach the foothills they pass a group of men knocking down the last of the olive harvest with poles. Leila drives slowly and carefully round each bend, and soon they leave behind the villages of Zghorta, Arjes and Ejbeh and enter the substantial village of Ehden.

The road winds in long loops as they continue to climb. Soon the pine forests are left behind and they reach the snow line, passing sparse clumps of holm oak and willow and a solitary poplar. Leila stops and gets out to gather a snowball for Alex. The child is surprised by its texture, having imagined that snow would feel like ice cream rather than this very light fluffy substance which adheres firmly to itself.

The route is kept permanently clear by snow ploughs, but on either side pale waves of snow billow up the bare mountain-side and merge with the pale sky. At a certain height Alex's ears go pop and she can suddenly hear more clearly. By the roadside a couple of herdsmen appear from nowhere, enveloped in tent-like capes against the wind. Only their dark eyes are visible.

Tom and Giles are discussing the cedars. 'I'm told that the grove of cedars near Bechare includes trees over two thousand years old, some of them over eighty feet high', says Giles.'

'It could be. The locals have always treated the grove as a holy place. If you cut a piece out of a cedar you're said to be cursed for ever. No one's allowed to cut down a cedar. People say while there's a cedar left in Lebanon the land will prosper. Let's hope it's true!'

'What a pity they didn't have that attitude from the start when these mountains were covered in cedars. What a sight that must have been!'

'The local peasants probably did revere the trees. It was the many invaders who came and cut them down without asking and carted them off to build their palaces.'

'It's a very useful tree, the cedar. The resin is good for embalming and for preserving papyri', comments Leila.

Fifty-five kilometres from Tripoli they arrive at the small town of Bechare, built in a large well-protected basin on the slopes of Mount Makmal.

'Isn't this the spiritual home of the Maronites?' asks Giles.

'Yes', says Tom. 'It's been a Christian town since the seventh century. Look, you can see it's full of churches, and there are numerous chapels and hermitages perched on the edge of cliffs. Their building skills are amazing.'

The road continues to climb Mount Makmal until they can see a green mist of trees huddled in the snow above them. After hearing so much talk of The Cedars, Alex is disappointed when they reach the grove of four hundred trees. She'd been expecting something more than this modest clump. But once they are amongst the trees the grove becomes a majestic snowbound forest filled with mysterious violet shadows. She's fascinated by the lower branches of each cedar which grow flat along the ground, each one bearing a plateau of shining frozen snow wide enough to sit on.

The chalet is only a two-roomed hut with kitchen and basic toilet, but sturdily built of thick seasoned logs. The large main room contains a rough wooden table, four chairs and a thick goat's hair rug, together with a kerosene stove and a pile of logs. The cold is so intense they have to keep their coats on until Giles has got a fire going in the deep fireplace. He finds it no trouble to light with some dry cedar cones. It's already getting dark, but the snow and the fire light up the room with a supernatural glow. Alex is thrilled by these unusual surroundings.

'Come and help me make up the beds', Leila says to Alex. They tackle a pile of sheets and blankets lying on four camp beds in the second room.

'Will we all sleep in here together?'

'Yes, we'll be packed in like sardines.'

Alex thinks what fun it will be. 'Where will we wash?'

'We won't wash much. Just a splash at the kitchen sink.'

'Are there wolves up here?'

'There may be wolves much further up the mountains, but not here.'

'Abby told me that in the winter the wolves get hungry and sometimes come down to a village and kill sheep or a donkey.'

'I don't expect that happens often. There's a torch for each of us and I've brought you an old pair of snow boots to wear with two pairs of thick socks.'

Leila sets up the little Christmas tree and lets Alex decorate it with gilded pine cones, red silk balls and some little parcels wrapped in silver paper. Instead of coloured electric lights there are miniature white candles in a dozen candle holders. They have supper at the table —ham sandwiches, mince pies, chestnuts roasted in the embers and something new to Alex called Black Bun.

'Tom always insists on having Black Bun at Christmas to remind him of Scotland', Leila explains.

'Sheena made it once', says Giles, 'Just after we got married. In those days she did quite a lot of cooking.'

'This is excellent Black Bun', says Tom, 'Better than my mother used to make.'

'Of course', agrees Leila. 'You can get such juicy raisins in Lebanon, and I've put in double the amount of whisky!'

Alex can only manage a small slice of the rich, fruity filling in its pastry case.

The coffee Leila brews in a tin pot over the primus stove in the kitchen gives off a delicious aroma and for the first time Alex is allowed to have a mugful. After a few whiskies Tom starts to sing old Scottish songs. They remain huddled round the roaring fire with blankets round their shoulders, looking, thinks Alex, like the picture of Hiawatha's family sitting in their wigwam. Three cigarette ends glow in the dark.

'Read to us, Giles', says Leila, lighting the oil lamp and passing him a book. 'At Bechare one must read the poems of Khalil Gibran, the Lebanese poet who was buried here in 1931.'

Tom puts his arm around Leila as Giles's voice lulls them into contentment with readings from The Prophet. '...*The deeper that sorrow carves into your being, the more joy you can contain. Is not the cup that holds your wine the very cup that was burned in the potter's oven? And is not the lute that soothes your spirit the very wood that was hollowed with knives?...*'

Giles stops and says 'Heady stuff, but not great poetry. It reads like deep wisdom, but I don't think he's quite the Blake of Lebanon.'

'There are better Lebanese poets', agrees Tom

'It's good enough for me', Leila insists.

Alex is aware that this Christmas Eve is very special, she may never experience another one like it. She wants this night to go on for ever.

Leila pumps the primus stove and makes more coffee. They all feel wide awake, and when they hear a church bell tolling she suddenly suggests, 'Why don't we go to Midnight Mass? There's a church we could walk to from here. Tom can stay and look after the fire.' Alex is enthralled by the idea of walking through the snow to church.

'Yes, let's go', agrees Giles. With scarves wrapped over their mouths, and woolly hats pulled down to their eyes, they walk down through the powdery snow to a Maronite church lit entirely by candles, with its typical belfry and cross above the door. They stand apart at the back. Alex's eyes are dazzled by the gilding on the many statues, the ikons of beaten silver and the glint of mosaics. Presently a procession enters, led by a tall bearded priest with long hair and a pale face wearing a gem-studded mitre, golden cope and pectoral ornaments over brocade robes. He bears a snake-topped crozier.

The main drama takes place behind the ikonostasis, a ceramic wall of brilliant colours – green, turquoise, cobalt, white and gold. Acolytes in apparelled albs make entrances and exits through three doors in the screen – one swinging hot coals in a silver thurible, another bearing candles and a third a metal-bound book.

'What's behind that wall?' whispers Alex.

'An altar they call the Holy of Holies', Giles answers.

The spicy fragrance of incense wafts above their heads and they hear chanting punctuated with the clash of cymbals. The people cross themselves at intervals.

Coming out of the glittering church into the purity of the snow-clad mountainside they are overwhelmed by the immensity of the sky dotted with glacial stars around the waxing crescent of a moon.

'They call this moon *The Prophet's Eyebrow*', says Leila.

A man passes them and says, 'Dieu vous donne la santé!'

They walk back to the chalet in silence like sleepy ghosts, and Alex remembers nothing more until she wakes up at dawn. In the white snow-light she can see a hump in each of the other beds. Tom is snoring gently. She lies happily in the warmth, clutching Hatty, listening to the wind soughing amongst the trees. When she pokes her head above the blankets the air is cold and sweet. Stretching her legs to the bottom of the bed she can feel the weight of a full stocking. But for once there's no hurry, she can savour the pleasure to come.

Later she edges her way out of bed and pulls on a heap of warm clothing and the snow boots. No one stirs as she creeps into the living room. The fire isn't quite dead, one log still burns amidst wood reduced to a grey powder. Followed by Hatty Alex ventures out into the fairytale scene where a few stray snowflakes are drifting down. She marvels at the swathes of soft pristine whiteness which cocoon the hut. Her boots make deep footprints next to the tiny dog prints as Hatty struggles in the snow. The air's so crystal clear it almost takes her breath away. By the time she re-enters the chalet she's feeling quite light-headed. The dog slips back into the bed as Alex begins to open the parcels in her stocking.

The adults eventually wake and the day passes in delicious slow motion, each chore taking a long time, each meal savoured to its utmost. Tom insists on porridge and molasses for breakfast. The coffee heats slowly on the primus stove and the fire smokes for a while before shooting out welcome flames. Their fingers are blue with cold, but gradually the room heats up and the scalding porridge takes effect.

When they are thoroughly warm they go walking in the snow. The wind's dropped and beneath the great horizontal cedar branches the forest is an enchanted white cavern.

'Next week the skiing season will start, and continue to the end of May', Leila tells Alex. 'The snow's still very powdery. It needs to be hard for good skiing. Tom and I are planning to come up in February. I want to try skiing.'

Giles says skiing has never attracted him, he's quite content with swimming and walking.

'Tom's been an excellent skier in his time', continues Leila. 'Before the war he used to go to all the ski centres – Sannine, Laklouk, Baidur, Faraya and Hermon. The French have developed a good Alpine Club at Sannine, but Tom prefers Hermon. Unfortunately Hermon is in Druze country and they're not very friendly. But Tom never had any trouble with them.'

'What is a Druze?' Alex asks.

'Don't you remember my telling you?' says Giles. 'They're a group of Muslims who formed a secret sect of their own: a mixture of paganism and Christianity mingled with their original Muslim beliefs.'

'An eccentric and warlike people' adds Leila. 'They were responsible for killing large numbers of Christians in the last century. The odd thing about the Druzes is that they never tell an outsider anything about their religion. When it's convenient to do so they'll pretend to a different religion.' This strikes Alex as very sensible. She often wonders why the Christian martyrs didn't do the same to save their skins.

'The Druzes believe their souls turn into stars after death. I find that very poetic', says Leila.

As they return to the chalet the sun breaks through and the cedars sparkle in the strong light. Tom's waiting for them outside. He maintains he's never felt so full of energy, and suggests they build a bonfire and hang a pot over it to heat up the soup.

'Yes, let's do that and we can bake potatoes in the fire', says Leila. They carry pine logs from the store hut and get a fire going. At two o'clock they're ready to eat cold turkey and tangerines. Then they warm up with soup and crisp baked potatoes dripping with butter and sprinkled with black pepper. Alex judges it the best meal she's ever tasted.

After lunch it's past three and Tom goes to rest. Leila drives Giles and Alex higher up the mountain to the Qadisha Valley to see a famous waterfall which flows smoothly over a precipice like a shining horsetail. They get out of the car into the brittle air, dazzled by the walls of snow which seem to fuse into the pale sky.

'The Qadisha Valley is my favourite place in Lebanon', says Leila. 'It's so wild and isolated. Of course all these beautiful high mountain valleys were cultivated once. But so many farmers have emigrated over the years. The government has never been interested in agriculture.'

As evening approaches the mountain landscape becomes tinged with dark blue shadows in the foreground fading to a light blue in the distance. The small groups of wintry trees – oak, juniper and walnut – seem very meagre compared to the giant cedars.

'Are there cedars in other countries?' asks Alex.

'Oh yes, the best ones are in the Taurus Mountains to the west of Tarsus in Turkey', Tom tells her. 'The Qadisha Valley was once covered in cedars, and sometimes an altar was set up under a tree for Mass to be said.'

They spend the evening again round the fire in the chalet. Alex is permitted a small glass of hot brandy and water with cinnamon and sugar to keep her warm.

'Which is the best Christmas you've ever had?' she asks her father.

He replies rather sadly, 'In Alexandria. I met Sheena at a Christmas Eve party that lasted right through Christmas Day. We were married at the Consulate in Cairo a month later.' Alex is curious and intrigued. She pictures her mother in a long white dress with a lace train and a filmy veil carrying a bouquet of orange blossom and roses.

'Have you kept photos of your wedding?' asks Leila.

'No one had a camera. It wasn't an organised wedding. We just rang a few friends to come to lunch afterwards.'

'What did Sheena wear?' asks Alex.

'A cream suit and a coffee-coloured hat with shoes to match. I bought her a few yellow roses.' Giles laughs at his daughter's disappointed expression. 'Yes, I'm sorry it wasn't a fairy-tale wedding. We didn't have a honeymoon either, just a night at the Sheraton Hotel, and then Sheena was back on duty at the hospital. Later I suggested a trip down the Nile to see the Valley of the Kings, but for some reason she couldn't go.'

Late in the evening a wind gets up and they listen to the branches flailing about outside the chalet. They nibble chocolates and dates and watch the oil lamp flickering in the draught. Leila sings a few songs in Arabic. Alex isn't sure whether she likes them or not. The harshness of tone takes some getting used to.

'The longer I live among the Arab peoples the more interesting I find them, and the more exasperating, especially in politics', says Giles. 'We're trying to instil democratic ideas into them, but I doubt they'll ever adopt them. They can't take political opposition. An opposing party is always seen as a dangerous competing power which must be destroyed.'

'You're right', agrees Leila. 'Why should we adopt democratic ideas which are imposed on us. We're not good team players like you British. We have our own rules. We're too individual and must have a dictator to control our excesses. And as well as being very individual the Arab is reluctant to assume responsibility for government for fear of being shamed by failure!'

'It's the Arab's notion of truth which is the hardest trait for us Westerners to get used to', says Tom.

'But it can be done', insists Leila, 'If you keep alert to the nuances of the language. When an Arab states something it becomes true in his mind even if it's not so. And the good intention sometimes becomes the substitute for the real act of goodness. That's why we're such imaginative poets.'

Giles remarks that all the universities in the Middle East are being run by foreigners. 'There's a danger that the Arab identity will be lost in all this western education. I'd like to see what a truly Arab university would produce.'

'I hope it happens, and then perhaps we'll surprise the west', says Leila

The evening ends with a lively discussion about religion which Alex only half hears as she dozes, wrapped in her blanket.

'The future of Lebanon is going to be determined very much by the dissensions between the various Muslim and Christian groups. The Christians, with the help of the French, have been taking the lead for some time, but the Muslims are waiting their chance', says Tom. 'And they've no intention of giving in to western ideals.'

'Which ideal is going to be better for the Arabs?' asks Giles. 'Is the Christian ideal more civilised than the Muslim?'

'The trouble with us Christians', Leila points out, 'Is that we don't follow what we preach, we're such hypocrites. The Muslims would accept Mohammed if he appeared to them today. I doubt the Christians would accept Jesus.'

By this time Alex is fast asleep and has to be carried to her bed.

Chapter Thirty-seven

The day after Boxing Day they return to Tripoli, and then Giles drives his daughter back to Beirut. Basil opens the door, saying sombrely, 'Sheena's just had bad news. Her mother's died. She's very upset.'

That's my grandmother, Alex thinks. *I have cards with her writing on them. But I can't picture her at all. Sheena has never told me anything about her or shown me a photograph.* She remembers Sania's grandmother lying dead in the bedroom and the women wailing around her. She wonders if Sheena is crying.

Giles and Basil sit talking politely until Sheena comes downstairs. Her face looks strained but she hasn't been crying. 'The funeral is tomorrow', she tells Giles. 'All the family will be there except for me. She had a stroke. Not surprising after the hard life she led, bringing up eleven children on so little money.'

'I'm very sorry', says Giles rather stiffly. Alex feels she and her father ought to be putting their arms round Sheena and comforting her, they should be asking questions and saying sympathetic things. They just stare at her miserably, and Alex thinks, *if my mother were to die....* but no, it's unthinkable. Life without Sheena and Giles is unimaginable.

She slinks upstairs with her holdall. It seems cold and cheerless in her room, the wonder of Christmas shattered. She longs for her mother to come and talk to her, but Sheena doesn't come, and for the first time, neither does Giles. The next day it seems as though the death had never occurred. Sheena doesn't even mention her mother in the weeks that follow.

After Giles's departure the days drag interminably until school starts again. It turns colder and the Sannine Mountains are shrouded in grey mists. Alex receives a short letter from Giles and sits down to answer it. She remembers to write 1944 instead of 1943, but after that she can think of nothing to tell him.

The day after St Valentine's Day at recess, Annabel takes Alex into a corner and shows her a small square box containing a silver ring with a mother-of-pearl stone. 'Bobbie gave it to me', she whispers.

'Where did he get it?' Alex enquires suspiciously.

'His sister said he could have it. it's too small for her. He kissed me in our summer house and gave me the ring.'

Alex pretends to be impressed but in reality she's become bored by their romance.

'Actually', continues Annabel, 'I'll tell you a secret. I'm not in love with Bobbie any more. I may even get to like Jake better than Bobbie.' From under her cardigan she takes out a Valentine card with a large red heart pierced by a golden arrow. Jake has added the initials AH and JD.

Alex isn't surprised. If the boys in her grade are going to fall in love, obviously they will choose Annabel. 'What will Bobbie say when he finds out?' she asks.

Annabel inspects the ring on her delicate little hand, and then examines the neat shell-pink nails with their perfect half-moons. 'Bobbie won't know. We shall meet secretly.'

Alex looks at her own bitten fingernails, on which the moons are scarcely visible. It seems unfair that Annabel should have both Bobbie and Jake. She can't visualise anybody being in love with her. 'No one will ever want to date me', she complains to Sheena. 'I'm too tall.'

'Date you?' exclaims her mother in surprise and amusement. 'You're only nine! You won't need a boyfriend till you're at least seventeen, and by that time some of the boys will be taller than you.'

'Annabel dates now.'

'I wish she wouldn't fill your head with these silly ideas. Sometimes I wonder if she's a suitable friend for you.'

Alex regrets mentioning Annabel, and resolves not to do so again. Her life in Beirut has revolved around the Hittis and her own status at school has remained high because she's her friend. Annabel seems to have lost all interest in the games they used to devise together. She hates attending Sunday service and the Bible Class. When the weather turns hot and sticky she says she can't be bothered to do anything. She prefers to lie on her bed and pick quarrels with Alex. She will then receive her back into favour, promising fervently that they will be friends for ever.

'Are you going to have children?' she asks one day.

'I suppose so.' It isn't something Alex has given thought to.

'I'm never going to have a baby!' announces Annabel grimly. 'Mom told me it hurts terribly. Some mothers scream for hours.' Alex looks horrified and Annabel warms to her description. 'Blood pours out of you for days afterwards. You can even die!'

Since Zilpha told her how babies are born, Alex hasn't spoken to anyone on such matters. This new information is frightening.

'When our cat had kittens', continues Annabel, 'It was horrible to watch. Most of the time I just couldn't look. One of the kittens died.'

On her way home from Annabel's house Alex walks slowly, kicking a stone through the dust and pondering over what she's heard. The maple trees in the hedge are already turning yellow from lack of moisture. But the two private gardens she has to pass are vibrant with colour – vivid red poinsettias vying with lustrous sunflowers, giant ochre hibiscus trumpets peering through magenta bougainvillaea. Sprinklers revolve ceaselessly, casting a mist of fine spray over the lawns and dark red soil of the flower beds.

In the kitchen Abby is making ice cream, her muscular arms slaving over the wooden bucket, beads of sweat standing out on her lined forehead. A newly made pot of tea stands on a tray. 'Your mother came home early today. She's not feeling well. You can take that tray up to her.'

The door is slightly ajar. Without a sound Alex pushes it wide open and stands on the threshold. She's taken aback to see Sheena stretched out naked on her back on top of the bedspread. Her housecoat has slipped to the floor. For a terrifying moment Alex wonders if she's dead. She moves forward and sees that her mother is sound asleep, her smooth white breasts and stomach rising and falling almost imperceptibly with her breathing. It's nothing new to see her mother naked, but standing so close to her sleeping body it seems strangely unfamiliar, as though she's seeing it for the first time. Being so used to shades of brown skin the stark whiteness of her mother's flesh seems unreal, reminding her of the alabaster statues she's seen of the Virgin. She takes in the few minute brown freckles on the arms, the thinnest of blue veins down the legs, the thick auburn plait lying across the lace-edged pillow.

Alex puts down the tray, and when her mother still doesn't wake, walks round the bed staring more closely at Sheena's body – at the small tight stomach above the neat triangle of dark gold hair. She remembers what Annabel has told her. Looking at the narrow hips, the slender thighs, the perfect compactness of the whole body, she finds it almost impossible to credit that she herself emerged from this flesh. Some horrific change must have taken place. Maybe it's the reason why Sheena can't think well of her. After what must have been a terrible experience Sheena would expect a perfect child in recompense. The more she gazes at this matchless white form the more disturbing, the more alien it becomes, and the more guilty she feels for having defiled it. Picking up the satin housecoat from the carpet and gently draping it over Sheena, she creeps away.

A week later when Alex comes home from school she finds Abby in the lounge, listening to the news bulletin. She notes with amazement that tears are running down her papery cheeks. 'The Allies landed in France yesterday' wails the cook. 'The war's nearly over. Mr Carrington will go back to the States and I shall have no job!'

'Can't he take you to the States with him?'

'No, I can't leave my family.'

Alex thinks of Abby's pumpkin pie, ice cream, kefta, falafel, tabouleh, Maryland chicken – and wonders how Basil will do without her.

'Is Hitler dead?' she asks.

'No, not yet.'

'What will they do to him when they catch him?'

'Cut off his head or hang him.'

'They don't cut off people's heads nowadays.'

'Of course they do', replies the cook grimly. 'You have a lot to learn.'

The June evening is heavy with the scent of jasmine. Alex swings aimlessly on the balcony until Sheena comes upstairs. 'Abby says the war's ended.'

'Not yet', replies her mother wearily. 'We still have a long way to go.'

Basil, however, is jubilant. He can't stop talking about General Eisenhower's liberation of France. 'We must go out and celebrate, Sheena!'

'Do we have to? I'm so tired. We've been waiting so long for the end of the war; how can we be sure it's going to happen?'

'Aw, come on, honey, do cheer up. The end's definitely in sight, Japan can't hold out much longer...' But he can't rouse Sheena's enthusiasm.

For the past three months Basil's been teaching Sheena to drive near the golf course. After nagging her to learn for years, suddenly one weekend she agreed. But it's been an uphill task. Alex listens behind the sliding door to their furious exchanges on returning from these lessons.

'You're damned lucky there's no driving test here, but you'll have to pass one in the States. You just don't listen to anything I say!' shouts Basil.

'You don't have to teach me!' Sheena yells back. 'Norman has offered to give me lessons. I'll go out with him next weekend.'

'If you let that little jerk take you out then you can let him buy you a car. Don't come running to me for one!'

'I'll buy my own car, don't you worry!'

So Alex is surprised when her mother says at the end of the summer term, 'I'll be driving us all to Broummana this summer.'

'Have you finished learning to drive?'

'No one ever finishes learning to drive in Beirut', replies Sheena.

'Did Giles take a test in England?'

'No, he was lucky. He learnt to drive before they brought in the test. There weren't many cars on the road then. He just paid five shillings and got a licence.'

When they leave for Broummana with Sheena at the wheel, Alex realises her mother's very nervous. As she drives towards east Beirut along Avenue Clemenceau she's disconcerted by the constant hooting and the oaths shouted from taxi to taxi. Her face is flushed with concentration and for the first time her daughter sees her at a disadvantage. At the T junction Basil says 'Turn right', just in time. Further on Sheena is about to take the left fork down Rue du Maréchal Pétain when Basil yells, 'No, Rue de L'Armée! God knows, you've driven this way often enough!'

They proceed correctly along Rue Gouraud and into Rue Ain Nahr, and Sheena relaxes a little as they cross the stone bridge and turn right past river cafés and swimming stations onto the Broummana road. She drives slowly and carefully, letting the taxis pass her at breakneck speed.

Beyond Ain Saade, the village before Beit Mery, the road's clear and Sheena speeds up slightly towards isolated houses on the left. Suddenly a small figure hurtles out from one of the houses straight into the road. Sheena panics and fails to brake quickly enough. The child is knocked down.

The next half hour becomes a confused nightmare. The car's immediately surrounded by clamouring, gesticulating people. Basil opens his door and struggles to get out, trying to make himself heard. Two men carry a boy of about six or seven into the house from which he ran out so swiftly minutes before. Sheena, Alex and Janine sit ashen-faced in the car while women press against the bodywork and voices threaten revenge. Alex is far too frightened to cry. She stares as in a bad dream at the distorted face of a boy pressed close against the rear window. He grimaces at her, showing his white even teeth.

It seems hours before Basil returns with a policeman who speaks only Arabic and French. It's unclear to Basil whether the child is dead or unconscious. After much shouting an ambulance screeches its way through the crowd and the little boy is lifted in, wrapped in a blanket. The crowd falls back as the ambulance roars away and the policeman writes down endless details in a notebook. Basil opens Sheena's door and says, 'We're advised to give the family a substantial amount of money unless we want to go through the courts.'

'But it wasn't my fault the kid ran out.'

'No, of course it wasn't. But the villagers will say it was and a court case could be difficult.'

Sheena asks hoarsely, 'Is the boy dead?'

'I don't think so. We'll have to hope he doesn't die in hospital.' Basil passes a wad of banknotes to a man who counts them. Then the crowd disperses.

With Basil now at the wheel, the policeman waves them on up the road. Before they reach Beit Mery he stops and says, 'You take over now, Sheena. If you don't do it straight away you'll lose your nerve for ever.'

But Sheena refuses. 'I'll never drive again. Never!'

'You must. It's the only way. You can't waste what you've learnt.' But Sheena refuses to move.

'You're probably suffering from shock. Shall I take you down to the hospital?'

'No. Just take me to the villa.'

When they reach Broummana, Basil helps Sheena out of the car. Her legs buckle under her and he has to carry her up the many steps, his face becoming puce with the effort. After a couple of brandies Sheena revives a little and begins to unpack, while Janine serves cold ham and salad in the musty-smelling living room. Basil shouts at Janine to do this and do that. She scuttles around like a frightened hen. Everyone is on edge.

Sheena goes to bed for the rest of the day and Basil drives off in the car. Alex sits on the verandah with Hatty on her lap until bedtime. The summer vacation has got off to a dismal start.

Chapter Thirty-eight

Sheena continues to be nervous and irritable, although Basil assures her that the little boy isn't dead. Alex would like to offer sympathy but her mother is even more inaccessible than usual. She seems to be ignoring her daughter as though she was to blame for being a witness to her mother's humiliation.

For a week Sheena hardly leaves her bedroom. Basil is out most of the time, and Janine stays in the kitchen. An unbearable lethargy settles on the house. Alex walks down to Sania's house one morning but no one seems to be at home. The only signs of life are the hens pecking in the yard. She continues downhill but then has to retrace her steps in the midday heat. Hatty is panting hard and flops on the ground every few yards. Alex feels guilty for bringing the dog out at this time of day.

Finally Sheena emerges from her isolation and she and Basil go out for an evening. Alex wakes up in the early hours to the sound of raised voices in her mother's bedroom. Standing outside their door in the dark she listens as accusing words pour out of Basil, feelings she doesn't really understand. But she gathers enough to know Basil is still bitterly resentful of the time Sheena spends at the club and that he's exasperated by her moods.

'You want an adoring slave like Giles, Sheena, and I'm not playing that role... Frankly I think you've been utterly spoilt by that husband of yours and by all those immature boys at the club... You're beginning to embarrass me. When you've had too much to drink you even become cheap and vulgar!.....'

Alex hates Basil for confronting her mother with these home truths. She wants to rush in and protect Sheena. Yet she exults in their quarrelling. Maybe now the relationship will break up. Alex returns to bed quivering with emotion. A door bangs, and then another. The child lies awake until dawn, when she gets up and finds Basil asleep in an armchair in the living room. She tiptoes across to have a look at him. How different he appears when sleeping! His mouth is slightly open, his stubby, bleached eyelashes brush the top of his red-veined cheeks, his chin bristles with ginger hairs. The more she stares, the more she can see how he'll look as an old man. At the same time in sleep there is something boyish and vulnerable about his face. He stirs, and she flees into the kitchen, her heart beating violently.

Later that day, when Alex is sitting with Hatty on the verandah, she hears Basil and Sheena quarrelling again upstairs. This time her mother is shouting abuse and then, without warning, something heavy and black comes hurtling from the balcony above, just missing Alex's head and crashing down the first flight of terrace steps. Alex is struck with horror as she recognises the shattered object – Basil's precious camera. What amazing power adults possess! Anything could happen now. Such violence could provoke murder itself.

What does happen is that Sheena locks herself up again, and Basil tells Alex curtly that he's returning to Beirut. He'll be back in a few days.

When he's gone, Alex creeps up and down outside her mother's room, wondering what she can be doing inside. The minutes tick by slowly. Can she hear sobbing? She listens intently but can't be sure. If only Giles could come! She decides to write to him urgently, telling him Sheena's unhappy, and loves him better than Basil. He must come at once to rescue her. But having written the letter there's no means of posting it.

Basil returns to Broummana in a seemingly cheerful mood and resumes his holiday with Sheena. Reconciliation has obviously taken place, but Alex senses an atmosphere of tension whenever she is with them both.

The next day, Sheena asks Alex to come into her room. She sits on the bed and her mother says, 'Giles is trying to arrange to take you to England by boat. If he can get a passage in September you won't be going back to school.'

For all the talk of the war coming to an end, Alex is still stunned by this news. 'What about Hatty?'

'I'm trying to find a new home for her.'

'I don't want to go away without Hatty.'

'There's no alternative. Hatty will get used to a new owner who will love her and when you grow up you'll be able to have another dog.'

'No one will ever love Hatty as much as I do!'

Alex's next thought is nearly as desperate as her concern over the dog. 'I haven't said goodbye to Annabel. I can't go without seeing her again!'

'You'll have to write to her.'

'I can't. She's at Aley for the summer and I don't know the address.'

'Well, you might see her in Beirut before you go.'

Sheena isn't interested in Annabel, she has other things on her mind, and for once she talks about the future in a matter-of-fact voice without evasion. 'I have to tell you, Alex, that your father and I are getting a divorce so I can marry Basil. We shall be going to live in the States, in California, which is nice and warm. You'll be able to come and visit us when you're older. And of course I'll be coming to see you in England for the summer holidays.'

'Am I going to live with Aunty May?' Alex asks, already knowing the answer.

'No, she's got enough to do with her own two children. And she lives in the middle of a big town. Giles will find you a boarding school in the country, and a nice family nearby where you can stay in the Christmas and Easter holidays.'

The thought of life among strangers is terrifying. And the idea of visiting California is too unrealistic to be taken seriously.

She determines to spend every minute of each day with Hatty, and goes to sleep at night with the dog curled up in her arms in spite of the heat. One afternoon when Alex is returning to the villa from the village a car hoots loudly behind her and stops. It's Mrs Hitti with Annabel and the twins in the back.

'What a lovely surprise to see you, Alex! We're staying in Broummana for three days to attend a Presbyterian Conference at the college here.'

Alex has been taken once to the college in Broummana to watch a tennis tournament with Basil and Sheena and some friends of theirs. She recalls extensive gardens with a magnificent view of Beirut.

'Would you like to come and spend tomorrow with us?' continues Mrs Hitti. 'There's to be an open-air service on one of the tennis courts, and we shall have music and a buffet lunch afterwards.' Alex can hardly believe her luck.

At ten o'clock the following morning she walks the half mile down to the college. But when she's crossed the lawn and is standing before the tall, imposing doors she dares not ring the bell. She sits on a stone seat, and a few minutes later Annabel herself appears from round the side of the building. How grownup she looks in a red and white two-piece outfit! Her mass of hair has been cut very short, her nails are varnished and her sandals are stylish, with a slight heel. Alex feels awkward in her childish frock and Clark's sandals. Annabel has entered another world and left her far behind. But her friend is as chatty and charming as usual and the day promises to be pleasant.

She enjoys the service, sitting on the raked wooden benches ranged round one of the hard tennis courts. A huge congregation sings hymns lustily with no musical accompaniment. A young blond American preacher talks about the end of the war, making a new start, converting the East to Christianity. During the lengthy prayer session Annabel whispers, 'See that guy opposite in the second row? Isn't he just darling?'

Mrs Hitti says 'Shush' before Alex can give an opinion.

After the service everyone moves onto a large paved terrace blazing with scarlet geraniums in stone urns. A buffet lunch is laid out on two long trestle tables covered with snowy-white cloths.

Alex imparts the news that she is going to England in September. In return Annabel says her family are departing for the States in October, so she too won't be returning to school. She's very excited at the prospect of a journey on a liner and a new life in the America Mrs Kellaway has described in such glowing terms. Leaving Lebanon doesn't seem to worry her.

During lunch her attention is taken up with the boy she pointed out earlier on. This fifteen-year-old object of her admiration is wearing immaculate long white trousers and a silk cravat tucked into his pale blue shirt. When he strolls over to speak to Annabel, Alex realises with intense disappointment that she's not wanted. There's no point in her staying any longer. Annabel doesn't even notice when her friend slips away. Mrs Hitti is nowhere to be seen, but she catches sight of the twins, Jimmy and Konrad, knocking a ball around on the tennis court.

Alex shouts, 'Tell your mother I had to go home. Tell her a big thank you for inviting me.'

Konrad nods and as Alex walks away he yells in his usual mocking voice, 'So long, Alexandria, see you in Beirut!'

Alex trudges slowly up to the villa in the heat, red dust gathering on her white sandals, and tears pricking at her eyelids. The world seems a very harsh place, and the future stretches out, cloudy and uncertain.

The villa is unusually quiet. Basil and Sheena are resting. Janine is in her room. Alex senses something is missing. There's no sign of the dog anywhere. Alex calls her name all over the garden and then rushes up to her mother's room in a panic without knocking.

'Where's Hatty?' she shouts.

'I'm sorry, darling, but the lady who offered to have Hatty turned up here this morning instead of next weekend and she wanted to take the dog straight away. We thought it best to let her go, even though you weren't here. Having to say goodbye would have been so hard for you.'

Alex is outraged that the dog should have been given away in her absence. 'Hatty is my dog! Giles gave her to me! You had no right to let her go without telling me!' she screams at Sheena. 'I hate you! I'll always hate you! I love Hatty more than you! I wanted to say goodbye!' She bursts into hysterical weeping for the loss of her dog and for the loss of Annabel.

For once Sheena doesn't tell her daughter to control herself. She says quietly, 'Hatty will have a very good home with Mrs Taylor who adores animals. And it wouldn't have been easy for you to part with Hatty in front of a stranger.'

'It was going to be unhappy for you whichever way it happened', adds Basil gently. 'One day you'll have another dachshund.'

'I don't want another dachshund. There aren't any dogs as good as Hatty in the whole world, and I know she won't be happy with anyone but me!'

Alex rushes out of the house and begins to run up the road and into the pine forest without any notion of where she's heading. She follows a path at random and finds herself going over a hill into a small ravine full of thorn trees and grey cousinia bushes. She hastens up the other side, over another ridge and across an orchard, her anger giving her the energy to keep going. Thoughts of running away for ever fill her head.

At the top of the next hill she comes across a large mausoleum-type tomb, one of many in the mountains. She's noticed this particular castellated and domed tomb in the distance while driving with Giles. Now she has to clamber through dried bracken and prickly undergrowth to reach the rough-hewn stone building with its single small iron-grilled window at one end and a heavy arched iron door at the other. She stops for the first time, panting. There's no one in sight. The cicadas are silent for the moment and nothing stirs. Dare she enter the tomb to find some shade? Normally she might have fled such a place, but today she pushes against the door and it creaks open to reveal a dark space filled with an inexplicable odour of dried citrus fruit. When her eyes become used to the gloom she steps inside the whitewashed room with its neat vaulted dome. Within an apsed recess runs a ledge on which are stuck the stunted remains of many candles and dead flies. The air is stale, and dried flowers are turning to dust in a large brass jar covered in verdigris. Alex assumes the place is a shrine to a long-dead saint.

Her nose gradually becomes sensitive to some faintly foetid smell she can't identify. Below the dusty smeared window lies a dark rectangular shape. Coming closer she sees it to be a long wooden box with a glass lid. Within lies what looks like a body wrapped in black cloth. No flesh is showing, save for a patch of what looks like wrinkled blackened leather round two dark eye sockets.

Her heart thumps with violent emotion, the same emotion she felt on looking down at the dead djinn in the desert. She wants to escape but her legs feel heavy and her head is aching. On the wall above the window a malevolent little face stares mockingly at her from a faded blue, red and gold fresco festooned with cobwebs.

At length she turns and stumbles out of the door into the blinding glare. In her haste to be away from the tomb she bounds down the hill without looking to see which direction she should take. When she has to stop for want of breath nothing around her looks familiar and she wonders if she'll ever find her way home. She hurries up the next steep incline and from the top sees the red roofs of Broummana in the distance, and thankfully, the main road a few yards below. It's surprising how far she's come from the villa.

When she finally limps home, sweaty and covered with dust, Sheena doesn't ask any questions, and Hatty isn't mentioned. At supper Basil asks 'Did you have a nice lunch at the college?'

Lunch at the college seems like a month ago. 'Yes', says Alex without enthusiasm, and anticipating the next question, 'We had cold chicken and cake and potato salad and jelly and ham and ice cream.'

'Not in that order, I hope', says Basil, smiling.

A letter from Giles arrives, informing Sheena that he's managed to book a provisional passage for the middle of September. The date remains uncertain. He and Alex will have to hang about in Cairo until the last moment.

Basil and Sheena go back to work in Beirut and Alex is left once again to amuse herself in Broummana. Now that going to England has become a certainty, the days suddenly seem to fly past. The sights, sounds and smells of the mountains have seeped into her subconscious and she wants the summer to go on for ever. She becomes obsessed by a series of 'last times' – the last time she will visit this village or walk through that vineyard – the last time she will touch a certain tree or eat a particular Arab food. Every new day in Broummana is sad and filled with nostalgia for Hatty.

Before the end of August a bulletin on the wireless announces that Paris has at last been liberated by the Allies. Owing to the strong French influence still prevalent in Lebanon, this news generates great rejoicing among the Christians. Bonfires are lit in the villages and fireworks are let off at night. Huge posters of General de Gaulle and General Leclerc are pasted up on walls. The war against Hitler really has ended.

In September Giles arrives in a hired car with more luggage than usual and clarifies what they will do until they board the ship for Liverpool. 'We'll spend another week here and then we'll take the train to Cairo from Beirut and stay there until we're given our sailing date. If we're lucky we may have time to explore the pyramids and other places in Egypt.' He pauses and then says, 'I think your mother has explained to you that she and Basil are going to the States, probably in October. I'll be able to stay in England until the new year, and then I'll have to go back to Kirkuk and later to Bahrain. By that time I'll have settled you into a good boarding school out in the country.'

'You said once', Alex accuses him, 'That I could live with Aunty May and go to a day school.'

'I know I did, but your mother and I have since decided you'll get a better education at a boarding school.'

'It's because Sheena doesn't like your sister, isn't it?'

Giles looks surprised. 'Of course she likes May. They don't know each other all that well.' Alex is yet again frustrated by her father's unwillingness to admit that Sheena could be mistaken about anything. It is the one unsatisfactory aspect of her own relationship with him.

Giles says he too is sad at the thought of leaving Lebanon. He has brought Alex a Brownie box camera with the idea that they should see as much as possible and take snaps. They visit Harissa, high above Jounie Bay, to see Notre Dame de Liban, an enormous white figure of the Virgin Mary twenty metres high. Many dizzily winding steps lead them round and round a terraced stone tower up to the statue. The view, when they reach her feet, is the most spectacular in Lebanon. It seems as if they can see the whole country laid out around them.

'I'm glad England is a small country', Alex says suddenly. The idea of living in enormous places like America or Russia doesn't appeal.

During their last night but one – a Saturday – Alex wakes hearing loud voices. Is it quarrelling, or just talking? Getting up, she pads across the tiled floor and listens intently outside her mother's door, trying to catch what's being said. A stern whisper from behind makes her jump.

'Alex, go back to bed! You've been told time and again not to eavesdrop!' She slinks past Giles, shamefaced at being caught out. Her father follows her into the bedroom. 'You must stop this habit, Alex. Your mother is entitled to her privacy. She'll tell you all you need to know in due course.'

'She never tells me anything.'

Giles sits on the bed and says, 'What do you want to do on our last day? We can't go far as I have to pack.'

'Let's go really early and have a picnic breakfast at our secret tree.'

'Very well. Go to sleep now and I'll get you up at six.'

As they leave the silent house they notice the Buick has gone. When they turn the corner of the track leading to the abbey, expecting to see the familiar gnarled olive tree growing out of the rock, all they can see is a gaping hole.

'It must have been brought down at last by a winter storm, and then taken away for firewood', says Giles. 'It was bound to happen sooner or later. It was a very old tree.' Alex is upset. She's become superstitious about the tree. Its demise seems to symbolise the end of the happy times she's spent with her father in these mountains.

Walking back to the car they see a small black goat standing on the branch of a sycamore tree, bleating as though to say, 'I'm stuck, I can't get down!' Alex moves towards it in concern and plunges into a bed of stinging nettles. She lets out a shriek and the kid leaps lightly from the tree and bounds away. Giles finds a clump of dock plants and she sits amongst them, rubbing the leaves over her stinging bare legs. After a while the pinpoints of pain subside.

Alex lies back amongst the dock leaves and stares up at the empty blue sky. Shutting her eyes against the glare she suddenly hears her father cry out. 'Look, look, Alex, just look at those cranes!' She opens her eyes to see a flock of large birds with tufted heads, flying low in close formation, their long legs and necks stretched out gracefully, their short wings powerfully whirring.

'They're on their way from Russia down to Egypt for the winter. There must be sixty or seventy of them.'

Father and daughter gaze up in wonder until the birds are no more than specks in the distance. 'You can't imagine how amazingly lucky we are to have seen that rare sight!' exclaims Giles. 'Just think, cranes have been flying south over these mountains from Scythia to the Upper Nile every September for thousands and thousands of years, like clockwork. One of the first historians, Herodotus, who died before Jesus was born, mentions seeing the cranes flying when he was travelling in this area. It's a sight you'll probably never see again.'

Alex is duly impressed by the birds, and on another day she might have been exhilarated as well. But today the migrating cranes have a depressing effect on her. She feels overwhelming sadness for the past and great anxiety for the future.

Chapter Thirty-nine

Before taking Alex home Giles drives further up the mountain to a small crowded outdoor café beside a miniature waterfall. Lebanese families in their Sunday best are tucking into arak and mezze. The cheerful proprietor is famous for his ice cream and Alex chooses her favourite flavour – pistachio. They sit for a long time enjoying the coolness of the café until Giles says they must return to the villa to finish packing and to discuss a few things with Basil and Sheena.

As they reach the villa Janine comes running down the steps shouting urgently, 'Madame! Madame! Isbataliyeh! Come! Come!'

On the way up the maid informs them Basil left for Beirut at 5 am. Sheena's bedroom door is open. She is lying very still on the bed in a satin night-dress, apparently asleep. But a half empty whisky bottle on the floor and an empty bottle of pills on the bedside table indicate to Giles what's probably happened, and he hurries downstairs to telephone the hospital in Beirut.

Alex sits on the bed in agitation. She's heard her mother talking to Basil about people taking overdoses of sleeping pills. Giles's panic leads her to assume the worst, and she takes Sheena's limp hand, whispering, 'Wake up! Wake up!' The next ten minutes tick by impossibly slowly on the bedside clock. She must be dead or she'd wake up. Her father returns and puts an arm around his daughter, saying, 'Your mother's not dead, she's just unconscious. They're sending an ambulance.'

'What's wrong with her?'

'She probably took too many sleeping pills by accident.' He takes his wife's pulse and then father and daughter remain close together beside the bed, watching Sheena intently. Giles is tense with anxiety. His face looks grey, almost old. He takes out a cigarette and then returns it to the packet.

'Why don't we take Sheena to hospital in the car?' whispers Alex.

'She may need medical attention on the way.'

'How could she take too many pills by accident?'

'She's been very tired and overworked lately. I expect she had a drink of whisky which made her so sleepy that she didn't realise how many pills she was taking.'

When the ambulance arrives, Sheena is lifted onto a stretcher and carried with difficulty down the steps of the villa. Giles tells Janine he's going to Beirut. He hands her some money and instructs her that if Basil doesn't return by dusk she can take a taxi back to town in the morning.

An hour later, after hastily throwing Sheena's clothes into a case, and putting it with their own luggage into the car, they start their drive to Beirut. During the journey Alex is silent, still certain her mother is dead.. As they begin to negotiate the traffic in town she asks, 'Are we going to the hospital?'

'Yes, we'll go to the hospital and find out how Sheena is. Then we'll go to the apartment and see if Basil's there.'

Giles leaves his daughter in the car while he goes into the hospital. On his return he looks almost cheerful. 'She's going to be all right', he tells Alex.

'Is she awake?'

'Yes, she's awake.'

'How did they wake her?'

'I don't know. But she's going to get well. That's all we need to worry about at the moment.'

Alex suspects Giles isn't telling her everything. There are many questions she wants answered. What's happened to Basil? Why has he gone without saying goodbye? What treatment did the doctor give Sheena? Why did she take too many pills? Is she unhappy because Basil's gone?... And foremost among her thoughts is the hope that Basil really has gone out of their lives for ever.

Back at the apartment Abby opens the door to them looking very dismal. She tells them Basil has already left. He's going to Jerusalem, and from there to the States. He's paid her two months' wages in advance and written her an excellent reference. Janine is to be paid until the end of the month. She herself is expected to stay on till the Kinleys depart and someone comes to pack all the possessions Basil wants shipped to America.

'Oh, Mr Kinley', wails Abby, 'How can I leave this house? It's been my home for so long.'

Giles consoles her by saying that the next tenant will probably be more than delighted to keep her on, and the cook cheers up enough to busy herself making a meal.

After supper, Giles and Alex go out to sit on the top balcony. Giles drinks a couple of whiskies and they watch the lights going on all over Beirut.

Then comes a phone call from the hospital and Giles tells Alex he's going to see her mother, and she must amuse herself till bedtime. 'You'll see her in the morning.'

It's strange to be back in the apartment, hearing the constant noise of a big city after the quiet of Broummana. She listens to the trams rumbling down Avenue Bliss, and when she goes to bed she misses Hatty's weight at her feet.

On waking, she finds a note by her bed. *You mustn't worry any more. Sheena is going to be all right.* Then Alex imagines visiting the hospital. Will her father hold her mother's hand, and will she smile at him the way she used to smile at Basil? Perhaps she herself will be able to give her mother a big kiss and a hug and tell her how glad she is that they're together again.

But when Giles takes her into the ward nothing happens the way she'd imagined it might. They walk between two rows of stiff iron bedsteads and narrow lockers over an expanse of scrubbed linoleum smelling of ether and Jeyes fluid. The severity is only a little relieved by the September sunshine lighting up the grey walls, and a glimpse of scarlet poinsettia outside the window. They find Sheena in a small private room off the ward. She's propped up against her pillows looking very thin and frail, no colour in her face at all. Without make-up she looks strangely faded, like a pressed flower. Her lips are almost as white as her skin. But her eyes are still green, her hair the same glorious auburn gold.

Sheena smiles wanly, but she doesn't kiss Giles or hold his hand. Alex wants to kiss and hug her but the bed seems to be in the way and Sheena makes no move to encourage her. The opportunity never comes, and father and daughter stand there looking down at her, not knowing what to say.

'They're stuffing me with mugs of sweet hot chocolate! Can you imagine it? All I want is a cigarette and a whisky!' It's a predictable remark, yet there's something chastened about Sheena. Beneath the bravado she's in a state of collapse for the first time in her life but she's determined to keep up the pretence. If she allowed husband or daughter to comfort her it would be a confession of failure. Her recent unhappy experience with Basil has only served to distance her from Giles and Alex. For the first time Alex begins to cry. She can't stop, and almost chokes over her tears. Sheena lies stiffly on her pillow, unable to respond, and Giles has to drag his daughter away. Alex weeps herself into exhaustion in Giles's arms.

In the morning, after a long sleep, Alex seems less unhappy. Giles asks her to start sorting out her things to take to England. Toys will have to be left behind but she may take all her books. 'You'll be happy to hear your mother will be coming to Cairo with us', Giles tells her. 'I hope to get a berth for her on the same boat as us. How would you like to fold her clothes very carefully and pack them into her trunk? Put the shoes and other heavy things in first.'

Alex enjoys laying out all her mother's suits, frocks and underwear on the bed. She pulls out the shoes from the bottom of the wardrobe and empties all the drawers. At the back of a cupboard she finds a large photograph of Giles as a very young man. She inserts layers of tissue paper between the clothes as she has so often seen Sheena do.

In her own room, Alex wonders what will happen to all Sally-Ann's toys stuffed away in the cupboards. She plonks the golliwog back in the wicker chair where it grins inanely at her. *He's glad to see me go,* thinks Alex. *How I hate him!*

She enters Basil's room. The drawers are empty, the photographs have gone, the row of smart suits no longer hangs in the wardrobe. All that remains of the man she's lived with for over three years is a whiff of cologne and a pile of American magazines. Alex drags a chair over to the wardrobe to stand on, so she can feel along the top in case he's left a box of chocolates. But there's nothing but dust.

She climbs up to the roof for the last time. She's long since grown tall enough to see over the parapet. From this height Beirut looks neat and tidy and colourful in the sunshine – the black and white lighthouse in the distance, the red roofs, the purple bougainvillaea, the emerald bean fields, the dusty tracks between the roads, the yellow blocks of flats, the tall dark trees on the campus, and the glimpse of sea in the distance. Down the spiral staircase and along the trellis the morning glory is still in bloom, its blue flowers tightly closed at this time of day. Alex descends to the balcony and sits idly on the swing, picturing some other child using it. She's been so bored, so unhappy, so anxious in this apartment, but strangely enough, now she doesn't want to leave it.

Early the next morning Giles and Alex say goodbye to Abby and Janine. The cook kisses Alex fondly and gives her a box of sugared almonds. Then they take a taxi to the hospital to pick up Sheena.

'Is she better now?' asks Alex.

'Almost better.'

If only her father would tell her more of the state of his relationship with her mother. Does Sheena still love Basil? Did she deliberately take too many sleeping pills? As a nurse, wouldn't she know the dangers? On what terms is she coming to England? Once, Alex would have flung questions at Giles, nagged him for an answer. But now his mood tells her it's too sensitive an issue. She's excluded from her parents' relationship. But at least Basil has gone out of their lives.

Sheena looks more like herself in a navy tussore suit with a deep white collar. Her face is carefully made up, her hair coiled and shining. Alex sits between Giles and Sheena as the taxi hurtles alongside the tramlines, crosses the Place des Canons and hoots its way down Rue Ein Nahr to the station. Immediately half a dozen porters vie with one another to carry the luggage. The platform is crowded with all types of people. Vendors push amongst them, selling hot bread and peanuts and freshly picked fruit.

The train chugs in slowly, enveloped in clouds of steam. They climb into a first class carriage and search for their reserved seats. Alex is squashed next to a tearful British woman clutching a Moses basket with a tiny baby in it. What looks like a small furry animal is curled up at the bottom of the basket. On closer inspection it turns out to be a fox stole with a glassy eye and a hard shiny nose. A man waves a green flag and the train moves out of the station and through a seedy part of Beirut they've never seen before. Then it gathers speed and in no time they have crossed the Awali River and are approaching Saida, looking from a distance as if rising out of the sea, its minarets and roofs bobbing on the waves. Alex enjoys the movement of the train in combination with the countryside rushing past. It's much more exciting than travelling by car.

'How far is it to Cairo?' she asks Giles.

'A long way. About six hundred and sixty kilometres.'

As they pass the Crusader castle Alex last saw on the way up to Beirut from Palestine, she expects her father to tell her its history, but he says nothing. They run on to Sour, the old town of Tyre, where they can see a line of classical columns beside the sea and once again Alex is surprised that Giles makes no attempt to explain their origin. Sheena's presence preoccupies him. He enquires constantly whether she needs anything, but she always shakes her head and continues to gaze out of the window, deep in her own thoughts. Alex is amazed at how anyone can keep silent for so long.

They cross another river, the Aqrab, then on to Acre and Haifa, where they are to await the overnight train to Cairo. They spend the interval at the Appinger Hotel. As before, the hotel is crowded with civilians and servicemen. By chance the very table where Alex sat with Sheena and Zilpha on her seventh birthday has just been vacated and they sit in the garden amidst heaps of dried pine needles. Memories of Zilpha come flooding back to Alex, who hasn't thought of her nanny for many months.

Now for the first time Giles does begin to talk about the journey. He opens the old, well-thumbed atlas, and shows Alex the route they'll travel overnight to Egypt. Tel Aviv, Gaza, Khan Yunis – then into the desert of the Sinai Peninsula to Qantara. 'It will be dawn by the time we reach Ismailia on the Suez Canal, so we shall see something of the Egyptian countryside.'

Giles has only been able to obtain two berths on the night train, so he'll sit up all night and let Sheena and his daughter have the sleeping quarters. Alex becomes wildly excited at the thought of going to bed in a moving train.

By the time they return to the station darkness is falling and the platform is packed. It seems everyone is on the move now that the war is nearly over. Most of the travellers look tired and irritable. Sheena is deathly pale, and Alex is flushed and feeling slightly sick. It's hard to believe this is the same Sheena of a year ago. Alex watches a harassed-looking mother with a strong Scots accent dragging along her toddler son who in turn is pulling along a wooden lamb on wheels. Another woman nearly falls over the toy and exclaims impatiently, 'What a damn stupid thing to take on a train!'

In the compartment there are two narrow bunks, a number of hooks on the polished wood wall, a small fold-up table and a minuscule wash basin. Blinds made of oil cloth are pulled down over the windows. In spite of a ventilator the air is stuffy. Alex climbs up the ladder to the top bunk and plans to stay awake so she can enjoy the whole journey. But as soon as the train starts to move she falls asleep. Only once does she wake, to the sound of a child crying in the adjoining compartment.

The next thing she knows, the train has stopped with a series of creaking jerks, and her father is speaking softly in her ear. 'Time to get up, Alex, we're in Egypt.' He switches on the tiny light above the washbasin. 'We'll let Sheena sleep on, so get dressed quietly and come to the restaurant car at the back of the train.'

They sit on either side of a table looking out of the window as they wait for hot rolls and coffee to be served. Giles looks exhausted after dozing in discomfort all night in crumpled clothes. The shell-pink sky is streaked with layers of orange and violet. For a few miles the train chugs through fields of roses, grown in rows like trees in an orchard. Giles says the flowers are being grown especially to make perfume. Then they move across the Nile delta, where the earth is rich and black on the flat oblong fields divided by green water channels – fields of flax, tobacco and barley followed by orchards of banana, pomegranates and mango. Yellow minarets peep out of groups of mud-brick houses like those on the Euphrates, and everywhere rubbish is piling up. Yet the landscape including the rubbish is bathed with an air of mystery in the dawn light. The sun rises, the flat terrain suddenly becomes monotonous and Alex begins to miss the mountains of Lebanon.

Giles buys a copy of the Egyptian Mail, which is full of war news. Troops have left North Africa, flying bombs and rockets are still falling over Britain, Greece will soon be liberated. Sheena joins them but shows little interest in the news. While Giles returns to the sleeping compartment to wash and change, Sheena drinks several cups of black coffee. She smiles at her daughter, but says nothing. Alex, too, is tongue-tied. There are so many questions she wants to ask, but never will.

They approach the Suez Canal at Ismailia. Ugly ships painted a dull umber loom out of an unexpected ribbon of eau de nil water running between sand flats. They can see the backs of grubby houses decorated with lines of washing flapping violently in the sudden wind coming up from the sea. The train halts alongside the bustling quay and there's a long delay while they transfer with their luggage onto the crowded ferry which conveys them across the canal. They board another train which moves on to Cairo through fields of cotton and more fields of roses. It stops for no apparent reason opposite a row of eucalyptus trees and a heap of rusty petrol cans. Alex catches sight of some children slinging stones from catapults at birds, and a group of men in blue robes moving along a track. At length the train seems to hiccup violently and shunts forward slowly. On a train going in the opposite direction they see boys hanging dangerously onto the couplings.

Eventually they reach Bab-el-Hadid station in Cairo and stumble out stiff-limbed onto a platform seething with life. Alex is intrigued by the long line of gharries parked outside the station, each one drawn by a couple of plumed horses with the inevitable blue beads sewn into their colourful trappings. Porters pile their luggage into a hot taxi, which makes its way at a snail's pace through a shabby area, hindered constantly by people and animals blocking the road. Women shrouded in black, with babies strapped to their backs, shove their hands through the taxi windows begging aggressively for alms.

'I hate Cairo!' she gasps, and Giles laughs.

'This is only one part of the city. Once we get out of this area you'll find it quite pleasant.'

'Isn't it strange to be back in Cairo after so many years?' Giles remarks to Sheena. She smiles, but makes no comment.

Chapter Forty

Now they are driving along the Nile, a wide brown river dotted with feluccas and houseboats. Up above flies a flock of white egrets. Alex keeps a look out for bulrushes and spots several clumps. Then they pass through suburbs of large white modern houses and blocks of flats, separated by avenues of flame trees and greyish-green eucalyptus. Even here a few beggars lie stretched out in the shade.

Giles says to Sheena, 'Sorry I couldn't get a room at a decent hotel. I tried Shepheard's, The Savoy and the

Continentale, but too many people are passing through Cairo just now.'

Their hotel turns out to be an unfinished, dusty block of grey concrete near the Bulacq Bridge, with no garden. Alex expects her mother to grumble, since she's become used to luxury hotels, but she says nothing. She continues to look tired and dejected, but she still looks beautiful, thinks Alex..

'We can go to the Gezira Club to eat and swim. It's really just a question of sleeping here', says Giles, trying to make the best of it.

The taps in the washbasin emit the barest trickle of brownish water and there are clusters of flies on the ceiling.

'There's no air conditioning', says Sheena.

'No. Thank God it's not midsummer.'

Outside the hotel they hire a gharry smelling strongly of horse dung. The inside is hung about with garlands of jasmine and miniature fluffy toys. The vehicle bumps them along over a bridge to the island of Gezira. Here one could live unaware that much of Cairo is a teeming, dirty, poverty-stricken town. Boulevards lined with tall shady trees lead past cool, spacious gardens and well designed private houses. Branches of frangipani and powdery mimosa balls hang over white fences into the street. In the centre is a large area of vivid green grass flanked by imposing white buildings and blue street lamps.

Giles points out the Zoological Gardens, but Alex is more interested in the Consulate where her parents were married – a gracious white crenellated edifice with fretted woodwork surrounded by tamarisk and banyan trees and well tended flower beds of roses and dahlias overlooked by ancient trees hung with creepers.

Giles pays for temporary membership at the Gezira Club and they try to find somewhere to sit near the pool. Most of the tables are taken by officers waiting to leave the Middle East. They have to share a table with a woman and her baby in a pram. At the next table sit four very tanned naval men in uniforms of dazzling white duck. They turn to stare at Sheena but she seems not to notice. She's too used to being admired. When she comes back from the changing rooms in a swimming costume of lime green Alex hears an officer make a flattering remark about her mother. Sheena cheers up a little and agrees to have some lunch.

'Are you going to swim?' asks Giles.

'No, the pool's too crowded. I changed just to keep cool. You take Alex and I'll sit and watch you.'

Giles and Alex slide into the aquamarine water amongst the many bronzed bodies. Tiers of diving boards prevent any serious swimming. Alex waves at her mother, and notices the woman with the pram is walking away, while two of the naval officers have joined Sheena, who's laughing. Alex is indignant, and wishes they would go away.

When Giles and Alex return to the table, Sheena says brightly, 'Meet Peter and Charles. They came to the club once in Beirut.' Alex has to sit for an hour, sipping a lemonade while half listening to the inevitable talk of the war. She watches the white-robed safragis gliding expertly and unobtrusively among the tables, balancing trays of drinks and miniature buckets of ice. She ventures to smile at one and is pleasantly surprised when he grins back. She feels sure none of the Europeans would respond if she smiled at them. Then she notices the only Egyptian guests, two smartly dressed middle-aged men who are looking towards Sheena. They obviously know her, but when one of them comes over to their table and bows, Sheena is very distant.

On the way back to the hotel they make a detour to show Alex the American hospital where Sheena used to work – a long white building at the end of a drive lined with blue gum trees and casurinas. Outside, scarlet poinsettias and blue jacaranda provide vivid splashes of colour against a cactus hedge. But Sheena doesn't want to stop.

Their hotel room seems even more uninviting on their return. The shower in a tiny cubicle is either much too hot or icy cold. The single window looks out onto the back of another block of concrete. Sheena lies on one of the twin divan beds and becomes silent and morose again.

After a rest, Giles says, 'Come on, let's go and have tea at Groppi's patisserie. There might be someone there you know.' Alex is delighted with the lovely walled garden where they sit eating mille feuilles using tiny forks with mother-of-pearl handles. Giles informs Alex that Groppi's is one of the most famous cafés in the world. They linger amongst the thick-petalled zinnias and the huge asters and the flowering creepers until the sun's rays lengthen across the gravel under the coloured umbrellas.

Before leaving they go through a bead curtain into the tantalising smell of the cake and sweet shop. Beribboned boxes of Turkish Delight in all shapes and sizes are piled on stands. Under the cellophane covers they can see the green pistachio nuts embedded in the delicate slices of pink jelly, dusted thickly with icing sugar. Giant golden boxes of hand-made chocolates remind Alex of Basil. Giles buys Turkish Delight for his sister's family. It's Behind a gauze hanging Alex watches a man grinding coffee beans in a bucket with a large pestle.

'I can't face going back to that hotel yet' says Sheena. 'Let's stay on here for a while.' So they return to the garden and order ice cream. A group of Egyptian men in silk suits and buckskin shoes carrying briefcases come in, on their way home from work.

'Amazing how these chaps carry off their European clothes', remarks Giles. 'They never seem to wilt in the heat as we do. Even our uniformed men look scruffy in Cairo.'

Sheena agrees. 'The British, in particular, have no idea about style.'

They watch a safragi watering the flowers after the heat of the day. 'Enjoy your ice cream', says Sheena. 'You won't get any in England.'

'Is there still rationing?' asks Alex in surprise.

'Oh yes. We'll all be issued with ration books.'

They emerge from Groppi's after dark into a city lit up with neon signs in Arabic and English, most of which have letters missing, and walk part of the way back to the hotel. All around them wafts the intangible, indescribable odour of an eastern city, where so many delicious scents mingle with the sickening stench of decaying matter. In the streets and alleyways the sound of life never ceases – cars honking, wirelesses blaring out insistent Arab music, dogs fighting, soldiers singing bawdy songs, trams rattling. Someone is banging a tambourine. Up above, the sky is distant, cold and clear. Alex, holding Giles's hand tightly, shivers, thinking how terrible it would be to be lost in this city.

No sailing date has yet been given and Giles hopes to show Alex the pyramids.

'I should have thought Alex has seen enough ancient monuments to last a lifetime', comments Sheena. 'If you're going to the pyramids tomorrow, I'll go to the club.'

'On your own?'

'Why not? There were several women there on their own yesterday. If you're late back I might go to the Metro-Roxy. Someone said there was a good film showing, with Greer Garson.'

They plan to visit the pyramids after an early lunch. In the morning Sheena says she'd like to visit the oriental bazaar known as the Muski. They walk through the Esbekiya Gardens to the Place Atabet and then into the eastern city, where they search for small souvenirs to take to England – sandalwood perfume, a carved string of camels, a bracelet in the shape of a serpent. Each purchase takes so long that Alex becomes bored with shopping.

While Sheena continues to shop, Giles walks on with Alex across a spacious courtyard towards a large handsome mosque. It's a white building surmounted with a dome in forget-me-not blue, gleaming through a geometric pattern in cream. Through the open doors she can see a row of bottoms as a group of men kneel on the marble floor. A series of lamps hanging on gold chains and the oriental carpets are the only decorations in that vast space.

'Which do you like best?' asks Giles, 'Mosques or churches?' Alex has no hesitation in choosing the mosques. 'Why?'

'Because they're emptier and more peaceful, and so cool.'

'You're quite right. It's wonderful how the Arabs can create an impression of coolness and peace in hot places. They use the same simple but beautifully proportioned design over and over again. But in England I'll show you some exquisite churches that are as lovely as any mosque. It's sad that Christians have built some very ugly churches and over-decorated them inside with tawdry ornaments.'

'Which would you rather be, a Christian or a Muslim, if you had to choose?' asks Alex.

Giles laughs. 'It would be a hard decision. Both Jesus and Mohammed had the right ideas about how we should live good lives.'

After an early lunch Giles and Alex take a tram from the Place Atabet to the pyramids at Giza, a distance of some eight kilometres. They rattle through ugly suburbs of whitewashed clay boxes with no glass in their windows. Then come villas surrounded with flame trees. These give way to paddy fields and corn fields until finally they reach the yellow vastness of the desert. A man is shovelling camel dung onto a cart to use for fuel.

A string of camels on their left is carrying bundles of feathery sugar cane. On their right, kites hover over a dying donkey. The tramline comes to an end at the large, pseudo-Moorish Mena House Hotel surrounded by its beautiful garden. From there they can see the pyramids in the distance. People are hiring gharries to drive the last quarter of a mile, but Giles suggests they ride a camel instead. Alex is both thrilled and afraid. She's never been so close to a camel before. Its smell is overpowering and the

403

look in its heavy-lidded eye seems malevolent. Giles has warned her not to go near the camel's head. She stands well back, looking at the beast's gaunt, mangy body and its wicked-looking yellow teeth. Yet it kneels down meekly enough for them to climb onto its back. They share a wooden saddle covered with a large sheepskin dyed red. Giles, in front, hangs onto a polished metal peak rising from the front of the saddle, and Alex clings to his waist.

At an order the camel rises in four movements, lurching them back and forth and making a strange noise. As the animal ambles forward Alex feels sure she's slipping, but gradually she becomes used to the disjointed movement, and enjoys travelling at such a height away from the burning sand. Every now and then the camel snatches up a twig of dry thorn which disappears between its rubbery lips.

The wide landscape of bright yellow sand and rock against a deep blue sky is being traversed constantly by gharries, jeeps and camels conveying travellers all anxious to see the pyramids in case they should never find themselves in Egypt again. They approach what are known as the three great pyramids of Giza, the largest being that of Cheops. The top is missing and the outer facing has been removed so that the stones underneath form a series of steep steps, each limestone block several feet high. Alex wants to climb to the top but her father says the authorities no longer allow tourists to climb the pyramids.

'Why not?'

'Because the stones would eventually wear down. There are Bedouin guards hanging around who'd come to stop you climbing.'

It is, however, permitted to go inside. Together with other visitors they pick their way across the piles of bricks near the entrance to Cheops' pyramid and follow a guide into a dark musty passage leading to a burial chamber of great height. Alex is disappointed there's nothing to see inside the chamber. Giles explains how the pyramids were once full of furniture and precious ornaments and jewels buried with the royal families. Most of the artefacts have been stolen over the centuries. Those found by archaeologists have had to be put in museums for safe keeping. He told her about the most wonderful recent discovery made in 1922 when a man called Howard Carter discovered the tomb of King Tutankhamun at a place called Thebes, south of Cairo. Luckily no robbers had entered that tomb, and everything was just as it had been well over a thousand years BC.

As they retrace their steps in single file along the dark passage, a woman behind them suddenly lets out a yell of terror as a bat flies past. Alex gives a scream too, remembering the bat on her bed.

'Just keep going', says Giles, 'It won't hurt you.' Nevertheless, she's intensely relieved to be out of the pyramid. There's something threatening about the immensity of this structure with no beauty inside, nothing on which to focus the eye.

'Now we must go and see the sphinx', says Giles eagerly. Inwardly Alex groans, imagining that the sphinx will prove as uninteresting as the pyramid. But when they gaze up at the great recumbent lion with the enigmatic human face guarding the kings' cemetery, Alex is filled with awe in spite of herself. This gargantuan carving is more fascinating than any antiquities she's seen so far.

Before setting off back to Cairo they have drinks and sandwiches in the garden of the Mena House Hotel. The place is buzzing with excited English and North American accents. Everyone is waiting to see a desert sunset. The pearl pink sky is streaked with wispy bands of violet, orange and cerise. A sudden hush descends on the garden as the sun slips down behind the flat horizon leaving the yellow sand glowing with light. The pyramids loom out of the dusk, incomprehensible excrescences on the face of nature.

They hire a gharry for the return journey. Now there's only the barest hint of light in a soft sky against which the palm fronds form stark black patterns. A brilliant evening star begins to twinkle. Alex watches the blue flash on the wires as the last tram plies its way back to town.

When they reach Cairo their driver asks if they'd like to be taken to Harafa, the City of the Dead. Giles is hesitant, but Alex begs to be allowed to go. The very name – *City of the Dead* – conjures up fear and romance. He agrees and the horses clip-clop slowly through the town and out beyond the eastern wall to the huge mausoleum built to house Cairo's dead. The moon has risen and in its clear metallic light row upon row upon row of white tombs rise eerily from the dark ground. They sit in the gharry and listen to the silence, broken only by the single screech of an owl.

Then, much to Alex's surprise, a light appears in one of the tombs – and another, and another. Giles explains that many of the tombs are actually lived in by some of the poorest people. As her eyes become used to the dark she can see that most of the tombs are like tiny houses with walls round them.

'Do the poor people really live with the dead bodies?'

'They must do. The poverty is terrible in Cairo and at least they get shelter in a tomb.' Alex is amazed and horrified at the lengths to which people can be driven.

When they return to the hotel there's a message for Giles at the reception desk, a note from Sheena. She's moved to the Hotel Continentale with all the luggage, to room number sixty. Their sailing date has come through. They have two nights left. She'll explain further when they arrive.

Alex is tired and doesn't want to settle into another hotel. She's half asleep when her father helps her out of the gharry into the luxurious foyer of the Continentale. Giles is told his wife's in the cocktail bar. Alex follows her father into the smoky atmosphere to find Sheena sitting amongst a group of noisy people drinking champagne. She smiles at her husband and daughter, but it's her 'pretend' smile. She's ashamed of their dusty clothes and dirty faces.

'Did you like the pyramids?'

'Not inside', replies Alex.

'I bet you've both got fleas from sitting in a gharry.'

Sheena takes them up in the lift, and they emerge into a wide hall furnished with pale leather sofas and a massive arrangement of roses and lilies. Their feet are soundless on the thick carpet. Room sixty seems to Alex like the bedroom of a princess. Her mother is saying, 'I met an old friend, Bill Carey, at the club. He's having to leave Cairo unexpectedly today, but was booked in here for the next two nights. So he offered us his room. Wasn't that lucky? I was going mad in that dreary place.'

There is a long white leather settee for Alex to sleep on. In the morning a chambermaid brings them a pot of tea, and later some breakfast on a huge tray. Giles and Sheena discuss what they will do on this last full day in Cairo. Giles is disappointed there won't be time to take a trip down the Nile to Luxor and Thebes.

'How about visiting the Egyptian museum?'

'Good God, no!' exclaims Sheena. 'I don't care if I never see another museum.'

It's decided he should take Alex out to explore Cairo while Sheena has her hair done at the hotel. She'll meet them for lunch.

Giles leads his daughter across the crowded foyer past piles of luggage – suitcases of Damascus leather, dressing cases and hat boxes in crocodile skin. As they step out onto the sunny pavement they see a couple drive away in a Bentley, followed by a shiny limousine with outriders. 'Who's that?' asks Alex.

'Some important member of the government, I expect! Shall we take a walk through the old city?'

They stroll down narrow streets with projecting cornices and hanging balconies of intricate woodwork supported by large brackets and corbels. They pass under arches of fretted stone, and glance through windows surrounded with a delicate lacework of wood. Prosperous looking Egyptian men dressed in vivid silk and brocade embroidered in gold give the streets an added charm and colour. But the beauty is marred by poverty. Alex's main impression of old Cairo is of filth, rags and disease, sunken eyes and skeletal figures. Because it's more congested it seems far worse than the squalid parts of Beirut. There are just too many deformed beggars, too many children with sores round their eyes or mouths, too many scurvy donkeys and mangy dogs.

'Some of the children suffer from trachoma', Giles tells Alex. 'A virus they get from lice, and it eventually leads to blindness.'

'Can't it be cured?'

'There's no cure as yet.'

Alex shudders. 'I don't like this part of Cairo', she says.

Giles suggests they take a walk along the river.

But Alex thinks the Nile is ugly too. She doesn't like the emaciated buffaloes lying on the yellowy-grey banks of mud.

'No, it's not a beautiful river, like those in Lebanon', admits Giles, 'But if it wasn't for all that fertile grey mud Cairo would never have been one of the world's great early civilisations. Each year the Nile overflows onto the fields in the delta and provides rich soil for the crops.'

They leave the river and turn into a boulevard of golden acacia trees bearing strongly scented cream blossoms. Strolling along in a slight breeze is very pleasant after the stifling air and unpleasant smells of the old city. Suddenly Cairo doesn't seem such a bad place after all. It's so easy to forget its horrors in the spacious residential areas.

At lunch Sheena says there's to be a dinner dance at the hotel that evening, and she'd like to attend. So they'd better pack their cases this afternoon. Later, Alex watches her mother dressing for the dance. She wears blue velvet with beige lace trimming, and for the first time since leaving Beirut her eyes are bright, with a suggestion of colour in her cheeks. Giles dresses up in his red cummerbund and starched shirt and Alex thinks yet again how very much better looking he is than Basil.

When her parents have gone downstairs Alex lies on the settee, listening to the faint strains of the dance band. She wonders if Sheena will dance romantically with Giles as she used to do with Basil at the various hotels in Lebanon. If only she could fathom what was going to happen to their relationship!

Chapter Forty-one

Anticipation at the thought of sailing the next day makes sleep impossible. Alex gets up, searching for something to pass the time. The suitcases lie on the floor almost packed. In her father's old revelation case, under a Harris tweed jacket and a mackintosh she locates the inevitable box containing the little green packets of Polo mints. At the bottom of the case are a number of books including an Everyman edition of *The Woman in White,* which looks promising. She settles down to read a few pages but finds the book heavy going.

A sudden thought comes to her – a diary; surely Giles still keeps a diary. After much rummaging around she finds it in the pocket of a holdall. Now at last she might find out all the details of her mother's illness and Basil's sudden departure – and, above all, whether there's been a genuine reconciliation between her parents. Giles's writing is minuscule and hard to decipher, but she's had long practice in reading his letters. She flicks through the pages until she finds the day her father arrived at the villa:

September 2nd: Arrived at Broummana. Managed half an hour alone with Sheena to discuss the future. She seems very much on edge. She persists in not wanting Alex to live with May and attend a day school. Strange how detached she can be from Alex, how unemotional, while at the same time she's so jealous of her daughter forming a close attachment elsewhere. Alex will need special affection from an adult while we're abroad, and May, who is so anxious to have her, could fulfil this role. But Sheena insists I choose a boarding school and ask the headmistress to find a suitable family to take Alex as a paying guest for the holidays. It's just conceivable such an arrangement might work, but more likely it'll be a disaster...

Giles goes on to describe briefly the various outings with his daughter. Alex skips most of these and moves on to the day they left Broummana:

September 8th: Back at Basil's apartment after the longest and most terrible day of my life. Returned from our walk at Broummana this morning to find Sheena unconscious on the bed and no sign of Basil. She'd obviously drunk too much whisky combined presumably with an overdose of sleeping pills. Impossible to know whether it was deliberate or an accident. She was taken to hospital by ambulance and we followed in my hired car. The doctor said it was fortunate she arrived in time. He assumed it was an accident and I didn't pursue the matter. It's hard to know how much I should tell Alex. The poor child is very upset and mystified. Abby told me Basil had dropped in to pack his clothes and was now en route to Jerusalem prior to going to the States.

September 9th: Visited Sheena late last night and was glad to find her sitting up and looking slightly better. To my surprise she's thinking of coming to England. Now Basil has gone she obviously can't afford to live in his apartment. She refuses to say how her relationship with him came to an end. I suspect she's wishing that he hadn't gone. I feel sorry for the agony she's going through. If she does come with us we might make a go of it for Alex's sake if nothing else.

I took Alex to see Sheena today and the doctor says she'll be well enough to travel to Cairo tomorrow.

September 10th: The armistice with Italy was signed on the 7th. We're on our way to Cairo by train. Sheena is very quiet. She looks deathly pale and hardly eats anything. I know Alex would like to show her sympathy but Sheena remains unapproachable. Why won't she allow her own daughter to show affection? Perhaps it was a mistake for her to have had a child. She's so terrified of appearing vulnerable. She doesn't seem to realise that Alex is no longer a baby, and in some ways very precocious and quite able to understand what's going on. At the same time I don't want to say too much to Alex myself. She mustn't be driven to take sides.

September 11th: So strange to be back in Cairo. So many happy memories! Sheena still very subdued. Our hotel leaves much to be desired.

September 12th: Took Alex to the pyramids. Sheena as usual refused to go sightseeing. She must be the only European in Egypt with no desire to visit the pyramids. She went to the club and met old acquaintances, which seems to have cheered her up a little. Bill Carey has let us have his room at the Continentale. It will cost the earth but it's worth it to see Sheena smile again. How beautiful she looks in spite of losing weight. I hope to persuade her to come out to Bahrain with me after my leave. The prospect of life abroad in a pleasant house may tempt her once she accepts that the affair with Basil is over. At the moment she seems to need me and I still love her against all reason. If only she could realise her potential she might become more contented with life. She's an excellent nursing tutor, and I found among her papers a glowing commendation from the British Minister's wife, Lady Spears, for looking after the welfare of servicemen so well at the British Club. But I realise we have so little in common. It's puzzling how *anyone so intelligent can lack any intellectual curiosity. We do at least share a sense of humour and we both hate stuffy pretentious people. Will it be enough?*

Alex reads through these extracts twice and then sits quite still thinking about them for a long time. Nothing she's read in the diary has altered her own view of her mother. There are still unanswered questions. There must be a way to please Sheena, but Alex has no idea what it is.

She replaces the diary in the holdall and regards herself in a huge ornate gilded mirror. She's more dissatisfied with her appearance than ever. Her body, too tall for its years, is awkward and angular, and her mousy hair is thin and wispy around her plain face. Without glasses she looks myopic. Her complexion will never have the close-grained porcelain texture of her mother's. It seems grossly unfair that some people are born ugly and others so pretty.

In the early hours of the morning Alex wakes to hear a muffled sobbing coming from Sheena's bed. Her heart begins to beat violently. Now is the chance to show her mother how sorry she is for her misery, how angry she is with Basil for deserting her. At this moment she would almost have welcomed Basil back. She gets up very slowly, with no sound, moves towards the twin beds and listens. The sobbing has ceased. Now in the throbbing silence she suspects from Giles's breathing that he too is awake. But he doesn't speak and she creeps back to bed knowing she can do nothing to help her mother.

They breakfast at seven before departing by train for Port Said. The interior of the carriage is old and shabby and they're squashed in on slatted wooden seats with too many people. Alex recognises the Scots woman with the small boy still clutching his lamb on wheels.

'I do apologise!' his mother keeps saying. 'I know wee Jimmy is being a nuisance, but I couldn't leave his toys behind. I've a rocking horse in the luggage van.'

'A rocking horse!' exclaims Sheena. 'You'll never be allowed to take that on board.'

'Oh, but I will! You just have to slip a few notes into their hands.'

Alex thinks suddenly of Hatty. Perhaps a few notes would have got her into England.

The train runs alongside the Suez Canal and finally deposits its passengers in front of the customs shed on the dock at Port Said. Notices *'Not Wanted on Voyage'* are pasted onto their trunks. Their ship is an ugly greyish-brown with no visible name. In wartime, explains Giles, ships carry no identification. Everyone is talking about the voyage as they stand around in brilliant sunshine. 'It's a troopship', someone says. 'We'll be sleeping with men and women in separate cabins so they can cram in as many people as possible.'

Sheena and Alex find themselves directed to a poky cabin with four bunks. A Mrs Duncan and her seven-year-old daughter are to share the claustrophobic accommodation. Numerous pipes run across the ceiling and down the walls, and a loud thudding noise issues from the ventilator. A tiny washbasin, thin hard mattresses, flat pillows, skimpy sheets and grey blankets complete the furnishings. Alex can sense Sheena's horror at the prospect of sleeping in this space for weeks. In the limited room between the bunks only one person at a time can get dressed.. They have to climb a great many iron gangways following numerous signs to reach the top deck. It takes half an hour to locate Giles.

'God, isn't this ship awful!' mutters Sheena as they stand on the open deck looking down at the quayside where a handful of people wait to wave goodbye. 'The thought of that musty cabin and then Liverpool and rationing and the cold grey British winter makes me shudder. Don't let's stay in England a minute longer than we have to!'

'You're right', agrees Giles sadly. 'We've become too used to life in the Middle East. We don't really belong to the UK any more. But it will be interesting to see it again.'

'Bombed out cities! A heap of ruins! Just up your street!' taunts Sheena.

Finally at midday the ship sails. As the vessel begins to move away from its berth, Alex watches the gap between it and the dockside growing wider and wider. The few people on the quay turn into black dots waving white squares.

They hear a hooter, the signal for lunch. In the packed dining room they sit at long tables and are served with a lukewarm stew, mashed potato and cabbage, followed by the inevitable pink blancmange and lurid red jelly. 'You can tell we're already on British territory!' jokes someone.

By the time they climb back on deck Egypt has almost disappeared. Alex stands between her mother and father at the stern rail. She puts her small hand into Giles's almost identical large hand, and unexpectedly Sheena takes her other hand. She knows she's saying farewell, not only to the Middle East, but to her childhood. Shortly she'll have to face the world without her parents.

The blue-green water turns dark and deep and treacherous. Soon nothing can be seen but sea and sky in every direction. A sharp breeze blows up, and huddled together, the three of them gaze down, mesmerised by the pale frothy wake trailing behind the ship.

Printed in Great Britain
by Amazon